"Borderzone gonzo charged with ————
ulated with a charismatic cast of '————
through the postindustrial lands————
Exile is a fun read and Lisa M. Bradley is an exciting ———

—Christopher Brown, Campbell and World Fantasy Award-nominated author of *Tropic of Kansas* and *Rule of Capture*

"Taut and fast-paced, *Exile* sets you down in a chemical disaster zone that has become a petri dish for violence, sex, and sublimated dreams. Bradley's characters struggle to define consent in a town where survival demands acquiescence and government interdiction kills hope. Sharp, smart and provocative, Exile grabs you from the first page and never lets go."

—Sabrina Vourvoulias, author of *Ink*

"*Exile* is a thrilling adventure that snags the reader on page one and never lets up. Bradley offers sharp examinations of how our society forces marginalized people further into the margins, and the community and complex relationships within Exile are as gripping as the action sequences. Heidi is a fascinating narrator whose flaws and strengths are equally compelling. I've never read anything quite like this, and I loved every moment of it!"

—Julia Rios, editor, *Fireside Magazine*

"Brutal and sensual in equal measure, Lisa M. Bradley's debut novel *Exile* offers a tightly paced near-future speculative story that had me on the edge of my seat. With elements of horror, the post-apocalyptic, and science fiction, this novel set twenty years after a chemical disaster shows street warfare with visceral intensity. Heidi tries to get away from her quarantined town and her abusive family, while everyone hides grim secrets. The living, breathing characters and snappy dialog make the intense violence feel eerily plausible, and the plot doesn't let up until the final twist of the knife. Can I get a sequel?"

—Bogi Takács, Lambda award winner, Hugo and Locus award finalist

"A hard-bitten and fast-paced dystopian adventure that will keep readers up all night, twitching and watching the skies."

—Meg Elison, Philip K. Dick Award winner

Exile

Lisa M. Bradley

ROSARIUM

Cover art and design by Vincent Sammy

Rosarium Publishing
P.O. Box 544
Greenbelt, MD 20768-0544

www.rosariumpublishing.com

Exile

To the Rio Grande Valley

Fight the Wall!

Chapter One

THE MAN HAD BEHEADED my brother. I couldn't stop
imagining it as I sat nearly recumbent in the passenger seat
of his steel-gray Stingray.

Tank ignored my inspection, avoided even glancing
my way as he drove us to Mute's Roadhouse out on Maiden
Lane. Before the Spill, Maiden Lane had been a quiet
cul de sac; now it was more bottom of the bag than ever,
despite being in the Outer Radius. Still, getting there
didn't require half the concentration Tank was faking. He'd
designed Mute's, had gotten down and hauled sheetrock
and hammered nails with the sulking townies Mute arm-
twisted and blackmailed into working. Tank had even
blacktopped the parking lot, raked that stinking asphalt
soup in the middle of an August night. So he knew where
Mute's was and how to get there. He just didn't want to
look at me or my blue mini dress or the line of my thighs
pressed together.

Maybe I scared him.

He pulled into the parking lot, headlights glitzing off
the rhinestone and spangles of the hooker promenade in
front of Mute's. The tires crunched over broken beer bottles,
and I winced in spite of myself. Sure, Tank was an Outsider,
but he'd been in town three years, plenty long enough to
have puncture-proof tires. Even so, a 1970 Corvette Stingray
coupe deserved better.

Tank must've been checking me out because he caught
my flinch, mistook it for fear. "You sure you want to do

this?" His craggy voice filled the small space, deeper than the Stingray's muted engine.

This? I looked across the lot bleached by floodlights, watched couples emerge from the shadows alongside the roadhouse to scope us out. This: appear in public with my brother's killer, burn the last bridges to my family, spray paint my suicide note in letters six feet tall.

I took a deep breath, inhaled the sandalwood spice coming off Tank. "I'm sure," I said, unbuckling my seat belt. "Are you?"

He didn't say anything. Didn't have to. Uncertainty cocked his jaw—an eight on Luciano's American masculinity scale, I decided. But he got out, met me in front of the sleek silver beast, and escorted me through the gauntlet of leaning motorcycles to Mute's door. His hand didn't quite touch the small of my back, but I felt its heat. And the answering heat on my cheekbones, the hollow of my throat. The hooker crew chiefs paused negotiations to marvel at Tank, then dropped their gazes to me. Tank and I nodded as we passed through their beer-and-blunts miasma.

Inside, the jukebox blared The Doors' "Peace Frog." No one noticed our entrance, but the moment Tank started crossing the sawdusted floor, the crowd parted for his immense form. And then the whispers started, audible even over The Doors. The roadhouse felt bigger inside than out, and it was packed with people who knew me, knew my brother, knew my brother's killer. My skin tingled. Mute's was one of Exile's only no-kill zones—that's why, when I'd propositioned him, Tank had insisted we have our "date" here; that, and Tank had some arrangement with Mute— but that was small consolation with everyone eyeing us like steaks. The street wars whet powerful appetites.

Tank ignored the crowd's gawking more convincingly than he had my staring. He guided me along a curving honey weiss wall that divided the bar from the dance floor toward a spiral staircase that looked like the bastard of a conch shell and a baby grand piano. Black, gleaming, and pearlescent, the staircase embraced us, buffered us from the riffraff. Even so, I had to concentrate as we ascended the polished treads; I was wearing newish fuck-me pumps, and vibrations—Tank climbing behind me, The Doors' mad organ music—funneled up my already trembling legs. Then we reached the surreal stability of the Guinness-black mezzanine. It jetted glassy, seemingly unsupported, over the muffled dance floor.

We sat at Tank's table—off-limits to anyone else—and a little breathless, I peered over the edge of the mezzanine at the dancers below. Plenty looked, stared, glared right back. A knot of warriors, part of my dead brother's crew, muttered near the bar. Their new leader, Chazz, bared nicotine-stained teeth at me and grabbed his crotch. I turned back to Tank. Studying me, he hadn't noticed Chazz's threat.

"So how does this..." I gestured around at the mezzanine, not needing to shout, the jukebox acoustically squelched. "How does it not crash down onto the dance floor?"

He gave me a longer answer than I expected: ksi yield requirements, seismic loadings, psf live loads, and I don't know what else. Most people would've been running off at the mouth, nervous. He, however, was one of those no-bullshit characters who assumed that if you asked, then you really wanted to know. When he finished, his mouth squeezed up. Not a smile exactly, more like a facial shrug: ripple of the zygomatic major, slight pucker of the incisivi labii, no movement of the orbicularis oculi.

"I don't know what you just said," I admitted. "But I think I get the gist. It's physics."

"Physics," he agreed.

We sat eyeing one another, silent, for a couple of minutes. He knew that I knew that he'd murdered my brother William. Hell, the whole town knew. You can't race down a residential street on your motorcycle swinging an ax at people without *somebody* taking notice, even in Exile, even during a street war. I looked away.

And looked right back. Tank was the most beautiful man I'd ever seen. Granted, I'd spent most of the last six months locked in my bedroom, the room farthest from the street, working on my thesis—but my thesis *was* on male beauty in mainstream American cinema, so I wasn't easily awed.

His head was shaved, the crescents of parietal bone pleasingly juxtaposed with the planes of his long, brown face. I mentally traced the temporal lines down the subtle slopes of his zygomatic bones (no jarring "chiseled cheekbones"), over the baby-smooth philtrum, down his mental protuberance (that number-eight chin), over a delectable Adam's apple, and down-down-down to that massive chest. He was so muscular that, despite his loose black T-shirt, he looked like an illustration from *Gray's Anatomy* ... had Gray been a lusty spinster with a predilection for multi-ethnic men.

From the look in his near-black eyes, I knew that he knew I wasn't thinking of my headless brother. It seemed to make him uneasy. He hailed a waitress so she could bring me a glass of ice water. I drained it, and a few minutes later, he called her again. And then again. I tried to slow down. The glasses were the size of cannon shells, and my bladder was maybe the size of a hand grenade. Something had to give.

"Excuse me," I said, and pushed away from the table.

I hurried downstairs, my legs trembling, bladder near bursting. "Peace Frog" played on a loop and surged over me as I joined the clot of bodies on the dance floor. I hadn't gotten halfway to the facilities when someone grabbed my wrist and yanked. I would've toppled, but there were too many bodies. As it was, I flattened my nose against someone else's biceps. That person shoved me off, and suddenly Chazz was in my face, close enough I could count wiry black beard hairs, tally steroid-acne scars.

Unlit cigarette clamped between his lips, he muttered, "You got time for a dance, Heidi?" He ground my carpals in his fist.

I braced myself, used my free hand to shove him in the chest. "I don't dance with William's friends," I said. "Not even now."

Chazz's cigarette bobbed as he glanced at the mezzanine behind me. "But you'll dance with that Outsider killed your brother?"

"I ain't dancing with anybody," I said, lips twisting in disgust. "I'm trying to get to the can."

"What are you up to?" He cocked his head. "Your mama know where you are? You guys plotting something?"

"What do you think?" I stomped his foot. My heel skidded off his steel-toed boot. "Or do you think?"

Behind me, a guy said, "You okay, Heidi?"

I turned around, found Romero Cantu at my back, his dark hair gel-scrunched like permanent bedhead and on his sleek brown cheekbone, a new, crescent-shaped scab. Maybe from the end of a metal pipe?

"I'd be better if I could get to the bathroom," I said.

Romero took my arm, his calluses a familiar grit against my skin, and pulled me out of Chazz's grip. "C'mon, man, let her through. You don't want her pissing on your boots, do you? That's kinda kinky."

Romero jostled us past, and Chazz stepped back, though Romero was smaller than him and not jacked up on steroids.

"Kinky? Shit," Chazz hollered after us. "You'd know kinky, right, Cantu? Slurping up your brother's—"

We didn't hear the rest, weaving through the crowd, but it was a classic refrain, mindless as a KISS chorus.

Romero whispered in my ear, "You okay?" His breath curled sweet with cardamom and Coke. I'd licked the taste from his lips often enough to know. It still made my mouth water.

I gritted my teeth. "Gotta go is all."

When we spotted the line of women leaning against the wall, Romero groaned. "Sweet Sue. C'mon, I'll take you to the men's." He started to tug me in the other direction, but I resisted. Not enough to go timber in my heels, but enough that he stopped.

"I don't think that's appropriate tonight," I said, looking toward the mezzanine, though not long enough to see Tank.

Romero sneered, and the scab on his cheekbone cracked, began to bleed. "You know what'd be appropriate? If your *date* bothered to protect you from William's thugs. What's he doing letting you walk into this rattler den?"

"It was his idea," I said. Then, when Romy's dark eyes flared, I amended, "No one's going to start shit at Mute's."

"What did I just haul you away from, burra?" Romero's grip tightened on my arm. "A Tupperware pitch?"

Out of the corner of my eye, I saw the line to the women's room growing longer. "Come on, you're not mad at Tank, you're mad at me. And I need to pee."

Romero huffed, but he let me join the line. He even waited with me, despite dirty looks from the other women. Maybe they thought he was going in with me. He turned me loose, leaned against the wall.

"Sammy asked about you the other day," he said. "Wants to know why you don't come 'round no more. Didn't know what to tell the kid, don't know myself."

I sighed. Were we still on that? I hadn't been to the Cantus' house in six months, since the last time I'd failed the exam that could've bailed me from Exile. "You know why I don't come around," I said.

"Not really. Carlos ain't dating like you wanted him to. He just works harder."

"Well, that's his choice," I said, trying not to frown.

Carlos talked around things, not his brother Romero.

14

"What about me, huh?" Romy didn't bother to keep his voice down, either. "Even if Carlos did start dating some nice girl—" He flashed the sneer again, and a thread of blood trickled down his face. "—some girl suitable to his 'position' as liaison, what about me?"

I reached out, gently swiped at his blood with my ring finger. "Maybe you need to find a girl and settle down, too."

Romero scoffed, dodged from my touch. "I'll settle down when I'm dead." He jerked his chin in the general direction of Chazz, then Tank. "You want me to wait for you?"

I shook my head. "I'll be fine. But keep Chazz distracted when I come out?"

"You sure Chazz is the one you need to worry about?" Though not circumspect, Romero left it at that and stomped away.

I CHECKED THE CLOCK as I left the can. Van Damme it. I'd been MIA almost fifteen minutes. Tank would think I'd ditched him. I hurried back upstairs, this time unmolested by any of William's friends, although Chazz watched me from a corner of the bar.

Tank was still at his table, but he'd been joined by an Asianesque woman and a slightly grimy white guy in a motorcycle jacket. The guy had taken my seat across from Tank. I smiled uncertainly, smoothed my dress over my hips as we were introduced.

Serena: I recognized her. Apple-round cheeks, semi-permanent nasolabial creases, no epicanthic fold, slightest of upper lid creases topped by pencil-stroke eyebrows. About ten years older than me. Not really a native, but more than an Outsider. She'd had the misfortune to be in our southwest Texas town with her mom on the day of the Spill, and she'd been quarantined like the rest of us. She was clearly attached to Sweeney, almost literally. Her burgundy-polished nails winked in the light as she squeezed his arm.

Sweeney: Long, oval face that looked all the longer for the frequently broken aquiline nose and his slightly cleft chin, the droopy eyes and slanting eyebrows. He was mouth-breathing, so I saw one too many teeth, an extra lateral incisor on the upper right. Older than me, but that didn't account for the permanent forehead furrow. When he smiled, the furrow deepened, as did the crow's feet around his muddy, yellow eyes. So far as I could tell, it was a genuine smile.

Tank pulled out the chair beside him so I could sit, then rested his arm along the back of the chair behind me. I soaked my panties, but it wasn't my bladder's fault. To distract myself, I imagined Sweeney with his head cut off. Aside from the yellow eyes and extra tooth, he was standard-issue street warrior. It could've been his headless body in the street two days ago, rather than William's. I felt a little better about the confusion I'd experienced then, how nothing had made sense until some thug matched William's head to the rest of his body and it dawned on me why Mother was hugging a bloody, bony duffel. Why she was screaming on her knees.

Serena curled black hair around two fingers and nodded. "Yeah, Heidi Palermo. When'd you become such a hermit? I mean, what do you do in that house all day?"

Sweeney kicked her under the table, but she ignored it. So I did, too. No way was I telling the truth, that I'd been messed up since failing the exit exam again, so I mumbled a little about my studies. Carefully avoided the word *thesis*, of course—no point in exposing myself as even more of a freak. I felt Tank looking at me and reddened, resisted the urge to toy with the earrings that spiraled up my helix cartilage, but Serena announced that she *loved* movies. A lot of folks in Exile do. Escapist, you know?

After ten minutes or so, more Serena's yakking than mine, Sweeney nudged her and said it was time to go. Serena pulled a face but scooted her chair back as Sweeney and Tank shook hands. Tank half waved, tensed his zygomatic major at Serena as they left.

I thought about reclaiming my original seat. After all, I wanted the best view of Tank. But before I could decide whether or not to move, he spoke.

"You want something to eat?" he rumbled.

I shivered, shook my head. Not hungry—partly because I kept remembering the way Sweet William's neck had oozed arterial blood; more because I was crazy horny. Around Tank, my sex drive—always pretty generous—ramped up to ridiculous.

"Can we go?" I said.

He raised his eyebrows. "Go where?"

"Look," I said, "Chazz is here, and he's confused enough he's not going to follow us. Nobody else in my brother's crew will dare jump you without his say-so. And I think most everyone else is waiting to see how this shitstorm flies. So can we go now?"

"Go where?" he repeated.

"Home. Your home," I said, and considered dousing myself with the ice water.

He blinked, opened his mouth as if to speak. Didn't.

But when I pushed my chair back, he stood and gestured "after you."

Chapter Two

MOTHER WAS PREGNANT WITH Sweet William when an unregulated semi biffed the turn into the parking lot for the QuanTex mixing plant. I was three, and we lived close enough to the industrial park that I heard the truck's 6,500-gallon cylindrical tank rolling like a giant beer can across three lanes of traffic. Father, who'd been leaning under the hood of a pickup in our backyard, said I scrambled up his leg and onto his back like a chimp, said he nearly severed his thumb in the fan blade.

The semi's tank wasn't properly annealed. It crumpled and cracked, spilling a toxin (to this day undisclosed) that ate into the surrounding vehicles, some of them ferrying other chemicals for QuanTex. Within minutes, a gangrene-yellow fog blanketed half the town. The neighborhoods nearest ground zero, like my family's, became the Inner Radius; the ones farther out became the Outer Radius. Both zones were indefinitely quarantined by the federal government due to what the media called "Spill-Induced Rage." Technically, Exile was half of an already-existing town (the other half cleared out by mandatory evacuation), but we rezoned and renamed ourselves. And if anybody called Exile by its old name, they got schooled fast with a blunt object.

The way I heard it, even though Mother was working the phones at QuanTex that day, the EPA and FEMA agents assigned to her case had insisted she'd be all right—until she got into a fistfight with one and broke the lady's cheekbone, blinding her. Granted, socking a FEMA agent is no sign of mental imbalance, but it grew hard to argue the diagnosis. Before the feds managed to place Mother (waddling pregnant) under house arrest, she'd beaten several more folks senseless. The feds finally strapped monitoring bracelets on her and a few other felonious troublemakers, and Mother was confined to a quarter-mile run around the house. Still too much leash, if you asked me. In any case, William soon came out into the world to crack more-distant kneecaps for her.

William was twenty years old when Tank drove by him on a black Kawasaki Ninja and whacked his head off with an ax. So ended my brother's short but otherwise unremarkable life. That he lasted as long as he did—with no particular speed, strength, or menace other than the glitter-kill eyes and brute body stench of your typical warrior—might've seemed uncanny, but really it was the product of my grudging expertise and his weaseliness.

I was the family medic, though I refused to sit on the sidelines and watch like other crews' medics. I figured if William croaked in the few seconds it took me to run down from my bedroom, I couldn't have saved his sorry ass, anyway—which, yeah, QED. In any case, William rarely attacked uninjured warriors, and seldom alone. But the week he died, the usual street psychosis had cranked up tenfold, and William must've been swept along by the bloody tide. He'd ditched Chazz and run across the street to yank a crowbar out of some guy's chest, left him to die of a sucking chest wound, when Tank came along.

Was I supposed to cry for Sweet William?

≈

BACK IN THE INNER Radius, I twitched when I realized which path Tank was taking. Rather than cruising northbound on Cricket and using the side entrance to his lot, he drove west on Raven. He steered around chunks of battle debris, sometimes nearer, sometimes farther from the concrete traffic barricades lining the streets, a cursory attempt to keep the fighting off people's lawns. Not that much of anything grew anymore, even dandelions. The 'Ray's headlights glittered over the broken bottles that spiked my parents' barricades. I shrank in my seat, wishing my atoms would merge with the leather upholstery.

The wars had shattered the street lamps up and down the block, but every bulb in my parents' house blazed. Mother paced, screeching in front of the living room windows. At least she wouldn't be able to see beyond her own crazed reflection. By now my family had to have known I'd snuck out, despite the mandatory mourning period decreed by Mother. They probably didn't know where I'd gone or with whom. Even if Chazz had called them, they wouldn't have heard the phone over Mother's screaming.

Still, I held my breath until we'd safely passed my parents' place. Tank turned into a narrow driveway between concrete barriers on his side of Raven. He pulled up to the closed garage, lowered the 'Ray's pop-up headlights, and unbuckled.

"Wait for me," he said, getting out.

I did wait, dumbfounded. Why wasn't he driving into the fortified garage? Why would he leave the car unprotected in the driveway? Maybe he'd been in Exile too long, I thought as he came 'round the front. Maybe he was as nuts as any of us now.

He opened my door, reached for my hand. "Watch your step," he said.

So he expected us to saunter right up to the front door? We were practically across from my parents' house. I raised a skeptical eyebrow, but silent, I let him lead me down the dark path.

On our right, on the northeast corner of Tank's property, loomed eight-foot-high timber-and-concrete palisades that formed a V, buffering the house from Cricket and Raven—and creating a dead end. Panic prickled my heart like stripped electrical wires. What if Chazz—what if all my brother's crew—showed up and cornered us on Tank's gravel lawn? I imagined the sheen of starlight on machetes. They didn't even have to come that close; if they dug up a contraband shotgun or rifle, they could stand in the driveway and gun us down. The feds might storm in afterwards, impose martial law, but tell that to my perforated corpse.

I resisted the urge to peek over my shoulder. Sweat collecting on my upper lip, I focused on the sidewalk, sidestepped rocks.

"You okay?" Tank said at the door, his breath a puff on my shoulder.

I shook my head. "Yeah, fine. You?"

He paused, hand on the lock, and squinted at me in the dark. I didn't know what he was looking for—or at—and before I could figure it out, he turned to the door, let the optical scan do its thing.

Inside, a row of track lights glimmered at our entry. He closed the door, and I sighed in relief. Walking past me, he glanced my way and almost laughed, it seemed. I felt pinned to the ground by his suggestion of a grin; that micron of tension in his outer orbicularis oculi the only thing holding me up.

"Come on," he said. "I'll show you my deck."

I blushed, and then he did laugh.

"My *deck*," he enunciated.

We crossed the living room, our shoes quiet on the cork floor. We passed a dark kitchen that smelled of nothing, walked down a hall carved with empty alcoves, into an echoing den paved with flagstone, and back outdoors to a patio austere with shadow. He led me toward stairs rising into the dark. A tube of white light wrapped around the handrail, illuminating the steps, so I didn't have to stick *quite* so close to Tank, but I did. My thighs were slippery, my nipples tight.

Up top, dense, fire-resistant canvas cloaked the cedar deck on three sides. The house's second story provided the deck's fourth wall. The south side, hanging over the backyard, had a built-in bench, but I gravitated to the point farthest from my parents' house. A breeze blew, creaking the stiff canvas, and I wondered if it was like being on a ship. Maybe one docked in concrete.

Somewhere out of sight, the moon had climbed over Exile's meek skyline. Gray light filtered through the tarry smoke of the tire fires ringing the Inner Radius. Behind me, I imagined the smoke stacks of the abandoned QuanTex plant throbbing like a toothache. I could still hear my mother, faintly. Near enough to hold hands—though we didn't—Tank and I stared out at the sooty night.

"Why are you here?" he finally asked.

Moonlight shone off his scalp, and I wanted to stroke those cranial lines, but I was too short. I shrugged in reply.

"You fascinated with me because I killed your brother?"

"I'm fascinated by you because you're fascinating," I said, too earnest to be embarrassed.

"Anybody could've killed your brother," he said, head cocked as he searched the sky, maybe for stars. "If not me the other day, then Sweeney today, somebody else tomorrow."

"I know. That only makes William unremarkable, not you."

He took my wrist, pulled me to stand against him. My nose was on level with the middle of his chest. I had to crane my neck to look him in the eye.

"You hear your mom crying?" he asked.

I nodded.

"Why aren't you crying?" he said.

I shrugged again. "No one ever cried for me."

He held my gaze a moment—a long one—before nodding. "No one ever cried for me, either."

I slipped my arms around his neck. I had to tiptoe, and he had to lean down. I kissed him. His lips were dry, like he'd been licking at them, nervous, when I wasn't watching. He didn't close his eyes. His lids drooped three-quarters of the way, but he didn't let me out of his sight. Fine with me; I couldn't get enough looking at him.

I stepped back, holding the kiss, holding him, pulling him toward the railing so he could brace his arms. We'd need the leverage. When he realized where we were going, what I was doing, his legs locked. I stopped. I waited, heart loud and annoying in my ears, my fingers hooked in his belt loops, my mouth open on his chin.

He seemed to reach a decision. He turned us and walked backward until we hit the edge of the bench. Okay, good. He sat and I straddled him, my back to the house, my hips aching over the span of his thighs. He ran his hands up my arms as we kissed, his thumbs grazing my biceps, seeking the telltale bump of my contraceptive implant. I wondered if he felt me smiling into our kiss. Didn't my reputation precede me?

He watched my face as we fucked. I watched back until it felt too good. If he closed his eyes when he came, I was too far gone to notice.

After, he led me to his bedroom. I staggered after him, cunt-sore and dead-tired from the chaos of the past two days. We crawled into bed and lay like meth spoons. I tried to wait until I heard him snoring, but failed.

Of course, I'd drunk all that water at Mute's, so an hour later I woke with my bladder in silent-scream mode. Slowly, carefully, I tried to ease from the bed. Tank's hand shot out and grabbed my arm.

"What's wrong?" he said, his voice even gruffer with sleep.

"Nothing. I have to pee."

His hand relaxed, but maybe only one ksi. I still had to pull free.

23

When I crawled back to bed, he clenched me to him, my back against his solid chest.

"Miss you," he mumbled, the words nearly lost in my hair.

He wasn't talking to me. More likely someone in his dream.

"Shh, it's all right," I said, anyway. I patted the arm he'd coiled around me. "We're all right."

Chapter Three

AWAKE, TECHNICALLY, I LAY still, eyes closed. Not playing possum—just a sleepwalker's habit.

I listened to the shower running, inched my fingers out, testing. The mattress felt cool; Tank must've been up for several minutes. The guy was a radiator and left everything he touched, especially me, hot. I yawned, wondering where I'd go when he gave me the boot. Home was out of the question—Chazz *had* to have tattled by now. I rolled over and fell back asleep.

It felt like seconds later that I woke again. Tank stood at the side of the bed, leaning over me. "... pick up some stuff before they start up out there," he was saying. "Go back to sleep."

I think I nodded. I tried to. I fell asleep again, half-smiling at the warm tickle of his rough fingertips against my lips. My imagination, surely, but sexy nonetheless.

I woke again when the garage door closed with the Stingray safely inside. Hallelujah. That car deserved a military escort. Hearing Tank move through the house, I sat up to rub my eyes clean, brush my hair behind my ears. Didn't matter if I'd hardly slept the last two days, I had to snap out of it. Tank might offer me breakfast before kicking me to the curb—he was odd enough—but where was I going next?

"Hey," he said, appearing in the doorway.

His gravelly tone rattled my blood, as did the sight of him standing there, carpenter pants clasping his thick thighs, black T-shirt skimming his broad pecs.

"Hey." I clenched my legs together, hoping he couldn't smell my lust from across the room. I noticed my knees were scuffed from dancing on the deck.

He took a few steps closer to the bed, ratcheting up my pulse again, and tossed a sack in my lap.

"What did you bring me?" I asked, voice hoarse from sleep.

A toothbrush: red. A hairbrush: black. A bottle of shampoo: vanilla. Glycerin soap: also vanilla, my favorite. None of it government issue.

"Why vanilla?" I asked, hazarding a smile.

He shrugged. "That's what you smelled like when you tracked me down." His voice was so craggy, it was almost unintelligible. I wondered if that was why he spoke so little. "When you asked if I was the one who ..."

"Killed William," I said, remembering also.

The day after William's beheading, I'd snuck out of the house. Not that I'd had to be that stealthy: my family was still reeling, his crew moping, so nobody noticed I wasn't in my room, grieving on demand. Thus, I was free to follow the gossip I'd gleaned from the crew. The same details that disgusted William's thugs intrigued me.

Tank, an intermittent warrior, had already gone back to work. The very concept of *choosing* to work was anathema to my brother's crew. In exchange for a government salary plus hazard pay supplied by QuanTex (part of a settlement hammered out in the twenty-teens), Outsiders were supposed to implement jobs programs in Exile. Tank was one of the few Outsiders who didn't just go through the motions; his building company got shit done. "Motherfucking Outsider ran back to his Legos," the crew had complained. "He's out at the building site like nothing even happened!" Clearly, they felt insulted by Tank's unwillingness to hide but weren't sure what to do about his unconventional behavior.

Rather "unconventional" myself, I'd skirted the battles junking up the streets (because, despite the crew's outrage, the street wars didn't stop so we could mourn the likes of William) and hurried along Gatling Drive, unsure how much time I had before Mother noticed my absence. Gatling Drive was a scrubby, jaundiced path that looped around Exile. About every twenty yards a stolen street or traffic sign stabbed the droughty Texas dirt. The signs marked how close you could get to the trench before setting off the feds' alarms. The trench—eight feet wide, nine feet at its deepest—served as an open grave for any fool who charged the feds' electrified fence. On the other side of the fence loomed mirror-glassed panopticons, each with an observation deck studded with mounted machine guns: the Gatlings.

The panopticons cast shadows every quarter mile. I kept my eyes to the ground, held my breath as I dashed through each unblinking darkness. No one knew how many of the towers were actually manned or if they had to be. After the Spill, all Exiles had been injected with subcutaneous ID chips in their thenar eminence, that meaty bump under the thumb. Some folks said it was your chip crossing a magnetic threshold that really set off the alarms, not a shmuck standing guard. Still, I hated those watchtowers, hated the shadow noose they looped around us. Everyone else did, too, so Gatling Drive was the path of least resistance. Not that anyone could've stopped me; I was burning down a fuse that led straight to Tank. I had to see him, talk to this bizarre Outsider who'd sideswiped my family, who'd unwittingly released me from my medic duties.

Brain crackling with such thoughts, I must've veered off course. A warning siren blasted from the feds' towers, and I near leaped out of my skin. Hands over my ears, I skidded over loose gravel, hit the ground hard. I scrambled away from the trench and the noise, remembering the last guy who'd danced with the Gatlings.

As I shuddered on the ground, the siren cut off mid-squeal. I waited, but the robotic recording never started its

Judgment Day countdown. I blew sweaty hair out of my eyes and stared at the impassive face of the nearest tower. Was there someone staring back? Had I gotten too close, had a guard slipped and hit a button, or were sunspots witching the supposed magnetic field ...? I scowled and waited for my heart to settle. Then I got up, took two showy steps away from the cordon of signs and walked on.

At Tank's work site I lurked behind the foreman's trailer, studying Tank. He leaned against a truck with his company logo on it: a dense, black capital "T" locked inside a circle. Arms resting on the lip of the truckbed, he conferred with a tall, sunburned woman about jackhammers. The position cocked his left hip, tightened his jeans over his ass, cleared my mind of the mortal terror I'd just experienced. Above his leather belt a spread of sweat stained his gray shirt black. I followed the narrowing black strip to its apex between his shoulder blades. The vertical line accentuated the angle of those wide shoulders. I imagined extending the line all the way to the base of his shaved scalp. With my tongue.

I'd squirmed then, and hearing my boots scrape gravel, he turned around. The sun glinted off his wristwatch, blinding me. I blinked to clear my sight, and suddenly he was standing close enough I could smell him: limey sweat, caliche dust, trace of sandalwood.

And evidently, he'd smelled me.

Could he smell me now in his bed? I swallowed, found my voice. "Most guys think I smell like cookies. From the waist up, anyway." When he said nothing, I thought I'd gone too far and tried to get back on track. "So I can use the shower?"

He pointed. "My robe's on the back of the door," he said, watching me slide out of bed. "Toss your clothes out and I'll throw them in the wash."

Clean freak? I wondered. Or control freak? But gift horses and all that, so I didn't argue.

The water stung my scuffed knees. I figured my soap and shampoo, more than niceties, were suggestions that I keep my mitts off his stuff. After my shower I sat on the commode and opened the drawers of his vanity anyway, found his shaving supplies, slathered aloe on my abrasions. When I emerged from the bathroom toweling my hair, Tank wasn't there. I listened for the washing machine, but the wars were raging outside. I couldn't hear much more than motorcycles and screaming. I walked down to the living room.

Where would the laundry room be? Basement?

I wandered past the kitchen and down the alcoved hallway. In the light of day, I saw one alcove was actually a doorway with steps leading down to darkness. I didn't see a light switch.

"Looking for me?"

I whirled. Tank stood right behind me, a half-eaten apple in hand.

"Give me a fucking coronary," I said, pressing a palm to my chest. "Where are my clothes, Copperfield?"

"You're on the right track."

He gestured with the apple down into the dark. I hesitated. He reached from behind me and flicked a switch on the sloped ceiling. A series of lights low on the wall illuminated the treads, but I still didn't move. Confession: I liked the sensation of him looming behind me. Maybe also the crazy fear he'd push me to my death.

"Go on." He sounded amused, whether because he thought I was afraid or because he knew I was enjoying the way he rubbed up against me, I wasn't sure.

At the foot of the stairs, Tank moved past me to the center of the dim, concrete room and pulled a cord overhead. Fluorescent light revealed a wall of storage lockers to our left, the laundry, and a semi-enclosed half-bath to the right. I blinked. The basement was nearly the size of the Cantus' whole house.

Tank walked over to the machines, checked the time left on the cycle. "Almost."

I joined him beside the washer. I thought about him handling my underwear and felt my cheeks redden. Stupid to be embarrassed. He'd handled them a lot more the night before.

"You want me to walk you home?" he asked.

I shook my head. Water from my hair sprinkled my hands and face, his T-shirt. "They'll kill me," I said, not meeting his gaze. "I mean, after they've torn *you* apart."

He bit his apple. Reflected. "I thought maybe this was your elaborate form of suicide."

"I'm not elaborate." As if to demonstrate, no plan occurred to me. I simply blurted, "Can I stay here?"

Another bite, then he pitched the core into a wastebasket by the washer. "How long?"

"As long as you'll let me," I said, shameless as ever.

He turned to me, and I had to look, had to lift my eyes to gauge his reaction. He wiped a drop from my cheek with one knuckle, finished chewing.

"I won't throw you to the wolves," he said. "I don't drown kittens or kick old people either, so you can stop with the eyes."

I hadn't meant to give him the velvet-painting orphan eyes—not that I could help it, the width of my eyes being nearly a third greater than the interpupil distance—but I averted my gaze.

"Besides," he said, picking me up, setting me on the washer, "I'm not quite done with you yet."

I looked up and saw a slow smile spreading across his face. I grabbed fistfuls of his T-shirt and tugged him into the V of my parted legs.

His mouth tasted of apple, his skin of street smoke.

≈

ONCE I WAS WELL and truly fucked and my clothes were dry, Tank showed me the rest of his house. It was the largest on our block, in all the Inner Radius.

Three years before, Tank had paid off the previous tenants and scraped two lots clean, then built his house to be as intimidating as he was. Not an unwise strategy for an Outsider, though back then, I'd thought it pretty pointless since most Outsiders died within five years. That was one reason I hadn't paid much attention to Tank when he first arrived, though his physical charms were visible from a distance. Also, I'd been hyperfocused on studying for the 4-S test that could spring me from Exile. Tank and I hadn't been neighbors so much as two workaholics passing in the night. Then I'd failed the exam and gone hermit, as Serena had so helpfully pointed out.

But now as we walked the halls, I discovered Tank's house wasn't a brute bulwark. He'd outfitted it with technologies heard-of but usually impossible to maintain in Exile. On the ground floor he'd embedded an immense tele screen in one living room wall. Near the front door, a control panel streamed three video feeds simultaneously: one from the door-mounted camera that panned the front yard and two more swiveling atop the palisades. Other labeled switches on the console indicated that cameras swept every angle of Tank's property. He could arm or disarm the security system or specific points of entry from the panel. He had sound dampeners, too, which created an invisible dome to buffer the house from street noise. The dampeners weren't on at the moment.

I followed Tank in silence, trying to calculate how much all this tech had cost. I couldn't. I didn't know enough about the economy Out There. Because of my thesis, I could rattle off the cost of restylane treatments, an Asian blepheroplasty, or sliding genioplasty, but I had no context. Nevertheless, I figured the energy gobbled up by this electronic rampart had to dwarf the monthly kilowatt ration each household in

Exile received. Tank must've been wealthy Out There to be paying that much here.

Under the stairs a guest bathroom featured the same hypnotic tiles and sleek chrome fixtures as in Mute's bathrooms, which made me feel a little better. A sign of frugality. Across the hall a guest room echoed, empty but for a floorlamp. Another relief.

On the second floor near the top of the stairs, a fortified picture window overlooked Raven Street. I'd rarely had a bird's eye view of Exile—my bedroom in my parents' house faced the backyard—so I couldn't help slowing, then stopping to stare.

I scanned the horizon, seeking signs of life Out There beyond Exile's triple border. The tire fires raised inky curtains of smoke, obscuring any glimpse I might've caught of Gatling Drive. I saw the watchtowers, but their blank stares disarmed me, sent my gaze scuttling back to the street below. Down there, Sweeney punched a thug in the face. Nearby, knots of warriors fought for weapons, vehicles, pride, and—most elusive of all—dominance.

Tank stood beside me, the usual heat radiating off him. "Does it bother you? I can roll down the steel siding." He indicated a crank in the wall.

I realized my mouth was hanging open. I closed it, swallowed, opened up again to say, "It only bothers me when I'm working." I chose not to explain that I was almost always working, with brief forays into the wild for food and sex. "Even then, I just set the noise dampeners."

I looked to the right, searching for my parents' house, and wondered what was left of my old room, where I'd work from now on. Tank shifted his weight, arms over his chest, but said nothing.

"Speaking of work, I guess it's too late for you to get to your job site. Unless you want to wade through that." I waved at the tangle of warriors and bikes below.

He nodded, staring out at the fights, mouth turned up in that facial shrug.

"Sorry to inconvenience you," I said.

"If you've been inconvenient," he said, completely deadpan, "I can't wait 'til you become a real pain in the ass."

I lifted one knee to the window seat and side-eyed him. "Careful what you wish for."

He didn't pull his gaze from the fighting. I couldn't quite read him, and I suspected he was equally baffled by me; but I might have unnerved him. The masseter muscle in his jaw flexed one, two, three times.

"You can go if you want," I said, trying to ignore the tips of a bonfire on my parents' lawn. "I can entertain myself."

He shook his head slowly. "Naw, it's out of my system for a while."

I toyed with my earrings, considering. If Tank's violent energies built up over time, then unlike my Rage-y cohorts, he could make a conscious decision to purge those homicidal tendencies. That explained the "intermittent warrior" thing. It also suggested some ... *interesting* possibilities.

The quarantine imposed on Exile was semipermeable. Just as we couldn't see into the panopticons but the guards could see us via one-way glass, we couldn't leave town unless we passed the feds' 4-S test: you had to be strong, smart, sane, and sterile. (All defined, of course, exclusively by the feds.) But Outsiders who agreed to implement jobs programs could get visas and move into Exile for five years at a time, so long as they didn't have criminal records. Generally, any Outsider who didn't turn tail and run in the first two weeks ended up in the street wars. Guess you had to be a little insane to begin with to want to come to Exile, or the feds' screening measures left something to be desired. In any case, most Outsiders expired before their visas did.

But not Tank. He'd been in Exile for three years, and I guessed he aimed to stay more or less intact. Intended to leave again one day. He seemed to like me at least as far as he could throw me. Maybe when that "one day" came ...

"What about your stuff?" he said.

It took me a few seconds to understand. I was plotting—shit, in my head I was already halfway out of town. I shrugged, forced myself to focus.

"Tonight. Mother might be exhausted by then." As if. "There's not much to get," I added. "Even less if she's broken into my room and started demolishing things. Mostly, I want my thesis stuff."

It was out before I knew it. Tank tilted his head, looked at me.

"Thesis? What you were telling Serena about last night?"

"Yeah," I mumbled, face going red. "Probably sounds stupid, studying anything in this hellhole ..."

He shook his head, thinned his lips in what physiognomists call an AU14: the "meh" expression. "I put up buildings so they can burn 'em down again. Who's stupider?"

That shocked half a laugh out of me. Which he traded for half a smile. When he spoke again, it was with a measured, careful quality I envied.

"I didn't realize the telestudy program covered college, let alone grad school."

"It wasn't meant to. But half-ass as the guidelines are, there wasn't anything to stop me." Like common sense? Hoping to outpace my inner snark, I said, "I would've preferred pre-med, but there wasn't a way to do the labs. The feds don't exactly trust us with chemistry sets. Anyway, even if I finish, it won't mean anything. Not here."

He shrugged. "It's your work. That's enough." Given the brutal work schedule I'd heard he kept, I didn't think the sentiment was merely job-maker propaganda. He nodded at the street. "If you want, I can go over with you. Help you carry stuff."

I glanced toward my parents', relieved to change the subject. Only now a flagpole leaned in the front yard, a burning effigy of Tank dangling from it. Mother smacked the scarecrow body, sent it spinning 'round the flagpole like a tetherball of death. The twins, Thing One and Thing Two, stood on the roof, hurling rocks at Tank's house. Their missiles didn't touch the barricades on Tank's side. But given time and the right materials, that would change.

"You want to carry your spleen?" I said. "Don't bother. I can smuggle a flash drive across the street." I should've brought it with me. But who could think straight with Mother sobbing and slamming things? I'd figured I'd get back home before the crew ratted me out.

Tank nodded, seemingly unaffected by my family's display or the street battles. Hand on his smooth scalp, he drifted toward his study, down the hall from the bedroom. "I've got some drafting to do," he said, uncertain.

"Then go do it." I turned on my heel and headed downstairs.

"There's stuff in the fridge."

Yeah, there was. Mostly fruits and vegetables—and not just the hardy root stock from the government dole. I drank a glass of filtered water and carried a handful of dried apricots back to the living room. I had to study the control panel for a bit before understanding how to work the noise dampeners, but I thought Tank might appreciate the quiet also.

In the engineered calm I lay on the couch and wondered how the hell I'd get in and out of my parents' house alive.

≈

COMPARED TO TANK'S, MY parents' home was a toad abode. Father worked more than most Exiles. His mechanic skills were in high demand, plus the terms of Mother's house arrest required his gainful employment. Still, almost all our money—the government stipends all households received and whatever Father earned working for RatRod at the junkyard or doing odd jobs in town—got funneled back into the street wars. William always needed new elbow pads or another Kevlar vest or bigger brass knuckles. We didn't even have sound dampeners, in spite of living on the sidelines. The savages didn't care; they loved the noise. I had to rig my own localized dampeners from specs I found on the Internet, and I ran the damn things night and day.

There were, of course, drawbacks to that bit of DIY. One night I got back from a good time, and Father ambushed me in the kitchen.

"What the hell are you doing up there?" he yelled. "We exceeded our kilowatt allowance for the next three months. Where am I supposed to get the money to pay for that?"

"The feds aren't gonna cut our power. We're the only people on the block who pay the difference." I tried to dodge around him.

"We're the only ones with a person under house arrest! We can't afford to flip off the powers that be. You really want to take the chance that they'll cut us off? With your mother and her hot flashes?"

I froze.

"And don't think you can run off to the Cantu boys and avoid the consequences." He nuh-uhhed a finger in my face, lowered his voice. "You pitch us into that circle of hell, and I'll tie you to the banister, Heidi. You'll share every screaming minute of it."

A fate worse than death. After that, I was more judicious about running the dampeners. And I soon discovered another drawback: the dampeners allowed my twisted siblings to creep up on me. Mostly, I had to endure Thing One's bizarre booby traps; easy enough—except for his minor success with the Crisco and homemade pepper spray. But there was one time with William ...

Hence, my rule about not dancing with William's friends.

I was sixteen, the Things were three, and Mother was enjoying a brief reprieve from house arrest. Every month, the free medical clinic in the Outer Radius opened for three days, staffed by the Red Cross. When Mother had a doctor's appointment, the feds loosened her leash, assigning her a specific route through town and a carefully calculated itinerary. Any deviation from the feds' plan, and Mother's monitoring bracelet powered up. A field of static electricity coalesced around her body; every hair writhed at attention. She looked like a hair-throwing tarantula preparing to strike. That was her only warning before a cocktail released into her bloodstream started poaching her insides.

That day, Father was scouring abandoned houses in the Outer Radius for a water heater to replace ours, so I got stuck babysitting. I strapped the twins in their kiddie harnesses and hitched them to two legs of my bed. Then I got to work on my latest project, an autopsy of Fievel, the neighbor's cat.

I knew the cause of death: William. My brother stomped anything smaller than himself that crossed his path. But even before Fievel's brush with Sweet William, the cat had looked scrawnier than usual, his hair thatchy. I wanted to know why. So I turned my desk into an operating table and set it up so the Things could watch while I worked. Thing Two seemed especially interested.

I was excising a lump in Fievel's large intestine when I heard a wobble from the dampeners. Even that might've been too late—I should've known better than to turn my back to the door—but I had an X-Acto knife in hand and a cat peeled open in front of me. That gave William pause, gave me an advantage when I turned and saw him sneaking up on me. I didn't stand or bolt, simply reached up and slashed.

"Bitch!" He hissed and sucked the wound across one palm. "What was that for?"

"What are you doing creeping up behind me?"

"I wasn't going to hurt you—"

"Then why didn't you knock? Why didn't you call my name?" Something chinked, metal on metal, and I glanced down. "And why is your belt buckle undone?" I slashed again.

"Stop! Shit! I just wanted to know what all the fucking fuss about your fucking pussy was all about!"

I watched him suck his palm again, my cheeks hot and my ears pounding as I parsed his panicked syntax. I did get up then, brandishing the knife. Though three years younger than me, William was taller, heavier, sturdier ... and apparently horny. Thing One sobbed and sucked on four fingers. Thing Two wailed, straining to reach Fievel's broken tail.

William retreated a step, then two, still licking his cut. Meanwhile, his other hand dripped blood on my floor. I stared him down, a strategy that always made him babble.

"I mean, if you don't want the attention, stop dancing with everybody. The guys are always bragging about what they've done to you, where you did it. What you do to them. Why shouldn't I get some? A look at least. It won't kill you! My own house and all. Hell if I know what they see in you anyway, you skinny skank, 'cept you don't charge for it."

"There's a difference!" I said, but I stopped, too amped to finish the thought.

"Why?" He paused, a gleam in his eyes. "'Cause I'm your brother?" As if that opened up the matter for negotiation.

"Yes! No!" I shrieked. "Just get out before I cut off your balls!"

He flinched from my swinging blade and backed out of the room.

I slammed the door behind him, locked it, then turned, shaking, to stare at the Things. "You believe this shit?" I asked. Rhetorically. They had some mysterious twin-speak but wouldn't speak English until they were five.

Thing One stopped sobbing but kept sucking his fingers. Thing Two grinned up at me, hopeful. But I slumped in my chair, all desire to dissect gone. Well, maybe William ...

It took a while, but later that night, lying in bed fully clothed, knife under my pillow, I figured out what the difference was, what I'd started to yell at William.

There's a difference between giving it away for free and selling at a loss.

Chapter Four

AFTER SUNDOWN, BLACKJACK (TOWN preacher turned bruiser) revved out of the neighborhood with his motley flock. That signaled the unofficial end of the day's bloodshed—too hard to fight in the dark. Half an hour later, Tank opened the side gate for me, and I hurried down the sidewalk. South on Cricket, away from Raven Street and my parents' house. My heels clattered, the sound echoing off concrete barricades. I had no weapons and no Kevlar, though Tank had offered both. My best bet wasn't fighting but fleeing, and Tank's body armor would have slowed me down. Or smothered me—it wasn't one-size-fits-all.

I had nothing like a plan, either. As I'd lain on the couch, my thoughts had quickly veered from sneaking into my parents' house to weaseling into Tank's future ... and out of Exile. I'd taken the 4-S test every two years from the time I turned seventeen, the maximum anyone was allowed to take the exam. After the third try, the cool-off between tests ballooned from two years to five. Despite my monomaniac efforts, I always came up one S short.

I had Sterile under my belt—or under my biceps, more accurately. The contraceptive implant sufficed for testing purposes. Surgical sterilization was a prerequisite for actually leaving town, but no prob there, as far as I was concerned. I mean, have you ever seen an anencephalic baby? I held one once. Her name was Lourdes, but I called her ET. She was a cousin of the Cantu boys. She was dead. And thanks to the Spill, she wasn't an anomaly in Exile.

I knew I was Smart. I'd done well when I took lessons from Miss DeeDee, and getting as much education as I had kinda proved the point, I thought. In any case, I'd tested myself online, consistently scored above average.

Which left Strong and Sane. I'd been surprised to find that Strong mostly meant Not Sick. Another condition of Mother's house arrest had been that us kids had to report for regular checkups and submit to all recommended immunizations and procedures. Done and done. 'Sides, I'd survived Exile long enough to take the test, right? So a doctor's physical was no sweat.

The hang-up, the motherfucking rub that blistered my ego, was Sane. "Inconclusive?" What the hell kind of result was that? Anyone could see my family was insane; *I* was not. I was the opposite of those wild-ass, battle-crazed pyros. I'd never taken a crowbar to anyone's kneecaps, I'd never gone looking to maim someone. Clearly, the test was flawed.

Whatever. I was stuck waiting five more years before I could test again. Well, I'd been sulking for awhile, so more like four and a half. But still.

I wanted to be a plastic surgeon. I knew I'd have to work shit jobs Out There to pay my way through an associates' degree in nursing (not like I had an impressive resume). But then, even if I got a job in a plastic surgeon's office, who knew how long it'd take me to get through med school while working? I'd already wasted twenty-three years in Exile; I couldn't spare another five. Life in Exile rode you hard. I knew from watching my father.

Tank had been in Exile for three years, so he'd have to leave in two, if only to re-up. In the meantime maybe he could help me figure out how to snag my last S. Or plan an escape. Maybe I could ... ingratiate ... myself enough that he wouldn't want to leave without me; he could smuggle me out ...

Such conniving gave me the creeps—a little too déjà vu—so that's as far as I got. My whole plot to infiltrate my parents' house ended up being my usual frying-pan-to-fire thing.

At the corner of Cricket and Flint, I turned right and clambered over the concrete buffer, across the street, and over another barricade. I walked a block on Flint, stopping when Red Sonja dashed out from under her porch to greet me.

"Hey, what are you doing under there?" I said, squatting to pet the Pomeranian. We'd gotten to be friends when I was dancing with the family's oldest boy. I wiggled my fingers under Sonja's armored helmet to scratch her auburn ears, under her body armor to let a breeze in. "Stay out from under the porch, girl. You don't know what's lurking down there." I shivered, thinking of worms and spiders, but she grinned, bathing my fingers in discount Milkbone breath.

"Gotta go. Be good." I scurried off before her people caught sight of me and called my people.

At the corner of Flint and Hornet, I turned right again and promptly snagged my heel in a tangle of jump ropes, nearly broke my ankle. Goddamnit, Sammy! Did he never put his toys away?

Limping, cursing, I cut through the Cantus' yard. The motion sensor was busted, or the light bulb burned out, because the porch held its darkness as I approached and sank on the age-worn boards. Nobody home, otherwise I would've heard *Bambi*, Sammy's favorite movie, chirping from the chinks in the wood siding.

I flexed and massaged my ankle, felt shitty for cursing Sammy. What next? Call him "retard" like Mother and William did? If Sammy had been there, he would've been rubbing my ankle for me, tongue tripping over apologies. Didn't matter that I'd ditched him without explanation. I hadn't wanted to, but the Cantu boys were kind of a package deal. I couldn't break up with only Carlos.

I shook my head. Not my fault. Carlos or Romero could've explained it to him, could've told him the same story I'd told them: Carlos would do better as a city liaison, one of the few Exiles considered reliable enough to act as an intermediary between the feds and us if he weren't connected to my family—and he needed to do better, for all three of them.

A pack of kids crept up on a blackened go-cart in the street, helmet lamps stabbing their prey. For now, they were too busy to notice me, but not for long. Most crews fought to burn off some Rage. They didn't hate each other any more than the average hockey team hated another in their league. But a few crews tended true, long-standing grudges. I didn't recognize these kids, so I doubted they had any truck with me, but a buck was a buck, and who knew what my family might pay for a tip?

I got up, tested my ankle. When it held without (much) complaint, I moved on down Hornet. A block and a half later, I turned right again and hastened down the glass-flecked alley between the houses on Raven and Hawk. Skulked until I came up behind my parents' house. I lifted the corner of our chain link fence, same as I'd been doing since I was twelve. On the back step, my heels gritting in the remains of a garden gnome, I imagined my family knotted around Sweet William's shrine.

Before I'd left they'd laid him out on the couch in the living room, a forever fountain of Pabst bubbling on the credenza behind him. Mother had safety-pinned his head to his neck, reinforcing her work with one of his studded dog collars—an improvement, style-wise. Father had taped a can of beer in William's clasped hands. Thing One had queued up an endless stream of AC/DC, Metallica, Kontagion, and American Riot for the wake, and Thing Two had sacrificed a few mangy squirrels in William's honor.

And I was walking into that shit. Oh, for the love of Jason Statham.

I wiped sweat from my upper lip and slid my key in the lock. The slamming rhythm of "Master of Puppets" covered the squeak of the hinges, my steps through the tacky-floored kitchen, but as I tiptoed upstairs, rusty nails rained down on me: one of Thing One's stupid booby traps. Like most of his thumbless fumbling, it would've been harmless, but the racket gave me away.

"What was that?" Father said.

"My trap," Thing One crowed.

I sucked a deep breath of Pabst and putrefaction and raced up the rest of the stairs. My family's feet thundered across the living room floor. I dashed through the broken door of my room, then reeled in horror. My pictures!

Fluttering scraps were all that remained of the full-color prints of my thesis subjects that I'd pinned to the walls: an inch of Clark Gable's smirk tilted at a fraction of Paul Newman's left Aqua Velva eye drooping over a swatch of Brad Pitt's scruffy cheek. My stomach cramped. Even so, I couldn't help noticing the serendipitous combination of features. Kind of my job.

Thing Two's war cry jolted me into action. I tripped over the wreckage of my desk to the nearly empty closet. My meager wardrobe must've been added to the bonfire on the front lawn. I leaned into the closet and jumping, groped over the doorframe for the secret panel I'd carved out.

"Get her!"

Mother wasn't as fast as the kids, so she barked her order at the Things as they tore up the stairs. I pushed in the panel and reached inside. Then sixty-five pounds of pure hatred rammed my side. Theo: Thing One.

"Fuck." I grabbed the clothes rod for balance before another 65 pounds barreled into me. Thea: Thing Two. Always hesitant for hand-to-hand, but she'd warm up.

I jangled into the clothes hangers, and the Things, clutching my legs, slid down in a jumble at my feet. Holding the rod, I kicked frantically. One of my heels stabbed Thing One's cheek—that's why they called them *stilettos*. Before Thing One could escape, I used his head and shoulders as a stepladder. With a final leap that rammed his head into the floor, I managed to grab the lockbox hidden overhead.

"What's she got?" Father yelled from the doorway.

Thing Two, skinny ass now in gear, backed up and charged again. This time she grinned, lips peeled back over chiseled teeth. I punched her in the face with the lockbox, and she went down, out.

I whipped my head around. Thing One panted on the closet floor, a twisted hanger skewering his right hand. I turned to see Mother push past Father, who teetered on one bare foot, trying to pull a rusty nail from the other.

Mother's green eyes flashed. "You little bitch! How dare you show that cocksucking face after taking up with your brother's murderer. Did you think we wouldn't find out? That Chazz wouldn't tell us?" She flew at me, red claws splayed, ratty robe flying open to reveal stretch-marked skin.

"Look out!" Father warned. Her, of course, not me.

I bashed her hands aside with the lockbox, praying the handle wouldn't break and my thesis—and one weapon— go flying across the room. Mother shrieked and shook her stinging hands, but she kept coming after me. I bolted for the Jack 'n' Jill bathroom that linked my room to the twins'. I stumbled over the remains of my printer and crashed to the bathroom floor. Pain flared from my scraped knees. I grunted, squeezing my eyes shut. And then Mother started kicking me.

Gritting my teeth, I hugged the lockbox and marine-crawled over the mirror shards littering the linoleum. Mother punted my tailbone so hard my eyes watered, but it must've hurt her, too. She was wearing slippers. She howled.

I scrambled to my feet in the twins' room. I veered around their bunk beds, heard a seam rip, wished I'd had more than a mini dress to wear into battle. The floor shook—Mother hopping after me on one foot—then there was another crash.

"Stop her, you asshole!" Mother shouted.

I careened out of the twins' room. Father blocked my path, the rusty nail now pinched between two thick fingers. He held the stair rail, one foot arched, bleeding. Head down like he'd gone ten rounds with Dolph Lundgren when I wasn't looking. I plowed ahead. He glanced up, stiffened for a second, wide eyes matching my adrenaline-blown gaze. (I'd inherited my manga eyes from him.)

But when we collided, he folded. He did punch my left eye. Mostly by accident, I think, his hand curled around the nail. I swore, momentarily blinded by a bolt of red and green, and we sprawled at the head of the stairs. He grabbed my waist, but he didn't hold tight. He didn't even try.

I got to my feet and raced down the first flight of stairs. I spun around the corner, screeching when an empty drawer hit my shoulder. I half fell, half jumped the rest of the way down, missed most of the nails. Mother hurtled down the stairs after me, but by then I was pretty much scot free.

I still toppled the beer fountain on my way out.

Principle, you know?

≈

USED TO THE CARNAGE of the streets, Tank didn't blink when he met me in the driveway. Although he *was* holding a shotgun. I stopped short, amazed to see contraband on such obvious display, never mind the dark. The slightest bit of gunfire and the feds swarmed down on us, as if worried we'd break quarantine and raid the neighboring town— over forty miles away.

"You get what you need?" Tank said, looking behind me. "Any clothes?"

I glanced over my shoulder. Braying, Mother leaned as

far over a concrete barrier as she could without stabbing herself on broken bottles or leaving Sweet William behind. Thing One, under no such restraint, leaped the barrier, shrieking incoherent yak threats.

"Thesis, yes," I panted. "Clothes, no."

I grabbed Tank's wrist and yanked him behind the palisades before this thing could escalate. The feds wouldn't care if Tank fired a warning shot or splattered brains on the street. They'd storm in, and it'd be feds versus residents, simple as that.

"Guess I don't mind if you go without," Tank said. He closed the door on my family's rage, easy as switching channels on a program he'd already seen. "Let's clean you up."

A well-prepared warrior, he kept a first aid kit in the kitchen. He left his gun on the counter and got to work. First, he cleaned the cuts on my arms and legs. Cold, stinging sweeps up and down. I could've done it myself, but having someone attend to me was weird enough that I simply leaned against the counter, watching. The dry tang of rubbing alcohol prickled my nose hairs and cleared the stink clogging my head. Tank touched the bloody holes in my dress.

"These hurt much?" he asked, meaning the gashes beneath.

"Not much." I wanted to be brave.

He pulled aside my collar and bra strap to examine my aching shoulder, ordered me to move it a few different ways, and apparently unconcerned, went on to my face. His huge hands were surprisingly gentle, particularly on my fast-swelling eye. He hadn't touched me that way before—not last night and not in the laundry room. Jealousy crept up on me as I thought of the construction materials he worked with day in and day out. Stupid, but I had to say something to quell the emotion.

"So," I blurted, "you still like me?"

He looked quizzical, lateral frontalis muscles lifting his eyebrows at the outer edges. Embarrassed, I indicated my bashed face.

"Oh." He doused another cotton ball with alcohol and touched it to my cheek. "Yeah, sure. I'll just do you from behind for a while."

I punched his shoulder, and he winked, walked to the freezer for an ice pack. Only then did I realize I was still clutching my lockbox in one hand. Reluctantly, I set it beside his gun. My bruised knuckles cracked.

"You took a pretty good beating," he said, handing me the ice. "What was it, four against one?"

"Three," I grumbled. "Thing One and Thing Two equal one human being."

"That what you call the knee biters?"

I looked him up and down. On him it might've been the knees, but Thea had been going for my gut.

"William called them Thing One and Thing Two. From his favorite author." I held the ice pack to my eye, gingerly at first, then more confidently when I felt the blessed cold. "Fucking animals," I muttered.

"I'll break their legs tomorrow."

I was pretty sure he was joking, but it was hard to tell. That craggy voice, the stony face I had to dissect for clues. "I don't need vengeance," I assured him. "I'll settle for a hot shower."

"Hang on, I'll come with you," he said, packing the first aid kit. But the simple chore took too long, and his eyes moved too much, the furrows in his forehead too deep. He turned to stow the kit in the cabinet, and his back to me, said, "I may have given you the wrong idea earlier."

My stomach flipped. Was he going to toss me out after all? With my family all riled up like that? "Yeah?" I managed. "How's that?"

"I'm not going to stop fighting in the street wars."

I stared at his back. "You said it was out of your system."

"*For a while*," he stressed.

"Right," I said slowly, not understanding.

"I ain't like your brother, it's not my entire life." He turned, but rather than meet my gaze, he scanned my wounds. "But now that I'm here in Exile, it's a part. A big part."

My turn to look quizzical. "I never expected you to stop."

He finally met my eyes, seemed faintly pissed. What did he want? I was agreeing with him, right?

"I'm not invincible, you know. I could get hurt. Die, even."

"I know!" What, did he think I was five? I lowered the ice pack so he could see my frown. "Look, Tank, I'd never ask you to stop. Who the hell am I to ask anything of you? I'm already staying here. Isn't that pushy enough? Besides, I can't imagine a household where someone didn't go out to fight—maybe wherever the fuck you're from, but not here. I just don't want it to be me."

"You sure?" He studied me, blank faced, practiced. "You took a smackdown from your whole family without a weapon."

I thought of Thea knocked out bloody on my floor. But that was different. I braced myself against the adrenaline still jittering through my veins, insisted, "I'm not a warrior."

"Well, I am. So long as you understand."

"I do."

He did the facial shrug again, but this time it looked like he was faking a smile. I thought I should be flattered that he bothered to try and appease me, but instead I was confused. Had he *wanted* me to argue with him?

He started to leave the room.

I said, "Wait," and touched his shoulder.

"What?" He shrugged my hand off but let me study him.

I scanned his eyelids, measured the vertical crease in his glabella, assessed the puckers at his chin. I couldn't figure him out fast enough. I decided to joke it off. "Do me a favor, huh?"

His eyes went steely. "Like what?"

The transformation shocked me, sent a ripple straight through to the cesspool at the back of my brain. Tank expected people to take advantage of him. But he wasn't going to lie back and take it. He'd go for first blood, and then he'd keep right on going until he got last. I swallowed hard, tried to silence my ever-pulsing desire to escape Exile.

Slowly—slow enough he could've stopped me, slow enough it wouldn't hurt me if he did—I reached out. I stroked his cheek, attempted a smile. "Don't mess up this pretty face of yours. I don't want to have to do *you* from behind."

"What?" His jaw relaxed. A glint in his eyes warmed his whole face. I held back a spasm of relief. "What does that even mean?"

"I don't know," I said, really feeling my smile now.

"Maybe you got hit harder than I thought." His expression went from warm to sizzling in point-two seconds. "You should lie down."

I nodded to the oak table at the center of the kitchen. "Think that will hold me?"

"Are you kidding? I made that table myself."

For a second I was jealous of an inanimate object again. Then he led me to the table, pressed me down, and proceeded to demonstrate exactly how sturdy it was. And somehow during that vigorous demonstration, all my plots and petty jealousy simply ... evaporated.

So what if he never closed his eyes?

Chapter Five

WILLIAM WAS FOUR MONTHS old before I managed to be alone with him. Mother hip-carried him everywhere, paranoid "They" would take him away. And who knows? It was the bastard sort of thing the feds would do, even to families not helmed by convicted felons. The few times Mother peeled William off and tucked him in his bouncy seat while she washed or did chores, I was afraid to go near him. He had colic and she was breastfeeding, and half the time he was covered in bloody, milky barf and screaming his damn head off.

But one day, after a prodigious fart, William relaxed and slept long enough that Mother put him in the crib. When she stumbled away to shower, I crept into my parents' bedroom to study the little monster. In the dim, curdled-milk atmosphere, I didn't see the appeal. He was so angry, so loud, so insistent. Even in sleep, his mouth was pressed in a grim, red line.

I was still getting used to the stranger in Mother's skin. Father had tried to explain, but I suspected it was really William's fault, that he'd given her the Rage somehow. He was always angry, too, right? Standing over his crib, I didn't want William to catch me staring at him. That would piss him off for sure. So I reached one hand through the bars and carefully covered his eyes. Gently at first, not to wake him, then a little harder. Could I keep him asleep by pressing his lids down? William's mouth wiggled. What if he screamed?

I reached my other hand through the bars and covered the lower half of his face to keep him from crying. I was trembling, terrified he'd bite me the way he was always chomping on Mother. So I held on tight, jailing his lower jaw. That left only his nose exposed. His nostrils flared.

I noticed that my hand flattened the bridge of his nose. I pressed his nose flatter, watched it inflate again when I loosened my grip. He was squishy! And if I spread my lower hand a little wider, I realized, I could cover his whole face. So I did. I felt warm suction on my palms.

He was really wriggling now. He was making a small sound, too, but not so much that it bothered me. For the first time since William was born, I felt relief. I could look at him all I wanted. I could take my time to see, understand. I could move a finger here and see one eyebrow. A finger there and find his chin. And so quiet!

I was fascinated. So much so, I didn't hear the shower go off, didn't hear Mother shuffle into the room. One second I was enjoying my baby brother, the next, I was flying through the air. I slammed into a wall. Mother's screams competed with William's, and I covered my ears, bruised arms aching with the effort.

Mother bent over the crib to frisk William head to toe and back. I started to crawl away, but finding William intact, Mother spun around and grabbed me by the hair. I screamed. She dragged me out of the room, cursing and shaking me. I kicked at the floor, clawed at the walls, seized carpet like the fraying edge of my very short life.

"But I didn't do anything!" I screamed. "I was just *looking!*"

≈

WHEN I WOKE THE next morning, I was pinned. Tank lay on his stomach, half-on/half-off me, one hand gripping "my" side of the bed. Perhaps that was why I hadn't gone sleepwalking. I'd been expecting an episode since William died—stress seemed to bring them on—but so far, nothing.

I blinked a few times, trying to get my left eye to cooperate, before turning my head a fraction of an inch to see if Tank was awake.

He was.

"Your eye," he said, voice muffled by his pillow, "looks terrible."

"Gee, thanks."

The cheek I could see lifted in a semi-smile. "Thought you should know before you saw it in the mirror. Less of a shock?"

Concern for *my* feelings? My brain might've slipped a gear.

He propped himself up on one elbow. "I got to be at a site today," he said, peering down at me. "Can I trust you?"

I frowned. "To do what?"

"Nothing in particular. Just, can I trust you?"

He was staring right into my eyes. I blinked, trying to keep him out. I imagined, quite vividly, him putting his forearm across my throat and snapping my neck. I swallowed hard.

"Yeah, sure," I said.

"Not a very ... *enthusiastic* response," he said, still eyeing me.

"I don't know what you're getting at."

"I mean—" He leaned more heavily on me. "—when I come home tonight, will I still *have* a home? Or will you and your family have burned it down?"

I scrambled to sit up, but fighting Tank was like fighting a brick wall. "You think I'm scheming with my family? They beat the crap out of me!"

"Maybe it was for show." Tank squeezed off one of his trademark facial shrugs.

"For show?" I jabbed a finger at my swollen eye. "You think I sat back and took this willingly?"

"I offered you a weapon, and you wouldn't take it. I offered to go with you, and you refused. Like you knew you wouldn't get hurt too bad."

"What have you been huffing? I'm not here to avenge William's death. I hated him!"

"So you say." He examined me like I was a wonky set of blueprints. "But you don't seem too concerned whether I live or die in the streets, either."

"That again? If you don't trust me, why am I even here?" My face burned; I didn't know what pissed me off more, that he thought I was conniving with my crazy family or that I was so *not* intimidating, he'd decided to keep me around as a toy. "Why did you meet me the other night? Take me to Mute's? I could've stabbed you in the car, or ... or ... knifed you on the doorstep!"

He rolled onto his back with a sigh. "No, I was ready for it."

I sprang into a sitting position, ignoring the ache in my bruised coccyx. "Oh yeah, well, how about when we were on the deck? I bet you were a little bit distracted—"

He shook his head. "Sweeney had my back."

"What?" I grabbed his arm, tugged until he looked at me instead of the ceiling. "What?"

"Sweeney was on the roof before we got here. He kept quiet, watched, waited until I gave him the signal to leave."

"But, wait ..." Suddenly, every single moan and groan of that night echoed in my head. I felt the heat in my cheeks draining away. "Where was he? When did he leave?"

"He was in the eagle's nest on the roof. You would've seen him if *you* hadn't been a bit distracted. He left when we came to bed."

"Sweet Sue, then he heard—saw?—everything?"

He shrugged. I felt like throttling him.

"Tank!"

I jumped out of bed. He snatched my wrist.

"Hold up—" he said.

"Well, what about yesterday?" I pried at his fingers. "When you left to go to the store? If I was out to get you, wouldn't I have done it then?"

He blinked a beat too long, as if silently cursing himself. "Wait, look, Heidi—" He knelt on the bed and grabbed my other wrist. "Stop fighting!"

"You first!" I said, twisting uselessly. "What about all that time you were holed up in your study? How do you know I wasn't lying in wait? Were you watching me the whole time? Do you have cameras everywhere?"

"Not everywhere."

I stopped. I stared. I couldn't tell if he was joking. Maybe, I slowly realized, being the Outsider didn't automatically make him the sanest person in the room.

"I figured if you were up to something, I'd hear." He released one of my wrists, his focus skating off me and onto the wall. "Besides, you're pretty small. I think I could take you."

So he was kidding. I rolled my eyes at the understatement of the decade. "If you don't trust me, why do you keep fucking me?"

He gave me side-eye, like it was a trick question.

"Don't give me that 'I'm a guy' bullshit." I groaned. "Fine! Then why'd you let me move in?"

He shrugged. "It was the easiest way to keep an eye on you. And if things really went south with your folks, I figured I could use you as a hostage."

I snorted. "Like they'd want me back."

He looked at me: measure twice, cut once.

"I don't get it," I said, ignoring his scrutiny. "If I'm a hostage, why tell me you aren't going to stop fighting in the street wars? Why be pissed when I give you the 'wrong' answer? What do you care?"

He shrugged again, defensive now. But he was still clutching one of my wrists. I took a deep breath. I didn't want him to throw me out. I didn't have anywhere else to go. And hell, so long as I was careful—very, very careful, I thought, remembering his eyes the night before when I'd asked him for a favor—I might still be able to work this.

One knee pressed against his on the bed, I lowered my voice, lifted my gaze. "Come on, Tank, you *do* trust me on some level, or I wouldn't be here. You want excitement, you've got the street wars. You want a lay, women'll line up around the block. Hell, the hookers would do you for free, for the glory."

He raised his right eyebrow. "The glory?"

His hint of a smile forced a curve to my lips.

"You know what I mean," I said, trying to stay serious.

His hand loosened around my wrist. "I got to get cleaned up for work. You want the bathroom first?"

Feeling whiplashed by the change in topic, I pulled my hand free, crossed my arms over my chest. "No thanks," I muttered.

"Don't pout." He twisted out of bed, a scowl creasing his face. "It doesn't suit you."

"Neither does being treated like a spy. Or a hostage!" I called as he stalked away.

I dropped face-first onto the bed and tried not to imagine Tank's slick, naked body under the shower spray. Obviously, not too successful. When he emerged from the bathroom wearing a towel and a sandalwood-scented cloud of humidity, I rolled to face the wall. I heard him rooting around in the closet, then the muffled thump of his towel hitting the floor. With Herculean effort I resisted turning around.

He came into my line of sight, tightening his belt. "You can use my computer if you want."

"Are you sure? I mean, I might wipe your hard drive."

He frowned, dimpling his chin in three spots. But he only asked, "You gonna be here when I get back?"

I almost snapped, "Where would I go?" But I didn't *want* to go anywhere else, except Out There. So I nodded.

He dipped down and kissed me hard. Our teeth knocked, and I tasted mint toothpaste, breathed in the spicy vapor still rising from his skin. The second I was hooked, he pulled away.

"See you later, Heidi Heidi Ho," he said, and left me floundering.

≈

I TOYED WITH THE idea of getting dressed and stepping out back, so he'd have to look for me when he got home. But then BlackJack's war cry split the morning peace, and ... no. BlackJack didn't bear me any grudges, but once he hit the streets, our neighborhood went all Mad Max. Not that I was judging, exactly.

For Exiles with Spill-induced Rage, the street wars provided structure to otherwise tedious days. Whatever changes unfolded Out There, in our quarantined wasteland, months blurred in an endless wheel of cloudless blue skies and scorching sun, starless nights and smoky moon. Romy Cantu was a warrior, and even Carlos had brawled alongside his cousins in the Cantu crew before, at age fourteen, he opted for the extra government pay that came with training to be a city liaison. So long as bloodshed wasn't the end-all-be-all of a warrior's existence (like it was for my family), I didn't begrudge warriors their way of marking time. Not everybody was built for work like me and Tank. But why expose myself to the stinky, dirty ruckus now that I had somewhere to hide?

Besides, what if Tank didn't bother to come looking for me?

I swaddled myself in Tank's robe, pitched my underwear in the wash, and grabbed my lockbox.

The study smelled slightly musky. And no wonder, with the desk that dominated the room.

If the Stingray was sex on wheels, then Tank's desk was an office orgasm. Boomerang shaped, dark wood wrapped around lighter, both overlaid with glass, it made me think of two-tone '57 Chevys, hairpin curves, the wind in my face, and furtive fucking in backseats. Tank must've made the desk himself. No one in Exile sold office furniture, much less office furniture that made you cream your jeans.

I glanced around. A pair of free weights sat in the corner. That explained the musky smell: Tank seemed the type to work his body when working things out in his head. I, on the other hand, would've been humping the desk.

The windows were sniper slits overlooking the streets, but between that and the track lighting, it was plenty bright. Against one wall stood a large drafting table and on a pedestal nearby, an architectural model. Cross-section of an office pavilion. Surely, no one in town had commissioned such a thing, so ... maybe a piece from Tank's past, his life Out There? I knocked my lockbox against one thigh, considering this memento. Then I turned back to the porny desk.

When I sat in Tank's chair, my feet dangled in the air. His grandiose computer monitor, perfect for CAD, blocked my view of the east wall. The OS defaulted to a three-dimensional GUI—intuitive to Tank's spatial mindset, but a puzzle to me. Eventually, I figured out how to download my files. And then I waited. State-of-the-art as Tank's computer was, shinier than any hardware I'd ever touched, my photo files still forced a cranky, churning sound from it. I twisted in the rolling chair until I caught a glimpse of my silhouette on the screen.

Quasimodo!

Even on my best days, I wasn't beautiful on any scale: dull brown hair; small, misaligned ears studded with piercings; featureless forehead; straight nose; decent columellar-labial angle; mismatched lips, the bottom one like someone had pressed their thumb in before I'd quite set. My eyes— light brown like Father's, rimmed with thick lashes—were my most notable feature, but only because they were out of proportion to the rest of my face. My interpupillary distance was comparable to the average fifty-five millimeters, but the width of each eye, inner to outer canthus, was nearly a third greater than the IPD.

And now, as if that weren't freakish enough, I had a massive periorbital hematoma. This would not aid my mission of sweet seduction. Groaning, I fetched an ice pack from downstairs, then returned to review, one-eyed, the last paragraphs I'd written before William died.

Chapter Six

ONLY WHEN I HEARD the side gate ratcheting open for the Kawasaki did I realize the street wars had receded for the night. I'd given myself a Cyclopean headache at the computer, then sacked out on the couch to watch soaps—on mute, of course, so I could admire the men without having to listen to them— but I'd spaced out. If Tank actually had cameras hidden about the place, they'd captured a whole lot of nothing.

He clumped into the room, reeking of sweat, sawdust, dirt. I stretched but didn't sit up. He walked across the room and peered over the top of the couch at me.

"You're here," he said.

I looked up at him, stereoscopic vision restored. "I said I would be."

"You always keep your promises?"

It was too much like his trust question that morning. I sat up, and he leaned down, his elbows on the couch, his breath on my forehead.

"I don't know," I said, not budging. "I've never promised anything to anyone."

His brown eyes flickered to the tele, a commercial for a nutritional supplement. He didn't say anything, didn't call me on the lie, so maybe I wasn't as transparent as I thought. But I felt sorry for picking a fight where there didn't have to be one. Could've been careless banter on his part.

"What did you do today?" I said, trying to make up.

He rolled his eyes, wrinkled his brow. Three horizontal furrows. "Catapults."

"Catapults?"

"Don't ask." He came around, leaned one hip against the couch. His khaki carpenter pants, blackened with oily spots, strained against his thighs. Seemingly oblivious to my lust, he nodded at the limp ice pack in my hand. "How's your eye?"

"Doesn't feel so bad, but it looks terrible—which, incidentally, is a big improvement over what it looked like this morning, you big liar."

"I was trying to spare your feminine vanity."

I made to swipe at him, then realized my sleeve would hike up, revealing the cuts I'd gotten in yesterday's knockdown drag-out. I settled for a scowl.

"What did *you* do today?" He leaned over and grabbed the remote. His stink rubbed up against me, prickling my nose, but I didn't mind. Better than blood and rot. Better than William.

"I transferred my stuff to your computer, made corrections, but I couldn't do much more." I watched Tank instead of the strobe of switched channels. "I had photos of my subjects up on my walls before my psycho family shredded everyfuckingthing. Hard to write without *seeing* what I'm writing about, you know?"

"I've got photo stock by the printer." He shrugged. "You can use it if you want."

"I saw it," I said tentatively. "I'd need a lot more."

"It's for work, right?" He shrugged again, stopped fiddling with the channels, and tossed the remote beside me. "I'll get more."

It didn't seem like a big deal to him, which made my chest ache a little. It'd been hell scraping together enough cash to pay for my previous stock. But then I envisioned my pictures wallpapering his study, and the ache faded. Mostly.

"I can't repay you," I said, a warning probably undermined by my grin. "I've got nothing but my underwear and what was on that thumb drive."

"You're earning your keep." He tugged the front of his sweat-darkened shirt to fan himself and parted with the tiniest of smiles.

Seems I'd been wrong about my black eye hampering the seduction phase. If I'd thought for one second the battered look turned him on, I'd've hightailed it outta there. But he wasn't looking at my bruises; he was looking *through* them, as if talking about my work had established some rapport that a few busted blood vessels couldn't diminish.

"You going to shower?" I said. I couldn't help the flirty lilt in my voice.

"Yeah. And I think you're coming with me. Or I'll take my robe back."

I smiled, already unknotting the belt. "And how exactly is that a threat?"

≈

AFTER SHOWERING, I SLIPPED on one of Tank's white oxford shirts and a pair of boxers that I cinched with one of ten identical black ties. Tank said he'd make dinner. I said, "Fine," and headed to the study to reprint my photos.

Given my limited resources, I started with the analytic batch. I taped up the first succulent specimens—How I missed you, Cary Grant. Too, too long Ramon Novarro!—then, as the others printed, I sat to reread a few paragraphs I'd brooded over earlier. Soon, I was off on a mad revision streak: masculinized phi masks, vermilion borders, neotenous cues, Johnny Depp's hair, sex-identification algorithms skewed by visual merchandising—

"Hey."

I screamed.

In the doorway, Tank smirked, held up a hand: We come in peace.

"Fuck!" I said, catching my breath. "You scared me."

"Don't know how. Been calling you for the last fifteen minutes."

"What for?" I turned to the wall and sized up Val Kilmer's torso, pre-1995.

"Dinner's getting cold."

"I'm not hungry," I said, flipping through the stack of torsos on the desktop.

"That's not what you said an hour ago." But he didn't sound annoyed. "What are you up to?" He stepped into the room to examine my wall of flesh.

"I told you, I need to get my glossies up again." I reached around him and placed another Kilmer torso, post-2000, beside its brother.

"These are people?"

I nodded. "Men."

"Why are they all marked up?"

I glanced at Tank. He had a "look" on his face. That gave me pause—I'd thought he *liked* that I was serious about work? But headshots were piling up in the printer tray, so I didn't have time to puzzle him out.

"The black lines form graphs that allow cell-by-cell comparisons," I said. "The solid blue lines indicate lines of symmetry, dotted blue lines indicate variation from ideal. Yellow for the golden ratio, and the red lines show changes over time. Solid for time alterations and dotted for chemical or surgical alterations."

"But they're all just parts," Tank said, sounding craggier than usual. "How do you know who they are?"

"There's a code on the back." I flipped over the upper right quadrant of Denzel Washington's face. "See? First and last initial, last two digits of the year, a source variable—press release, tabloid shot, screen cap, et cetera—and body part."

Tank's outer canthuses wrinkled, not unlike Denzel's. "When do you put them all back together?"

"Back together?" I paused to pick up Denzel's upper left quadrant. "Well, I have sections where I discuss whole packages, but it's much easier to provide coherent analysis if I have pieces to point to. Probably like when you talk about a building." I cocked my head at the model office pavilion behind me. "I bet it's more useful to point to specific walls and ducts than to wave your hands at the whole thing." I paused again, distracted by the wrinkles around Denzel's eyes. Not a single dotted red line. You had to admire that.

"Yeah, but then I make the buildings."

"Yeah ...?"

I looked up. Tank was studying me, but he dropped his gaze before we made eye contact.

"Dinner's getting cold," he said again, and left the room.

"I'll be right down," I said. But I forgot.

Later that night, when my vision blurred so bad I couldn't type anymore, I crawled into the Tank-warmed bed. Tank was curled up facing the wall. I pressed my naked body to his back and waited for the inevitable response—which turned out to be quite evitable, actually.

"Tank?" I whispered.

Silent.

I ran my hand down his side. He was wearing pajama pants, his hands folded between his knees. When I stroked his bare chest, he grumbled and turned into the bed.

I rolled away with a sigh, tried not to assume I'd said or done something wrong. He could've been tired after a long day of work. Or tired of keeping up with me in the sack. There were rumors about who he'd danced with and when, but I figured he'd danced with three women, tops, since coming to town—and none of them the ones who'd bragged about it. By my reckoning, Tank was practically a monk. I was lucky I hadn't killed him yet.

Later, he found his way over to me anyway.

"Where were you?" he mumbled, and laid his head on my breast.

I remembered the first night, when he'd said he missed me.

"Right here, baby," I whispered, kissing his stubbly head. "And I'm not going anywhere."

It just slipped out. It was the right thing to say; it soothed him. But it frightened me.

It felt too much like a promise.

Chapter Seven

FATHER WAS ALWAYS THE one to stitch us up. Not that he was all that good at it, his big grubby mechanic hands cramped from years of wrenching cars into submission. But Mother was impatient at the best of times and frothed at the mouth if William got a hangnail. Even William didn't want her coming at him with a needle. So we all had crooked scars winding like barbed wire over our skin. Clumsy but loving in their way. He could've let us bleed out, right?

That changed when I was thirteen. Father was searching the junkyard for parts for the neighbor's sink—who knows what they'd shoved down the disposal—but really he was avoiding Mother and her knocked-up hormones. We weren't neighborly, as a general rule.

Mother hollered up at me from the kitchen. Reluctantly, I paused the movie I'd been watching, studied the freeze-frame of Matt Dillon's bare teen back. I cocked my head, shriveled a little when I heard Mother calling William, too. Why did she need both of us?

I dragged myself downstairs and smelled William before I saw him panting in the back door, squinting against the sweat dripping in his eyes. Mother sat at the table, legs spread to accommodate her pregnant belly, her tent of a sundress clinging sweaty wherever it could. Her face heat-rashed and swollen.

"Yeah, Mom?" William wiped his forehead with his arm, then smeared his arm along the back of his white-gone-gray T-shirt.

"Come in. Sit down." She nodded at the chair in front of her. "You, too, Heidi. I've got a test for you."

"What kind of test?" William squinted at me as he sat, like the summons might've been my fault. "I don't do school. I don't take tests."

"This is different," Mother said. "A different kind of test. One I made up for you. Both of you," she amended. She eyed me as I scooted my chair a few inches from William and his ground-in summer stink. "We've each got a role in this family. You, William, are our warrior. You'll represent our family on the street in a few years. You, Heidi, are our medic. You'll care for William."

I wanted to protest, but the words backed up in my throat—sure, I was taking lessons with Miss DeeDee, a lady in the Outer Radius; sure, I'd completed basic Red Cross training, but I had no intention of "caring" for William. But I couldn't open my mouth. I felt hypnotized by Mother's green eyes. Snake eyes.

She continued. "You don't wake up one morning, and BAM! you're a warrior or a medic. You've got to grow into your roles. Practice, so you're ready. Heidi, go grab what you need for a stab wound. Bring it here and set up on the table."

I started to stand, paused. "Is this an emergency scenario?" I choked out. "Or do I have early warning?"

She smiled. I nearly fainted from the approval.

"Let's pretend you have warning. But be quick." She turned to William, dismissing me. As I left the room, I heard her say, "You have your switchblade?"

Like that, my blood felt spiked with refrigerant. I should've run away. But my body cruised on, fueled by the fumes of Mother's respect, the delusion that I knew what she had planned.

When I returned with my kit, William's chair was pulled up alongside Mother's, close enough their thighs pressed. His nose, salt-crusted from dried sweat, hovered inches from her milk-heavy breasts. They'd clasped arms. She held his elbow, and his fingers twitched on the pale skin of her forearm. He smelled worse. Neither of them looked at me. William's knife waited on the table in front of them.

"Set up," she told me. She didn't watch, so I figured this wasn't part of the test. She stared into William's wide eyes— into William, it seemed—and said, "When she's ready. When I tell you."

Her tone matched Father's mantra when he stitched us up, if not the words: *Just sit tight. You'll hurt yourself more trying to get away.*

She picked up the knife, and William shivered. "No fear," she told him. "No hesitation."

"But, Mom," he whined, and I looked up, startled. He wasn't even *trying* to sound tough. He leaned in like he might bury his face in her chest, but instead he looked up at her. Tears washed some of the grime from his face.

"Be brave," Mother said.

"B-b-but ..." William gave off a wave of wretched heat like he'd wet himself, but I didn't smell piss. "But I don't want to hurt you, Mom!"

I almost gave myself whiplash. *He* was going to hurt *her*?

Mother didn't spare me a glance. She locked eyes with William, bored through his panic like a diamond drillbit. Their foreheads nearly touched.

"William." She sounded as certain as Charlton Heston. "You can't hurt me. I'm your mother."

William kind of spasmed. But he took the knife. His eyes were hubcap huge, he still shivered, but he swallowed, churning up his courage. Meanwhile, my stomach dropped down around my knees. My heart jacked against my ribs. My mind screamed like a buzz saw, every single synapse insisting I get the hell out of that kitchen *now*.

I couldn't move.

William grasped Mother's elbow. His spine straightened. His thighs flexed as he twined his legs around the legs of the kitchen chair. He braced his sneaker soles on the linoleum. He gazed up at Mother, his fear seeping away, replaced by awe. He breathed out, and Mother inhaled. She exhaled, and he sucked it down.

My chest ached. There wasn't enough air for me.

William focused on Mother's bloated forearm. He set his jaw and pressed the blade into her skin midway between wrist and elbow. Flexor carpi radialis.

Bloodscent flooded the kitchen.

William stared at the rich black blood welling up around the knifepoint, breaching the flesh. He pressed harder, dug in, drew down. Palmaris longus.

Blood pattered onto the linoleum and speckled his jeans and shoes. He looked up at her. She hadn't flinched, hadn't pulled her gaze from his face. She merely clenched her teeth and smiled, press-lipped, at him: permission granted. William grinned. He pulled the knife out. Released her.

Then they turned to me. I stared back, my cheeks impossibly hot, my hands clammy in their gloves.

She rested her bloody arm on the towel I'd laid out. "Heidi," she said, jaw still tight. "Move it. We don't have all day."

Hands trembling, I grabbed a gauze pad.

My work made Father look like a surgeon. Over the next two days, the wound turned pink and ropey, infected. Mother made me redo it and said, less forgiveness than not-so-veiled threat, "Better you messed up on me than on William."

William had passed Mother's test. I had failed.

≈

THE NEXT MORNING, TANK left for work before I woke. At least he didn't bother me about trust.

I stumbled downstairs. On the dry-erase surface of the fridge, Tank had printed "EAT SOMETHING HEIDI."

Inside, last night's leftovers were neatly packaged. My guts twisted, but not in hunger. It'd been a while since anyone gave a damn whether I ate or not. And Tank knew that, given our "Nobody ever cried for me" conversation. Was my seduction plot already an amazing success, or had I miscalculated? Was Tank playing *me*?

I was thinking maybe I oughtta put on the brakes, at least until after my brother's funeral burn, when I heard a motorcycle approach: a Yamaha Dual Sport, it sounded like. It zipped right up Tank's driveway, cocky as you please, and triggered an alarm that honked like an embarrassed but insistent donkey.

I scurried into the living room and glared at the security panel. Between the alarm's *hee* and *haw*, I heard the bike idle beside the house before coughing off. The door-mounted camera caught the driver, zoomed in on his sunburned neck as he hung his cracked helmet on one handlebar. Then he turned around.

Sweeney.

The doorbell *blurp-blurp*ed like the synthesized heart monitor in that ancient Soft Cell song. I didn't want to open the door. But it wasn't my house. Sweeney was part of Tank's crew, and the mutant moral code, such as it was, obliged us to provide refuge. That and I wouldn't win points with Tank by pissing off his brass. The braying alarm and the blurping bell must've scrambled my brain because suddenly I thought, *What if something happened to Tank?* I jerked open the door. Immediate, assaultive, the summer heat slammed into me.

Beyond Sweeney, bikes flickered past the gap between concrete barriers. Some dumbass hurtled by on a streetluge; not five seconds later I heard a *thwonk* and scream. Probably racked himself.

I glanced at Sweeney's bike parked beside the house. Red and white WR250R, blood in the treads. It wasn't a shiny bike liberated from an Outsider; it predated the Spill.

I looked at Sweeney. Same as the other day, a little cleaner. Like Adrien Brody in his heyday, but with those yellow eyes, that extra incisor. Deeper crow's feet. A less-often-broken nose—

"Hey, Tank home?" he said, grinning. Wasn't self-conscious about that tooth at all.

"You know he's not." I watched, and his grin hardly faltered. Between the permanent forehead furrow and the crow's feet, I guessed he was near-sighted. "Did he send you to check on me?"

"What?" He squinted like maybe he hadn't heard right over the alarm. "Naw. I was just curious how you're settling in. Tank says you're staying a while."

I nodded, my gaze straying over his leather-jacketed shoulder to monitor the visible half of my parents' house. The Things were wrestling on the roof, fighting over a spyglass they were more liable to shatter than share. No sign of Mother or Father. Probably inside, mooning over Sweet William's corpse.

"Can I come in?" Sweeney asked, and moved forward.

I grudgingly stepped aside. I held my breath but still smelled leather, hair gel, motor oil, cigarettes as he passed.

"Nice shiner," he said.

"Walked into a fist." Despite the threats from outside, I hesitated before closing the door. I didn't know how smart it was to be alone with this guy. He wasn't near as big as Tank, but he was taller than me. Heavier. No doubt stronger.

Even with the door shut, the alarm kept hee-hawing. Sweeney gestured at the security panel. "You gonna get that?"

"Be my guest."

He smirked, understanding I didn't know how to silence the alarm. He swiped at a toggle, and Eeyore shut up.

"You look cozy." He nodded at my get-up: Tank's button-down shirt and a pair of cinched boxers.

"Dress got messed up."

"Too bad. Looked good on you." He walked backwards into the living room, boot spurs clicking. He looked away from me long enough to scope out the kitchen, glance up the stairs to the second floor. Satisfied, he leaned against the couch. "Yeah, you look quite at home."

"What do you want?"

"Aww, why you wanna be like that?" He cocked his head and turned those muddy yellow eyes on me as if hurt.

I forced myself to move from the front door. I started to head for the security panel like a security blanket, but realizing that, I veered away, positioned myself between Sweeney and the kitchen. Where the knives were. I was sick with a knife.

He heaved an exaggerated sigh, nodded. "Tank tell you I was here that night?"

My face and neck flushed. My arms crossed over my chest of their own accord.

"Yeah, well," he said, "a little surveillance was necessary. He had me check you out before that night, too. I talked to a lot of folks, trying to get the lay of the land ... so to speak." He pretended to check his spurs before grinning up at me. "Wasn't exactly a surprise what I saw."

"So I sleep around. So what?"

"So Tommy Vai told me some stuff."

That. I looked at my bare feet, damning the lump in my throat. "Thomas is an idiot," I muttered.

"But he's alive."

I snorted, bracing myself. "Not my fault."

"And his brother's dead."

Couldn't snort at that. Couldn't even whip up sarcasm when I said, "Not my fault, either."

"Didn't say it was." Sweeney examined his right hand, flicked one fingernail against another. "But Forrest seemed fine before he took up with you."

I rolled my eyes. "Nobody in this town is fine."

"But see, that's the thing." Sweeney's grin dimmed. "Forrest *wasn't* in town anymore. He had his four Ss, he'd tested out. But then he came home for a visit, hooked up with his little brother's sloppy seconds, and next thing you know, he's—"

"Shut up!" I sucked down a breath, held it behind locked teeth. Damned if I'd let him see how much this fucked me up. I shook my head, repeated, "Nobody in this town is fine, okay? Even the 4-S board can make mistakes. Why else—" I clamped down before finishing: *would I still be here?*

"Right ..." He filed his fingernails against his jeans, studying me.

Given one near miss, I should've kept quiet. So of course I snapped, "What? You think I'm going to fuck Tank suicidal?"

He leaned his head back and laughed. I watched his Adam's apple hitch, his hips roll slightly against the couch. "No," he snickered. "I confess, that particular method never occurred to me."

"There is no method," I said, walking to the front door.

"Oh. So I'm dismissed?"

I turned back. He was still smiling. Or pretending to. I twisted the doorknob.

"Well, I'd hate to wear out my welcome." Sweeney pushed off the couch and swaggered toward me. "But don't get any ideas, Heidi. You stick around, you're going to see a lot of me. Maybe as much as I've seen of you."

I refused to retreat, so I couldn't avoid his fingers in my hair. He tilted my head, forced me to look up.

"I gotta say, though ..." His eyes saccaded, miniscule recursive sweeps left to right, over my features. "I can see why Tank likes you. You got moxie, girl."

≈

TANK KEPT NO LIQUOR in the house. Believe me, I looked.

I was in the study, cutting up Rick Yune and Daniel Dae Kim, when the side gate opened for the Ninja. The gate moved slow enough I had time to push away thoughts of Forrest. The back door slammed, and a few minutes later, Tank stomped up the stairs. I squeaked my chair to signal my presence in the study. He popped his head in. He didn't say, "You're still here," but he looked it. I resisted the urge to pitch the scissors at him. At best, I was a lousy hostage; at worst, a fucking mutant. What did Tank care whether I left or not?

"Gonna shower," he said.

I grunted and started cutting Yune again.

He came back later, still wet, and asked from the doorway, "You gonna eat tonight, or am I gonna have to run you an IV?"

I watched a line of water trace his sternocleidomastoid. My teeth itched. I forced myself to meet his eyes. Once I did—red from dust, a thin veil of weariness—I softened. I wasn't mad at Tank. I was mad at Sweeney for threatening my progress with Tank. And furious at my own stupidity for thinking Tank would never find out about Forrest.

"I'll eat," I said. "Come get me if you have to."

"Easier said than done."

Over dinner—plum-glazed chicken, nutty rice pilaf, roasted broccoli; did he always eat like this?—Tank said little, which was normal enough. I didn't realize I was quieter than usual until he said, "Something wrong?"

I sighed, didn't have the energy to dissemble. Anyway, better to suss out Sweeney's influence on Tank sooner rather than later. "Sweeney came by."

Tank rubbed his fingers on his napkin. Contemplatively, if that was possible. "Yeah?"

"Yeah."

He waited. Drank water. Swallowed. "What for?"

"Said he wanted to see how I was settling in." I watched Tank, my napkin over my mouth.

"I wondered why he wasn't on site this morning," he finally said. "What'd you tell him?"

"Nothing."

He looked at the edge of my plate. "You okay?"

I shrugged. He went on eating.

"You don't have to let him in if I'm not here," he said, mouth full.

I leaned forward. "No?"

He shook his head, swallowed. "Not if I'm not here."

"But ..." Was it possible I'd miscalculated Sweeney's sway over him? I invoked the warrior code. "He's your right hand. What if he's hurt?"

Tank scoffed. "Shit, who ain't hurt?"

"Really?" I wondered if we had a translation glitch, native nuance lost to Outsider-speak.

"Really," he said, half shrugging. "It's up to you. You feel safe ..."

I couldn't help pushing it. "But I thought he was your friend."

Tank looked at the edge of my plate again, his chin pushed out. No answer.

≈

THAT NIGHT, TANK, DROWSY, watched TV. Documentary about the largest skyscraper in the world. I wondered if he wanted to see it in real life, if he would one day. If I would ...

On the opposite end of the couch, my feet braced against his thigh, I held a reader Tank had lent me. Instead of studying outdated physiognomic markers of criminality, however, I was cataloging Tank's profile: the droop of his eyes after a long day, the softness of his jaw, his lips slightly parted. I started to see ... not crevices, exactly, but ledges in his rocky facade. Edges, fingernail-thick, where I might get a grip. He must've felt my attention because he turned, cocked his right eyebrow at me.

"Creeps me out when you do that."

"Do what?" *I'm just* looking, I thought.

He shook his head and turned back to the tele.

I followed his gaze and seeing a welder with a blowtorch reminded me. "William's burn should be in a couple of days."

Other than dawn to dusk, the street wars didn't follow a set schedule. But there was a rhythm to the wreckage if you tuned in to it. About a week after someone died in battle, Exile's collective Rage stalled long enough for the family to light a funeral pyre. Then the streets around the family emptied out for a few days, letting the warrior's crew regroup. Once the smoke cleared, I might see how to proceed with Operation Break on Through.

"Figured." Tank nodded, a little out of sync with his words. "I arranged a few days off."

"Yeah?" I lowered the reader to get a better view of him, though he didn't return my gaze.

"Yeah. Things might get ... intense. I think it's best if we hunker down."

"Here?"

"I got a room at Mute's," he said, surprising me, "but really, this is the best place to be. Safest."

"Of course. I didn't mean ..." I stopped, not sure what I had meant, stunned that his plans included me.

"You 'bout done?" He tilted his head, indicating the reader. "I'm fading fast here."

I blinked. "Were you waiting for me?"

He seemed too tired to smile, but it was in his voice. "You got pretty big eyes to be missing that."

Chapter Eight

Every time I called the Vai house, Thomas picked up. "Forrest's not here," he'd yell over my protests, then hang up.

I'd hit redial, and he stopped even saying hello. He knew it was me and what I wanted.

"Put Forrest on," I snapped.

"No! He doesn't want to talk to you."

"No, *you* don't want me to talk to *him!*"

"He hates you, Heidi. He doesn't want anything to do with you. He knows what you're really after."

"Damn it, Thomas!"

But he'd already hung up.

I yanked on my boots and ran to their house in the Outer Radius. My hands shook so bad I could hardly get the key Thomas had given me into the lock. I ran into the living room. There was a body on the flowered couch, and at first I thought it was Forrest, that I was too late. But it was Thomas, his head pillowed by his ever-present football.

"You asshole," I hissed.

"He doesn't want to see you," Thomas called as I ran down the hall. "He hates you."

The hall was long and dark and smelled of sweaty socks, spunk, Skittles. I passed Thomas's door, flung myself at Forrest's: locked.

"Forrest, it's me. Let me in!" I pounded the door with both fists, felt it give not a bit. "Don't do it!"

The door was as solid as a bank vault. The doorknob was gone, the hinges had disappeared, not even a sliver of light shone around the edges. My fingers scrabbled, fingernails snapping as I sought some crevice. I banged my forehead against the door, squeezed my whole body against the unyielding grain, tried to wade through the wood.

"Heidi," a voice said, so soft it was like my conscience—the scrap I had left.

I moaned, tried to speak, heard only whimpers, and couldn't move.

"Heidi, wake up!"

I blinked through my tears, and Tank was there between me and the door, me and Forrest.

"But," I said.

"You're dreaming. Sleepwalking." He shook me a little.

"But ..." I squirmed, craning to see around him. It was the wrong door. The front door. Tank's. I looked down at my fingers. Bleeding nails, scuffed knuckles. "I have to ..."

"You were sleepwalking. Come back to bed." He turned me, led me, arm firmly around my shoulders, back upstairs.

"But ..." I tried to look back; he wouldn't let me.

"It's over. You're awake now."

He sounded pretty sure. So I took his word for it.

THOMAS VAI PLAYED FOOTBALL. Which was stupid. Why scramble after a pigskin on a field when you can skin your opponent in the street and steal his bike?

Even so, I couldn't help staring when, at age nineteen, I passed the field behind the old high school. Two teams dodged across the field, shirts versus skins, no helmets or pads, just that ball and fighting over it, the closest thing our mutant town had to jocks. Mostly kids from the Outer Radius. The guy in possession, sweaty and bare-chested, outraced his opponents like nothing. As he sailed into the end zone, he had this grace I'd only ever seen in old musicals. Was it a touchdown or a tango? I couldn't tell.

I wandered closer to the sagging bleachers. When the star slouched to the sidelines to guzzle homemade Gatorade, I did a quick survey of his face: white boy with gently straight eyebrows low over green eyes, a broad forehead ("plenty of room for thinking," I thought, but "this space for rent" turned out to be more accurate), fine bones, and hollow cheeks—one smeared with mud—strong Greek nose, and soft lips straight as those eyebrows.

Used to being ogled, he didn't notice me at first, but I was the single point of stillness in the eddies of excitement. Scuffed football under one well-muscled arm, he looked at me, tilted his head to appraise. I stood my ground. Tit for tat.

Turned out, Thomas carried that football everywhere. Normally, it would've been a deal-breaker, but I wasn't in the best headspace. I'd failed the 4-S test for the second time. Two more years—two agonizing years trapped in Exile with my mutant family—before I could retest. And if I screwed up again, the span between tests would expand to five years.

Desperate for distraction, I asked around, found out Thomas was a Vai, younger son of Meris and John. They'd served as liaisons for a time, volunteered in our rundown school. Rumor had it that their son, Forrest, was the last person to test out of Exile. Clearly, his brother, Thomas, would never test out. I mean, he could read and write like you'd expect from the Vais; otherwise, he was about as sharp as a marble.

Luckily, Thomas was very, very pretty. I'd've pounced on him even if he hadn't been my key to Forrest.

≈

TANK PINGED ME AROUND noon. I wondered how he knew my addie, or that I'd be online. Then I remembered I was using his computer, that I hadn't asked for privacy or passwords, that he knew I was a workaholic bad as him.

Have to work late. Don't wait up. Delivery this pm, rooftop. Sign, open.

Weird. I guess I hadn't said anything too revealing while sleepwalking, not if he trusted me to open his mail. But if last night's episode hadn't triggered Tank's suspicions, it had sure set my hamster wheel of memories spinning.

Thomas used to run errands every afternoon for Miss DeeDee, who was agoraphobic. Once we'd been dancing a couple of weeks, he gave me a key to his house. The deal was I would greet him naked and ready in his musty-smelling bed every day after his run for Miss DeeDee. (We never went anywhere because of his girlfriend. And he was probably scared of the Cantus, though Carlos and Romy were more protective than possessive.) In exchange, I got to have mind-blowing, noncommittal sex with the most popular guy in town. Or I suppose that's how he explained it to himself.

The sex *was* pretty good. But better was getting to the house early and snooping. Thomas's parents, Meris and John, had been profs at a nearby community college. Living in the Outer Radius, they'd seemed to escape the effects of the Spill. They both had all four S's—smart, strong, (voluntarily) sterile, supposedly sane—but they chose to stay in town until their boys could test out, too. They were the ones who'd gotten the feds to upgrade our WiFi to offset the isolation of the quarantine. Even after they were gone, we all benefited from that cyber lifeline.

But the Spill left behind this invisible slick that sullied everything and everyone. John's attention slowly swiveled from the outside world. He started braving the Inner Radius on humanitarian missions, badgering families to keep their kids in school, to reject the settlement of the class action suit against QuanTex. And though it was like reasoning with berserkers, John kept coming back, as if drawn by the silent beacons of the defunct smokestacks. Meris followed, dragged him home again and again. One day they got caught in the street wars—wrong place, wrong time—and it was over.

Forrest was three or four years older than me. Same age as Carlos Cantu, I guess, but I'd never laid eyes on him. First he was a loner, then he was gone.

Thomas didn't like talking about him, so I spent time in Forrest's old room, trying to get a sense of the guy. He hadn't left much behind: a butterfly knife, an old atlas that fell open to Nepal, posters of the Grand Canyon and coral reefs. Sometimes I sprawled in his bed, staring at those posters, imagining him roaming rocky gorges and saltwater vortexes. It was hard because I didn't know what Forrest looked like. So sometimes I imagined it was me.

One afternoon I let myself into the house, and *It's A Wonderful Life* was projected on the living room wall. I frowned, key in the back door, head cocked at Jimmy Stewart's stutter. *Thomas must be home*, I thought. But he didn't have the irony to watch Capra.

"Thomas?"

No response.

I walked into the TV-blued living room. A man slouched on the couch. Not Thomas. This guy was bigger all over—like a zoom shot—and he had no football. He looked up at me—lazily, I thought, used to Thomas. But this guy was like the original that Thomas had been copied from: thicker black hair, broader brow, darker eyebrows, wider cheekbones, crisper lips, squarer jaw, larger shoulders, bigger hands. I kept staring even after he turned back to the movie. Once I was capable of rational thought, I said, "Forrest?"

"Who are you?"

He didn't turn from the movie, not caring about the answer. Not lazy, I realized; more like switched off. But I didn't let his lack of affect faze me. I couldn't believe my luck—what was he doing here?

"I'm Heidi." I watched him a moment before adding, "Thomas and I fuck."

"Wow." He blinked but didn't glance my way. "Not even my parents called him Thomas."

"I couldn't come if I thought of him as Tommy."

Forrest didn't react, but I was content to stand there staring, so I did. Until Thomas got home.

"Hi-deeee," Thomas called from the kitchen. He waded, languorous as always, into the living room, his grin slow as a steamboat, his gaze sliding down my body. Then he saw the movie, his brother. His grin cracked, his spine stiffened. "Bro," he said, obviously with effort. "What are you doing here?"

Forrest didn't respond to the forced cheer in his brother's voice, didn't glance at him, either. "Spring break."

My spine went ruler-straight, too. Forrest was *studying* Out There?

"Yeah, in two weeks," Thomas retorted. "They kick you out?"

"Finished early."

Before I could say anything, Thomas curled his arm around my neck like he never did, said, "'Kay, man, I'll catch up with you in a few. Me and Heidi need to scratch an itch."

He yanked me to his bedroom, and we fucked fast like a Hail Mary pass. When Thomas hustled me out the front door, Forrest didn't look up, let alone say goodbye. He watched the shadows projected on the wall like he didn't believe in happy endings.

≈

BETWEEN MY THESIS AND memories of Forrest, I forgot about lunch and dinner until I was starving. Then, too lazy to cook or forage, I drank water until my stomach shut up. I turned off the dampeners to get a sense of the street. UTL wouldn't deliver until about an hour after the fighting stopped. Outside, it wasn't quiet yet, but the screams were fewer, the individual engines easier to identify.

I headed out back. On the deck, I scanned the roof for this eagle's nest. Way above my normal sightline, a narrow balcony like a widow's walk jutted from the steel roof. It had no door leading into the house and no ladder up from the deck. Tank probably didn't need a ladder, could hoist himself up there. With a shotgun, if needed.

I sighed and went inside to grab a chair. I hauled it back up, stood on it, and then with a brief prayer to Tank's building prowess, I lunged for the gutter. It shuddered but held as I clambered onto the scalding hot roof. I shook my scorched hands, danced on tiptoe 'til my soles adjusted. Then I vaulted over the half-wall into the metal box of the eagle's nest. I imagined Sweeney hunched here that first night, waiting for the show. Bastard.

Cinder block walls topped by oscillating cameras separated Tank's property from the neighbors'. I checked my quadrants, orienting myself by the feds' watchtowers. Trickling from the sunset-stained south and west, warriors approached Raven Street. Battle fever tended to wane last in our neighborhood, but this evening's congestion was worse, exacerbated by the bad blood between Tank and my family. In the east the QuanTex smokestacks loomed like powered-down golems. North, Tank's roof blocked my view of my parents' house and, more important, their view of me.

Below, a blue Suzuki I didn't recognize cruised through the smoke and knife fights. The driver—slight, female?—impossible to tell with the ghost-faced helmet skin—tipped a glance at Tank's house and traced its lines to the top, to me. Then gunned the engine and disappeared. Odd.

Half an hour later, BlackJack peeled out of the neighborhood with his bloody flock. I started to relax. Soon, the *whump-whump-whump* of a 'copter filled the purpling sky, and a bright yellow beast drifted down, the familiar UTL logo emblazoned on its side. A year after the Spill, UTL had secured the government contract to service Exile.

The chopper sank within range. Floodlights on the landing skids speared Raven Street, blinding anyone left on the ground. I held back my thrashed hair and watched the delivery guy—nope, girl—twirl down like a spider on a thread, a wide flat box clasped to her body, a gas mask on her face.

"You've got to be kidding," I screamed, taking the box. "It's not airborne. Half the country would be mutants!"

"Sign, please," she said, nasal and echoing behind her blue-lit window. She held out an electronic clipboard.

I appraised the package stretching my arms—my name on the label. Huh—and shook it. Not a sound and not heavy, so probably not food or supplies. I tossed the box onto the deck, took the clipboard. There was a certified letter for Tank clipped to it.

"Feds reported tear gas," the courier hollered.

"Lady," I said, clamping the letter under one arm, "we don't have it that together."

"Wouldn't matter anyway." She twirled for a more panoramic view, her combat boots not touching the roof. "Company's hellbent on milking the last of its contract."

"What?" Last I'd heard, UTL's contract had been renewed.

The courier looked at me, sour expression dissolving. She shook her head. "Union stuff."

I frowned. When had UTL unionized? But then the clipboard beeped, my subcutaneous ID scanned and accepted. I thumbed *OK*, and the courier practically ripped the board out of my hands.

"Have a nice day," she yelled, zipping back up her cord. "Thank you for using UTL."

As if we had a choice.

In the kitchen I tossed Tank's letter on the counter and sliced open the package. Looked inside and frowned. Clothes?

My cheeks burned so hot I might as well have stuck my head in the oven.

≈

I FOUGHT TO STAY awake until Tank came home. Instead, I fell asleep, cranky as a little kid, on the couch. I dreamed of my last night with Carlos, of whisper-fighting with him so we wouldn't wake Sammy, so Romy wouldn't barge in and try to make everything better with sex.

Then Tank was towering over me, nudging me with his knee. "Heidi. Bedtime."

I pawed my eyes open—ouch, still the black eye—and sat up. "No, talk time," I snapped.

"Tired, Heidi," he said. Him or me? I didn't care.

"No, damn it. Why did you do that?" I gestured at the box spilling out its obscene luxury: smocked bodices, kimono sleeves, Hepburn trousers, lace-lined bikini underwear. A week's worth of brand new clothes that probably cost his monthly stipend. "I can never repay that. I don't need that. I'll wear secondhand and your boxers."

He sighed. He'd been smoking, despite not being a smoker per se, and I wondered if I was dreaming. Then he sat on the footlocker that served as a coffee table. It creaked under his weight, so I thought no, it's real.

"You don't have to pay me back," he said. "It's a gift."

"What? But ..." This was so much worse than the photo stock. "I don't deserve gifts!"

He started to laugh. "Says who?" But seeing my glare and reddened cheeks, he palmed his forehead. "Look, don't make this a big deal. I have the money, and I don't want you to feel trapped here because you don't have clothes."

I leaned forward, my smidgen of pride smarting. "You think that's why I'm still here? You think I'd let myself be trapped by a lack of clothes?"

He said nothing. My groggy brain processed the beer and cigarettes on his breath, his story about working late. What if he'd been drinking with Sweeney, listening to stories about my slutty past? Or worse, about Forrest?

"Wait a minute," I said, squinting. "Are you 'suggesting' that I go? Is this a payoff?"

He heaved another sigh, massive shoulders sinking. "I don't want you to go. But I want you to be *able* to go if you choose."

Some of my tension siphoned off.

"You got all over my case about me trusting you," he continued. "How 'bout you trust me a little? I treat you better than your family ever did. You like me more, I think. Why not accept the fucking gift? Is it so bad to be taken care of?"

I choked a little, remembering dream fragments, Carlos whispering, "Heidi, no hagas esto. I can take care of you. Anything you want, todo lo que pidas, mija."

And that was what I was afraid of, that I'd ask ...

"I can take care of myself!" I snapped at him, at Carlos, at all of us.

Tank didn't flinch; shit, maybe I sounded like that all the time. Instead, he lifted one hand to say "Wait," and I yawned while he gathered his thoughts.

Finally, he said, "Houses get lonely, Heidi. I work. I fight. When I'm home, I eat, sleep, shower, that's about it. But houses aren't forts. They're meant to hold people."

"So are prisons," I grumbled, but I rubbed my face, wondering, Why was I fighting? Didn't I *want* to ingratiate myself?

"Not like that," Tank said, stroking my knee. "I mean, 'hold' like support us, shape us. Mold us into ... whatever we want to be. You know how hard I worked on this house only to find it didn't hold me? Come on, Heidi. Live here like I can't. Let this be a real house."

"A home," I said. When he shrugged, I added, "You want someone to come home to?"

Again, the shrug.

"Tank, if the door only works one way ..." I blushed, remembering how he'd found me sleepwalking, banging on the front door. I tried again. "If I can't leave without *leaving*, why should I stay?"

He stopped rubbing my knee. "I ain't your jailer, Heidi. You're not a captive."

I raised my eyebrows. "How about a hostage?"

He groaned, rolled his eyes. "Shit, I should'a known that'd come back to bite me. I didn't mean it." To my skeptical look, he said, "I went out with you 'cause you asked! 'Cause I don't know anybody else who'd pull a stunt like that. You didn't even pretend to be sorry about your brother, and later, you didn't fake feeling sorry for your mom. It was weird, prob'ly even psychotic, but honest, y'know? Not so far from what I'd do, if it'd been me. And the way you work, I thought we understood each other ..."

He jerked to his feet, yanked me off the couch. "Y'know what? Fuck it. Come here."

He pulled me past the kitchen, down the basement stairs, and then to the left, to the wall of lockers. In the dark he slammed his palm against a locker near the top, and a section of the wall slid aside, revealing a metal door he hadn't shown me before. Inside: a tiny room, bright and loud with electricity. A bank of video screens, a phone, a cockpit of switches, toggles, dials.

Holy Sean Connery! A panic room.

Tank dragged me inside. I couldn't stop blinking.

"Here." He shoved something small and sharp into my right hand. A key.

"Here." He pulled me by the elbow, my bare feet cold and slow on the concrete floor, and slapped my left hand onto a scanner. He punched buttons. I cowered from a flash. Then he yanked me over to a viewfinder.

"Look." He pushed my head down to the port. I heard a whir. I remembered that slasher flick where the guy spiked women to death with a blade in his camera. I nearly shit myself.

Tank released me. "There. Wear whatever the fuck you want, Heidi. Come and go as you please, just ..."

I gaped up at him, stupid with shock. Had he really given me an all-access pass?

"Just come back, okay?" He faltered, clearly tired. "Please."

That last bit ... he didn't *request* things very often. Sounded rusty. But he meant it.

"Okay," I mumbled. After a moment's rummaging, I found my own rusty pleasantry. "Thanks."

Chapter Nine

AT AGE TWO SWEET William didn't walk. He oozed across floors like a slug, but despite an overabundance of toes, he showed no inclination to join the upright. I'd long since grown bored of studying my brother the blob, and thinking I hadn't made any further attempts on his life, my parents finally moved him into his own room upstairs.

Predictably, Sweet William was pissed.

The first night, he screamed his guts out, and no one slept. The second night, he screamed for five hours, but I was wrecked enough I slept, anyway ... for a while. Then William found his motivation. He climbed out of his crib. He inchwormed to my room. And then he cruised over to where I sprawled, one leg sticking out from the covers, and clamped his teeth into my calf.

I screamed. I writhed and clawed the mattress and shook my leg, howling. And that diapered leech just dangled there.

Mother and Father ran in. One of them slapped on the light. Frozen, they swore in unison, boggling at my blood bright on the bedsheets.

William, jubilant, finally unlocked his jaw and thudded to the floor, grinning like a cannibal clown. Mother scooped William up. She ran him to the bathroom to make sure none of the blood was his. Father stayed behind to clean and close me up.

Sit tight, Heidi, he'd said. *You try and get away, you'll hurt yourself more.*

Afterwards, he struggled to change the sheets with me koala-ed on his back, my arms strangling him. He promised me William wouldn't come back. He promised I wouldn't die. But I had my doubts.

≈

THE NEXT MORNING, THE bikes came orderly, single file, their mufflers echoing in the otherwise empty streets. Closest to church bells you'd ever hear in Exile.

Time for my brother's burn.

Listening in bed, I held my breath. Soon, Sweet William would be dead, really dead. Dust in the motherfucking wind. Even if Mother turned all her raging grief on me after, that was one less needle in my eye. I flexed my calf, the one with the old bite marks, and tried to release the memories with a sigh.

"What the hell did he do to you?"

"Huh?" I hadn't realized Tank was awake, too.

"Your brother." He planted one elbow in the bed and propped his head to study me. A quality of ... yes, protectiveness in the creases around his eyes. "What'd he do to make you hate him so much?"

Nothing happened, you're overreacting, Mother had said. Compared to what Tank faced every day in the streets, he'd probably agree. "Nothing," I said. "Not like you're thinking."

It didn't occur to me until later that he knew what *I* was thinking—or at least getting better at it.

We ate breakfast picnic-style in the den, the room farthest from my parents' house. It was supposed to be a day of mourning, but William's crew never acceded to the finer points of etiquette. Stuff kept crashing against the steel siding of Tank's house—hubcaps, beer bottles—and the dampeners complained with wobbles and *boing*s. The scents of burning plastic and rubber coiled down the cold, never-used fireplace. I expected my yogurt to curdle with the stench. After I gave up eating, Tank swallowed the last of his orange juice and beckoned me, drew me into his lap.

It was ... different. We'd never taken the time to exactly luxuriate in each other. Mostly, we shoved aside clothes and jumped each other's bones. This time I kissed him, really kissed him, until he no longer tasted of reconstituted oranges but slick-clean and nearly metallic. He let me tongue along the edges of his lips into the corners of his mouth, along his teeth. As if I could build a wall against my family's hate with each secret of spit and sinew, flesh and bone. When he turned to kiss my hairline, dipped down to lick my neck, I felt his quickened breath. Not aroused ... or not *only* aroused. More like I'd overwhelmed him. Maybe he wasn't used to being laid open like that, wasn't comfortable being the center of such unmitigated attention.

I relented. I pulled back to tickle kisses along his scratchy cheeks, lip his earlobes. I reclined into the circle of his arms and let him see my face. *Want you*, I thought. *Want this. Just this.*

He rubbed my stubble-scrubbed lips. "You're so red," he murmured, eyes dark.

I wondered at his chagrin. He'd never been gentle. I didn't want him to be. I shook my head. "I like it." The stinging, I meant. Like saltwater on a sunburn from an ocean I'd never seen. But maybe one day ...

I let him kiss me, let him hold my head in his big hands as he investigated my mouth, my tongue, my patience. I read him with my fingertips, traced his scalp like the finest sandpaper, his corded neck, the broken altar of his collarbones, memorizing. My neck ached under his kisses, vertebrae grinding, each pang beading into a pearl.

His lips skidded up my cheek, and I thought he'd come up for air until he whispered, "You're shivering."

I shook my head again. My neck creaked with relief. I steeled myself against the shudders—not shivers—he'd felt. My muscles were like hungry eels for him.

"Want me to stop?" he asked.

I squirmed in my panties and felt his cock throb through layers of fabric, burn the back of my thigh. I scanned his lust-slanted eyes, his swollen lips. "*Can* you stop?" I teased.

He growled and poured me onto the blanket. I flailed out of my burgundy blouse as he swept down my body, tongue flicking each scratch, gash, bruise, scar. Taking inventory. Under new management. He nuzzled the subdermal knot of the contraceptive in my arm while I ran my hands up under his T-shirt and over the range of scar tissue rippling his back. He nibbled new bruises on my chest while I probed the pitted scars in his sides. I wrapped my knees around his waist and rocked to loosen my hips. He stopped, lower lip caught between his teeth, and watched me grind my satin-and-lace panties against his flannel pants. He'd thought about this, I realized, imagined this when he bought my clothes.

So his little buying spree had not been completely charitable!

I grinned, and he looked up, feeling the change. He hooked two fingers in my waistband, his thumb under a leg hole.

"Get these off," he pretended to complain.

"And this?" I tugged his shirt, delighted with my power over him. "And these?" I stroked my legs up and down his pants.

"Now," he breathed.

Once we were naked, he squeezed my left hip to hold me still, legs spread. The flagstones bit into my ass, jutted against the ridges of my ilium, but I absorbed the pain, savored it like salt. Tank slipped his chrome-hot cock inside me slow enough to tattoo each inch in my sense memory. I hissed and clenched. He groaned. I wiggled my legs, as if I could shake loose the overwhelming urge to come. He seemed to understand. He let go of my hip long enough to slap my thigh. One. Two. Three. I gasped and relaxed. He pushed deeper, and we had to slap-relax all over again.

He put his hands on either side of my head, bent his elbows to bury his face in my hair. "Fuckin' hell, Heidi." He sounded pained.

"What if I move?" I murmured. "Turn over or something?"

He twitched inside me, and we both moaned. After he caught his breath, I rolled onto my side, and he curled behind me, pressed inside. That helped. Slowed us down, reduced the particular friction threatening to wreck us. Tentatively, I rocked against him. When I didn't spontaneously combust, didn't push him over the edge with me, I started to fuck back in earnest.

He held my hip, his grip growing tighter, his thighs tenser the longer we danced. My throat burned, and I realized I was panting. I clenched my lips, trying to hold back the sound. He leaned closer and whispered in my ear. My blood pressure spiked.

More, more, I needed more. I twisted until I was on my knees, never mind the stones biting through the blanket. He followed—he didn't have much choice, but he didn't complain, either. He coiled one arm under me, grasping my shoulder for leverage, and sank his teeth in the meat of my other shoulder. I shuddered, thighs threatening to give out as I got off. He held me up, licked the bite, pumped me through rapid-fire second and third orgasms. I kind of hazed over then, felt like I was dissolving into the vowels he mouthed against my broken skin. Then he came, and the new heat set me off again.

He collapsed, crushing me happy between a rock and a very hard place. I smelled blood on his breath, but I didn't hurt yet; I was still coming. Eventually, he pulled out, rolled onto his back. I followed, sweaty, to rest my head on his chest. He looked down, smeared his thumb over the bloody dents in my skin. I think I purred.

"Don't let me do that again," he said.

"What part?"

Disapproving growl, then his hand moved. He thumbed the birth control implant through my skin. I traced the quarter-sized scars, smooth with age, that pitted the skin between his pectorals and armpits.

Forrest hadn't tried to get away after sex, either. Like Tank, he lay there. Not cuddling like the Cantus or biding his time. Accepting. Maybe stroking the implant like Tank was doing now. It was reassuring, I guess. To know our actions began and ended with us. A simple circle, no ricochet. I remembered Forrest's flushed skin under my fingers, the warm miasma of our bodies. I could almost taste his beer-and-Skittles breath. For the first time I didn't fight the memories. I didn't relish them, but I lay patiently, waiting for them to pass.

They didn't.

The supposedly simple circle was getting crowded, Forrest radiating a silent *Don't do it. Don't use him like you did me.* To shut him up, I said to Tank, "You told Sweeney to ask around about me before Mute's."

"Yeah," Tank rumbled. I felt it in my ear and jaw, felt it in Forrest's sudden disappearance. After a pause, Tank added, "Seemed prudent."

"Yeah." I wondered how to formulate my question best, hadn't decided before I found myself saying, "He told you I've danced with lots of guys?"

Tank didn't quibble about *lots*, only made this affirmative noise in the back of his throat. Guess the word choice wasn't that subjective.

"And that doesn't bother you?" I asked.

No pause this time. "Nope."

I pondered. That soon after sex, thought didn't come easy. Less so with Forrest's warnings echoing in my head. "Does it turn you on?" I finally asked. With most guys it was one or the other.

Tank raised his head to look at me. His eyebrows lifted quizzically from the outer edges. *Like cranes taking flight*, I thought as I blushed.

"Never thought about it that way." He dropped his head again, relaxing.

"So you're neutral."

"I'm Switzerland."

I smacked him on the chest, surprised he was teasing so easily.

"Hey," he said, though it probably hurt less than a mosquito bite. "I mean it. Far as I'm concerned, you and me started at Mute's. Before that? Nothing existed before that."

He made it sound so easy. I smoothed my hand over his chest, as if to erase the earlier smack, and found those nearly perfect circles again. Whatever he said, we weren't blank slates. These scars weren't from the street wars; they seemed older, deliberate. Wasn't it supposed to be saner Out There? But if young Tank had been ... if Forrest went Out There and ...

"Quit thinking so loud," Tank said.

I lowered my mouth to kiss one of his scars. He flinched. I lifted up and looked at him, my smile loose and easy to soothe him, but for once, his eyes were closed. And he didn't open them.

"You gonna ask for my dossier now?" he said.

"Nope." *Three women since he came to town*, I thought. Definitely no men; you couldn't keep that a secret around here. I tucked my head against his chest.

"Y'sure?"

"I'm sure."

≈

WHILE TANK WASHED DISHES—by hand; who was he, the Brawny paper towel guy?—I knelt in the window seat and counted the bikes lined up outside my parents' house by the handlebars I saw glinting over the barricades. I tugged my earrings. Even if Tank's crew came out in full force—and I wasn't quite clear on who was "crew" crew and who was just construction crew—that was shitty odds if William's burn jumped the track. Which these things sometimes did, enforced as they were by habit and battle fatigue.

I sucked in my bottom lip. Tank wanted the house to be more than a fort; but like a fort, it let you see any mobs coming from a mile away. I should've felt safe, but seeing all the threats laid out before me like a bloody smorgasbord made me feel worse. How did the feds in the panopticons stand it? Was that why they were so quick to smack us back down? Maybe that's why the alarm had gone off when I was jogging down Gatling Drive. From up there, even I might've seemed a threat.

In the street Chazz leaned against one of my parents' barricades, swapping a joint and a bottle of whiskey with his cousin, Keith. I couldn't look at Keith without feeling dirt under my nails. He was the last of William's friends I'd danced with. He'd had a thing about the not-so-great outdoors.

As I brooded, the blue Suzuki pulled up alongside them. I rose higher on my knees, watched the rider—no helmet this time, it would've crushed his faux-hawk—talk to the welcoming committee. Eventually, they nodded, waved toward a barrier shoved out of alignment. Faux-hawk angled in and parked on my parents' lawn. Chazz called out to him, but Faux-hawk lifted one hand in acknowledgment, then headed inside without tilting his face into view.

I sank back. Tank's doorbell rang—*blurp blurp*—and I jolted around, "Tainted Love" in my head. Tank emerged from the kitchen and checked the security panel.

"Sweeney's here. At the side gate."

I snorted. "Why?"

"Moral support?" His face gave absolutely no expression, no hint as to whether he was making a joke or admonishing me or what.

After a befuddled moment, I said, "You going to let him in?"

"Might as well." But he didn't sound decided yet. Not until he said, "You going to put some pants on?"

≈

SWEENEY FOLLOWED TANK INTO the living room, a case of beer dangling from his fingers. "Good day for a burn!" he announced.

Tank turned to look at him. I was already staring down at our guest from midway down the stairs.

"Dry," Sweeney explained, glance shifting from Tank to me. "If we're lucky, maybe your brother will take the whole fucking town with him."

I was inclined to agree, despite my distaste for Sweeney, but Tank said, "Yeah, I ain't quite ready for that."

"Where's Serena?" I asked.

The caninus muscle in Sweeney's left cheek tensed. "Said she didn't want to be this close to the powder keg. She's a nice girl," he added, as if the insinuation might distract me.

Rather than press my advantage—he must've wrangled with Serena—I retorted, "No such thing as a nice girl. Not in Exile."

Sweeney smirked. "Think you might be biased there, Heidi?"

Tank crossed his arms over his chest, mumbled something to Sweeney that sounded suspiciously like "Play nice."

"Anyway," Sweeney said, flashing me a fake grin, "you're looking good."

"Funny," I said. "You just look the same."

"If it ain't broke." He aimed a laugh at Tank, who twitched a tolerant smile. "Seriously," Sweeney said, assessing me. I'd pulled on black slacks and ditched the burgundy blouse for one of Tank's Henley shirts, dress-long with a grease stain on the sleeve. It felt safer. "Your eye looks better. Must feel better, too, if you can glare like that."

Tank's smile lasted a beat longer this time. He gestured at the beer. "Let's put that on ice," he said, heading for the kitchen.

"Ice?" Sweeney winked at me before following Tank. "Hell, just let Heidi hold it for a second."

I let them go, let them have their stupid boys' moment while I scuttled downstairs to check the security panel. One of the thugs had pitched an old tire at the door-mounted camera while I was dressing. The view slanted uselessly at the sidewalk now. Quiet as it was, I didn't have to eavesdrop; I heard Tank and Sweeney clear as day.

"Jackson and Kier said they were staying home today, laying low," Sweeney said.

"Figured." Glasses clinked onto the counter. "I don't mind."

"Puppy skipped out, too. Said he'd see us the regular time at Mute's. But Rain's on site like you asked, and everybody else. Even Cam and Isaac."

"So things are moving along," Tank said.

Hiss-crack of beer tabs. Slight gurgle of pouring.

"Yeah, though I don't know how Cam'n'Isaac get shit done when they can't be ten inches apart." Sweeney lowered his voice then. Not quite enough. "So ... she upset about her brother?"

"'Course."

"You sure? 'Cause she don't look distraught to me. More cranky."

"Ask her," Tank replied, and I imagined him shrugging.

"Right. Except I'm kind of fond of my balls where they are."

I grinned in spite of myself, until Sweeney asked, "You sure this is a good idea? Dancing with this girl while her Spilltastic family raves next door?"

"I've had better ideas," Tank allowed. "And worse."

Sweeney paused, smacked his lips. Must've been drinking. "You two serious?"

"Aren't I always?"

"And her?"

A longer pause this time, almost unbearable. It took every speck of my scant self-control not to barge into the kitchen to see Tank's face.

"Ask her," was all he said.

I SAT AT TANK'S sexy desk, empty beer glass in one hand, a trio of photos in the other: Joaquin Phoenix, Heath Ledger, Benicio Betancourt. Technically, if you couldn't tell from a still, they weren't beautiful, but how could you argue with Hollywood? I stared at Heath Ledger. Thought about Forrest. If only his death had been so neat ...

Tank and Sweeney stood drinking at the picture window, talking in low voices. Not trying to be discreet, but comfortable, little to say after an hour keeping watch.

"Here we go," Sweeney said.

Tank came to the open study door. "You want to watch this?"

"Much to see?" I stood, leaving the glass and photos. Forrest came with me.

"From this angle? Mostly smoke. Almost dark, too."

Sweeney edged over to make room for me, and I knelt on the window seat. Behind me on my left, Tank stood close enough that I felt his warmth; on my right, Sweeney rocked his weight from one leg to the other, nudging my bare foot now and then. I might've jerked away, but it was a useful distraction. The sky was hazard orange, the smokestacks faceless totems. Kids piggybacked in the neighbors' yards and along the barricades to watch.

"You want to hear it?" Tank asked me.

I shook my head. What would we miss? Semper fi lite shit from the crowd, chants cribbed from movie versions of *Beowulf*. Better to leave the dampeners, run my own silent laugh track. They'd burn my brother like a Viking while better men decayed in the dirt Out There alone with the worms and spiders. My skin prickled at the thought.

First, twists of flame burst from behind my parents' roof. I tried counting the bright spikes like counting the steps Mother could take from our house before tripping her leash, but I lost count when bits of William's charred cerements spiraled up. They drifted across the street, disintegrated into goth lip prints on the window, making me blink.

Three hours of those plague kisses, and I never stopped blinking: mini flinches, as if William were toxic enough to penetrate glass. Oily gusts erupted over the roof whenever part of the pyre collapsed. Three feet deep, three feet wide, six feet long. Fifteen hundred to seventeen hundred degrees Fahrenheit.

Eventually, there was more smoke than ash, and even that was hard to see in the dark. Still, I knew from previous burns that black silt had dusted the street, probably Tank's driveway. I clenched my fists. Imagined driving over those last particles of William, grinding him deep into the pavement, deeper even.

When the smoke petered out, my knees creaked, hesitant muscles decompressing. I was going to be so fucking sore. I opened my mouth to complain, but then the sky sizzled red. I yipped, almost tipped over. Tank caught my shoulder.

"I'm okay," I said, despite shuddering. Another bottle rocket unzipped the dark, and I grumbled, "Didn't expect a fucking light show."

"I think it's kinda cool," Sweeney said. Immune to my glare, he swallowed the last of his third or fourth beer, licked his lips. "Wouldn't mind some Black Cats for my party," he added.

The fireworks scribbled glee across his eyes.

≈

THE CROWD RESUMED ITS lackluster rioting as it left the burn. Tank rolled the siding up over the window, and he and Sweeney settled on the couch to watch *The Crow*, sound cranked loud to cover the *ping*s and wobbles of the assaulted dampeners. I grabbed another beer and cuddled up to Tank, mostly to be sure Sweeney wasn't bashing me out of earshot.

During the end credits, I glanced over to find Sweeney asleep. Slumped in his corner of the couch, cheek on his fist, empty glass tucked between his legs. No wonder he'd been blessedly quiet. He didn't look so bad now: wrinkles shallow, lips pink, the thin flesh over his carotid artery endearingly exposed.

"He was drinking before he got here," Tank muttered.

"You want to wake him, or should I?"

Tank shook his head, a reluctant sympathy tightening one cheek. "Let him stay the night, sleep it off."

My jaw clenched, but if Tank noticed, he ignored it. He leaned over me and eased Sweeney's glass free.

In the kitchen I washed and rinsed the glasses, and Tank dried. The soapy water spread warmth up my arms, loosened my jaw. Also jogged loose a realization: we'd made it. We'd survived William's burn. A few days and the street wars would rev up again, fresh blood overshadowing William's death. I could start testing Tank's pressure points, plan my escape in earnest. The epiphany coalesced with the beer I'd drunk and made me tipsy and warm.

I scrubbed the sink, then leaned against the counter, drying my hands. Tank was peering into the living room to check on Sweeney. I studied his silhouette limned with TV light. The warmth in my belly ribboned into my crotch.

I went to Tank, stood on tiptoes, levered up with my fingers in his waistband. He turned and kissed me, tongue a mere suggestion, gone too soon. I reached for his chin, pulled his mouth back down and held him, used my teeth when he tried to get away.

"Hey, cool it."

"Too hot already," I whispered. "Want to feel you." I tucked my fingers in his waistband again, tugged him backwards with me until I bumped the kitchen counter. He went willingly enough but rested his forehead against the upper cabinets, looked down at me, and did nothing to move the game along.

I smiled. "I know how to make you play." And I started to slide down.

He caught me under the arm, yanked me up before I could get my face in his crotch. "Not now, Heidi."

"Why not?" I whined.

He glared at me so hard, he probably saw bone marrow. "You know why not."

"I can be quiet. Can you?" When he kept glaring, my cheeks went hotter than my cunt. "So *now* you're shy? Just tell Sweeney to stay in the other room and he will. Better yet, make him leave!"

"We can go upstairs."

"Why do you get to call the shots? Why do you decide when we have an audience?"

He grabbed my jaw. "This is why I don't keep alcohol in the house."

"Why?" I struggled to pull away. "'Cause you think I'm a lush?"

"No! It's not you, it's ..." He worked to loosen his grip.

"Too many variables," he said, softer now. "Too many ways things can go wrong."

I curled into his touch and rocked against him. "Oh, Tank."

He faltered, held his breath ten seconds ... fifteen. I rubbed harder.

"Heidi, stop it! I am not doing this. Not here, not now. And never when you're drunk." He pushed me away, as if wiping his hands of me, and stalked to the den.

I slapped the counter, clit throbbing so hard I thought I'd split my pants. I had half a mind to stick my hand down there and take care of myself. But Sweeney was in the living room, which drove me upstairs. Once there, I charged into the closet for my fuck-me pumps.

I'd leave. I could. I could duck out the side gate. William's crew would be stuporous around the smoldering remains of his pyre. I could move fast, get to the Cantus' house. They'd take me in, they'd be fucking *thrilled* to see me. And once I hugged Sammy and promised to watch *Bambi* with him for the millionth time, I could haul Romero or Carlos or both into a bedroom to get me off.

I grabbed a shoe. The house key Tank had given me flew out, glinting, and I caught it against my chest.

Yeah, frying pan to fire. Typical. And then what? I lowered my hand, stared at the key. How long before I got tired of the Cantus' cramped little house, remembered I couldn't stand this cramped crazy town? How long before I started plotting again? Before I asked Carlos, city liaison, for that tiny little favor? How long before I ruined everything?

Eyes wet, I squeezed the key. Tank trusted me this much, this finger-long bit of metal that could bring his whole fucking fortress down. Who knew what he'd be willing to do later? With the right pressure, on just the right spot?

Sit tight, Heidi. You'll only hurt yourself trying to get away.

I dropped the key back in my shoe, tossed the shoe in the corner, slammed the closet door.

"Sit tight," I told myself, and I forced myself to go to bed.

Chapter Ten

THE DAY AFTER I met Forrest I walked fast and got to the Vai house early. Forrest was in the same position as when I'd left—might even have been wearing the same shabby sweats—but now he had a beer bottle in his right hand. The label looked so dry he must've been nursing it all day. *It's A Wonderful Life* again.

"Heidi," he said, a verbal nod.

"So you tested out?" I jangled my key ring, hoping he'd face me instead of the wall, where a snooty young Mary scorned my girl, Violet, for liking *every* boy.

"Yeah, lucky me," Forrest said, and didn't spare me a glance.

He *was* lucky. Smart, strong, sterile, sane—four out of four. But you don't argue with self-pity. "What are you studying?" I said.

"Rocks."

I thought of his old maps, the posters. "You mean geology?"

"Yeah."

"When I test out, I'm going into plastic surgery. I want to be a surgeon, but that takes four years of med school and then a five-year residency, and who's got time for that? So I'll go the nursing route."

I knew I was babbling, but damned if I could stop. He finally dragged his gaze over, studied my face, not my body. And not like it took an effort.

Cheeks warming, I said, "It only takes two years to get

105

an associate's degree in nursing, and then you can bridge and get your bachelor's while you're working. I can't do pre-med from here, so I'm majoring in film theory. Gives me an excuse to study faces."

He blinked, head angled as if waiting to see if I was done. Which I was. But all he said was, "Truth is stranger than fiction," and turned back to *It's A Wonderful Life*.

Not so fast, I thought. "Why'd you come back?"

"Told you, finished early."

"No, I mean, why do you *ever* come back? When I get out of this town—"

He looked at me again, so blank-faced I started to stutter. Before I could reset, Thomas crashed in from the mac-n-cheez-scented kitchen, early also.

"Hey, baby." His arm snaked around my waist, and he kissed my ear, whispered, "You smell good." He turned to his brother. "Dude, are you still on the couch? At least get up and take a shower, man. It ain't pretty."

Forrest sipped his beer and flipped off Thomas, who fastforwarded his lazy grin and pushed me to the bedroom. I was on my back in record time, hands braced so Thomas didn't ram me through the headboard. I discovered that, if I squinted, Thomas looked like Forrest. I came so hard my ears rang.

Maybe an angel got his wings.

≈

THE DAY AFTER WILLIAM'S burn, Tank sagged the edge of the bed. I'd been awake for awhile, cunt throbbing from my wet dream, head throbbing from Tank's kitchen clatter.

"Making coffee shouldn't wake the dead," I said, pulling the pillow from my head.

"Actually, I'm pretty sure that's the purpose. You hungover?" he asked, a touch too innocent.

"No! I'm just not a morning person. Hadn't you noticed?"

He shrugged, coffee mug steaming. "Not really. Most of the time you seem ... perky enough."

"Horny is not perky."

"Can be."

I raised my head and scowled at him, the mug in his hand. "Is that for me or what?"

"What." He sipped, then said, "Sweeney's gone."

"Great. Spectacular. Hooray and Harrison Ford." I drooped onto the mattress again.

"What's with you two? What did he say that day I wasn't here?"

Did I really want to explain? Repeat the insults? Make Tank reconsider our arrangement after I'd decided to sit tight?

I sighed. "Never mind. You're right. It's stupid."

He shook his head. "Didn't say it was stupid. Don't even know what it is."

The way he so effortlessly gave me the benefit of the doubt? I blushed and wanted to hide my face. I sat up, knees to my chest, and took the mug. I drank, then tried to hand it back.

"Keep it," he said, half smiling. "It *was* for you."

I blushed even redder, nearly sank into myself. "Way to make a girl feel sheepish."

He smiled all the way this time. He rested his hand on my knee. "We good?"

I looked him in the eye. It was harder than you'd think, harder than scanning his face through the grid my mind superimposed. He wanted us to be good. Hell if that wasn't hope shining from those dark eyes.

"Yeah, we're good. Better than most," I said.

He squeezed my knee, then kissed it.

It was better than makeup sex.

≈

TANK WAS ON MY good side until he insisted we leave the house.

"I don't like being cooped up," he said. "Makes me nuts. Got to get out for a while."

I sulked behind the reader. "I've got work to do."

He finished clearing the breakfast dishes around me. "Me, too. My crew's got a standing date at Mute's. And I ain't wasting another minute 'cause of your brother."

At least he didn't invoke warrior honor. I might've decked him.

"'Sides, the longer we're holed up in here," he called, heading into the kitchen, "the more time your family has to plot."

Sweeney's smell still lingered on the couch cushions. That was as close as I wanted to get for a while. "You go."

"Like hell. People'll start talking shit like I killed you, too."

I snorted. "No one cares if I'm rotting in your closet."

"Maybe I want to show you off."

I rolled my eyes, caught him standing in the kitchen doorway, hands braced overhead. "Very funny, Tank. I don't go out unless I'm hungry or horny."

"Way I see it," he said, looking smug, "I'm in a position to make you both."

"You wouldn't."

But we both knew he'd won.

Later, he scoped out the scene while I dressed.

"One of the knee biters rigged spike strips at the front and side entrances," he reported when he returned to the bedroom.

"That would be Thing One. Theo." I fussed at my belled sleeve. "Won't I be overdressed for Mute's?"

"We both will," he said, watching me in the mirror. "But I prefer overdressed to tinfoil hats. Now I figure the 'Ray can take the spikes—"

"Wrong. Theo's not counting on popping your tires. He makes the strips gnarly, so they tangle up in your axle and gank your suspension, maybe even the clutch and transmission."

Tank's normally stoic mouth fell open. "Okay ... Moving the strips'll take time and expose us. Probably the point."

"Probably."

I admired his body armor, the way it clasped his T-shirt-clad torso before disappearing down his black slacks. I thought of arming typology scenes: Jason Momoa donning a blessed shield, Mel Gibson smearing on blue war paint, Bruce Willis strapping on a terrorist's MP5 in Nakatomi Plaza.

"You want to risk it?" he said.

"Can't you jump the spikes on your bike?"

"Naw. Wrong angle, too close to get up the momentum. But," he conceded, "I could carry it over. Still, we'd better get those strips out of the way."

"Can't we stay home and fuck?" I smiled at him hopefully.

"Don't try to sweet talk me."

He slid into his dress shirt. The cotton weave did nothing to hide his armor. But then, nothing about Tank's physical appearance was meant to mollify. He knotted his black tie and flicked a knowing half-smile at me in the mirror. "Not looking bad yourself, Heidi Heidi Ho."

He walked the Ninja out the back of the garage and over the patio. I followed, kicking dust in the twilight, wishing I had boots instead of heels. Tank straddled the bike, studied me.

"Wear my jacket," he said, shucking the skid-proof gear.

I shook my head. "It's too big." That, and why should he give up his protection when it was my family posing the risk?

He held out the jacket, implacable. "I'd make you wear the helmet, too, but it'd fly off your head if anything happened. Wouldn't do either of us any good."

I groaned, but feeling childish in the face of his practicality, I took the damn jacket. "Damn, make me wear the whole fucking cow next time. It'd be lighter."

But it wouldn't have smelled musky with sweat and smoke, sharp with blood on leather, sweet as sandalwood and sawdust. It wouldn't have smelled like Tank.

He tucked his tie between the buttons of his shirt. I thought of a few, more interesting places for that tie while he strapped on his helmet. Then he pushed the button for the gate. As the titanium panels accordioned open, Tank rolled the bike out. I spotted the spike strip blocking the gap between concrete barriers. Another slithered down the sidewalk, nearly all the way to the corner of Flint. Tank was right; the strips didn't pose much danger now, but if we didn't grab them, my siblings would find a more unpleasant use for them later. Sighing, I hurried to drag away the one blocking the exit. And of course, the racket alerted Thing One and Thing Two, who jumped out from behind the concrete barrier across the street.

With Molotov cocktails.

"Crap!" I hurled the strip into the backyard and slapped the button for the gate. The titanium curtain, still opening, shuddered to a stop, seemed to think a moment, then reversed.

Tank kicked the bike to life. The coin-sized speaker on his helmet crackled. "Forget the other strip. Get on."

"You think?" I clambered up behind him.

My butt barely hit the seat before we zipped through the exit gap and into the street to face the Things.

"Cocksucking whore! Goddamn murderer!" Theo screamed.

A step behind, Thea said nothing, summoning reserves she never needed when she aimed her crossbow. I almost felt for her. Then, as Tank revved the engine, she bared her picket teeth.

The first cocktail missed us completely. The bottle chipped on the asphalt, then rolled away, smoky. Gasoline and Quaker Oats: a good sticking combo, but trapped inside a bottle much too thick for splash and flash—Thea wasn't incendiarily gifted. The second bottle smacked the bike's fender, bounced off, and shattered on the street. The flaming T-shirt wick ignited the splatter, and cursing under his breath, Tank paddled the Ninja back out of range of the flaming pond.

"C'mon, let's go!" I screamed.

He shook his head. "Gotta wait for the gate."

I twisted and saw the gate sliding shut, slow as FEMA. Still three feet to go. I could've hauled it shut faster myself.

The third cocktail actually hit Tank—I didn't see it, but it sounded different—and his right sleeve flared. He snapped his arm out, reflexive, and the bottle flew to the right. The bike tipped that way, too. I clung to Tank and slapped at his burning shirt with the floppy sleeve of his jacket. Tank steadied the bike, kicked us farther from the flaming splatter. Gas burned up the side of a graffitied concrete barrier before snuffing out.

My parents tore 'round the corner. Mother raced toward us, pipe-and-chain flail held like an Olympic torch. With every stride something dark strung around her neck (a rock?) bumped against her black battle jersey. Father kind of … loped, as if his torque wrench weighed too much. For a split second I wondered what was wrong with him. Then I started counting, calculating how far Mother could get before her monitoring bracelet charged up.

Tank glanced behind us, doing some calculating of his own. Annoyance at the slow gate knotted his back and shoulders. He revved again, and the bike leaped forward. Thea jumped back, slamming into Theo. Theo was trying to light his next cocktail. Instead, he lit the back of Thea's dress.

Tank grumbled something that got lost in his helmet speaker and didn't flinch. But my blood felt hot as lava, my skin too tight as I craned to look over his shoulder.

"Shit shit shit," I muttered. The flames raced up Thea's back, coloring and crisping her matted hair. Why hadn't she stuck with her bow and arrows?

Theo tossed his bottle aside and kicked Thea to the ground. I gasped, but then he stomped a boot in her belly, and rocked her back and forth to put out the flames. Not exactly Stop, Drop, and Roll, but close enough. Father veered to help. Mother did not.

"Fucking bastard murderer," she screamed at Tank.

The shape bouncing against her chest with each stride. ... It was one of William's hands, black with rot and stitched into a fist. My stomach lurched. I lost count.

"Holy shit," Tank said quite clearly.

"I'll kill you, you goddamn foreign pig," Mother screamed. "I'll kill you and mash your balls in my fist and cram them down your throat! No, I'll cram them down Heidi's throat. You hear that, you cocksucking trai—"

She staggered, arms pinwheeling, black hair rising as she blundered against her invisible leash. My thighs quivered. It must've been fear, but my quads only went warm and loose like that when I was drinking. Or getting bent over in an alley.

Father's head jerked up. His attention swung back and forth from Thea to Mother in anguish. Unencumbered with empathy, my little brother dashed to a concrete barrier on their side. He leaned over and snagged one of his contraptions, a backpack dangling with PVC pipes and plastic tubing. A blowtorch swung from the end of a long nozzle.

"Heidi?" Tank said.

"Flame thrower," I said, still craning to see past Tank.

Theo slung the backpack over his shoulder. Mother had retreated a step or two behind her invisible barrier, but she still bristled like a hair-throwing tarantula.

"Not that," Tank said. "The gate!"

"Oh!" I yanked my stare from Mother's prickly hair and gruesome pendant to peek over my shoulder. "Umm, foot and a half?"

The bike shot forward. I seized the back of Tank's shirt. Theo might not have had thumbs, but his trigger finger was itchy as any warrior's. Yellow flame burst from the blowtorch. Mother shrieked. Tank ducked. I lifted an arm to cover my eyes, but the blast curled and disappeared in mid-air, fast as a dragon sneeze. I blinked, trying to clear the black blob from my retinas.

Around the afterimage, I caught movement. I turned and peered out the corner of my eye. Mother was clawing herself upright. Theo dropped the trigger and ran to help. She shoved him and his apologies aside. He picked up the flail, trying to hand it to her, but Mother locked eyes with me. Face damp and pink, she took a hair-raising step forward.

"She can't come any closer." Tank tilted his head, doing the same thing I was, straining to see past the retinal burn. "Right?"

Not without poaching her insides, I thought. But nothing came out of my mouth.

"Right?!"

"Go." I pounded his back. "Go go go!"

Tank hooked the bike around. As we rocketed away, Mother screamed. Metal clattered on asphalt, and I tried to squeeze through Tank's back. It took me a second to realize the noise was the flail flung, that Theo had missed. It took me even longer to understand that Mother's scream was one of frustration, not triumph or pursuit.

No matter. I buried my face between Tank's scapulas, and I didn't come out until we pulled into Mute's parking lot.

THE POSTER TAPED TO the front of the roadhouse read *Closed for "Private" Function* in purple marker. I rolled my eyes at the quotation marks, Mute's bizarre sense of humor.

Sweeney had been holding up the wall, but seeing us, he sauntered along the row of bikes glinting in the bleach-bright parking lot. Sweating beer bottle in one hand. Right eyebrow cut since yesterday, now raised.

"Thought you'd bring the 'Ray," he said.

Tank shook his head, unstrapped his helmet. I forced myself to peel my fingers from his shirt. My hips popped when I unclenched my knees from his sides.

"Everything okay?" Sweeney studied the scorch marks on Tank's sleeve, maybe my fingerprints chiseled in the cotton weave. "Something happen?"

"Heidi's family," Tank rumbled.

Both Sweeney's eyebrows went up. He whistled. "They're not letting this thing drop, huh? Guess they really don't like you."

Tank huffed dry laughter. "Ahh, we get along like a house on fire." Resting his helmet in his lap, he twisted to watch me slide off the bike. His right eye narrowed when I teetered on my heels.

"Well, then." Sweeney turned to me. "Guess it's you they don't like."

"It's not my fault," I snapped, almost grateful—easier to be mad than scared.

"But you're not helping any," Sweeney said, head cocked. "Are you?"

We both turned to Tank, seeking support. He squinted at Sweeney a moment before scanning the parking lot, as if counting the bikes and the trucks with his company logo on the side.

"Well, hey, you're here now." Sweeney walked backwards, the jangle of spurs like my jangled nerves. "Come join the party."

Inside, Tank's crew cheered his arrival. I frowned at the sawdusted floor and people's boots, twitchy with so many eyes on me. A guy with a ginger faux-hawk and spiderweb tattoos on his long, smooth neck offered to take Tank's jacket. Suckered by sincere blue-green eyes, I let him. Anyway, no one with two brain cells was going to steal from Tank. Who, incidentally, was still studying me with narrowed eyes, as if checking for injuries.

Serena wormed her way between us, lipstick and sundress the same dried-blood color. "What the hell happened to you?" she said, hand on my arm. "Never mind. Come get cleaned up."

Chapter Eleven

IN THE WOMEN'S ROOM, empty but for me and Serena, I had no idea what to expect. I'd only ever had one girl friend, and only for a few months; she'd ditched me when she thought I was flirting with her dad ... which maybe, yeah. Force of habit.

Serena slicked her hands under the faucet and came at me. I goggled and took a step back, but couldn't avoid her squashing my hair.

"You're so windblown," she said. "Why didn't you wear your helmet?"

I tried not to dodge. "I don't have one."

"Then tell Tank to get you one. Hell, tell him to get you one for every outfit. He's got the money."

I noticed my frown in the mirror and tried to wiggle it off. Me being defensive would probably play worse—more angles for her to work there—than me being a moocher.

"So," she said, still squashing. "What's it like with you and Tank?"

I hesitated, wondered if this was girl talk. "What do you mean?"

"How long have you been dancing?"

I frowned again. By now, I'd've thought everyone knew I'd hooked up with Tank two days after William's death and never gone home. Or did *dancing* not mean what I thought it did anymore? Finally, I mustered, "Isn't it obvious?"

"Kinda." Serena shrugged. "You're living with him now, so you two must've been dancing for months, right? How did you keep it a secret? Did he kill William for you?"

"What?" I pulled out of reach, wished I could as easily distance myself from the suggestion. I didn't have much real world knowledge, but I suspected "family killing family" fell on the wrong side of the sane/insane continuum. "I had nothing to do with that! I'm not a part of the street wars. Tank and I didn't even know each other!"

"Oh."

Serena stared at me in the mirror, apparently puzzled. "But there must've been something between you two. When William died, you could've gone nuclear like your parents, but you didn't."

Actually, I sorta had. But a flashpoint in my pants wasn't what she meant and saying so wouldn't have helped my case.

"Gotta say," she babbled on. "I didn't see it coming. Nobody did. You always kept to yourself, didn't seem like the others."

"You mean crazy?" I was still imagining the continuum, me in the "Inconclusive" section.

Serena barely paused. "Yeah, sure. But then this? How did Tank know you'd be okay with killing William? Was it like him bringing you roses?"

"No!"

She flinched, and I realized I'd yelled. I lurched forward, slammed the faucet to have something else to focus on. "It just happened," I said, scrubbing my hands. "Tank didn't know I existed, and I didn't know he was ..." What? Worth falling on a grenade for?

The lust must've shown on my face. Serena said, "I bet he's an animal in bed," and I heard the smirk in her voice. "Is he cut?"

Fury razed all worry about sane or insane from my mind. How dare she! Mentally undressing Tank, speculating on the terrain of his body ...

"He's scarred like everyone else," I said, shooting death glares in the mirror.

"No, I mean—"

"I know what you mean, and I'm not talking to you about it."

"Right," she drawled, studying me. A beat later she grinned. "Have you tried the Russian car bombs?"

≈

SERENA HAD BRUSHED UP on her movie chat. And maybe snorted some meth. She talked instead of breathing, pressed me into the bar every time I started to excuse myself. Finally, I gave up and climbed on a bar stool.

The whole time we discussed pseudo-documentaries she yanked at her eyelashes. As we critted full-frontal nudity, she twirled the hair over her right ear. I watched, hypnotized in spite of myself, and realized why her eyebrows were so thin: trichotillomania. I kept my glass away from her, lest the hairs she obsessively plucked ended up in my whiskey and Coke.

The guy who'd taken Tank's coat for me came up on my other side and ordered a fucking *spritzer*. Mute's daughter, Vanessa, was tending bar. She shook her overgrown bangs, the better for him to see the glint of her gray eyes: I'm *this* close to pissing in your glass. But then the guy tilted his head and smiled. Vanessa sighed, world-weary as only a sixteen-year-old can be, and poured the sissy drink.

Checking him out, I understood why. The guy had a mouth like a nineteen-thirties film star—Fredric March, maybe: pale, thin, nearly invisible lips that made his smile seem extra-special, like you'd dragged it out of him. A narrow goatee ran from lower lip to sharp chin. The black ink of his spiderweb tattoos—I suppressed a shudder; why'd it have to be spiders?—disappeared past his blue polyester work-shirt, down the V neck of his white T-shirt, and dragged my gaze farther on down. From his battered hands, I guessed he wasn't too good with a hammer, so why was he part of Tank's crew?

He didn't wait for Serena to pause but leaned over and asked me, quiet-like, right through her blabbing, "Your eye okay?"

I bit back, "What do you care?" After a minute said instead, "Better, thanks." I still gave him the hairy eyeball. Did he cultivate that soulful blue gaze? Did he know how tempting those stingy lips were? And how far down his slightly fuzzy chest did those tattoos go?

"What?" Serena said, leaning over.

He ignored her and nodding thanks at Vanessa, walked away with his spritzer. Since he walked around the crowd rather than through it, I had time to measure his shoulder span, the angle of his hips in his saggy-seat, bleach-splotched jeans. He was an Outsider, newish in town, or I would've known him already.

"Heidi!" Serena said.

Grudgingly, I turned to her and said, "I'm going back to Tank."

≈

WATCHING SWEENEY AND TANK, if I hadn't known they were friends ...

... I wouldn't have known they were friends.

Sweeney shifted his weight back and forth, sucked a fresh beer, occasionally interjecting while Tank conferred with the steady stream of his sunburned, rock-muscled crew. In the infrequent lulls Sweeney talked to Tank, tried to draw him in with beer bottle gestures. Tank, who'd rolled up his sleeves to hide the scorch marks, scanned the empty mezzanine, head tilted toward Sweeney but eyes checking the joists overhead. Tank never walked away, though. Probably an alpha male thing, punishment for Sweeney mouthing off at me in the parking lot.

I hung back, skimming the walls so I could watch Tank

among his crew, a nearly even mix of Exiles and Outsiders. Two guys, blond from the same bottle, approached Tank. Lanky like skaters, they walked in step, hunched shoulders nearly touching. Tank shifted slightly to interpose the Doublemint Twins between him and Sweeney.

Sweeney saw me checking them out and scanned the bar for Serena, now spewing her verbal diarrhea on long-suffering Vanessa. Sweeney excused himself. Tank didn't stop talking even when one of the guys lifted his chin at Sweeney in a silent "See ya later."

I made my way closer to Tank. The blond guys didn't really resemble one another, I decided, aside from slightly cleft chins and blue eyes. It was the way they mirrored one another that blurred the differences. They were impressively foul-mouthed—even by Inner Radius standards—and not knowing them, I couldn't tell if they were really pissed or not, so I held back.

"Shit, you're never gonna believe this shit, Tank," said one.

"And what shit would that be?" Tank said, unruffled.

"This load of sorry horseshit went down on Gatling Drive," said the other. Hollered, actually, to be heard over Tank's increasingly rowdy crew.

"Nowhere near the motherfucking signs," said his friend. One was Cam and the other Isaac, I realized.

"Me and this fucktard right here—" Cam or Isaac hitched his thumb at the other "—we were walking along Gatling Drive—"

"Nowhere near those son-of-a-whore signs," stressed the other.

"And we got to wrestling a little, got to keep this bitch in line, you know." A retaliatory punch in the arm started the two of them smacking each other until Tank cleared his throat. "Anyway, out of fucking nowhere, the sirens start blaring like we're making a run for the border—"

I should've been more sympathetic, since I'd nearly

stroked out on Gatling Drive myself, but I'd have blasted the sirens just to stop Cam'n'Isaac's relentless blue streak. Tank tried to extract more info from the pair, but all he got was that they'd been yards from the street signs when they got joybuzzed. Not that they seemed halfway reliable witnesses. I got a little more from their story: the sirens must not be triggered by ID chips, or they wouldn't have gone off for Cam'n'Isaac; Outsiders didn't have them. I waited until they shook hands with Tank and took off in matching strides toward the bar. Whereupon, I joined Tank. He gave me a final once-over, probably wished he'd bought me armor instead of underwear.

"How you doing?" I had to really enunciate, or scream over the din.

He shrugged. "You?"

I shrugged back, traded drinks with him. He'd hardly tasted his beer. He sniffed my glass.

"You have a nice chat with Serena?" he said.

"As riveting as your discussion with Sweeney."

I considered telling him about Serena's suspicion, that he and I had plotted William's demise. I decided Mute's wasn't the place to talk. Exile had few taboos, but offing a fellow crew member was borderline. Killing family? Wrong side of the continuum—even for Exile. The fewer folks caught wind of Serena's theory, the better.

"Was that Cam'n'Isaac?" I hinted.

"Yeah." He didn't elaborate, looking into my drink like he might read its chemical signature. "You met—?"

"Who?" I yelled. Could've sworn he said "puppy."

"Kid with the mohawk, his name is Puppy. Skinny Puppy if you're bigger than him ... or old enough to know who that is." He checked my eyes for recognition. "Never mind, they weren't in many movies."

"It's a Joke," I said.

"Not that funny."

"I meant my drink. A Joke. Jack and Coke?" Once I saw a flicker of humor in his eyes, I asked, "Show me your secret room?"

"Nosy." But he smiled and cupped the back of my neck.

"It's not my nose that's interested," I said, leaning into his touch.

"No room for acrobatics," he warned, still with the smile.

"All we need," I said, pulling on his tie, "is something you can truss me up to."

He looked over my head like that'd prevent me from seeing the blush spreading over his face. I started to laugh, but his smile melted as he made eye contact with someone across the room. I turned and caught the tail end of a significant glance from Mute, his Brillo-thick brows low over gray eyes, before he disappeared into a room behind the bar.

"What's wrong?" I said.

"Give me a minute." Tank tried to loosen my fist from his tie.

"Like hell." I hung on and followed him to the bar.

"You got a not-very-welcoming party waiting for you down at the intersection," Vanessa reported, no hesitation. Serena stared from her bar stool, wide eyes looking all the wider for her overplucking, but Sweeney moseyed over to our end of the bar. "Problem?" he said.

"Yeah," Vanessa snapped. "Your crew's too predictable. Chazz is out there waiting to slam ya. You'd best head 'em off before they bring the fight here, or Dad's gonna revoke your party privileges." She waited for Tank's nod before leaving to pour another round.

"I told you," I said, yanking Tank's tie. "We could've been dancing back at your place. Now we're headed into another brawl." Remembering the last one, Thea's face twisted with flames, made me shiver. Tank's beer bottle fizzed over in my hand.

"No," he said, wresting the bottle from me. He plunked it on the bar and shook the drizzle from his hand. "*We're* not going anywhere. *You're* going to the house with Sweeney."

"I'm not going anywhere with him," I said, same time as Sweeney said, "Dude, I ain't leaving you to run Cinderella home."

"Then you'll go back with Puppy," Tank told me, setting my drink on the bar.

"I don't know him from Adam," I shrieked.

"Never stopped you before," Sweeney snarked.

"Stop talking like you know me!" I said.

"Everybody *knows* you."

"Silence!"

The crew at the bar hushed, eyes sharpening at the violence in Tank's voice. Irked by the attention, Tank gave my shoulder a less than affectionate squeeze.

"You're going to my place," he growled. "We'll decide who with later."

In the quiet spreading through the Roadhouse, probably everyone heard me gulp. While I tried not to squirm in his grip, Tank turned to point a finger in Sweeney's face.

"And you," Tank said. "Don't let your tongue get your teeth knocked out."

To my satisfaction, Sweeney gulped, too.

≈

TANK SENT TWO GOFERS—Beto and Belen—to assess the threat posed by Chazz's crew. Then he summoned his brass to the long table under the mezzanine, near the back wall, for a conference. Used to my brother's rules, I didn't expect to be included, but I lingered by the jukebox, hoping to listen in. Tank beckoned me with one hand. When I approached, he jerked his head at a chair against the wall. I was to sit under the mounted hubcaps: an observer, not a participant. Well, we'd see about that.

Sweeney sat at Tank's right hand. Rain, the construction crew's "foreman," sat on his left. I'd met her earlier, one of a dozen five-second intros I'd grimaced through. A redhead with close-cropped hair, Rain was tall and fair-skinned, though working for Tank gave her a consistent sunburn and freckles over her broad cheeks and straight nose. She avoided eye contact, so I barely caught that her eyes were brown.

Jackson tilted back in his chair, long legs bouncing restlessly despite his perpetual half-grin and amused right eyebrow. Unlike Rain, he had no problem meeting my eyes as he cast off jokes like spilled salt. His were dark brown, set wide over a scarred Nubian nose. I liked his ears, small and close to his buzz cut, and his full lips. He was young for brass, which made me think he must be smart. Or charismatic. Hell, I'd've followed him around—not into battle, but that was my idiosyncratic desire to see middle age, no reflection on him. Judging by the laughter at the table, he was well-liked.

Kier was the other Exile. Watery blue eyes, fine-boned cheeks, horseshoe hairline: like Jude Law on a bender. The way he muttered, his bulging knuckles, seemed familiar. But he didn't give me the usual knowing smile, so if we had danced, it'd been a long time ago, a whiskey-dick waltz lost in the haze of next morning's hangover.

The remaining brass were all Outsiders. Dahlia, a woman in her fifties built like a minotaur, sat at the end of the table. A nevus flammeus (port-wine stain) covered a third of her square face, and an elaborate cameo tattoo festooned her visible chest. Mostly brown hair, brown eyes, brown skin, and a lot of chunky silver rings on thick fingers.

Zeke was in his thirties, I guessed, but nearly bald. His eyebrows and eyes were dark brown, in contrast to the remaining feathery bits on his head. Long, thin nose, defined philtrum, narrow lips betraying long-term bitterness. He didn't seem as soused as Kier, but he rubbed his pitted face as if to sober up. I noted strong hands, the fingernails painted black.

Moss had eyes that color and matching calligraphy tattooed from one temple to the other. I couldn't read the words winding in and out of Moss's black hairline, but rumor had it, they were Nahuatl. Also as rumor had foretold, I couldn't determine Moss's gender. Thick, curling lashes, hawkish nose, smooth cheeks, firm chin. I didn't usually rely on hair for cues, since it could be altered so easily, and Moss's long, braided black hair didn't help anyway. The layers of torn T-shirts under a knit vest, the well-muscled shoulders, left me guessing, too.

Finally, there was Faux-Hawk, or Puppy. He flashed me a smile like he knew the color of my panties. I squirmed, wishing his smile didn't dampen said panties. I had enough craziness going on. My irritation must've shown because Puppy dropped his gaze. He took his seat, smoothing his ginger goatee thoughtfully.

Tank neither explained nor acknowledged my presence. Instead, he called order and described in typically terse speech how my family had ambushed us earlier that evening. I stared at my hands in silence. Anyone who didn't think I'd asked Tank to kill William for me before probably wondered now since I was there with them instead of at home, treating my burned little sister.

Tank finished with one of his facial shrugs. Puppy let loose a low but awed whistle. Tank frowned. "Questions?" he grumbled.

Kier had perked up at mention of my brother's flamethrower—engineer, I suppose—and though his request for design details seemed off-topic to me, Tank obliged. Afterwards, Dahlia said, "I'm guessin' you didn't tell us this to brag." Which gave Tank his segue to the threat awaiting us outside the Roadhouse.

Beto and Belen returned. They waited where the jukebox cast a golden orange glow over their crossed arms until Tank finished his explanation and waved them over.

"How many are out there?" he asked.

"Approximately?" Belen stuck her hands in her back pockets. "All of them."

"Two to one," Beto said. "At least."

"That's way more than William's crew," I blurted.

Tank tilted his head, aimed a heavy silence in my direction.

"Well, it is!" I said.

Belen backed me up. "Some of the breeders joined them. I saw Pops and his crew."

Pops wasn't her dad, he was an old white guy with a stupidly big family on the east edge of Exile.

Sweeney glared at me. "What do those guys have to do with William?"

"How should I know?" I ignored Tank's deep sigh. "I'm not talking to my family, let alone those—"

Tank grabbed one leg of my chair and yanked me to the corner of the table so fast I stopped mid-sentence.

"Join us. Please. I insist," he deadpanned.

I didn't say "Finally!" though I probably looked it. I adjusted my chair between him and Rain so the table didn't jab my ribs. I scanned the brass's faces, defiance ready, but Rain only blinked. Puppy winked at me, the fool. Dahlia actually gave me a thumbs up. Moss smiled but directed it at a spot on the table so's not to peeve Tank. Sweeney met my challenge, but that was old news so why waste my energy?

"My guess is Pops ain't here for William's sake," Tank said. "He's here 'cause of that demo job."

"We didn't do anything!" Sweeney said. "We left them their condemned houses, which they didn't even own in the first place, and that was months ago!"

"So Pops has a memory, and Chazz made an alliance," Tank said. "And they're ready to battle. Rain, thoughts?"

It sounded like a routine prompt. "I'm in," she said. "But not everybody came ready for a fight. There's Heidi and

Serena." She nodded at me, gaze skirting mine. "Marshall's arm is still in a sling from our last fight with their crew. And Hugo's leg is acting up."

"Noted," Tank said, which seemed the signal for the other brass to speak.

"Long as the odds are this bad already, we can split up," Zeke said. He had a slight accent I couldn't place. "Send the crew who aren't up to fighting as an escort for the girlfriends."

My brain stumbled over that one. Was I Tank's girlfriend? Really? And were Serena and I equals?

Tank shook his head, but his thoughts ran on a different track than mine. "If they ain't up to fighting, they're in no shape to protect Heidi and Serena."

"But Chazz's crew is here for *you*, Tank," Puppy said. "What do they care if a couple of guys get away with the girls?"

"Women," Dahlia corrected. Zeke turned to listen to her, and I noticed his hearing aid, understood his accent then. "And where are they supposed to go?" Dahlia said.

"Heidi's going to my house," Tank said automatically.

I huffed. "Nice to have a say in the matter."

Dahlia chuckled. More discreetly, Moss smiled down at the table again.

Tank tugged his tie a little looser, told Sweeney, "Serena's welcome, too."

Sweeney shook his head. "She's gotta get home. Her mom depends on her."

"I'll talk to Mute," Tank said. "See if he's willing to let her wait it out here."

"Why can't I stay then?" I leaned forward, trying to make him look at me, but then I felt Rain craning to see past me, so I settled back.

"Serena's clearly a civilian," Tank said, unconcerned by Rain's intensity. "Mute's not gonna get any shit for harboring her. He can't do that for you and still be considered impartial. He'd be jeopardizing the Roadhouse's status as a no-kill zone."

"Listen, if your brother's crew wanted blood *before* your sister got hurt," Dahlia said, "now they're going to want more."

Rain swiveled to Dahlia, and I realized she didn't avoid eye contact so much as hyperfocus on people's mouths. I thought she was speech reading, but any noise the crew made outside our inner circle hooked her attention so she didn't seem hearing impaired like Zeke.

"Tank's head, for sure. Maybe yours, too," Dahlia said, nodding at me. "They're gonna have people posted outside Tank's house to keep y'all from running home. They want you out in the street in the fight."

Jackson nodded, chair coming down with a business-like thump. "That sounds 'bout right."

"But we don't give people what they want, do we?" Chin in hand, Moss parted with a sly grin.

"Then let's talk strategy," Tank said.

His brass threw out ideas, cautiously at first, then with growing excitement as the impending fight became more real in their minds. Beyond the juke box some warriors stopped drinking, preparing for battle, while others started slamming shots—same reason, different approach.

Tank slapped the table. "Cross talk," he said.

Used to William's chaotic crew, I hadn't thought the overlapping voices that bad, but the brass settled down. I assumed in deference to Zeke's hearing.

"Rain?" Tank prompted again.

"Like Dahlia said, we need to remove any guards at your house." Between Tank's conversational cues and her attentive, if flat, expression, it dawned on me that Rain might have what used to be called Asperger's. "It won't matter if we fight off the crews outside the Roadhouse. If we have to fight again at your place, we'll be tired and those guys'll be fresh."

Jackson raised his hand, then spoke without being

called on. "They've got allies. Maybe we can call in ours? Plenty of folks owe us, for fixing their houses and stuff. Who can we ask to head down to Tank's place ahead of us?"

I raised my hand timidly, not sure I was doing it right. "I might be able to help with that."

I turned to Tank, and from the microscopic twitch at the outer corner of his left eye, I thought he knew what was coming next. I went ahead and said it.

"On one condition."

I WATCHED TANK'S CREW from a window of the Roadhouse, my finger to the glass and Tank's phone to my ear. For every ring Romy didn't answer, I smeared a tic mark until my fingerprints threatened to occlude the arming typology occurring in the parking lot. I hung up. The crew's trucks had been moved to create a wall, behind which Rain now unloaded nail guns and hammers and rebar, passing them out to eager warriors. For a split second I thought of taking a hammer to my fingers to stop me from making the second call. But I had promised Tank. I dialed the next number.

This time I got an answer before the first ring even finished. I considered hanging up. Instead, I forced myself to say, "Carlos? It's Heidi."

"Heidi!" The screech of tires told me he'd been driving. "Where are you? Are you okay?"

"I'm fine," I said, startled by his concern. Of course, I wasn't fine, and somehow he already knew. "I'm at Mute's Roadhouse. Why? What did you hear?"

"What did I hear? You mean what did I *see*, chica. And that'd be your little sister, getting hauled away in an ambulance by the feds."

"What? Why?"

"¿Qué carajo? What do you mean, 'Why?' Kid's got third-degree burns over half her body! Weren't you there?

Your parents said you were."

"Yeah," I said. Under the bright lights of the parking lot, Tank's white shirt glared, making him easy to follow. "But I didn't know it was that bad—"

"How could you not know? You're a medic."

"I don't know!" Tank had hidden the scorch marks on his shirt by rolling up the sleeves. It didn't seem possible Thea had been hurt so badly. "I was trying not to go up in flames myself. It was an accident, I never meant ..." I clamped down before he heard the tears in my voice. Deep breath. "Listen, Carlos, I'm in trouble."

Gears clashed as his SUV suddenly changed direction. "I'll come get you."

"No! It's a mess out here."

I closed my eyes, trying to think past alternating currents of relief and panic. I'd feared Carlos would hang up on me before we'd gotten this far. Hell, I knew I deserved it, the way I'd broken things off with him. Instead, he was trying to save me, and he didn't even know what from.

"I'm with Tank and his crew," I said. "William's crew—I mean, Chazz's crew—they're waiting outside the no-kill zone, and they're not alone. Pops' crew joined them. They've got a grudge against Tank."

While Carlos cursed, I spotted a blue Suzuki idling in the parking lot right beside Sweeney and his Yamaha. It was the same bike I'd seen outside Tank's house—and at William's burn. And straddling it was Faux-hawk/Puppy. Sweeney waved a nail-studded baseball bat, but not at Puppy. The two were laughing.

"What the hell?" I muttered.

"What?" Carlos said.

"Never mind. It's insane over here. More so than usual. Look," I said, more to focus myself than Carlos. "Tank's crew will stay and fight, but Tank and I are heading back to his house. Tank's pulling in favors, so we'll have cover while we take the long way 'round, but we need someone to check out the neighborhood, make sure none of William's thugs are waiting to surprise us."

"Wait a minute. Tank's crew is fighting, but he's sneaking out the back with you? What kind of fucking coward are you mixed up with, Heidi?"

"He's not—"

"And he can't even use his own connections? He made you call me?"

"It was my idea," I said. "I told him I'd ask you for help, but he had to promise not to fight. This whole thing with William's—Chazz's—crew has gotten way out of hand. Maybe if we lie low for a few days, it'll blow over."

"Blow over? No mames, cabrona."

I kinda wished I'd hammered my fingers, after all. "It's up to you, Carlos. We're heading over there in, like, ten minutes. You can help by clearing out those streets, or you can let me walk into another ambush. What's it going to be?"

Chapter Twelve

THE THUG ON THE motorcycle racing beside us swung his chain. I gasped and ducked, inhaling the sharp scents of sweat and licorice from the padding of my borrowed helmet. I felt Tank duck, too, helmet and body armor meeting to protect his neck. The links cracked against the rearview mirror, deflecting most of the sting before the chain hit Tank's chest. He gunned the Ninja, and the thug, a skinny white kid who'd styled himself after William, fell behind.

Knowing I'd likely be wannabe William's next target, I unhooked my arms from Tank's waist. I didn't need to hold on. We were bound by paracord. I hefted the pipe I'd gotten in the Roadhouse parking lot and turned to look behind us.

Before we'd reached the Inner Radius, another thug had jumped off his bike to tackle Puppy. They'd gone down in a cloud of dust. Cam'n'Zak had sped off into Frankie's territory, drawing off the breeders who'd spotted us making our getaway. I was grateful to the trash-mouthed duo, but I really missed the cool clothesline thing they'd used to yank folks off their bikes.

Wannabe William swung his chain at me. I retaliated with my pipe. The chain didn't wrap around the pipe like I'd hoped, but at least it didn't smack my back. Tank's skid-proof leather jacket was meant to prevent roadrash, not blunt force trauma. Before the thug raised his chain again, Sweeney drove up alongside him. He slammed his nail-studded bat into the thug's back tire, then let go. The bat hit the rear fender, and we shot ahead of wannabe William. Momentum must've kicked the bat out because I heard the bike's plastic undertail shatter before the guy skidded out with a scream.

Back in our neighborhood, the streets were quiet. My breath felt deafening in the confines of Puppy's helmet. Tank had borrowed it for me—Puppy hadn't wanted to mess up his 'hawk, the dope. Carlos's truck was nowhere to be seen, but neither were any of William's thugs, on bike or foot. Several blocks south of Cricket, Sweeney caught up with us.

"We good?" Tank asked. His helmet mic sounded so smooth, it was like he was in my head.

Sweeney nodded. "It'll be a while before the chainiac gets up again." Despite his staticky mic, I heard him grinning at his own pun.

"Puppy?" Tank said.

"On his way."

Minutes later, Puppy rejoined us, clothes dusty and 'hawk mashed in the back, but still in possession of his bike and a devilish grin. Dark pressed in on the cautious rumble of our bikes as we paused at the intersection of Cricket and Flint. No roadblock. No armed gauntlet of thugs. Red Sonja barked under her house, Mexican electronica cascaded from a window, but there were no war cries or whispers of ambush.

"Looks like your Cantu friend made good," Puppy said to me.

"Or we were overthinking it," Sweeney retorted.

He took the lead, driving in lazy loops down Cricket, and Puppy followed. They skimmed their headlights over the concrete buffers, alert for shrapnel and shadows. I didn't think they were looking high enough, but saying so would've sounded paranoid. People didn't grasp the diabolical nature of Thing One's booby traps. Wary, I squinted to make out houses, wondered which neighbors might've taken sides.

Sweeney stopped. His headlight glared off a spike strip that spanned Cricket, sharp but skinny, easy to jump. Beyond it, access to Tank's side entrance looked easy: the gap between concrete barriers inviting. Tank drove toward it. I took a licorice-tinged breath—it was like sharing Puppy's gum—and tried to swallow past my pounding heart.

"Wait wait wait," I breathed. Tank couldn't have heard me over the Ninja's engine, but he slowed down.

Puppy and Sweeney came back, circled us. "I'm gonna go 'round the front," Sweeney said. "See what's up."

He cranked up the speed to pop a wheelie over the strip. Puppy followed him. When Sweeney yanked his bike over the metal serpent, a blast of yellow flame spit across the street. Sweeney sailed right through it. Puppy hit the brakes and went skidding. I heard a high *thwunk*.

"Get down," I yelled.

Too late; Puppy yelped.

Tank threw our weight to the right. The bike was moving so slowly, we toppled over. Tank put out a knee and hand to catch us. Gravel screeched along the Ninja's black-ice paint, bit through my pant leg. I stifled a screech. Tank flexed to keep a grip on the handle, and I kept a grip on him.

Puppy was moaning. My eyes burned from the flash of fire, but when I yanked off my borrowed helmet, I didn't hear dragon's breath. Theo's flamethrower must've been rigged for a single blast. Sweeney's Yamaha sputtered back, stinking of scorch and ash, the scent stronger as Sweeney silenced the engine, dropped the bike, and stumbled over to us. "Fuckity fuck almighty fuck," he panted, pulling off his helmet.

Tank flicked off the Ninja. Sweeney helped him get the bike upright. I was too busy tearing at the paracord that bound us.

"You okay?" Sweeney said.

Tank muttered something, then looked over his shoulder as I slid free. "Heidi, wait. Stay down!"

I scurried to the nearest concrete barrier, hoping I was out of shooting range. I tried to answer Tank, but I couldn't get the words past my ridiculously enlarged heart. Like Theo's flamethrower, Thea's crossbow had to be a one-shot. She was the only one any good with it, and according to Carlos, she was out of Exile. But who knew what other death traps my family had devised? I stumbled along the barrier on Tank's side of the street, head ticking back and forth as I searched the street for triggers, relays. Sweeney yelled, "Hey, Puppy?" and I realized I was closest to the sprawled Suzuki. With a last glance 'round, I hurried over.

Puppy was still moaning. I twisted the key, shut off the engine, touched his shoulder.

"Did I get shot with a motherfucking arrow?" he said, eyes clenched shut.

"Looks like." I set down his helmet to free my hands. "Where'd it hit you?"

"Went right across my fucking back."

"Think you can move? If Carlos missed those traps, there could be others."

I missed his response in the sudden racket: the side gate opening, and then Sweeney hollering, "Move your asses!"

"Come on."

I pulled at the back of Puppy's dusty leather jacket. It gaped open, sliced through, and my eyes bugged at the blood. The fool wasn't wearing skid gear.

Q: WHO THE FUCK in their right mind ever looked at me and thought, "Ah, a medic!"

A: No one in their right mind. It was my parents.

I was nine when they had their epiphany. Mother had been escorted to the clinic for a checkup. Her monitoring bracelet needed tuning, had been—much to my delight—

strangling her in an ever-tightening spiral that most days stranded her in the kitchen. Father had gone with. So I was the only one around when Sweet William came home crying.

He'd staggered out of the house and into the backyard. I looked up from the dead crow I'd been prodding with a stick. Its right wing was busted, the bones showing through.

"What happened to you?" I said, none too sympathetic. William was always bleeding or healing, even at the tender age of six.

"Stupid Cantu boys," he sobbed, holding his arm. "I was playing with Sammy, and his brothers got mad."

Right, "playing." No doubt William had gotten what he deserved, but I dropped my corpse poker and went to check him out. Sooner he stopped moaning, sooner he went away.

"Where does it hurt?" I said.

"I can't move it," he blubbered, clutching his wrist. "Carlos grabbed this arm and Romero pulled the other, and they said they were going to rip 'em off!"

"Well, don't mess with Sammy anymore, you dope. Oh, come on," I hollered over his wail of pain. "I can't help just by looking."

Holding his injured arm, ignoring his screeches, I herded him to the house, pushed him against the heat-warped siding. I figured his elbow was dislocated; I'd seen warriors stumble out of scuffles with their arms dangling uselessly until a medic twisted something and sent them back into the brawl.

"Hold still," I said. I twisted his arm so his palm faced out.

"Wait, what are you—"

I rammed my shoulder into his chest, pinned him to the wall, forced his arm up. It bent at the elbow. Something slotted into place, and I let go. He sagged to the ground, his eyes (green, a little reptilian, like Mother's) showing white all around, mouth hanging open. He sobbed, tentatively flexed his arm.

"What did you do!" he shrieked.

"It's better now, right?" I backed up. I needed to get the lighter fluid before more ants caught the dead crow's scent. *Worms and spiders*, I thought out of nowhere, and shivered.

"I'm telling Mom," William said, running back into the house.

Little shit sure did. Soon as Mother and Father got home, the screaming started. I scuttled into the footwell of the 1965 Ford F-100 behind the garage to wait it out.

But when Father found me, he didn't look mad. A little excited maybe, but it was hard to tell. He and Mother had had a fight a few weeks before, and she'd scorched his eyebrows off. Come to think of it, could've been when her bracelet got jacked up, too. At any rate, my dad had looked slightly astonished ever since.

"Heidi," he said, sliding into the dusty driver's seat, "how'd you know what to do for William?"

I shrugged, shaking off the scent of naphtha. "Saw it in the streets."

He gestured for me to sit beside him on the sun-warmed seat. "But weren't you scared to try it?"

I blinked. "Why?"

"Didn't you think you might hurt him? Maybe make it worse?"

I frowned, retracing the afternoon's events. All I'd thought was to stop William's caterwauling—I mean, what was worse than that?

Father must've seen my confusion. "What *were* you thinking?"

"I dunno." I propped my feet on the dash. I remembered the dead crow, its hollow bones. "I know what my arms feel like. I've looked at other people's. William told me what happened, and I imagined his insides, how to rearrange them."

Father stared at me. If he'd still had eyebrows, they might've been high on his forehead; instead, his crow's feet just smoothed out. Eventually, he cleared his throat. "Heidi," he said, same jolly tone as when I got to choose dessert. "Your mother and I think it's time you began medic training."

"I don't want to be a medic." Sitting on the sidelines all day, watching my neighbors beat the crap out of each other, repairing the same dumb injuries over and over? No, thanks.

"Well then, what do you want to be?" Father asked.

I hadn't thought about it much—what was anyone in town? Mutants, thugs, stoners, victims ... No one had ever asked me before. I looked out the fly-specked window at our padlocked garage, considering.

"What do you want to do?" Father prompted.

"I don't know. Take faces apart?"

I felt him stiffen and turned to look. His forehead was wrinkled in a way that he didn't need eyebrows. My gaze shifted to his hands gripping the steering wheel.

"And put them back together again," I said. "Fix them. Like you and the cars."

Father's knuckles went a little less white, loosened around the cracked wheel. "You mean ... plastic surgery?" He laughed like he'd been punched in the gut. "Not much call for facelifts in Exile, baby." He went on, voice stronger. "Being a medic's better, anyway. You'll be helping your brother. You'll be useful."

"I don't want to be useful."

"Sure, you do," he said, but he was staring out the windshield at something I couldn't see. The future, maybe.

≈

LEANING AGAINST THE KITCHEN table, Puppy winced out of his jacket. Sweeney, clothing scorched but otherwise fine, took the torn jacket and handed it to me. I scowled at him and tossed it on a chair along with Tank's.

Tank ripped open the back of Puppy's bloody shirts. The arrow had slashed over the left trapezius and snipped some of the supraspinitus and teres minor. A spider was severed from its tattoo web, and Puppy needed stitches—lots—but the wound wasn't too deep.

Tank sighed in relief. Then he pointed Sweeney to the first aid kit and pushed me into the living room.

"I'm fine," I insisted.

He jerked me this way and that.

"Scared shitless," I added, "but fine."

He ignored me and stooped to check my torn pants, the scrapes on my leg. Came back up and tilted my chin left, right, to study my eyes and scan for bumps. "Yeah," he finally said. "Fine." He dropped his hand and glowered. "But, Heidi, this shit can't keep happening."

I tried not to twitch. "What shit ... exactly?"

"I am not going to examine you for injuries every time we come or go!"

"Umm ... okay." I blinked a few times, unsure.

"It's not even going to be an issue. You get what I'm saying?"

I squirmed. "No?"

"No one hurts you again, Heidi. Ever."

Before I could speak, Puppy screeched in the kitchen.

Sweeney popped into the living room. "Uh, Tank, drugs?" he said, half grinning. "I ain't exactly a light touch."

So I doped and stitched up Puppy while Tank and Sweeney commiserated in the backyard over their abused bikes. I tried not to touch Puppy's tattooed spiders, and he tried not to twitch and mess up my neat knots. When I finished, he slumped in his chair, one cheek flat on the table, faux-hawk wilted with sweat.

"What's your name?" I asked, repacking the kit.

His aqua eyes had gone glassy with Demerol and however many spritzers he'd had. I figured he was too far gone until he said, "Ha ha fuck. I thought Tank told you.

You can call me Puppy."

"No," I said, rolling my eyes. "I can't."

"Everyone does." He smiled, those nearly nonlips pale and goofy. I shook my head, and he drawled, "Oh, *now* you gotta problem with nicknames? What about 'Tank'?"

Well, shit. It had never occurred to me that that wasn't his real name. *Tank* suited him. I cleared my throat, carried the kit to the cupboard. "It's not nicknames in general. Just yours. So what can I call you?"

"Paolo," he puffed, mouth slack.

"Why do they call you *Puppy*?"

"I dunno. Someone said somethin' about some—some ..." As if begging me to read his mind, he aimed a soulful gaze at me ten times deeper than the ocean I dreamed of seeing one day.

I shook my head, prepared to stow my questions for later. But then, an idea. Dirty pool, but who knew the next time he'd be so unguarded?

"Paolo?" I hooked my arm under his and helped him stand. "Why were you at my brother's burn?"

He leaned into me, not an unpleasant weight. "Your brother burned? Thought that was lil sis ... ter."

"No. My brother William. Why were you at his funeral?"

"Oh." He panted, sweat seeping through my blouse. "Recon."

"For Tank?"

"No, f'r you."

I stopped shuffling him toward the living room. "What do you mean?"

"Wanted to know 'bout you. All 'bout you."

I frowned. "Why?"

He echoed me and closed his eyes. I shook his arm, but he was too sloppy drunk to be any use.

"C'mon," I sighed. "Let's get you to bed."

"Mmmm. Zoundss good. You come, too."

Chapter Thirteen

I DON'T KNOW HOW Forrest survived childhood in Exile. Butterfly knife notwithstanding, he didn't give off a warrior vibe. In fact, the fastest I ever saw him move was the day I arrived an hour early for my "date" with Thomas. He lurched halfway up from his slump on the couch, and asked, "What are you doing here?"

"What are you still doing on that couch?" I said, blocking his view of *It's A Wonderful Life*.

Forrest slumped back down and almost scowled. A real scowl would've taken too much energy. "What do you care?"

"Doesn't look very comfortable." I held out a hand. "Let me make you more comfortable."

His mouth tasted like beer and Skittles. In the hallway, he worked free long enough to ask, "Why are you doing this? To make Tommy jealous?"

I shook my head, pulled his hand up under my skirt. I pressed his fingers into my soaked panties. "No. Because of this, for you."

As I remembered, his bedroom smelled like Thomas's, only cleaner. I maneuvered him to the edge of his bed, then went down on him, thinking I'd get him off once to make the Tab A/Slot B last longer. Instead, seconds after his come burned the back of my throat, my cunt went off without so much as a tickle.

"Fuck," I said, feeling betrayed.

Forrest pulled me up to straddle his hips. "You okay?"

I nodded, still shivering. He kissed my clavicles, dragged my clothes off, and we lay in bed, staring at a faded poster of the Great Barrier Reef until we were ready to go again. Didn't take long.

When Thomas got home, slamming doors and calling for me, then for Forrest, we froze.

"He knows, he must know," I muttered. Forrest nodded, dropped his forehead to mine and thrust once more before Thomas barged in.

"Shit!" Thomas exclaimed. He threw his football, and Forrest ducked, still got hit in the shoulder. "Bro, if you wanted my sloppy seconds, you should've said so. I was done with her, anyway." He spit—actually spit—on the carpet before turning to leave.

"At least close the door," Forrest called, pulling the sheet higher over us.

"What for?" Thomas yelled. "Ain't nothing I ain't seen before. That a lot of guys have seen before. Hell, half the guys in town!"

Forrest regarded me, face suddenly blank. "Have you really danced with that many guys?"

My chest went tight, my breath stuck in my lungs. There was no use lying—I'd never bothered to hide my dalliances—so I nodded. Forrest studied me a minute longer, his features about as enlightening as a brick. Then he pushed deeper inside me, and we moaned together.

≈

BY THE TIME TANK and Sweeney stopped fiddling with their bikes, Paolo was asleep, spread-eagled on his belly on blankets I'd tossed on the living room floor. One look at him and Tank insisted he and Sweeney stay the night. I started to argue, but the flash of Tank's eyes shut me up fast. 'Sides, after all that had happened, I desperately wanted to close my eyes and forget everything for a while. So I didn't mention Paolo's attendance at William's burn.

Tank turned on the house dampeners, and upstairs, he locked the bedroom door behind us.

"What's that about?" I said, eyeing the doorknob.

"You. I don't want you sleepwalking down the stairs and breaking your neck."

"I didn't last time," I retorted. But I figured he was looking out for me, and he seemed to understand I argued mostly out of habit.

That night I didn't sleepwalk. I dreamed of Tank dead in the street, his body riddled with arrows like anatomic pointers. Forrest staggered into the street to claim Tank, and I couldn't fight him off. He'd been stitched back together again, but everywhere I touched him, worms spilled out. I backed up, flicking filth from my fingers, and fell over Thea. She was burning, her scrawny body turning into Mother's, then a cloud of black ash. I scrambled backwards, skin sloughing off my palms. The Mother cloud roiled and transformed into a ring of spiders around me. They chewed the asphalt in unison, paused en masse, then chewed again. I leaped to my feet, head whipping 'round as the prickly noose tightened. The street vibrated under their metallic teeth. A chasm opened up, and I plunged into a dark pit.

I gasped, opened my eyes.

I could still hear the rhythmic munching. No, wait. Buzzing.

Tank's phone. Buzzing on the bedside table.

I glanced at Tank. His eyelids twitched with dreams. He'd tossed and turned longer than I had. I leaned over and grabbed the phone.

"Hello?" I whispered.

"Umm ... Heidi? It's Carlos."

"Carlos?" I turned from Tank to let him sleep. "Where were you last night?"

"What do you mean, where was I? Me and Romy were clearing out the neighborhood, 'escorting' William's buddies home like you asked."

"Well, you missed a coupl'a things," I hissed. "We ran smack into Theo's booby traps—"

"Anybody hurt?" he interrupted. "I mean, 'dead' hurt?"

"No," I admitted.

"Then bitch me out later. I gotta talk to Tank. Stuff was stolen from city storage last night. Chain link fence, an old generator, traffic cameras—"

Beside me, Tank mumbled. Sounded like, "Jenna."

"Who cares about that junk?" I snapped.

"Pues, you should, chica. 'Cause all that stuff's outside Tank's house."

"What?" I checked over my shoulder, saw Tank blinking blearily. "Fucking Frank Sinatra. Don't tell me you think Tank stole—"

"No, I know it wasn't him. It was Chazz and the rest of your brother's crew. Thing is, have you looked outside lately?"

"No." I sat up, patted Tank's thick thigh to rouse him.

"Heidi, you're in deeper shit than last night," Carlos said. "Get up, look out the fuckin' window, and call me when you figure out what you're doing. The questions Sammy's been asking since you ditched us, they're bad enough. I don't want to have to explain your funeral, too."

≈

TANK CRANKED THE SIDING away from the picture window. I ran down to the security panel and slapped off the dampeners. Instantly, the chink of metal on metal and a series of barked orders invaded from outside. I squinted at the video monitors, not understanding what I was seeing. Sweeney rolled over and nearly fell off the couch before creaking into a sitting position. Paolo didn't budge.

"'Sup?" Sweeney croaked, rubbing his eyes.

I rushed up the stairs, putting on an extra burst of speed when Tank groaned, "Fucking hell."

Beside him at the window, I gawked. William's buddies swarmed in the dawn-smudged street, erecting a chain link fence around Tank's property. Chazz shouted orders from atop a ladder near the concrete-and-timber palisades. I leaned in, trying to find Mother. Then a black cloud splattered the window. I shrieked and jumped back onto Tank's bare toes. Sweeney bolted from the couch and stumbled over his own feet to join us.

Backed up against Tank, I watched an opaque slurry drool down the window. I shook myself—not a cloud, not my dream. I tiptoed and craned to the side, made out, beyond the toxic snail trail, Theo standing on our parents' roof. He hefted a new PVC-tentacled backpack. Another jet of tarry goo blacked out our view. Below, warriors cursed, mad about getting jizzed on. Behind me, Tank cursed for other reasons.

"What the hell's going on?" Sweeney said, morning hoarse.

"Oh, nothing," Tank said. "Except we're fucking trapped."

Chapter Fourteen

I BALANCED ON THE rolling office chair to peek out the sniper slit. We were in the study out of range of Thing One's super squirter. The chain link fence around Tank's property didn't quite touch the asphalt because the thugs were using old portable basketball hoops from people's driveways as fence posts. Perpendicular to the fence, a line of wrecked cars blocked off Raven Street. Their buckled chrome and smashed windows reflected early morning light. At the east end of the fence, the generator waited, guarded by Keith.

Tank stood at the sniper slit on my left, Sweeney at the one on my right. After a few minutes' observation, Sweeney turned from his window, then stopped mid-"damnit" when he noticed my photo gallery.

"What in hell?" he said.

Tank didn't turn from his window. "It's Heidi's work."

Sweeney's gaze jerked from fragments of Robert Redford to pieces of Errol Flynn, Gregory Peck to Zac Ephron. "It's messed up, is what it is. Who the fuck are you?" he asked me. "Dr. Frankenstein?"

"She studies actors' faces," Tank said. "How they're put together, like blueprints."

Surprised by his matter-of-fact tone, I glanced at him. He ignored me; neck craned, attention lasered on Raven.

"Whatever," Sweeney said. "So long as she don't study me like that."

"Too late," Tank and I said. I grinned despite Sweeney's epic bitchface.

"Is the generator for what I think it's for?" I asked, sinking in my chair.

Sweeney nodded. "Electrified fence." He stalked over to sit on the desk.

"And the traffic cameras?" I said.

"Must be hacked," Tank said. "So the minute we leave the house, they'll know."

"What's next?" I wondered. "They gonna start digging a trench? Like the feds did?"

"This shit can't stand," Sweeney said. "We gotta take them out now before they finish caging us in."

Tank turned from the window. "Not so fast. Let me call Rain. For all we know, brass has a plan. We charge out there without consulting, and we might screw it up."

He headed for the bedroom for his phone. Sweeney and I moved to follow him, but not slowing, not turning, Tank pointed behind him. "Stay. I can't have a convo with you two yelling in both ears. And try not to tear each other apart 'fore I get back."

Scowling, I sank into the chair again. This time I noticed the cool leather against my skin, remembered I was running around in my underwear and a nearly sheer shirt. I crossed my arms and spun the chair to face the wall. Sweeney slumped against the desk, staring in the opposite direction.

We couldn't hear what Tank was saying, all grumbly monotone, but it went on too long to be good news. Sweeney must've been as twitchy as I was 'cause Tank hadn't made it all the way through the door before he asked, "What's the rumpus?"

"They took a hell of a beating last night. Pops played dirty, sent in a bunch of kids whenever our guys got the upper hand, took advantage of the fact that our crew wasn't willing to beat down kids that ain't even shaving yet. Then the grownups came back all refreshed."

"How bad was it?" I said.

"Lucky if half our crew can ride."

Sweeney sagged. "So we got off easy. Chased all over the Outer Radius, flamethrowers and bows and arrows in the Inner Radius, and we still had it better than the rest of 'em."

Tank nodded. "And while we're bottled up in here, Pops is taking potshots at our guys, the ones who're still mobile."

"Then what do we do?" I said, looking from one man to the other.

Careful not to disturb my photos, Tank leaned against the wall. "For now, we're outnumbered. Best to sit tight until the street wars start up again."

Alarmed by the phrase, by memories of Father, I hugged my knees.

"Chazz and company, they got the attention spans of rabid squirrels," Tank continued. "They'll want to fight in the street wars, not guard us. Once they go AWOL, we can use the chaos to our advantage."

"But even if the warriors take a powder, we still got her crazy family to deal with," Sweeney said. "A dad with a grudge. Ain't that worse than a whole crew?"

"Not my dad," I said. "Mother's the one who'd gut a nun. But she's got that monitoring bracelet on, keeps her close to home."

Tank gave Sweeney a need-I-say-more shrug, and asked me, "What did Carlos say?"

Sweeney sat bolt upright, exposing the red ring around his neck where he'd been burned by the flamethrower. "What? Carlos Cantu called her, here?"

"Cool it," Tank said. "It wasn't phone sex."

That red ring on Sweeney's neck? Perfect for lining up a noose. Jaw tight, I said, "He wants me to call him when we know what we're doing. He'll help us out. They both will, him and Romero," I added, cheeks warming under Sweeney's squint.

Tank nodded thoughtfully. Sweeney shook his head, then used the cuff of his borrowed flannel shirt to rub crust from his eyes. The cut eyebrow I'd noticed at Mute's was barely scabbed now. I must've misjudged its depth. His legs dangled over the edge of the cumtastic desk, pale under cut-off sweats, and I mentally traced a long, jagged scar on his right shin, knee to ankle. I imagined slicing another line down his left shin. Purely for symmetry, of course.

"If we could just get around your mother, right?"

I startled, realized Tank was watching me, waiting.

"I mean, she runs that house," he said. "Your dad ...?"

I nodded, tried to focus on the conversation instead of imagining Sweeney flayed on that wet dream of a desk. "My dad ... yeah, he'd let it go. He's torn up about William, maybe more about Thea." And me? Did he miss me at all? I cleared my throat. "But Father's not one to settle scores, and he'd never drag anyone else into it. Not like Mother has."

"And the knee biters?" Tank asked.

"Batshit," Sweeney said, surveying my photos. "Runs in the family."

I closed my eyes a second, wished I could carve out his larynx. "They're easy enough to handle if Mother's not pulling their strings." My gut tightened as I added, "Thea's gone, anyway. Carlos said the feds took her away in an ambulance last night."

Tank didn't sound especially concerned as he said, "So if we take care of your mom," and looked out the window.

"Yeah." I scoffed. "Take care of her. I've been trying all my life."

"So let's do it," Tank said.

"Do what?"

Tank turned around, caught my eye. "Let's kill your mom."

Something felt broken in my throat. I couldn't speak. I stared at Tank, felt Sweeney watching me as Tank's suggestion squeezed the air out of the room.

"Are you crazy?" I finally managed.

Tank shrugged. "Practical."

At the edge of my vision, I sensed Sweeney perk up, but I forced my voice low and slow. "How is it practical to kill another member of my family?"

"Well," Tank said, equally low and slow. When I only stared at him, he seemed disconcerted, stopped. He sheathed the sarcasm. "It could end this fucking blood feud. Fast."

"Sweet!" Sweeney jumped off the desk. "Let's do it."

"Get out," I said, not looking at him.

Tank held my gaze. A few seconds later, he tilted his chin at the door. Sweeney sighed, disgusted, but he raised his hands and walked out. I waited until I heard him waking Paolo downstairs before I spoke.

"It doesn't work that way," I said, going to Tank. "Exiles don't care if you kill an opponent in the streets, but you can't kill a member of your own crew. Much less your family."

"But you're not going to do it. I'll do it," he said. Like it was changing a light bulb.

"Not enough degrees of separation."

Yet my belly warmed, as if with liquor or arousal, and that weird heat wiggled down my thighs. Same as the night before, when Mother reached the end of her invisible leash. I stepped into Tank's space, grateful when his arms wrapped 'round me. At least then I had a physical excuse for the tingles riddling my body. An excuse no one could label "Inconclusive."

"People already think you killed William for me. Serena said so. Killing Mother would make things worse."

Tank's gaze bored into me, speculative, suspicious. A Doors rhythm throbbed in my veins: "Five to One." The lyrics were scrawled on abandoned houses throughout Exile, a nihilistic rhyme assuring me I'd never get out, not alive.

"Worse how?" Tank said. "You're already Miss Popularity for fucking your brother's killer."

I blinked at his bullying words. "Epically worse," I said, warmth dwindling. "You know that tracking bracelet my mother wears? If she flatlines, the feds will know. They'll barge in to investigate and collect their precious tech. They'll see she was killed, and if they think I had anything—"

"We'll claim self-defense," Tank said. "Hell, it *will* be self-defense."

He didn't get it because he didn't know my 4-S status. Homicide—no matter how justifiable—might shift me from Inconclusive to Insane. I couldn't take that risk. Or the risk that Tank would turn on me if he knew the truth.

"But, Tank, the feds come in packs," I said, clutching his arms. "And they'll crack down like they always do. You've seen how aggro the streets have been. You think the crews are going to back down from a dick-waving contest? It'll be a massacre! I don't want to be the fool who brought the feds down on our heads."

Still, the idea of Mother gone ... Temptation kneaded my thighs, made the muscles warm and soft as rolled mesquite sap. It occurred to me that sane people didn't reject matricide on purely pragmatic grounds.

"You know what?" I said, changing tack. "Never mind all that. As awful as Mother's been to me, what about my dad? He wouldn't make it without her. He—"

Wrong tack. Tank's muscles tightened around me, and my nerves flared, every inch alert to how much bigger he was, how much stronger.

"What do you care?" Before I could answer, Tank grabbed my shoulders, pushed me to arm's length. "Where was he when you needed *him*? Your mother forced you to be William's medic, to lick his wounds and god knows what else, and where was your dad? She treated you like you were nothing, less than nothing. I saw it. Hell, I lived across the street, and I saw it clear as the moon."

I stared up at him. Clearly, I'd been on Tank's radar

longer than I'd assumed. Maybe I was the idiot, not Serena.

Tank realized he was shaking me, and he stiffened, as if trying to stop. "What do you care?" he insisted. "Your father didn't take care of you, he didn't protect you from William. And don't tell me William never touched you because he sure as hell did something. You practically jumped me before I even washed his blood off. If there was anyone—I mean, *anyone*—you cared for in that house, you wouldn't be here with me."

I closed my mouth. Face carefully composed, I tucked my arms a millimeter closer to my body, a hint that he was hurting me. He let go so quickly I wobbled on my feet. He grabbed me again, steadied me.

"I'm sorry," he said a minute later.

"Okay." I didn't mean it, but it was the correct noise at the correct moment.

He moved one hand to cup the back of my head. "It's just ... Killing your mom?" Tank stooped, whispered against my hair. "It's the best thing you could ever do for yourself, Heidi. Trust me, I know."

I went so cold, I thought I'd shatter.

≈

THE SECOND HE LEFT the room, I pulled the office chair to the computer. Shivering, brain stuttering, I told myself I'd misunderstood. Tank couldn't have, he couldn't have done that to his mom. The feds wouldn't have let him in, they didn't let criminals into Exile, they had weird qualms about pouring kerosene on our bonfire. But what if ...

I did a search for "Tank Benavides." *Did you mean "Hank Benavides"?* No, stupid search engine. I searched for "Benavides architect." Better, but too many hits. I didn't have the patience. I pulled up DataFace and inputted the three actors Tank most resembled, shuffled a few parameters for a reasonable resemblance, added the image to "Benavides architect."

And there he was: Noé Benavides.

My heart shuddered like a rusty muffler. It was one thing to know Tank had been Out There, something else to *see* him Out There. Thumbnail after thumbnail of him standing in front of strong, stable, sane buildings. He didn't belong in Exile building blast walls and biker bars. Not if he could do that.

But if he'd killed his own mother ...

I swallowed hard and started digging. I went chronologically, most recent pages first. The office pavilion turned up immediately. It didn't look the same as in Tank's model: Out There, the window glass was silvered, the courtyard had been chopped in half, and a turret—a fucking turret—topped the main entrance. I checked the date, did the math, blinked. Tank had come to Exile before the building was complete.

Tank leaving in the middle of a job? So wrong.

I heard a door close. Minutes later, a tedious stump-and-shuffle up the stairs. I kept searching, sifting through Tank's—Noé's—professional past.

"Hey, Heidi," Paolo said in the doorway. "You busy?"

"Not exactly." I didn't look up. "You need something?"

"Not exactly."

I glanced up, and he was half smiling at me despite the dark smudges under his eyes.

"I'm bored," he said, and limped into the room, stinky. "A little fried."

"What happened to you?" I quick-scanned his legs: elegant toes peeped from an Ace bandage wrapped all the way up over one ankle.

He shrugged. "Sprained it, maybe broke it when that asshole knocked me off my bike last night."

I nodded, scrolled through another list of certifications. "Where are Tank and Sweeney?"

"Out back, talking surveillance."

Perfect. Sweeney was no doubt goading Tank to commit a second matricide—did it count as matricide if it wasn't your own mother?—and I wasn't there to talk sense into him. But then, the idea of me talking sense to anyone ... Ha. Pull the other one.

Paolo cocked his head, studying my thesis photos. He'd raked the last of the gel out of his unwashed hair, but he still didn't have a shirt on. And I didn't have pants on, so I guessed we were even. The bandage across his back was blotched brown.

"You shouldn't be going up and down the stairs with your foot messed up," I said, closing search windows. My lungs, my heart, began to decompress. No articles titled "Blueprint for Murder." Nothing on Tank older than a college fraternity photo, even. "You're liable to trip and mess up the other foot. Anyway, this isn't the most exciting room in the house."

"Oh, I don't know," Paolo mused, still staring at the photos. "You're here."

But I should *be outside with Tank*, I thought. I closed the last search window and pushed away from the computer. "I remembered something. You going to be okay getting back down the stairs?"

"Sure." He waved me off, half smiled again. "Don't worry about me."

I did for a minute—damn his eyes. But then he said, "Go," and I did.

≈

WE'D TURNED OFF THE dampeners so we wouldn't be surprised again. As I stepped out the back door, still buttoning a pair of pants, an electric zap sizzled the air. People shouted in the street. Metal hit asphalt and rattled like a spinning dish. I scanned the yard and patio, didn't see the guys. Like thunder, a barrage of blunt objects slammed the house. Overhead, unseen, Sweeney cursed, then a thud shook the wooden deck, closely followed by another. Panic overriding survival instinct, I raced to the stairs. Tank and Sweeney came barreling down. Laughing.

"What did you do?" I said, jumping out of the way.

Tank leaped down the last few steps, grinning like a madman. Then he cleared his throat, rotated his shoulder experimentally. "We were on the roof, testing out their fence. To see if it was operational, yet."

"It is." Sweeney clapped Tank on the back, chuckling.

"Cut it out, it's not funny!" I shrieked; I couldn't help it. "You go around punching grizzlies, too?"

Tank shrugged. "No way they were going to hit us. We threw an old hubcab from the roof. It hit the fence, made it spark and fizz, and those assholes scattered. Once they spotted us, we—"

"Threw yourselves off the roof." I watched Sweeney flex his scarred leg, a new scrape already visible. Did he always lead with that leg? "And landed on the deck."

Tank nodded, clearly trying for solemnity. Minutes ago, I'd suspected him of killing his mother. Now?

"Well, what did you find out?" I said, exasperated. "Paolo said you'd come out here for surveillance, not fratboy pranks."

We moved out from under the shadow of the deck, and Tank explained that the chain link fence we'd seen from the study wrapped around the corner of Raven and Cricket. So now, in addition to the street barricades and the timber-and-concrete palisades that Tank had built, the thugs' electrified fence extended the length of Tank's street-facing property. We were triple-penned, our own defenses turned against us.

On the plus side, we still had functioning cameras on the palisades and atop the cinderblock walls that separated Tank's property from the neighbors'. And those neighbors seemed inclined to steer clear of the shitstorm, at least for now.

"What should I tell Carlos?" I said, my whole excuse for coming out in the first place.

Sweeney groaned. "Him again? How 'bout you don't tell him anything. For all we know, he's ferreting information for them!"

"He's giving *us* information, you stupid mutant. He's on our side, maybe the only one who is. Serena didn't bother to call!"

Sweeney's eyes flashed. "I don't trust narcs—"

Tank raised his hands, but I ignored him.

"Carlos isn't a narc," I said, fists at my sides. "He works with the feds because he's got mouths to feed. He's fucking responsible. Something you don't know shit about. Besides, I've known Carlos and Romero longer than I've known you."

"Or Tank," Sweeney said.

"Longer than you've known Paolo, and he's in here with us!"

"Hey." Tank stepped between us. "Cool it."

Sweeney leaned around Tank, yellow eyes nearly smoking. "Man, you got a problem with Puppy now?"

"He was at William's burn—"

"Yeah, right," Sweeney retorted.

"The Cantus weren't," I yelled. "So I think you can trust them at least as much as Paolo."

"If we've got to trust everyone you've fucked—"

"Stop!" Tank grabbed Sweeney's shoulder, squeezed until Sweeney switched his glare to him. Tank stared him down, told me, "Baby, go inside."

"But—" I started.

Sweeney jerked out of Tank's grip. But he turned away and sullen, silent, punched one of the wooden posts supporting the deck. I pinched off my protest and took a second to catch my breath. Tank looked at me, then the house.

I nodded. "Okay. But what do I tell Carlos?"

"Tell him we're not moving yet. We'll call him if we need them. And thank them for me."

I nodded again, and Tank relaxed, the furrows in his forehead smoothing. Maybe it was worth giving in, I thought, to see the effect I had on him.

I returned to the house, shaking my fists open. In the den Paolo leaned against the cold fireplace. Forehead on the bricks, bandage bloody bright. He smiled at me, grazing this side of ghastly.

"Hey," he panted. "You think you could prop me up in the shower? I ain't feeling too good."

ABOUT THE ONLY SATISFACTION I got from being a medic was the power of retribution. I could make a crew member's scars as neat or as nasty as I liked—nearly invisible if they got off on those badges of "honor," crazy-quilt lumpy if the warrior was a different kind of vain. And bitch as they might, how did they know how much hurt was really medically necessary?

So being a medic had its advantages, but I hadn't fled my parents' house to nurse some Outsider who didn't have the sense to stay put when he got hurt. I told Paolo as much while I hauled him to the guest bathroom and dropped him on the toilet. By the time I reached the back door, Sweeney and Tank were coming in.

"Paolo's bleeding in the bathroom. He needs help," I said, and left without caring who dealt with it.

Upstairs in the bedroom, I grabbed Tank's phone and dialed Carlos. First thing he said was, "I'm sorry."

"What?" I shook my head, irritated and confused. "Why?"

"That crack about your funeral, Sammy asking questions. I shouldn't even joke." He spoke in an urgent whisper, and I heard background voices receding on his end. He must've been walking away from people.

"Forget it. I did." But I knew his Catholic guilt wouldn't let him. Half to distract him, half because I wondered, I asked, "Is Sammy really still asking about me?"

"Of course! He's known you more than half his life. He's known you longer than he knew Mom. No seas tonta."

I ignored that last bit; Carlos was always telling me not to be stupid. For some reason he thought I was smarter than any of my actions indicated. "Didn't you explain why I stopped coming 'round?" I said. "Tell him what I told you!"

"I don't lie to Sammy," Carlos said, voice rising.

"It's not a lie that you're better off without me, that a city liaison shouldn't be consorting with the daughter of a convicted felon."

"Bullshit! I get any more respectable, and I won't be able to do my fucking job. As it is, half the town refuses to cooperate with me, calls me a traitor." He slowed down, perhaps catching scent of the red herring. "Anyway, who cares who I'm dancing with when Romero's out busting heads as bad as anyone I could be narcing on?"

"If you settle down, Romy will, too—"

"Girl ..." He laughed like it hurt. I imagined him tilting his face to the sky: little help here? "Romy can't settle down. If he slows down, he'll stall out."

I was pacing a rut in the bedroom floor. I dropped onto a corner of the unmade bed. "As long as I'm around, even if I'm only taking care of Sammy, everyone's gonna assume. No other woman'll set foot in that house. You know it's true!"

"It's true, but it's not the truth."

"What?"

"Te conozco, Heidi. I know what you're afraid of. But I don't care about that."

I stiffened. I wondered if he was finally going to say it. I couldn't tell if I was cold or hot.

He sighed. "But right now you're in Tank's house, not mine, and if we ever want to get you out, we need to talk strategy. So talk to me, chica."

Cold or hot, relieved or disappointed, I sagged. I covered the mouthpiece to take a deep breath. Once collected, I said, "Tank doesn't want to move, yet," and I explained.

"Who all you got in there?"

"Me, Tank, Paolo—people call him Puppy—and Sweeney."

"Four's good odds," Carlos said. I wondered if he was rubbing the shiny scar on his left temple like when he untangled the logistics of his work schedule and Sammy's care.

"Yeah, but Paolo's hurt, and Sweeney hates me."

"You okay?"

I smiled a little. "Unscathed."

"I meant with Sweeney."

I smiled wider. What was Carlos going to do, bust in all He-Man? "Yeah, I'm fine for now. Hey ..." I ran a fingernail over my hoop earrings, soothed by the familiar metal ringing. "I'm sorry about bitching earlier. About where you were last night. It would've been worse if you and Romy hadn't run the thugs out of here."

"Sorry I didn't check for traps. But when I drove by later, everything seemed quiet. Should've known they'd regroup. Didn't know they were still stirring up shit until Manny called at hell o'clock this mornin'."

"Hey, you gotta sleep sometime. Any updates on my sister?"

"Not an update, exactly, but I didn't get a chance to tell you last night." He paused, carefully choosing words. I tried not to yell at him. "When the ambulance came for your sister, well, your mom couldn't go with them because of her ... status. But the feds refused to take your dad, either."

"But they're supposed to," I said, childish though it sounded. "They're supposed to take a parent or guardian whenever a minor's removed. It's the rules!"

"I know, but he was so upset ... They said he was a security risk. According to Manny, there was an 'altercation.' Your dad, he, uh ... he kinda lost it. He ran off, so I don't think he's hurt bad—"

I exhaled, tried to laugh. "Shit, Carlos. So he's hurt. How is that an update?"

The doorknob rattled. I jumped and turned. Tank stood in the doorway, all slanty shoulders and droopy eyelids. Damn, the guy needed sleep. I waved him over.

"I gotta go," I said. "Thanks for all your help, Carlos."

"Thanks?" He scoffed. "Like I'm going to sit back and watch the angry villagers tear you apart."

"Still ..."

The bed bounced as Tank dropped beside me, kissed my shoulder.

"Still nothing," Carlos said. "Tonta."

Chapter Fifteen

I THINK I WAS twelve, so William must've been nine. I dreamed I was vomiting blood clots. I woke cramped in half, thought I was barfing already until I realized the retching wasn't mine. It was coming from the Jack-n-Jill bathroom. I clutched the bed sheets and willed my stomach not to erupt.

Someone in the bathroom—William—sobbed, and someone else murmured. I couldn't imagine who. A woman, I thought. Mother? But no, I had to be hallucinating. Since the Spill, Mother never crooned, was never so sweet.

I dragged myself out of bed and over to the cracked-open bathroom door. Most of my view was blocked by a wooden chair from William's room. Mother sat in the chair, her back to me, tending to William as he knelt beside the toilet. In the dingy yellow light, she patted his sweaty flattop, pressed a wet washcloth to the back of his neck. Between blasts of barf, she praised him, encouraging him to get it all out.

I clenched my lips against the stewed bile-and-bismuth stink and maneuvered around slowly so as not to toss my cookies. I stared into the dark of my bedroom, trying to make sense of this twisted tableau. So Mother never crooned anymore, never was sweet *to me*.

"Here, rest your head," Mother said. William's next sobs were muffled by her fleece robe. "Want me to read some more?"

He whimpered, and then I heard the slick rustle of magazine pages. She read in a soft, soothing voice. "To obtain maximum boost from most water/methanol injection systems, Davis says ..." It was an article from one of Father's old copies of *Hot Rod Magazine.* I remembered the graph of torque, rpms, and horsepower. I curled up on the floor and listened, too, lulled to sleep.

When I woke, the bathroom was empty. If it weren't for the stink in the towels, the feds' confession—weeks later— that they'd pawned salmonella-tainted peanut butter off on us, I'd still think it had all been a fever dream.

≈

AFTER HANGING UP WITH Carlos, I only lay down with Tank to help him sleep, but his warmth and the whirlwind of events conspired against me. When I emerged from dreams within dreams, it was so quiet I thought the dampeners were on. After a few moments, I registered Red Sonja's yapping, a UTL chopper in the distance. I figured Chazz and company had left a skeleton crew while they broke for lunch. Downstairs, Sweeney argued with the tele.

I shifted. Tank opened his eyes.

"Hey," he mumbled, mouth half buried in the pillow.

"Hey." I reached over, stroked the eyebrow I could see. "Paolo okay?"

"Pulled out couple a stitches. Maybe broke his foot when he dropped his bike." He didn't close his eyes, but I felt the whisper of his eyelashes against my hand.

"He probably fractured the base of his fifth metatarsal. It's one of the most common foot injuries among athletes."

Tank took a moment to process that, then asked, "You really worried about Puppy? I mean, not trusting him?"

"Well ... he was at William's funeral."

"I asked him 'bout that. Said he'd never seen a burn, was curious. Chazz didn't know he was part of my crew. Still too new to town, I guess."

I *hmm*ed. It was possible. Chazz was one of the larger, not sharper tools in the shed. But that didn't quite mesh with what Puppy had said in his drugged stupor. "You trust him?" I said.

"In what sense?"

Exasperated, amused—how many senses were there?—I squeezed Tank's shoulder. High up to avoid his chain-shaped bruises, of course. "How long have you known him? How long has he been in town? Where did he come from?"

Tank shrugged. Or squirmed, if someone that big could squirm. "His contract was to handle abandoned houses in the Outer Radius. Organize people to demolish the run-down ones, renovate others. I helped him with a few 'til he found out Exiles excel at demo, not reno. Then he ditched the urban renewal and came to work for me. Three weeks ago? A month?"

Right. Tank was too exacting to forget business details like that. And he'd completely skipped my question about where Paolo had come from. I must've looked dubious because Tank sighed and rolled out of the pillow. I let my hand slide down to his chest.

"Look," he said, "I trust him not to hurt you. That's all I'm worried about right now."

I snorted. "Like you're not in danger?"

"I'm used to taking care of myself. Other people ..." He clasped his hand over mine and squeezed. My heart twitched.

"And you trust Sweeney?" I said. "Not to hurt me?"

He inched closer, slotted himself against my hipbone, shifted our hands to my chest. "Sweeney does what I tell him."

"That why you keep him around?"

He exhaled, almost a laugh. "Yeah, 'cause you see how much I value obedience."

I bumped him with my hip. He ground against me.

"Seriously," I said.

"Seriously? He's a good beta. He follows orders, and he doesn't ask anything of me."

I frowned. "But he's willing to *do* anything for you. Why you think that is?"

"Bad upbringing?" Tank's breath puffed hot against my ear. "Point is, right now I ain't asking him to do anything but mind his manners 'round you. Which is harder for him the longer we're barricaded in here. You thought about what I said?"

I swallowed. That strange warmth I trusted less and less was creeping down my thighs. "Kinda hard not to."

"And?"

I thought of Mother reading to William. It should've made me reluctant, recalling that tender moment. Instead, I wondered, *Why the fuck not?* I'd never seen a flicker of that kindness for myself or Father or even the twins. We weren't going to talk her out of this vendetta. And to preserve a shred of street cred, William's crew needed to fight the Outsider who'd snuffed their chief. So why not get the murder ball rolling?

I clenched my eyes shut, exhorted myself to think, not react. If Serena's suspicions were anything to go by, people already thought I'd recruited Tank for fratricide. If we killed Mother, then the feds would rush in to retrieve their high tech tether—and probably bust some heads in the process. Plenty of Exiles would narc on me and Tank to get shorter beatings. Then my fourth *S* would be Screwed, rather than Sane. Goodbye, plastic surgeon dream. And goodbye, Tank. He wouldn't stick around for the crazy chick even if he was a mom-killing maniac, too. Why would he, when there was a whole wide world to explore?

Then there was Chazz. Had I been the typical town whore, he'd have eventually grown tired of this fight. But there was a certain valence to Chazz's hatred of me: the way he talked about the Cantus, the way he'd looked at me at Mute's ... Even if we killed Mother and nobody ratted me out to the feds, Chazz would keep escalating this vendetta. Depending on how seriously Tank took his vow to protect me, he might never get out of Exile alive.

And if Tank didn't get out, he couldn't get *me* out.

Suddenly, Tank's arms felt tight all around me. Like a cage I'd locked myself in.

"I can't," I said, rolling away. I didn't have to pull out of his grip like I thought I would, but he watched me so intently I didn't escape at all. "It's ... I—I can't."

I practically ran to the bathroom, his stare digging into my pores the whole way.

WHEN I EMERGED FROM my evasive-maneuver shower, the bedroom was empty. I toweled my hair at the head of the stairs, listening to a racket in the kitchen. Cans slamming the counter, tins and boxes rattling. I jogged down, ignored Paolo when he greeted me from the couch, tried to ignore Sweeney, but he scuffed my heels as I entered the kitchen.

Every cupboard hung open, every inch of counter space covered by jars of tomato paste, cartons of crackers and powdered milk, sacks of rice and beans. Like the pantry had barfed. Tank stood in front of the refrigerator, scribbling a list on its dry erase surface.

"What are you doing?" I said.

"Yeah," Sweeney said over my shoulder. "We got mice?"

Not turning, Tank asked, "How many calories a person need per day to survive? Two thousand, right?"

A scurry of panic tickled my chest. "For someone like you? More or less," I said carefully. "Why?"

"We're under siege, and you won't let us shoot the puppetmaster." Tank turned back to the cabinet upchuck. "So we'd better take inventory, start rationing the food supply."

"Whoa." Sweeney stepped from behind me. "You said we could wait 'em out, that Chazz's crew would get bored."

"They will. We can," Tank said. "But we got to be smart about this. We need to know what we've got, what we need, how to get it—"

"What're you guys talking about?" Paolo yelled from the living room.

"Mind your own business," Sweeney hollered back.

"I'm stuck in here, too, case you hadn't noticed," Paolo said. "Kinda *is* my business."

"Shut up, both of you," I said. "What do you know about UTL?" I asked Tank.

Still cataloging our victuals, he tilted his head in my direction but didn't look at me. "I know we can't assume they'll be willing or able to make deliveries. Not the way things are going lately."

"What do you mean, the way things are going?" I sharpened my voice, willing Tank to make eye contact.

"What do you mean, what do I mean?" Tank sounded harassed. "In the street, with William's crew."

"You haven't heard something about UTL?"

Sweeney's gaze prickled the side of my face. "What have *you* heard about 'em?"

"Nothing," I snapped. But finally Tank was looking at me, so I continued. "The courier said something the other day about UTL's contract running out. She said it was a union thing ..."

"And?" Sweeney said. "How do you know it's not?"

"I don't, but ..." I shrugged and waited to see if Tank would connect the dots I couldn't.

He nodded, but his frown held steady. "All the more reason to get a handle on what we got." He turned and gestured at the refrigerator list. "Two thousand calories per day per person means—"

I stepped forward, snatched the dry erase marker from

him. "Don't be ridiculous," I said, panic scurrying over my skin again. "Somebody your size, you need more than two K a day, and it's gotta be more than sixty grams of protein. And I don't need the calories you do, or even as many as Paolo." I smeared my fist over his figures.

Sweeney said, "She's right, man. If you're really worried, now's not the time for chivalry or any a that 'all men are created equal' shit."

"Thank you," I said, but Tank glowered at Sweeney.

"Although," Sweeney conceded, backing up, "what do I know? Math ain't my strong suit. I'm gonna ... yeah."

Sweeney practically moonwalked from the room. Tank scowled after him a minute before lifting a box of pasta to read the nutritional info.

"You okay?" I said.

"Yeah." His head didn't get the memo, shook "no" instead. "But we need to be prepared. And I need to do something, keep moving."

Cabin fever already? He *had* said he hated being cooped up.

"Water's more important than food," I said to distract him. "Half a gallon to drink per person per day, and then cooking, cleaning, showering, shitting, so ... a gallon per person per day?"

I didn't think water was really an issue, but I let Tank do the math. Once alpha waves were flowing, I excused myself and booked it to the study, where I resumed my search of Tank's past.

HE HADN'T BEEN KIDDING about needing to move. During college, Tank moved a lot. More than I thought was normal. He dodged cross country during freshman year, transferred a second time, then moved south for an internship. Moving for grad school seemed natural, but skipping to another halfway through?

At any rate, Tank must've sprung fully formed from someone's forehead. I couldn't find any record of him before age eighteen. No high school yearbooks on reunion sites; no Honor Society pix from newspaper archives; no digital altars frozen on once-adolescent girls' (or guys', anyone's) blogs. Had he changed his name?

I was still headbutting the wall in Tank's past when the kitchen racket settled. Soon after, the scent of grilled meat and seared rosemary wafted up from the kitchen. I heard Sweeney and Tank talking again, calmer now, work stuff. Maybe fifteen minutes later, Paolo stump-shuffled upstairs. I closed most of my search windows before he poked his head in the room.

"Dinner ready?" I said.

"No. Not yet." He frowned, quizzical. "Why?"

"Then why are you hoofing it up the stairs on that bad foot?" *Dumbass*, I almost added.

He shrugged, shuffled into the room. "Bored."

Again? "Why don't you talk shop with Tank and Sweeney?"

"Eh. Not into the details."

I raised my eyebrows. Hard to imagine Tank tolerating that kind of attitude around his work. I closed the last search window before Paolo came around to lean on the edge of the desk. He smelled better. Blood and sweat gone, jeans freshly laundered.

"Then why are you on Tank's crew?" I asked.

He shrugged, Tank's too-big T-shirt wrinkling over his chest. "Don't have to think. Don't have to put up with anyone's bullshit. Tank is a no-bullshit zone."

That he was. "What about Sweeney?"

Paolo smiled, eyes less shadowed with ache and insufficient sleep. "I don't deal with Sweeney much." He bent to check the computer screen. His hair, nearly shoulder length, fringed across his cheek, emphasizing the sturdy line of his cheekbone. "What you working on?"

"Nothing."

"Nothing? Or nothing I'd understand?" Before I could deny the implication—not that I was inclined to—he reached over and lifted my chin, held it. "Almost all better," he said, studying my black eye.

I stared back, felt the undertow of those blue eyes. I shifted my focus, got as far as the sweep of sparse ginger eyelashes. I waited for him to realize how inappropriate the contact was. More inappropriate by the second. He didn't. Our temperatures melded. I lost track of where his skin started and mine ended.

Downstairs, Sweeney called, "Puppy, Heidi! Dinner! Where you guys at?"

I pulled away first, proud of myself.

≈

TANK AND SWEENEY CARRIED the kitchen table out to the living room so Paolo could sit at one end with an extra chair to prop his foot. Tank sat at the other end, and I ended up across from Sweeney. We'd only been eating a few minutes when William's buddies started hollering in the street, clearly soused.

"Hey, Heidi," one guy called—Keith maybe. "Why don't you come out and play?"

"Yeah, come play with my balls," Chazz yelled, ever the rapier wit.

"We'll turn off the fence if you come out," another said.

Paolo fidgeted on my right, trying to catch my eye. I concentrated on spearing a steamed carrot.

"Come on, Heidi." Keith, definitely. I felt dirt under my fingernails. "We'll take *real* good care of you."

"Take care of my cock, baby, and I'll take care of your ass."

Sweeney swallowed badly, started coughing. What was his problem? If anyone should've been sputtering, it was me. He'd already seen me naked; now he could picture all this in 3D, triple-X glory.

"Hei-dee ... Hiiii-deeee ... Hiiiii-deeee ..." the thugs called.

Under the table I squeezed my napkin. Paolo set down his fork and after a darting glance at Tank, asked me, "Friends of yours?"

I laughed, grateful. "Not *that* friendly."

Sweeney cleared his throat, drank some water, added, "Can't blame 'em for trying. Heidi's the friendliest girl in town."

Paolo's glance flicked to Tank again.

"Yeah," I said, aiming for breezy. "But even I have standards, Sweeney. For instance, I'd never fuck you."

Tank lifted his napkin. I turned in time to see him smother a small smile.

Sweeney's cheeks reddened enough to match his neck burn, but before he whipped out a retort, Paolo asked Tank, "Can't we turn on the dampeners?"

I shook my head, preemptive, and finally stabbed that carrot. "I'm a big girl, Paolo. It's okay."

"But—"

"I'd rather they didn't catch us off-guard again," Tank said.

So we lowered our heads and kept eating.

But then Keith waxed nostalgic—and megaphonic—about the time we'd danced in the junkyard. I might've stopped breathing for a minute. I know Paolo did, the way he gasped. I tried not to choke on a chunk of green apple. Meanwhile, everyone at the table pictured me bent over the hood of a 2009 Camaro.

Then Chazz speculated aloud—very loud—about how I'd accommodated the Cantu brothers, and *there* was the valence of hatred I'd worried about. Sluttiness (or nymphomania, if you were more kindly, more clinically inclined) was one thing. Fucking brothers, quite another. It didn't matter how off-base Chazz's lurid imaginings were, I blushed so hard I thought my cheeks might stain permanently.

Sweeney swiveled in his seat, and I was startled to see he was blushing, too.

"Tank," he said, "this would be a helluva lot easier if you kept liquor in the house."

"No shit," I muttered.

Tank shook his head. "If you two agree, it must be a *really* bad idea."

Outside, the ruckus quieted. After a suspiciously peaceful two minutes, the thugs started chanting. "We want Heidi, We want Heidi, CUNT CUNT CUNT! We want Heidi—"

I couldn't help it, I laughed. But my eyes burned, and I didn't dare blink.

Paolo pitched his napkin on the table, the spiderwebs on his neck fluttering. "Tank! Come on, man!"

"All right, all right."

Tank pushed back his chair, touched my hair as he walked past. I choked back my laughter and angled out of reach, forced myself to chew, swallow, breathe. Cool as he.

But at the control panel, Tank paused, letting the thugs' chant continue. "Sweeney, come take a look at this."

Sweeney jumped up, napkin still in one fist, and jogged over. Uninvited, I followed. Paolo whined about being left behind but didn't move. "What's happening?" he said.

"Heidi's dad came out," Sweeney said.

I clawed past Tank's and Sweeney's joined shoulders to see the monitors. Sure enough, Father stood outside the electrified fence, arguing with Chazz. He looked different. Old. The sleeves of his cowboy plaid shirt fluttered, torn, when he gestured at the fence, then the generator. Chazz shook his head.

"About time somebody shut them up," Paolo said.

"He's not there to defend my honor," I said. "Trust me."

"Then what's he doing?"

The tendons in Father's neck stood out like when he used to wrestle stuff loose under the hood of an old beater. He was furious, but not yelling, not yet. "I don't know," I said. "He's been missing. The feds wouldn't take him when they took Thea. Carlos thought he'd make a break for it."

Instead, he'd come here. Why?

Chazz clapped a hand on Father's shoulder, brusque camaraderie. Unswayed, Father stabbed a finger in Chazz's chest, then gestured again at the fence. I glanced at the other feeds: William's crew watched, waiting, as if crew leadership might be in dispute.

"Tank, this is a fine opportunity to catch those motherfuckers off guard." Sweeney eyed me. "Especially if Heidi's up to being bait."

"Fuck you." I socked him in the arm. "Risk your own ass."

Tank held up a hand. "No bait."

Sweeney sucked his teeth. I stuck out my chin smugly.

Tank abbreviated my gloat by adding, "But maybe ... negotiation." He turned to me. "Your dad don't look any happier about this fence than we are, and you said yourself he ain't inclined to fight. You go out and have a few choice words, we might be able to return to our regularly scheduled program."

"Think I trust Heidi's porny superpowers more than her negotiation skills," Sweeney said.

Not even looking, I socked him again.

"Shit, you hit me one more time," Sweeney started.

"Shut up. I'll do it," I said.

≈

BAREFOOT, I STEPPED OVER the threshold. Hot concrete, even at this hour of the night. The rigid pores scraped the calluses of my feet. Sweat instantly beaded up on my skin. Beyond the traffic barricades crowned with barbed wire, past the electrified fence, Chazz and Father had advanced to yelling. Other thugs spotted me creeping down the front walk, and they hollered for Chazz.

I raised my hands, screamed, "Wait!" as he spun around. "I'm unarmed. I just want to talk to my father." Then the idiocy of appealing to Chazz of all people, my brother's underling, hit me. I switched focus. "Father, what are you doing here?"

"I'm trying to haul your ass out of the flames. Trying to fix this fucking family before y'all kill yourselves."

Some of the thugs chuckled and jeered at me. I might've been more embarrassed at being called out if I hadn't been shocked. Father was parenting up?!

"Calling off these headless chickens is a good place to start," I said, casting a sneer at the warriors. "Make 'em tear down this stupid fence and we'll talk."

"You'll be lucky if they turn it off for the five seconds it takes you to scramble over," Father said. "I'm not here to call a truce, I'm here to bring you home."

"What?" I shook my head, woozy from the sudden change in temperature. Or possibly the idea that Father had come to his senses, for me.

"Leave now and my crew lets you go," Chazz said.

"*Your* crew?" I said. "Seems like Mother's calling all the shots here."

Over Chazz's blustering retort, Father said, "It's none of your business what the crews do, Heidi. You need to stop this bullshit. Come home."

I thought my eyes would pop from my head. "To Mother? That crazy lady who was trying to kill us last night? Who didn't even notice her other daughter burning?"

"Enough! We've all been through enough. Your brother's dead. Your little sister's dying!"

I leaped forward. "You got news?"

"Not yet," Father said, desperation sanding his voice. "But we'll make calls and find out, together."

He was begging, looking at me and only me, needing me ... Maybe he could run interference between me and Mother? I could help Tank better if I was out here, couldn't I? Soon as I got some space, I could contact his crew, give them intel on Chazz.

Father was still talking. "Please, Heidi. Be smart. Come home and apologize to your mother."

I stopped. I hadn't even realized I was walking toward him. "What? No! She tried to kill us. She wants me dead—"

"Not *you*. Tank!" he said. "Stop being stubborn and come home, Heidi! It's that Outsider scum in there or your family."

"That 'scum' in there never beat me like Mother did, or tried to rape me like William!"

Father's eyes went wider than mine. I covered my mouth. I hadn't meant to tell him. Not ever. Not after Mother blew it off. I started to take it back, but Chazz sneered.

"Can't rape a whore," he said.

Father whirled and slugged him. Staggering more from surprise than the knock on the chin, Chazz didn't retaliate. One of the thugs ran toward my parents' house, however.

Father turned and pointed his finger at me like it was more lethal than all the weapons in Exile, like he'd walk through the barricades to turn me over his knee. "Don't you dare talk about your brother that way. That never ... I would've ... Don't you blame your problems on him! You come home and kneel in William's ashes right now. Beg forgiveness!"

Well, Kermit and Christian Bale. He'd finally sailed off the deep end. I'd pushed him off.

"Forgiveness? From you? From that sick fuck, William? From Mother, who'd rather avenge his death than protect the rest of us?" I backed up, hands raised again, this time wash-my-hands-of-you rather than please-don't-kill-me.

"You don't know what you're saying. *You* go home. Go back to Mother and whatever little box she keeps your balls in!"

Behind me, I heard swearing from the open doorway. "Heidi, that ain't negotiation," Sweeney yelled.

"I'm done," I shouted, at him and Father. "I'm coming back in."

I turned to the house. Father yelled, "Heidi, wait!"

I let his plea bounce off my back. "Forget it! There's nothing left to say."

Chapter Sixteen

THE NIGHT BEFORE FORREST was due back at school, we lay on his bed holding hands, watching *It's A Wonderful Life* projected on his ceiling. The room was dark, the posters of the Grand Canyon and coral reefs reduced to glossy black portals. Celluloid snow flitted overhead and melted into grayscale puddles on our skin while George Bailey talked Mary to death.

I turned to say something to Forrest, but he was gone again. His body warm and with me but his face—and everything behind it—shut down. It was the stillness I'd mistaken for laziness when I first met him that I'd grown used to over three weeks. Whenever I asked about Out There, it was like he flipped a switch and turned himself off. Even when I didn't ask—once I learned it was the surest way to lose him—he sometimes powered down, as if conserving energy for a task I couldn't imagine.

I didn't blame him exactly; I might've done the same if I were cast back into the pit after tasting freedom. But the thing was, he'd *chosen* to come back, and I was running out of time. Maybe he could coach me on the 4-S test or put in a good word for me with the review board. He had four out of four, his word had to count for something, right? But the longer I waited, the more afraid I was to ask. Would he freak out being in bed with a possibly insane girl? How could I even broach the topic without him shutting down, turning to stone?

Whatever. I'd figure that out later. First, I needed him to look at me, *see* me. I squeezed his hand. He blinked, coming out of whatever trance Capra worked on him. He sighed at the ceiling. *See me*, I thought. *Look me in the eye and see what I need.*

Then he turned, and he did look at me, his green eyes like searchlights through static-colored rain. My breath hitched. My heart thudded in my clit. And I forgot I wanted anything more than Forrest Vai looking at me like that always.

Later, the movie muted, he said, "I don't want you to feel bad if you don't hear from me. I've got this thing I need to do when I go back."

"What thing?" Sore in all the right places, I snuggled deeper into his sweat-damp pillow, thought about term papers, lab assignments, academic drudgery I'd love.

"Nothing to do with you."

I wrinkled my brow at him. "Well, I know that. You didn't even know me three weeks ago."

"I wish I had." His breath still smelled of beer and Skittles, bittersweet. "Really. But I mean it, don't feel bad. It's not about you."

My stomach cramped. I knew that tone from teen chick flicks. Forrest had a girlfriend. Of course—beautiful, smart guy; four out of four—he had someone else. I couldn't even pretend she was a snobby bitch from New England. All she had to be was normal to triumph in this "triangle." A normal girl from a normal town where people didn't brawl in the streets or need medical clearance to leave.

"Tell me?" I tucked a hand under his cheek, hoping to keep him connected. "What you're going to do."

"You don't want to know."

He tried to turn away. I curled my hand around the back of his neck and pulled him closer, pressed my forehead to his temple.

"I do," I whispered against his skin. "I want to know everything about Out There. So when I—"

"It's too late." He rolled away from me, onto his back. "Nineteen is too late. Seventeen's too late. Hell, seven might be too late."

I rose on my elbow, squeezed his neck to make him look at me. "But you got out."

"Did I?"

"Oh, spare me the Philosophy 101 crap. Just tell me what you're going to do!"

I expected him to retreat into his stony shell. Instead, he laughed. This pathetic exhalation I didn't recognize at first.

"I actually took Philosophy 101," he said.

I felt my face light up. He was talking, like a real boy! "Yeah? How was it?"

"I failed."

I laughed harder than he had. I flopped onto my back, and he came with me, propped himself on his elbow and looked down at me this time.

"Will you do me a favor?"

"Anything," I promised. I'd dance on the QuanTex smokestacks to keep him talking about Out There. Anything to get his help.

"Don't sleep with Tommy anymore."

I frowned. "He wouldn't have me back, not after the humiliation," I reminded him.

Forrest gave me a long, probing look, as if drilling through my strata. "It's more than that though, isn't it?"

"What do you mean?" I wondered if I didn't prefer his blank expression.

"You got what you wanted out of him. Me."

As it sank in, what he was saying, what he was calling me without saying a word, my heart caved in. Because he was right, it was true. Tears scalded my eyes, threatened to burn my reddened cheeks. I threw off the sheet, searched the floor for my underwear.

"You're not going to tell me, are you?" I said.

"It's better if you don't know."

"Forget it." I yanked on shorts and underwear together. I hadn't bothered to shimmy out of them separately, and now

I was glad. I'd get out the door before I cried in front of him. "Doesn't matter, right?" I said with fake cheer. "We'll always have Bedford Falls."

Except, of course, we didn't. And the next day, instead of crossing at the feds' checkpoint to return to school, Forrest walked (barefoot, some say) right across Gatling Drive. He ignored the panopticons' sirens and automated warnings. He jumped into the trench. And when he climbed up the opposite side, the Gatling guns fired six hundred rounds per minute apiece.

So maybe it wasn't four out of four, after all.

≈

I BLINKED.

Sudden brightness, a cracking echo, my face hot on one side.

I looked around, marveled at the bathroom light refracted through fat teardrops, wondered why we were standing in front of the sink, why Tank had that tense, slightly sick look on his face.

Then the heat on my left cheek exploded, needle-stinging. "Ow," I said. And my right wrist flared like I was wearing a molten bracelet. I looked down, saw Tank's hand gripping my wrist, my fingers clenched around a pair of silver scissors. Silence, I thought at first, listening for the echo that had woken me. But no, I was panting, and there was pounding on the bedroom door, Sweeney cursing on the other side.

I looked at Tank, started to understand. Despite my tears, my voice came out calm. "Did you hit me?"

"You wouldn't wake up," he said, jaw tight. "You were ransacking drawers. Muttering about knives."

"Huh." I remembered searching for a knife, but that was in the Vai house, their kitchen. I needed to get Forrest down, he was hanging from the ceiling ... But no, that didn't make sense. That wasn't how he'd died.

Stupid dreams.

My muscles ignored the signal a few times, then grudgingly dropped the scissors. "Is that why I'm crying?" I brought my left hand up—leaden, nearly useless—and touched my cheek, my tears.

"No," he said, loosening his grip. "You were crying before I ..."

"I'm okay," I reassured—him or me? The pounding had subsided, but Sweeney was still yelling outside the bedroom. "God," I sighed. "Talk to him before he breaks down the door."

"Yeah, okay." Tank swiped the scissors from the floor, closed the bathroom door behind us. Then he led me to the bed and made me sit before he opened the bedroom door a crack.

"What the hell?" Sweeney yelled. "Are you all right?"

"We're fine."

"Are you sure? All that banging and crying—"

Tank muttered something so growly I don't know how Sweeney understood him. Sweeney lowered his voice, too, but not enough.

"A bad dream? Tank, I didn't sign on for this, none of us did, being trapped in here with her."

More grumbling from Tank as he stepped into the hallway.

"No," Sweeney said. "But it wouldn't hurt *you* to be a little more worried."

Tank nearly closed the door behind him, and his usual grumble dipped to a more menacing register.

"I didn't say that," Sweeney exclaimed. "I wouldn't throw *any*body out there. But seems we're awful committed to her when you might be her flavor-of-the—OWWW!" Sweeney thumped against the wall. "Man, use your words. I'm just saying, be smart."

Tank slammed the bedroom door. He returned without the scissors and plopped beside me, shoulder bumping warm against mine. I scrubbed the tear tracks from my face.

"You want to talk about this dream?" he said.

It was all wrong. After my disastrous "negotiations" with Father, I should've dreamt about our fight in front of his garage or that time under the porch. Not about Forrest. Even my fucking neuroses were messed up.

"I don't remember," I snapped. But that sounded as nuts as Sweeney had implied, so I said, "Not enough to make sense."

Tank shook his head. "I don't care if you make sense."

The sweetness of him taking my side, asking about my dreams, sparked something warm in my chest. But Forrest was dead, and I didn't deserve sweetness, so the spark turned into rage, more than my withered self-esteem could absorb. Suddenly, I wanted to hit Tank, hurt him for trusting me, ask him who he thought I was in the middle of the night, who was Jenna?

"Hey." Tank reached out, held my chin, and fixed me with a stern frown. "Don't."

"I don't want to talk about it," I said, gritting my teeth.

"Okay." He let me go. "But don't do that, look at me that way. I'm on your side."

I eyed him; he eyed me back. Didn't so much as blink. Finally, I huffed a pent-up breath.

"Fine. I just need to ..." *sit tight,* I thought in Father's voice. I dropped my head to my knees, laced my arms under my legs and held on.

Tank kept me company, rubbed each of my vertebrae all the way down. Maybe testing load limits.

≈

AFTER THAT SLEEPWALKING FIASCO I wanted to hide upstairs. The thought of Sweeney's suspicious glare, of Paolo's increased attention, made my stomach ache. Tank seemed to understand because he invited me into the study. He said he'd gotten an idea for a new weapon and needed input. Which, unless he wanted a weaponized model of

Tom Welling's head within 2.5 degrees of accuracy, was so flimsy an excuse it should've been insulting. Humbled, however, by my earlier outburst, I followed him.

"The thing that's bothering me," he began.

"Only one thing's bothering you?"

"Smart ass." Sitting in his office chair, Tank said, "Those cameras. They got eyes on us all the time, means they can relax."

I boosted myself to sit on the desk. "You thinking of taking 'em out with a mega-squirt like my brother's?"

"I'd prefer something more permanent," he said, voice diving into menace again.

I suddenly wanted to play footsie with his lap, my still-puffy eyes notwithstanding. I settled for scritching his knee through his jeans with my toes.

"If I could get outside, I could clean my window, no problem." He started up his drafting program, one hand on the keyboard, one on the back of my knee. "They can clean their cameras, too. Better to destroy the things entirely. And if we can short out the fence while we're at it ... I'm thinking crossbow."

"Do you *have* a crossbow?" Didn't seem likely to have made it past the feds' checkpoint, but he had the shotgun, right?

"I can make one. All it takes is a two-by-four, rubber, paracord, a few screws, gutter spikes, a toothbrush ..."

I'd have been more surprised if my sister's crossbow hadn't been made from an old Mustang's leaf spring. "Where you going to shoot it from? They'll see you on the roof."

"Maybe not. I could rig a lighted scope for night use." He shrugged, no big. "But I'd have a better shot from in here."

"The sniper slits aren't wide enough for a crossbow," I said, rubbing my foot up his thigh.

"Bullpup design, like a long slingshot mounted on a gun stock."

"But will the gutter spikes be long enough to complete the circuit between fence and camera?"

He tilted his head, gave me the corner of a smile. I think he was impressed that I'd cottoned on to his design. "No, but I have some high-volt conductive thread." He made it sound like sex. Or it might've been the way he leaned forward and kissed my knee, tongued a path along my inner thigh. "It'll be like bowfishing."

The weapon wasn't a turn-on, but Tank's uber-competence? Totally zapped the highway between my brain and cunt. I couldn't even summon a quip about his "arrow." A bit breathlessly, I settled for, "What are you? Batman?"

"We can't all be superheroes." To my quizzical look, he cocked his head slyly. "You want to show me those porny superpowers Sweeney was talking about?"

"What, with him in the house? In the other room?" I teased.

"Case of blue balls would serve him right, way he was talking at dinner." Tank stood and dragged me to the edge of the desk.

I thought about Paolo, but with that busted foot, we'd hear him thumping up the stairs. Also, desk sex! So I unbuttoned Tank's pants, unzipped his fly, reached into his boxers before he reconsidered. I licked my palms and started to stroke. At the first twist and pump, he hissed. I glanced up to make sure it was the good kind of hiss. He was watching me, and oh yeah, it was good. I flashed a grin and went back to work.

Before long, I smelled it, felt the pre-cum slicking his dick. I rubbed the head all shiny, then licked my thumb while looking at him. The way he groaned, I thought he wanted me to suck him as bad I wanted to. I tried to slide off the desk to get on my knees, but he grabbed my arms. I stilled, awaiting his lead.

He bent to nuzzle my cheek, then moved on to my ear. His tongue bumped over the rings in my cartilage. I shivered as his hands slid down my arms. He cuffed my wrists, leaned in, pushed me down. The cold glass desktop shocked my back into an arch. He kissed me flat. I spread my legs to get the warmth of his cock against me. He ground against my soaked panties, finally let go of one wrist so he could rub my folds through the fabric.

"Please," I said, and he understood. My panties went flying. Before they even hit the ground, he pushed two fingers into my pussy. I lifted my legs to scrape his jeans down, so the zipper wouldn't catch on anything important. That made his fingers sink deeper, gave him room to thumb my clit.

"Tell me ..." he whispered.

I rocked on his fingers, tried to keep my thoughts intact. When he didn't finish his sentence, I managed, "Hmmm?"

"Say it."

But he didn't explain, only kept breathing against my breast. Was he embarrassed?

"I want it," I whispered. "Want you, Tank. Please."

He grabbed me by the ass, lifted until my shoulder blades were braced against the desk. He licked a thick stripe up my cunt. "Tell me. Want to hear it."

I had no idea what he wanted. He didn't usually talk during sex. He certainly never made me beg. And now he wouldn't meet my eyes. So much for my porny superpowers. Over his shoulder, I saw one photo-plastered wall. No clue in those dissected faces.

I squirmed to reach one of his hands. "I want you, Tank. I want to feel you. Want to forget everything but you."

Almost. He lowered me until the tip of his cock teased my cunt. I shook, and I was so dripping wet he started to slide in. I bucked. He pulled back. I hooked my legs around his waist, desperate to keep him.

"No. Please, Tank." My voice cracked with want. "Fuck me. Need you to fuck me."

His shoulders sank a millimeter, and whatever he'd wanted to hear, that wasn't it. But his arms were trembling, his cock twitching. I didn't think he could wait anymore. He pulled me down, and we hooked together, perfect.

I couldn't think much after that. I panted a few vague encouragements, but soon there was only our rasping breath, the slap of skin on skin. It took him longer to get off than usual. Normally, I'd've been pleased—more orgasms for me!—but in the rhythm of his thrusts, I still felt him insisting.

Tell me, Heidi. Tell me, tell me, tell me.

ON DAY FOUR, THE street wars started up again.

Outside the siege zone.

Paolo, the one officially on duty, leaned against the couch behind me as we watched the vidfeeds rerouted through the tele. The insectile buzz of motorcycles drifted from neighboring streets, as did the occasional crash or scream. Flickers of silver-edged movement streaked the edge of the camera feed aimed at Flint. Chazz took over as sentry, and Keith trudged inside. Each thug stationed along the fence had an open duffel bag bulging with barely concealed weapons.

"Fewer assholes, at least," Sweeney said from the other end of the couch. "Inside, too. Serena said some of Chazz's crew defected for the street wars."

"Nice of her to remember your number." Paolo nudged my shoulder, shared a smile when I looked up.

Sweeney side-eyed us. "Bitch."

"Still too many of 'em out there," Tank said, oblivious to our sniping. "Especially with those traffic cams."

He was pacing behind the couch. Lately, Tank didn't stop moving unless he was asleep, sometimes not even then. He took up the whole bed, tossing and turning. Cabin fever? More like cabin meltdown.

"C'mon, Sweeney," he barked. "We need that crossbow."

"I can think of a couple practice targets," Sweeney said.

But Tank didn't hear. He'd already stomped off to the garage.

≈

TANK SCHEDULED MY SHIFTS during daylight, and—no accident—the few hours he allowed us to use the sound dampeners overlapped with the hours I slept. But the electric fence interfered with phone calls, radio waves, even the dampeners, so we didn't always get a reprieve. On the contrary, sometimes the fence amplified the din outside.

That night, a mighty crash jolted me awake. I sat up in bed, straining to hear past my spazzing heart: jeers in the street, then a whistling missile, another crash of metal. Inside, I heard footsteps on the stairs, so at least one of the guys was awake. I breathed a little easier, fell back on my pillow.

Outside, the thugs cheered on one of their own. "Higher! Go for it, see how they like it!" I groaned and folded the pillow over my ears.

Then the rare but unmistakable blast of a gun.

I threw my pillow, batted aside sheets, stumbled out of bed. When I reached the door, I heard another shot, then a guy screaming for a medic. My blood iced over.

I lurched into the hallway. It was dark, but light shone in the study. I heard voices through the open door and charged in.

Tank stood motionless at one of the sniper slits, the butt of a rifle braced against one massive shoulder. The muzzle was outside, out of sight.

"What are you doing?" I shrieked.

Paolo caught my arm before I reached Tank, yanked me to stand beside him. "Hold it." The edge of the sexy desk cut into my bare hip. "Stay away from the windows," he added, and I felt the words on my clavicle.

Tank didn't so much as twitch an eyelash in our direction, all attention absorbed by the skirmish on the ground. His slingshot crossbow lay discarded on the floor. Modified gutter spikes twinkled dully beside it.

"Why are they shooting?" I screamed. "Why are we shooting? You want to bring the fucking feds into this?" I looked from Tank to Sweeney, who peered out another slit, to Paolo, holding the desk for balance as I struggled against him. To my great relief nobody was bleeding. Not inside, anyway.

"Some fuckwit tried to scale the wall," Paolo said.

"Of the house?"

Paolo shook his head, but Tank didn't budge, even when the fence rattled and threw off a sizzling flare that reflected off his sclera.

"The palisade," Sweeney said. "Dude was going after one of our cameras."

"Well, did Tank hit him? Is he dead? Why didn't you come get me?" I wrenched my arm free of Paolo, didn't miss the way his annoyed glance caught and lingered on the waistband of my low-rise panties.

"Wasn't time," Sweeney said. He finally turned to me as I was adjusting my collar. "Jeez, woman, you ever wear pants?"

The barest wrinkle of a smile teased the corner of Tank's mouth before he refocused on the street. I frowned, tugging the hem of my blouse over my underwear.

"No time?" I scoffed. "But there was time to drag Paolo up here with his bad foot?"

Sweeney pushed off the wall, stood in front of me, hands on his hips. "Hell no! Puppy was already in here giving himself friction burn."

"I was reading!"

"Yeah, one handed." Sweeney smirked.

"Shut up!" I pushed past them to pull at Tank's shirt sleeve. "Tank, get out of the damn window. Did you really shoot someone?"

He unhooked my fingers with one hand, brought his firearm in with the other. "Relax. It was one shot. I didn't hit him, just scared him, and he fell."

"But if the feds hear gunfire, if they saw—"

Tank shook his head. "I doubt they even noticed over the usual smoke and noise."

"You don't know that," I said, hands flapping. "And it's not just the feds. The neighbors don't want to deal with a standoff. They want this stupid fence to stop dropping calls and radio signals. They want the streets cleared so they can get back to their bloody business-as-usual. They might call the feds to hurry things along!"

"More trouble for them than us," Tank said, though he now looked uncertain.

"Not necessarily," Sweeney said behind me. "The feds crack down, you Outsiders might be safe, but me and Heidi, we'd be up Shit's Creek."

"Exactly," I said, whirling on Sweeney. "So why didn't you stop him?"

"I was barely awake!" Sweeney said.

The yelling outside had died down, so his frustration echoed 'round the study. In the relative calm I noticed that, despite Sweeney's basic-brown head hair, his fuzzy jaw glinted with a surprising amount of gold. I'd probably get to see more of it, too. After I'd gone looking for knives in my sleep, the guys had hidden all the sharps.

"Settle down." Tank touched my back so I'd turn to him. "I wasn't aiming for a shootout. I meant to take out their cameras and the fence."

"And?" I said.

"And the camera I hit was a decoy, all right?" The stillness he'd marshaled for shooting disappeared. He practically vibrated with frustration. "It wasn't connected to the power. Excuse me if Chazz has two more IQ points than I gave him credit for."

"But, shit." Sweeney checked the bolts on the floor. "You

only had enough high-volt thread for two arrows."

Tank gave a slight nod. "Second one was perfect. Bolt went straight through the cam, thread went through the fence. Just like threading a needle. Unfortunately, they cut the power first, avoided shorting out."

"But why the shotgun?" I said.

"Hey, they shot first," Tank said. "Must've dug up some relics from the basement. Good thing I was prepared."

"But why try in the middle of the night? Without telling me or Sweeney?" That languorous heat, that oily mixture of fear and thrill (sane and insane), was creeping down my thighs again. "Was my mother down there?"

I spun toward the windows, but Sweeney blocked me.

"What's her mom got to do with it?" Paolo asked. No one answered him.

Tank grabbed my shoulder. "Never mind. It's over. They stopped shooting, we stopped shooting, no more shooting. And no feds to be seen, right?"

If Mother were dead, Tank would've said so, or it'd be more chaotic outside. And could I blame him for trying to do what I secretly wanted him to? I almost relented. Then his cellphone buzzed in his pocket.

"You see?" I said, punching him in the chest.

"Whoa." Sweeney took my arm, dragged me back a couple of steps. "Don't slug Mr. NRA."

Tank scowled at Sweeney before checking his phone. He might've rolled his eyes at the caller ID. "Yeah?" he answered.

On the other end Carlos let loose a string of Spanish curses so loud, the guys outside probably heard it. Great.

"Let me talk to him," I said.

Tank pulled the phone from his ear. "I don't think he wants to talk."

"Give it to me!"

Tank gestured at Sweeney to release me. I'd barely caught the phone before Tank turned away, peering out the window once more.

"Carlos, shut up, it's me," I said, turning on my heel, into the hall.

Carlos faltered, his last "chinga" unfinished. "Let me talk to Tank," he yelled.

"Tank's busy," I yelled back. "Talk to me."

"Mierda en la leche, what the fuck is going on over there? Some anon reported shooting. Are you shooting? For real?"

"Tank was using a crossbow, they're the ones who started a fucking firefight!"

I careened into a wall, bounced off unfeeling as he screamed back, "They started it? What are you, ten? I don't care who started it, you better fucking stop it right now!"

"Then tell those pendejos to stop climbing over our walls!"

Someone patted my shoulder, and I nearly backhanded Paolo. He grabbed my wrist and pulled me away from the stairs. I let him; I hadn't realized I was a step from breaking my neck.

"I'll talk to Chazz's crew," Carlos said. "But you know I have to report this to the feds, right?"

"What? Why can't you just ignore it?"

"And risk your neighbors calling the feds themselves? And *then* how much shit am I going to be in, huerca chingada? I'm gonna have to lie my ass off and pray the feds don't bust in with tear gas and fire hoses, anyway."

"So do it," I said. "Nobody wins if the feds show up. And tell William's crew to put away their boomsticks! This siege was their idea. If they can't keep it up without shooting, they better pull out now."

Beside me, Paolo snickered. I elbowed him low. He cursed and let go of me to shield his balls.

"Fine!" Carlos said. "But you tell your trigger-happy boytoy if he pulls shit like this again, I'll come over and beat his ass myself, hijo de—"

"Fine," I snapped, though I'd do no such thing.

"Good! Now I gotta go put out fires, but when I'm done, I'm calling you back, mocosa. And you better answer 'cause I got some shit, totally unrelated, I got to tell you. Okay?"

"Okay," I said, winding down.

"Vas a matarme," he growled, and hung up.

Chapter Seventeen

I COULDN'T SLEEP AFTER my yelling match with Carlos. The guys stomped downstairs, but I grumbled back to the bedroom for pants and a wash-up. Carlos called back as I was drying my face.

"Okay, done," he said. "I put off the feds."

"They're not coming to clean up Dodge?"

"Not tonight. I told them the alleged gunfire 'could not be verified.'"

"Think they believed you?"

"Fuck if I know how normals think. Most of the time they're busting my balls about stupid shit—bikes backfiring, dinky structure fires. But tonight ..."

"Tonight what?"

"They didn't," he said slowly. "They asked the usual follow-ups, but then they let it go."

"Why? What does that mean?"

"Pues, válgame," he said, voice rising. "How the hell should I know? How'm I supposed to know what's going on in their pinheads?"

"Okay, híjole, I'm just asking!"

He huffed in frustration, but when he spoke again, his voice was lower, softer. "I'm sorry. How you doing, baby girl?"

I felt that old tug, heart to pussy. How long since he'd called me that? "How do you think?" I said, staving off a blush.

"I mean it. They treatin' you good in there?"

Let's see, the guys had hidden all the sharps from me, but Tank was toting a rifle. Sweeney treated me like a walking STD, and Paolo, always underfoot like his nickname suggested, thought I was his private nurse. I sighed. "Yes, Carlos. I'm their pretty, pretty princess. Did you talk to Chazz?"

"No, not personally. He wouldn't listen to me. Not when he knows—well, everyone knows me and Romero ... that we ... and you ..."

I rolled my eyes as he searched for a suitably oblique euphemism. "Don't hurt yourself, Carlos."

"Point is, I had Manny call and talk 'em down for now." Manny was another city liaison, not as smooth as Carlos, but more likely to be trusted by Chazz. "While he was at it, he suggested they clear the street so warriors can roll through before they pique the feds' interest."

"I hope he didn't say *pique*. They'd need a dictionary." I shook my head, tossed my towel over the rack. "So what was this totally unrelated shit you wanted to tell me?"

"Well ... *wanted* might be the wrong word." The way Carlos paused, I knew he was rubbing the scar on his temple. "Thing is, your dad ... He's been raving all over town."

"*My* dad? My dad doesn't rave about anything but the electric bill."

"No mames, Heidi," he said, stern as any big brother. "This is serious. He's threatening to break out of Exile if the feds don't let him see your sister."

I stopped, stunned. Hearing my own breath on the receiver, I forced myself to say, "Fuck him. He can fend for himself, just like he made me."

"He's your dad," Carlos said, each word separate, underscored. "Fucked up as he is—and believe me, he's as fucked up as anyone I know—he's still the one that called looking for you when you didn't come home. When you were fourteen, he threatened to beat me to death with a torque wrench if I ever hurt you, you know that?"

"Why are you telling me this? I don't want to know this. I can't do anything from in here!"

"Heidi, try to see it his way. One kid dead, another damn close, and you shacking up with an Outsider who's gonna get you killed. What if your dad takes a walk down Gatling Drive?"

I broke out in goosebumps. I wished Carlos would go back to talking 'round things.

"I'd give anything to have my dad back," he said. "The least you could do—"

"I told him, Carlos! Don't you know that? He came to the fence and begged me to come home, and I told him. What William did."

The line went so quiet I thought I'd lost him. Behind me, Paolo said my name. Surprised, I turned to see him in the doorway. Blue eyes deep with sympathy, he mouthed, "You okay?"

"Baby, I'm sorry," Carlos finally said. "I heard, but I didn't know what to believe. What'd he say?"

I closed my eyes, willing my voice steady. Didn't quite make it. "He told me to kneel in William's ashes and beg forgiveness."

"He must've misunderstood. He's crazy with grief ..." Carlos gave up. "That bastard."

I nodded, though he couldn't see me. It didn't ward off Paolo either, who reached out and squeezed my shoulder. I might've leaned into him. I was tired.

"So are we done angsting over my deadbeat dad?" I asked Carlos.

"Done as a doornail," he said.

≈

THE NEXT DAY I continued searching for cyber chinks into Tank's past. When, none the wiser, I slumped downstairs an hour later, I found Sweeney on the couch. He was keeping lookout while cleaning the shotgun—and other guns, too. Apparently, Tank had smuggled in a small arsenal.

"We planning something?" I said, unnerved. I'd never seen so many guns.

He shook his head. "Bored."

That did nothing to ease my pulse. "Where's Tank?"

Sweeney dropped a rag on the footlocker, spared me a sidelong glance. "Out back. On the phone. Business."

Stepping behind Sweeney, I admired the ease with which he handled the weapons. Squelched a thought of what else those fingers could do. The guns creeped me out, but all the testosterone in the house had me twisted up like whoa.

"What kind of business?" I said, and it came out a little tarty, though I really did wonder. Tank had been making calls earlier, trying to arrange a UTL drop off. But it didn't seem likely he'd suffer bureaucrats long.

"*Business* business," Sweeney said, thankfully immune to my tone. "Talking to Rain."

"Thanks."

"Don't go hang off the man while he's working," he called. "Pest."

I peeked into the kitchen as I walked by. Paolo sat on the counter, rewrapping his ankle.

"Heidi!"

He flashed that "these lips weren't made for smiling, but they'll do it for you" smile and waved me in. I gestured toward the backyard but entered the kitchen anyway. Paolo had been on my good side (however narrow) since promising not to tell Tank about my phone call with Carlos. He must've recently showered, since he was shirtless and his hair dangled wet against his cheeks.

"Check my stitches?" he said.

I considered choking him, but I didn't want to put my hands on his tattoos, no matter how good he smelled. "You want to need new ones?"

He smiled again, uncertain this time. "Sorry?"

"I'm not just a medic, I'm certainly not your medic, and I'm not at your beck and call," I said, retreating.

He gave me the puppy eyes. "Didn't mean nothing by it, Heidi. Can I help it if I like you touching me? I mean, compared to Sweeney," he hastened to add, seeing my nose twitch.

So much for my good side. Shaking my head, I left.

Chazz's crew had softened their auditory assault for the night. According to Serena, one of the thugs had gotten a beatdown from a neighbor over the volume. That was the only vaguely useful info she'd offered in her last call; she didn't want to ask questions around town, didn't want to be mistaken for part of Tank's crew. I didn't exactly blame her. Pops' thugs were stalking Tank's guys, keeping them from getting anywhere near us.

As I eased the back door shut, I heard Tank's rumbly voice from the patio.

"Wish I knew. Starting to feel a little tight in here ... How far behind are we?"

I leaned against the door, listening. My brain itched along the edges. For the first time in my life, I felt guilty about eavesdropping.

"No, that sounds 'bout right ... . Did he? No, better not. I don't want to schedule anything into next year. ... Haven't thought that far ahead. Right now I'm trying to figure out if we got enough spoons to tunnel outta here ..."

I worried at my earrings. Tank was logical about work, true. But maybe the siege had tipped an invisible scale. What if the real reason Tank didn't want to schedule new jobs was he didn't expect to stay in Exile—assuming we ever escaped his fortress of solitude. I might not have much time to worm my way into his heart. Should I bring up the 4-S test?

"Right, tomorrow, ten o'clock. I'll bring Sweeney, you bring Jackson, and we'll plan a jailbreak."

"Tank?" I called.

Half-stooped, he emerged from the shadows under the deck, beckoned me to join him on a bench. I waited until he rang off, then settled in his lap.

"Scheduled a video conference with Rain for tomorrow morning," he said. "I'll need the computer. If that cuts into your work time, we can juggle the lookout schedule."

I blew a raspberry. As if I had equal claim to the computer. He needed the conference more than I needed my internet prying. Anyway, if he really had a deep dark secret, wouldn't I have found it by now?

"Everything all right?" he asked.

I didn't figure it was a real question, so at first I said nothing. Then I remembered what he'd said to Rain, about it feeling tight around here. "If you need time alone ... I mean, I don't want to crowd you. I can go."

I started to stand. He held my waist, pulled me into his lap again.

"You can if you want, but I don't," he said. "Sit with me, Heidi Heidi Ho."

Right. Sit tight, I thought. But he was tense as an I-beam and more dangerous if he snapped. Better to release some of that tension.

I pulled off my shirt. "Why sit when we could dance?"

THE NEXT DAY TANK thumped weights in the study, stomped up and down the stairs, slammed kitchen drawers, banged pots and pans. The grouchier he got, the bigger he got, pushing me out of the way. It reminded me of living with William.

Before Tank and Sweeney even needed the study, I cleared out. Downstairs, Paolo slumped on the couch, supposedly on watch. The vidfeeds formed a frame on the tele, but in the center of that frame, the screen pulsed as Paolo channel surfed. Outside, Chazz and company blasted Rammstein. I would've sold my soul for some Barry Manilow.

I joined Paolo, cross-legged on the couch, cataloguing actors according to Lombroso's criminal profiles, the Merton

System of Face Reading, and the guidelines set each decade by the American Plastic Surgeons Association. Paolo's leg jogged my knee now and then, and he smelled good. Not fresh exactly but less like soap and detergent, more like himself. Sandy, like pear grit. Or the beach, I imagined.

"I can turn off the tele if it bothers you," he said. Peace offering, I supposed.

I shook my head. "Just nothing with men in it."

"Wha ...? That leaves, like, chick flicks and girl-on-girl porn."

"Shut up. You can watch NASA or MoMA or cartoons—"

"So I get space junk, scribbles, and ... *Animaniacs*?" He laughed. "What a relief."

I backhanded his arm but couldn't help smiling, too. "You get the whole fucking cosmos, just no men, okay?"

He slanted a glance at me, eyes lingering on my bra strap. My shirt, one Tank had bought me, kept slipping off my shoulder. "I'd rather look at women, anyway," he said. "Sexier."

"Speak for yourself, baby boy." I showed him Stallone in Rodin's *Thinker* pose.

He scoffed and turned back to the weather report for Maui. I puzzled over the plastic surgeons' decree of a nose with a "more natural-looking tip." Could a surgical alteration be more "natural looking" than one's original nose?

"Hey," Paolo said. "Does Tank have a secret candy stash? I'm jonesing for licorice."

I remembered the scent on his helmet's visor, shook my head. "He would've put it on the fridge list if he did. 'Sides, Tank can't maintain those guns of his on Gummi Bears and M&Ms."

"Or beer, huh?"

I murmured, vaguely affirmative. Tried to focus on whether Robert Patrick really looked like a 1940s company man or if I thought so because he'd played an FBI agent on *X-Files*.

"I don't think I could make the tradeoff," Paolo said. "Licorice versus pussy?"

I frowned at the interruption, then the implication. "You think Tank looks like that for sex?"

"Can't hurt, right?"

He grinned. I stared.

"Nah, I know better," he said, shrugging. "I only meant, well, he turned *your* head."

I blinked in disdain and went back to work. Then I stopped. I reached for the remote in Paolo's hand and touched the mute button. "Wait. What do you mean, you know better?"

He looked at my hand on his before meeting my eyes. "Well," he said, mouth pursed, as if debating how much to say. "You can't grow up in the system and not be affected. Sometimes, the bigger and badder you get, the better."

"System?"

"Yeah." His voice lowered. Eyes pinned to mine. "Foster care. Juvie. You knew that, right?"

I didn't have to shake my head.

"Shit," Paolo muttered. "He didn't tell you. Fuck, why would he? So stupid." He rubbed his mouth like he could erase his mistake. Despite the revelation, I noticed his goatee was neatly trimmed; he must've known where Tank hid the razors.

My throat felt dry as week-old toast. "Tank was in foster care?" I croaked.

"For a while, before he got thrown in juvie. We both were."

My eyes bugged. "Why would you keep it a secret?" *You* meaning *Tank*, of course. "I mean, look at us, this town, this freakfest. What's to be ashamed of?"

Paolo shook his head. "It's not shame, it's ... The way they move you around, like a nut under a paper cup, you learn not to get attached. Don't tell anyone more than you have to."

Upstairs, Tank's voice rose in irritation. Paolo blanched, then shifted to face me, close enough he didn't need to whisper, close enough his shin pressed the length of my thigh.

"Don't take it personal," he said. "The system changes you. Even once you age out, you can't help moving. Town to town, state to state. Not exactly a lifestyle that promotes intimacy."

"Age out? What does that mean?"

"Once you turn eighteen, you're no longer a ward of the state, feds don't have to take care of you anymore. You ain't been saving your money, don't have a place lined up, you're out on the street. They tell you you can change your name, start all over. Ha." Paolo's thin lips disappeared. He studied our hands, still on the remote, now on my knee. "Start over with what?"

"Blank slate," I mumbled. That was why Tank's— Noé's—history went no further back than age eighteen. And no telling what they'd wiped clean when they gave him his fresh start. Unless ... "You knew him back then?"

"No. Same shit, different states. But I guess that's why we get on so easy."

I nodded, tried to cover my disappointment. At least now I understood why Tank evaded my questions about Paolo, why he trusted him. Had more reason to trust him than me.

"Sorry to drop this on you," Paolo said. "I thought he'd told you. I would have."

I patted his hand. I think I did; everything from my heart down felt numb. "No, it's okay," I said. "I just need a minute."

And being on duty laid up with that foot, Paolo couldn't do much more than call after me when I bolted from the room.

≈

I SLAMMED INTO THE backyard, staggered a bit when the summer heat slammed right back. Sequestered in Tank's house, I'd forgotten the heat and decibels and stink that always plagued the Inner Radius.

I retreated under the deck, stumble-paced the shadowed patio. My thoughts bounced like spilled BBs. Tank in foster care, then juvie. No wonder the siege was flipping him out, some kind of PTSD. Those fucking feds—cops, whatever—putting kids in cages. Was that where he'd gotten those circle scars? Or had those come earlier? A gang? Or had his mom done that? Was that why he was in foster care? But wait, why was he in juvie? They didn't throw you in a juvenile detention center for killing your mom, right? You'd go to jail, a real prison for that, right? If they could prove it?

I must've done eighty laps around the patio before I threw myself in a corner. The walls of Tank's house felt good against my shoulders, cool on my bare skin. *Supportive*, I thought—which was stupid, because they were *walls*, of course they were supportive. I knocked my head back and shuddered a deep breath. My machine-gun glances around the patio gradually slowed, absorbing, understanding, disbelieving. How did I miss it before?

The patio was a golden rectangle.

And the stairs leading up to the deck, the shadow they cast, they created a golden rectangle within the golden rectangle. Which meant ... I cocked my head, squinting up. The deck was probably a golden rectangle, too, the lengths of its sides corresponding to the golden ratio: 1 to 1.618. The formula most often associated with beauty in paintings, shells, sculptures, pyramids, even faces.

I considered the house's rooms and floors. The den, for sure. The living room. Not the bedroom or study, but the entire second floor. If I had blueprints, I'd bet I'd find more. Maybe that's why—when I wasn't on watch—I could forget the brawls raking up the Spill-scoured landscape, why I was calming down now, in spite of the maddening half-history of Tank that Paolo had divulged.

Tank had talked about houses holding us, molding us. He'd said this house couldn't hold him, like he'd failed somehow, like he wouldn't need to fight if he'd gotten the boxes lined up right. But maybe the longer I stayed here, the more his house molded *me*. I'd rebelled when Mother and Father squashed me into the medic mold, but I could stand to have neat, orderly, actionable thoughts once in a while. Maybe if this house altered me enough, I could stop chasing my tail and see my way out of Exile.

I puffed sweaty hair out of my eyes and thought, *Tank carved out beauty, created harmony here—in the Inner Radius, the cesspit of Exile. Why here?*

All that research into Tank's past? Maybe I'd simply been stalling. Because whatever brought him here—even if it wasn't matricide—it had to be awful, right? What kind of nightmare would force someone as smart, strong, and successful as Tank into Exile?

And what kind of monster would beg him to go back just so she could go, too?

≈

I WORRIED ABOUT FACING Tank when I came in, whether I'd be able to look at him without betraying my new knowledge, but as it happened, he wasn't making eye contact with anybody. Sweeney and Paolo whispered in the living room, their words inaudible to me over the slamming in the kitchen.

"What's up?" I said.

"Some of your brother's crew trashed the job site last night." For once, Sweeney didn't bother with a glare. Narrow ass on the back of the couch, he watched the kitchen entry, Tank's figure blacking it now and then.

"Sweet Sue," I muttered.

I stood near Sweeney, looked to the kitchen, too. Tank wasn't out-and-out hitting things. But big as he was, he had to be careful not to break stuff, and now ... well, he wasn't being careful.

"The damage bad?" I said.

Sweeney cracked his neck. "Nobody's hurt. They hit the trucks, some equipment."

"Nobody's hurt, yet," Paolo added from his seat on the couch.

Sweeney peeked at me from the corner of his eye. "Now might be a good time for your porny superpowers."

Grimacing, Paolo raised an arm to smack Sweeney's back. "Yeah, throw the girl in the lion's den. Jerk."

"Let's just stay out of his way for a while," I said. "Go on, Paolo. Take a break. I'll keep lookout."

Paolo took his time about it, perhaps reluctant to leave me alone with Sweeney, but he shuffled to the bathroom. I flopped onto his spot on the couch. It was warm, smelled like him: antiseptic from his wound and that sugary sand smell I liked more and more. Sweeney lingered against the couch like a devil at my shoulder, spurs clicking as he tapped one boot against the other.

"Get Paolo out of the way," I said, "and I'll see what I can do."

"Atta girl." Sweeney pushed off the couch, half turned to muss my hair. When I ducked, he chuckled, yanked my earrings hard enough to make my eyes water. Then off whistling he went.

SWEENEY COULD THINK WHAT he wanted, but I didn't put any moves on Tank. All I did was accept the hamburger he served me for lunch—not a word about my allotted calories or protein. That was sufficiently unusual to bring Tank out of his funk. We ate on the couch, arms seldom bumping.

Then I offered to wash the dishes.

"Sorry," he muttered.

"What for?" I said, empty plate in each hand.

"Guess I must've spooked ya." He leaned forward, caught my eye. "If you're eating and all."

"A little," I admitted.

"It's not you." He reached for my arm, held my elbow.

"I know." I tried a smile.

"Thing is ..." He sighed, sagged back, let my arm slide from his grasp. "I hate being cooped up. Feel like my skin's gonna split open, like my head'll explode. I know it's the smart thing to do, it's our second-best option, I know ..."

He tilted his head at me almost wistfully. I knew what he wanted, knew more than he realized: he might not be so eager to ice my mother if he hadn't been in juvie or shuffled from home to home; if he could sit tight without going crazy and grasping at any bullet to end it. But killing Mother would bring the feds and sink my 4-S chances. I couldn't risk it. In a way I was resisting for his sake. I wanted to get out of Exile on my own by testing out. I didn't want to use Tank if I didn't have to. I adopted that facial shrug of his and waited for him to continue.

"... but that doesn't make it any easier. Especially not when William's crew is wrecking my hard work."

I shrugged, a pathetic reply hardly bolstered by, "I don't like being cooped up either."

Tank's upper cheeks tightened: skepticism. Before he pointed out I'd never left the house even when I had the chance, I asked, "You sure it was Chazz and company that did the damage?"

"What? Who else would it be?!"

I edged back, legs hitting the footlocker. "Is there proof, though? Did anybody see it? Do you have security footage?"

"No," he said, squinting. "Why?"

"I don't know. It could've been them or Pops' crew. But things are weird. Weirder than usual."

He didn't say anything, only wagged his hand: *Gimme more.*

"Like the thing with the UTL courier. She said their contract was running out; but I checked, and they don't have a union. And there's no official statement about their contract expiring or being cancelled. And," I said, consolidating plates and my thoughts, "Carlos said the feds bought his line about not being able to verify our gunfire, even though they usually ream him about shit like that. And I don't know if this is part of it, but when the feds sent the ambulance for my sister, they refused to take my father. I don't care how crazy bereaved he was, that's standard operating procedure: if a minor's taken from Exile for medical treatment, a guardian has to go, too, or the feds make them sign off."

Tank nodded, adding things up. "You think the feds trashed my worksite?"

"Maybe. I don't know why, seeing as how you bring order to the savages."

He shifted, as if to study the corner of the footlocker. More like to avoid my eyes.

"What?" I said, goosebumps rising. "What haven't you told me?"

He rubbed the bridge of his nose. I was ready to kick him when he said, "I got a letter. Day your package came. It was a recall warrant."

"What?" I half sat, half fell on the footlocker. I'd forgotten all about that certified letter. Tank took the chattering dishes and set them on the floor before I dropped them.

A recall warrant revoked an Outsider's visa. It didn't happen often, mostly because Outsiders were practically DOA. But every once in a while, some jerkwad committed a crime Out There and then slipped through the background check and into Exile before the feds wised up. Had the feds found dirt on Tank that I hadn't?

"What did it say?" I asked.

He shook his head. "I don't know, some bullshit about inconsistencies in my paperwork. There weren't any. I had a lawyer go through it all when I applied."

"So what did you tell the feds?"

He shrugged, about to rise from the couch, but I grabbed his knees.

"You ignored the warrant?" I said, eyes feeling saucer-wide.

He must've known it was pointless to walk away, that I'd chase him around the house until he caved. He burrowed back against the couch and huffed at the ceiling. I followed, straddling his lap and clutching his shoulders.

"You ignored it," I said. "Why?"

"It's bullshit. Cam'n'Isaac got recalls, too. Same non-explanation as mine. The feds don't play fair, why should I? And now they got to get through Chazz's crew if they want me, so what's the worst that could happen?"

"Never ask that in Exile," I grumbled.

The feds wanted Tank out of Exile. And he saw being separated from them by a bloodthirsty crew as an upside. While I tried to wrap my brain 'round that, Sweeney popped in, grinning big enough to bare his extra incisor.

"Not interrupting anything, am I?"

Tank shot me a warning glare as he moved my hands from his shoulders. "Nothing much."

Sweeney must not have known about the warrant, either. Fine, I'd keep Tank's secret. I climbed off his lap, digging one knee into his groin in the process. Clench-jawed, Tank bit back a moan. I gathered the dishes again. Swiped Tank's phone from the footlocker while I was at it.

"I'll wash the dishes," I said.

And I did—muttering the whole time—but then I snuck into the den to call Carlos. When he realized it was me, not Tank, his tone shot from gruff to worried.

"¿Qué pasó, mija?"

"Nada, nada," I assured him. "No mas tengo una pregunta."

"Pues, ¿puede esperar?" he said, voice now strained in a different direction. "Tengo una tormenta de mierda en mis manos."

"Y, ¿qué más hay de nuevo?" I teased. I wished I knew more Spanish, so the next part would be somewhat encoded. "It's about recall warrants."

"Sweet Sue, I don't have time for this, mocosa. I've got a water main break in the pinche Outer Radius. Speaking of which, you might want to boil your water until I talk to you again. Cuidate bien."

He hung up. I cussed him out. But I did go to the kitchen to dump the ice from the freezer into the sink. I also drew a skull-n-crossbones and arrows pointing at the fridge's water dispenser, then filled a kettle and stock pot and put them on the stove to boil.

Back in the living room, Sweeney was stirring up his own shitstorm. Straddling the couch back, he told Tank, "C'mon, man. I can jump the back wall, run through your neighbor's yard—"

"No!" Tank stood in front of the tele wall, staring at Sweeney so hard I expected to see smoke curling off the guy's edges.

Sweeney groaned. "But I'm out of cigarettes. I'll be a ninja, I won't get tagged or shot—"

"Go ahead, get shot," Tank said. "That's not the point."

Stifled laughter. I turned and saw Paolo sitting on the stairs, chin in hand, knuckles hiding his smile.

Ignoring him, Sweeney said, "Your neighbors aren't taking sides—"

"And we're not taking advantage of that," Tank said, glowering. "You run through the neighbors' and Chazz finds out, he's gonna post sentries in front of their places, and they'll turn on us, too. No, we don't pull anything like that 'til we're ready to go full throttle."

"Then why not use those catapults?" Sweeney said. "Have our crew send us a care package?"

Paolo stood and smile fading, beckoned me. I hesitated. Much as I hated to admit it, Sweeney wasn't an idiot; he knew everything Tank was spelling out for him. Worse, he'd given Tank an irresistible engineering problem. What was his angle?

"Heidi?" Paolo and his puppy dog look. "Come check my stitches?"

That again. I tried to catch Tank's eye, but he was too busy explaining how long it'd take to get a catapult in and out of position from the right distance even if their crew could sidestep Pops' stalkers.

In the bathroom under the stairs, Paolo pulled Tank's white T-shirt over his head, left it hooked around his arms and leaned against the sink, head down. I shivered a little—all those spiders etched into his skin.

"You okay?" he said, quiet.

I shook my head. "Fine," I whispered, mindful of the bathroom's acoustics. "Although my brain's a little backed up."

"My fault?" He looked at me in the mirror, cocked his head. "Sorry."

Weird how his revelation about Tank's childhood had blown over. "No, forget it," I said. I wondered if *he* knew about Tank's recall warrant. But the way the tiles amplified everything, I wasn't going to risk asking. "We're under a boil water order, FYI."

"Of course, we are," he said, smiling bitterly.

I visually traced his webs down to the bandage hiding his ripped tattoo. I edged a nail under the tape and peeled. His shoulders tightened as he tried not to flinch. Beneath the gauze, bristles of black stitches glistened with the antimicrobial that we took turns slathering across his back every day.

I put a hand on his hip, shifted his angle so light ran

along the wound. "Looking good. We should be able to pull 'em soon."

Paolo sighed. "Great, I miss my faux-hawk."

I smiled, surprised. "Me, too, a little."

I leaned sideways to flick the old bandage into the trash. He tracked me in the mirror, eyes blue as the ocean I'd kill to see, pupils widening when he got to my bra strap. He smelled good, like my daydream of sweet sand. In the other room Tank's voice rose. I realized I was still holding Paolo's hip. But now my leg rubbed the back of his, and my breast pressed his arm.

I backed up, hands off. "I'll apply a fresh bandage if you hold still."

"I'll be as still as you are gentle, sweetheart." And damn if he didn't wink.

When I finished bandaging him up, I smooshed down the last piece of tape with feeling. He squirmed against the sink, teeth gritted, and I grinned. He caught his breath, looked up through his lashes. His tongue skimmed his lips, leaving a spit shine before he grinned back.

Bitch, he mouthed.

Cheeks hot, panties soaked, I flipped him off and slapped my other hand over his bandage. His knee knocked the vanity, but he held back a hiss.

"One of your spiders got ripped off its web. My friend Romero can hook it back up for you."

He shook his hair back. Another open-mouthed grin. "You treat all your friends this nice?"

"Who said we were friends?" To avoid his gaze I glanced down. He had dimples of Venus—lateral lumbar indentations—that peeked over the waistband of his saggy jeans.

"Everything all right?" Tank said, suddenly standing in the doorway.

I jumped. "Sweeney on a leash?"

Tank nodded. "Short one. You got one on Puppy?"

Paolo pulled his shirt over his head, down over stitches and dimples. "I need a leash?"

Tank didn't answer; he looked at me and cocked his head toward the living room. "Come keep me company."

Chapter Eighteen

THAT NIGHT, ONCE WE were alone, I tried to grill Tank about the warrant.

"You know as much as I do" and "Said all there is to say," he insisted, unable to escape while on watch. Then growling about how many TV channels showed nothing but static, he reached into the footlocker for a sketchpad and pencil.

My brain felt clogged with info I didn't want anyway, so I watched him draw. It wasn't random scribbles or caricatures of the onscreen thugs he simmered at now and then. More like plans for a rocket launcher. Why was I surprised?

"What's that?" I finally said.

"Just some ideas."

Flashbacks to the crossbow fiasco. "For what?"

"Message delivery system."

Well, that didn't sound too heinous.

"Can I see?" I scooted along the couch and wiggled my way under his arm. He didn't fight it, only switched the pencil to his other hand and kept drawing. *Hotter than lava*, I thought, and snaked my arms around him. After a minute of my cheek on his chest, he relaxed, his hand moving from the back of the couch to my shoulder. I hummed, *Hell yeah*, and sensed him smile. The callused pad of his thumb slid under my bra strap. I warmed, all awareness centered on the heat at my clavicle.

I kissed a line up his chest. Didn't quite get to his collar before he ducked down and caught my mouth in his. We were doing so well, I slid one hand under his sketchpad and into his lap. He pressed a remonstrative "Heidi!" against my lips.

"What?" I murmured, squeezing. "You're not interested?"

"You kneed me in the balls." He shifted his legs but sounded amused.

"I'm a medic." I licked his parted lips. "I can make it better."

He laughed, turned from my questing tongue. "I'm supposed to be on watch."

Feeling him settle deeper into the couch, happy and relaxed, was almost as good as a quickie, so I relented. "In that case, I'm gonna get a drink of water and head upstairs. See if I can't get a bit of my own work done."

I was drinking in the dark kitchen when Sweeney entered from the garage. His hands and forearms nearly glowed, freshly scrubbed with pumice soap.

"You still up?" he asked, rubbing his forehead with his T-shirt hem.

I lowered my glass. "I was heading to the study. Unless you plan on getting Tank all riled up again."

"Huh?" He looked up, flat stomach still exposed.

"That shit about running out to get cigarettes? The catapults?" I glanced over my shoulder, made sure Tank wasn't looming. "What was that about?"

He dropped his hem and leaned into my space. "That was about distracting him. Which is what I told you to do." Over my protests, he growled, "You were supposed to make him feel better, supposed to get his mind off the damage at the site. Instead, I come back in, and he looks, I don't know ... harassed!"

"You don't tell me what to do, Sweeney. And whatever I've done in the past, I won't use sex to manipulate Tank. I won't manipulate him at all." I'd made my decision on the patio, and it felt good to say it.

"Like hell." Sweeney shook his head, addressed the floor like my idiocy burned too hot to look at. "You already do,

Heidi. You can't help it, it's your fucking nature. Every word, every glance. Even," he said, lifting his chin to point, "that damn shirt that don't cover you up."

I remembered Tank's hand on my shoulder, his thumb under my bra strap. How good it had felt and how it relaxed him. Was that what I'd been doing? Manipulating, scheming?

"Shit," Sweeney continued, "you oughtta be blind from the eyefucking alone."

Face burning, glad of the dark, I slammed my glass on the counter, sloshing water all over the place. "Fuck you," I said.

Tank called, "Heidi?"

"I'm fine!"

Sweeney snagged my arm, pulled me close. I wrinkled my nose at his stink, leaned back.

"Heidi, I'm ..." A subtle whine, perhaps his version of regret, crept into Sweeney's words. "All I'm asking is you use your superpowers for good, not evil. You keep Tank from combusting, I won't care how you did it. We're on the same side here, yeah?"

I wrenched my arm free. "Are we?"

THE NEXT DAY WE lost the Internet. Normally, I'd have shrugged it off—Exile's lines to the outside world were never that reliable, and now Chazz's electric fence was mucking up reception. But given the feds' recent squirreliness, I told Tank. And though I'd done all there was to do, he sat in the study and tried it all over again. When his cell phone rang, he handed it to me. I answered—Carlos—and edged into the hallway.

"You boiling your water?" he asked.

"What kind of pervy question is that?" I said.

"Heidi, no me jodas, I'm serious! We got that water

main patched, but I don't know how long it's going to last, and the engineers can't get here until next week."

"Yes, Carlos Killjoy." I heard Tank suppress a chuckle in the study. I smiled but moved farther away. "We're boiling the water. Conserving, too. What happened, anyway?"

"Pues, let's see. In my unprofessional opinion? Twenty years without maintenance."

"That it?"

He scoffed. "That's enough, cabrona."

"And why can't any engineers get here?"

Still audibly scowling, he said, "Because we're always the feds' last priority, 'member?"

"Are you sure that's all?" And having his attention, I ducked into the bedroom to share the clues Tank and I had hashed out earlier.

Afterwards, sounding grim, Carlos said, "Last time you called, why'd you ask about recall warrants?"

I didn't hesitate to tell him, then asked, "Why? What do the warrants have to do with ..." I didn't know what to call the feds' latest weirdness.

He sighed. "You wouldn't remember, I guess. You were still little the first couple of times the feds cracked down."

"I remember one time," I said, bristling. It's not like I was Sammy's age. True, I'd been young enough to be locked in the hall closet, punishment for slugging William because he'd scribbled in my books, but I'd heard the National Guard's Humvees rumble down our street, blasting curfew orders from PAs.

Carlos didn't acknowledge my protest, continued grim as a reaper. "The feds issued public recall warrants a week or two before they stormed in. Outsiders hadn't done anything, the feds just wanted them out of harm's way, but the liaisons didn't know that. They helped track down the Outsiders, tossed 'em to the feds. Of course, that only worked once. The next time the feds sent recalls straight to the Outsiders, tried to keep the liaisons out of the loop and let the Outsiders choose their fates."

"You think they're issuing warrants like that again to clear people out?"

"I don't know, the feds haven't hit us that hard in a while. Would they risk sending recalls? I mean, one mouthy Outsider could tip their hand." Before I could feel too reassured, he added, "But then, we're always outgunned. Could be the feds are simply covering their asses 'cause the element of surprise is trivial."

"Wow, Carlos. Your optimism rocks."

"Hey, you try wading around in the fucking sewers for thirty-six hours, see if you've got a happy hard-on."

"Sorry, baby. You're right. I'm sorry." I wished I could squeeze his arm like I used to, make him look at me until he calmed down. "Do you know if the feds are still issuing visas to those idiots who *want* into Exile?"

"I don't know, there's been no official freeze."

"Well, when did the last Outsider come through the checkpoint? Last week, last month?"

"I don't know! I've been busy."

I said nothing—waiting, wishing.

He sighed. "But I'll find out."

THAT NIGHT, LONG AFTER Tank fell asleep, my brain kept grinding like a car with a sticky clutch. Crap about Tank and his recall warrant and why he was in juvie, who'd really trashed his work site and what the hell were the feds up to and how badly was my little sister burned? Against my will I worried about Father: where he was and if he'd make a break for it, if he'd even have to or if the hair-trigger feds would aerate him for getting too close. I imagined bloody chunks of him in the trench—a feast for the worms and spiders—and I shook hard enough my teeth rattled.

I tried to sneak out of bed so I wouldn't wake Tank. He reached for me, said my name instead of Jenna's, but I shushed him. "I'll be right back," I said. And he was so burned out he let me go.

Paolo was on duty. As I crept down the stairs, he brightened, switched on the spotlight of his smile. Stupidly, automatically, I smiled back.

"Where's Sweeney?" I said.

"Sweeney has temporarily escaped my radar." Paolo's attention returned to the tele. "But my spidey senses tell me he's in the den phonesexing Serena."

I *ewwed* out my tongue.

"Hey," Paolo said, "better there than here."

"I guess."

He patted the cushion beside him and I sat, propping my feet beside his on the footlocker.

"How's your foot?"

He grunted. "Sometimes better, sometimes worse."

"You want me to take a look?"

"Nah. I think I've used up my nursing chits."

I raised my eyebrows, surprised he'd come around. "I'm kind of a bitch about it," I said, "but it's not you. My family crammed it down my throat, always expected me to take care of William. So I don't deal well when you guys assume I'll take care of you."

"I get it." He didn't turn from the tele, and his profile offered no clues. "We all got shit from our pasts."

I sat processing that for a minute. Then I realized I was probably supposed to ask a follow-up question. "What's your shit?"

He shrugged, and I thought I'd guessed wrong until he said, "Romero ever tell you what spider web tats mean?"

I shook my head.

"Means you feel trapped."

My heart winced. "Boy, you picked the wrong town."

Head tilted, he picked at the frayed inseam of his jeans.

"Wasn't so bad at first. I liked that I could leave whenever I wanted and you guys can't."

I gasped before laughing. "Bastard!" I slugged his arm, only half affectionately.

He sniff-laughed. "Yeah, but then this siege thing happened. Guess it serves me right."

"Don't." I stopped him tugging a loose thread in his seam. "Don't say that."

He twisted his hand around and twined his fingers in mine. "I'm sorry I acted like it was your job to take care of me."

I squeezed his hand. "Eh, I can think of worse. Like taking care of Sweeney."

He snorted again and let me pull my hand away. The only stations we got were Mexican, so we settled on a telenovela. Compared to its convoluted storyline, our situation seemed almost normal.

I'D NEVER TOLD THE Cantus my birthday. I wanted to avoid the fuss of a cake and "Las Mañanitas." But once he became an official liaison, Carlos had access to public records. So he probably knew when I was old enough for the clearance test and that I'd scheduled to take it. He never said anything about it, though, like he never asked what I was studying for or who else I danced with. Even after I failed the first test and sank into tar pits of despair, he said nothing.

He coaxed me out of my parents' house and dragged me to a kegger at Tia Vela's. I remembered trying to keep my liquor down while Sammy hoisted me over his shoulder in a boisterous bear hug. Next thing I knew, I woke in a tangle in Carlos's bed. It wasn't big enough for the three of us, but we made it work. Romero spooned me, and I hugged Carlos, my head on his shoulder. The arrangement was familiar enough. I recognized it without cracking an eyelid.

The bed shook. Again. I realized that was what had woken me.

"Carlos?" someone whispered.

I opened one eye. Sammy leaned over us, shaking Carlos's shoulder.

"Hi, Heidi." He smiled down. His hair stood on end, and he wore the same clothes as the night before. Like us, he reeked of bonfire and barbecue. "You going to live with us now?"

"What?" I closed my eye, burrowed back into Carlos's shoulder.

"What's wrong?" Carlos moaned. He covered his face with one arm.

Sammy shook him again. "I'm hungry. Can I make breakfast?"

"Breakfast?" Carlos uncovered his face. "Shit, Heidi. Wake up, girl. It's morning."

He hauled himself out of bed, searched for his shirt—which I was wearing—but I rolled over into Romero, who snuffled.

"Your phone's been ringing and ringing," Sammy told Carlos.

"Where'd I leave it?" Carlos said, stumbling after Sammy into the kitchen.

I blinked, listening to the growl of motorcycles outside. A new tat, a candy-colored calavera, grinned at me from Romero's pec. What Carlos had said gradually sank in.

I'd never not gone home before.

Amid the toaster and coffeemaker noises, I heard an electronic trill, easy to ignore: Carlos's phone. He answered, rumbly. His voice came clearer as he walked down the hall toward the bedroom.

"Yes, sir." Carlos had found a shirt, but he'd pulled it on inside out. He mouthed "Tu padre" at me and waved me out of bed. I groaned and sat up. "She's right here. You want to talk to her?"

I shook my head like a wet dog. Instantly regretted it, beer burning up my throat. But Father must've refused, too, because Carlos said, "Yes, sir. I'll tell her," and hung up. "You gotta go home."

"Might want to shower first," Romero yawned, scratching something off the back of my arm.

I brushed his hand away. "Is he mad?" I asked Carlos.

Carlos screwed up his face: *No seas tonta.*

I went home the back way to avoid the fights in the street. Of course, this way I ran into Father and a fight behind the house. Couldn't be helped.

He was leaning in the dark rectangle of the open garage door, cleaning a torque wrench that didn't need cleaning with a rag that did. He looked up but didn't meet my eyes, his gaze skirting my collar. His mouth twisted. I wondered if I'd missed a dry patch of jizz.

"You sleep well?" he asked.

I focused on his work boots, knowing a rhetorical question when I heard one—at least when it came from him.

"Sure hope so," he said. "Least one of us should, and I know goddamn well it wasn't me."

"I didn't mean to fall asleep," I said, hands going to my hips, defensive. "I'm sorry."

"Which one of those boys are you dating, anyway?"

Dating? I looked up, smirking, but he glared a warning, so I wiped the smile off my face. "What does it matter?" I said, studying the grease-smeared knees of his jeans. "You don't have to wait up for me anymore."

"It matters, Heidi. If it's Carlos, he's old enough to know better. If it's Romero, he's too stupid for you."

"What if it's Sammy?" I said, arms crossing over my chest.

"Not funny, Heidi! I'm getting too old for this—"

"Oh please, you're forty-five!"

"Yeah, but I live with you. And your mother. I can't be up all night wondering where you are, Heidi. I can't deal with getting up and seeing you never made it home. It's like the sleepwalking, but worse."

"You don't have to wait up for me," I said, resisting the ache in my chest. "I didn't mean to fall asleep. And now you know, if I don't make it home, I'm at the Cantus' house. I'm not stupid. I can take care of myself."

"I know you're not stupid ..."

He trailed off like I was something else but he didn't want to say it. The ache in my chest went razor-sharp, splintered my heart.

"What really bothers you?" I said, hands going to my hips again. "That I didn't come home, or where I was? Or what you think I was doing?"

"Pretty clear to the whole town what you're doing. As for who or how many ..."

My throat closed up. When I didn't protest, only goggled at him with wet eyes, he reddened.

"You know what? Fine!" He pitched his rag on the ground and pointed the wrench at me. "I don't care if you come home at night or who you're messing with. But you damn well better be ready when William needs you. And don't expect me to haul your ass out of trouble because trust me, there's gonna be trouble the way you're carrying on. Always is with girls like you. And don't—"

I watched him, as if through a pane of safety glass, his rant muffled and the razor dulling in my heart. I studied the crimp of his mouth, the wrinkles around his huge, brown-as-mine eyes. He wasn't mad, I realized. More frustrated that he couldn't make me do what he wanted. Never could. And it wasn't a matter of reasoning or pleading or exerting his will.

What good's a scalpel when you want a blowtorch?

≈

I GUESS I FELL asleep, the novela blurring into a memory, the memory into a dream. Then Paolo sat up straighter, and my head bumped on his shoulder.

"Heidi. Think you need to see this." He moved one of the smaller pics to the center of the screen, where it replaced Spanish-language news.

I sat up, squinted, rubbed my eyes. Wondered for a split second if I was still dreaming.

"What is that?" I said, jerking my sleep-numb legs off the locker.

Three of Pops' boys—his actual boys, blood kin—carried an old blanket. A mottled thing weighed down the center so it nearly scraped the ground. *An improvised stretcher*, I thought with a spark of panic. The boys, teenagers who all shared the same lurch as their permanently stooped father, lowered the blanket to the ground beside the sentry ladder. Chazz jumped down, listened to the boys for a minute before nudging the thing on the blanket with one boot. Then he turned to yell at Tank's house. We couldn't hear it. The dampeners were working for a few blessed hours.

Paolo said, "Should we get Tank?"

I swallowed back my pulse. "Not yet. He's not been sleeping well. What's Chazz saying?"

"You want me to turn off the dampeners?"

I stood, ran a fingernail up and down the earrings on my left ear. "Shit, I don't know. What *is* that?" But I was pretty sure it was a body, and a familiar pattern was emerging from its blood-black jumble.

"Hey." Paolo reached over, squeezed my waist one-handed to get my attention. "You don't have to take lead on this. Let's ask Tank, or we can go get Sweeney."

Sweeney? I shook my head, rapped my fist against my forehead, as if to jog loose an idea. Instead, words spilled out like a collapsed house of cards. "But that's a stretcher. They have a body. What if it's one of your crew? Zeke or Moss or ... maybe I should step outside, see what's happening."

"You want to see my insides?" Paolo said, voice cracking. "'Cause Tank'll skin me alive if I let you out there."

I turned to him. His low eyebrows were pinched together, forming two knife-sharp vertical creases at his glabella. If I cut there and peeled ...

His blue eyes flicked back and forth like he knew what I was thinking. His thumb slid down and pressed my pelvic bone. "Focus, Heidi."

"On what?" Sweeney said.

I turned the same time as Paolo yanked his hand from my waist. Sweeney entered the living room from the kitchen, boot spurs jangling. "What's going on?" he demanded.

I pointed at the tele, but Sweeney seemed more interested in my face, then in Paolo's.

"Something's wrong," I said. "Outside. Someone's dead."

That got his attention. Sweeney hurried around the couch and grabbed the remote, zoomed in while Paolo explained.

"When did these guys show up? Any sign of her mother?" Sweeney asked. "Go get Tank," he told me.

I nodded, and that should've tipped him off, me taking orders from him. But he was so engrossed in the televised danse macabre, I walked to the door and stepped outside before he or Paolo caught a whiff of a clue.

A MUTED CACOPHONY MUMBLED 'round me as I padded down the sidewalk. The zone of noise-cancellation waves emitted by Tank's house dampeners. It sounded like Mute's Roadhouse under water.

The humid night rubbed up against me. I remembered I wasn't wearing anything but one of Tank's T-shirts and some silk boxers. Sweeney was right; I needed to wear more pants. I gritted my teeth, preparing to walk through the bubble formed by the dampeners. It was there somewhere.

WHOMP.

Instant nausea. I clamped my hands over my ears, cowered as my ears popped from the sudden change in sound fields. I clenched my jaw, closed my throat against bile. Once I managed to raise my head, I saw half a dozen twenty- and thirty-year-old shotguns pointed in my direction. The floodlights on the other side of the fence sent bright bolts gleaming down the black barrels. My ears adjusted, as if zeroing in on a pirate radio station, and I heard thugs yelling at me to get down on my knees.

I spotted Chazz and the lump on the blanket. Actually, not a blanket. A rag rug. But definitely a body. Very bloody. Not intact. Chazz swept out an arm to call off his crew. Pops' boys retreated to the shadows.

Behind me, Sweeney hissed through the open door. "Heidi, get your ass back in here. If Tank—"

The guns hitched in Sweeney's direction. Something happened, and the hair on my head and arms and legs tickled. I thought of Mother's bracelet, her bristly tarantula look. Sweeney ducked back inside and started ripping Paolo a new one. Paolo had turned off the dampeners. A thug took off running, but I didn't turn to see which one or where to. With Sweeney gone the guns all flicked back to me, dead black eyes.

"I hope you're satisfied," Chazz yelled.

"What shit are you shoveling now?" I tried to ignore the guns, squinted through the chain link fence at the rag rug and body. Specifically the brown work boots. One was twisted a hundred 'n' eighty degrees from its proper position. "Who is ... *was* that?"

"It's your dad. Don't you recognize your own dad?"

My heartbeat throbbed in my ears. I fought the panic clamping my lungs and studied the body. The head was a massacre. Even I, with years of facial analysis and numb-to-nonexistent sympathy, couldn't bear to look for long. I scanned the bullet-riddled torso instead, the arms exposed by rolled sleeves. It could've been anyone of a certain height and weight range, lighter skin. Why should it be Father?

"Who the fuck do you think those Gatling guns went off for?" Chazz said. "The president?"

"We had the dampeners on, dumbass." The shirt—blues and cream and brown drenched in blood—looked familiar. But lots of Exiles wore cowboy plaid, same as those work boots. "We didn't hear anything. We saw Pops' boys, the commotion ..."

"Well, now you see what you've done. You could a stopped this if you'd gone home when he said. Just a matter of time 'fore he did something stupid. But no, you cared more about fucking that Outsider than about your own family."

Trust me, Father had said. *There's gonna be trouble ... always is with girls like you.*

"But ..." My vision flickered. I blinked fast, struggling to push past the memory. "If it was the Gatlings, how ..." *is there anything left?*

"Oh, ain't you heard?" Chazz summoned a snide grin. "The feds don't wait for you to get to the trench anymore, 'specially not if you're raving. Pops' boys saw him go down on Gatling Drive and dragged his body back. Shit, they're more loyal than you were."

I didn't reply. I'd caught a silver shine from the body. Father's silver wedding band? But this was on the wrong side, the wrong hand. I sighed in relief.

"Fucking those faggot Cantu boys ain't kinky enough? You had to add an Outsider notch to your belt?"

Again with the Cantus. I started to snark about Chazz's hard-on for that particular "abomination." Then the splatter on the rag rug shifted into focus, knocked the wind out of me. *Two* hands on that side of the body. The left hand, severed by gunshots, had been jostled over to join its brother. But more than the silver ring, I recognized those hands. My vision wavered again, this time from tears, but still I saw those hands: cramped from years of fixing machines; swollen knuckles; strong, thick fingers; black grease forever embedded in the loops and grooves. Father.

Behind me, I heard more swearing in the open doorway: Tank cursing Sweeney to the festering backwaters of hell. I tilted my head back, sniffed hard, and willed my tears to soak back in, for Tank to stay in the house. If he came charging out, I'd be the one thing between him and all those fucking guns.

Down the street the front door of my parents' house slammed open. Mother howled. Distracted, the thugs let their guns dip. I stumbled backwards. I couldn't tear my gaze from Father's body, but I couldn't be there when Mother saw him, when she blamed me. I knew she would. I did.

I backpedaled, tripping, skinning my bare toes on the concrete. As soon as I was within reach, Tank leaned out, grabbed my wrist, and yanked me inside.

"JesusFuckingChrist, Heidi! What the hell were you thinking?"

Tank slammed the door behind us, twisted me back and forth by the wrist to look me up and down. I grimaced back a whimper.

"It was my dad, Tank—"

"The hell it was! It was a stunt, and you fell for it. You could've been killed."

"It was my dad! You think I don't know my dad?" Echoing Chazz, however unintentionally, soured my spit, made me shudder with disgust.

"That could've been anybody," Tank insisted. "If Sweeney'd gone out there, they'd have said it was Kier or Zeke. It's just somebody they beat up to draw us out."

I flailed, trying to yank free and scrape tears off my face at the same time. "He was dead," I screamed. "Not beat up. His head was a pothole. His hand was shot off."

"Tank's right. They've got to be bluffing," Paolo said. "Who hauls around dead bodies as bargaining chips?"

"What show have you been watching?" Sweeney snapped. "Shit, if she's so keen on joining dear old dad, let her go. Good riddance."

Tank lurched forward. Paolo shouted at him. Tank must've pulled his punch because Sweeney staggered and spit blood but stayed standing. Yanked along behind Tank, I slammed into the control panel. The house alarm *blurp-blurp*ed at ear-splitting volume.

"Sweeney, shut up," Tank yelled. "You shouldn't have let her out to begin with!"

"*Let* her? She bolted like a fucking jackalope!"

But Tank wasn't listening. He turned to me, eyes scary black, and shook me again. "Even if it was your dad, you couldn't have known that before you went out!"

"I could! I did," I said, believing it. The cowboy plaid ...

"So what?" Tank shouted. "What was the point of running out there, risking yourself like that? Shit, Heidi, I never took you for a daddy's girl. Think he'd run out in front of a fucking firing squad for *you*?"

I imagined Father stalking toward Gatling Drive. Had the sirens gone off? Had he gotten any warning? How many bullets before he'd stopped feeling? Before he'd bled out?

Before he died?

Suddenly, I was shivering. I couldn't stop no matter how stupid I felt.

Paolo hissed, "For fuck's sake, Tank! That's exactly what he did!"

I shook my head. Not that anyone could tell, the way I was shivering. "No, Tank's right. He didn't go King Lear for me. That was for Thea."

"And that's why he ain't worth the shit you'd scrape off your shoes, Heidi." Tank wrenched my wrist hard enough to hurt. "When's the last time he gave two seconds' thought to you? Useless prick let them barricade you in here—"

"Don't talk about him that way!" I stomped Tank's foot, yanked my hand free the same time he let go. Stumbling, I said, "It's not his fault he couldn't end this stupid siege. You can't. I can't."

"The hell you can't," Sweeney said. "Let's kill your mom!"

Paolo rounded on him. "What?"

"Not now, Sweeney," Tank warned.

"Why not? The bitch is out there. We've got sniper slits, we've got guns, we can take her out and be done with this bullshit."

Paolo sputtered. First he'd heard any of this, I guessed.

"How can you be so stupid?" I said. "If Tank kills Mother, her monitoring bracelet will alert the feds. They'll swoop in like vultures, and everyone will turn on us! Tank might never get Out There again."

Paolo turned to me, eyes wide, spider webs flexing on his neck. "What?"

"Oh right, it's all about Tank," Sweeney sneered. "If the feds crash our party, nobody will care about us. They'll be too busy fighting the Guard. Pretty sure Tank can fend for himself until the feds take him home. You, on the other hand?"

My face burned. With shame or rage I couldn't tell. "Shut up, Sweeney."

"That's it, isn't it?" He paused to spit blood again. "A crew traitor who killed her mom? When the feds come, William's friends will rat you out in a heartbeat. You'll probably inherit her monitoring bracelet. Then you'll never leave Exile. That's what you're really worried about, isn't it?"

"Wait a minute." Paolo asked me, "You could leave town?"

I looked up at Tank. His eyes had lost that dark rage, but there was nothing—*nothing*—there now. Just a blankness eerie as the end of a shotgun.

"I told you!" Sweeney crowed. "Remember Forrest Vai? Heidi must a thought he was her ticket out of here, but she pushed him too hard, or he flipped when he found out she was using him. Whatever, he got wire fever and went dancing with the Gatlings. And now she's got her claws in you, Tank."

Tank hadn't taken his scary-blank eyes off me. "You think I could get you out of here?"

It took me a few tries to get my throat to work. Even then, my voice sounded grated. "I don't need anybody's help. I can test out on my own. Unless you fools kill Mother and get the feds involved. Sweeney doesn't know what'll happen, nobody does. This blood feud could turn into a bloodbath. If Chazz decides he hates us more than he does the feds, you might never get out of Exile, even without me."

"We could all die?" Paolo turned to Sweeney. "And you're willing to take that chance?"

"All we have are chances," Sweeney said. "Better we kill that ringleader bitch and get out of this house than rot in here. But I guess that wrecks your plans to get into Heidi's pants."

Tank didn't acknowledge either of them. We stood staring at one another, as if we'd rewound all the way back to that first date, when we'd peered into one another's eyes and hit solid rock.

Not taking his eyes from me, Tank grabbed Paolo's collar. He whipped him around and pushed him toward the couch. "Back on watch," Tank growled. "And you," he said in Sweeney's direction. "Back. Off."

Tank reached for me. I flinched. He heaved a sigh and grabbed my sleeve, pulled me into the kitchen. Once we were out of sight, he let go. He stood about a yard away— like I was contagious. I thought of Father, Forrest. Maybe I was.

"Is it true?" he asked. "You think I'm your ticket out of here?"

I must've gone a little crazier, bloody images of Father and Forrest fusing in my head. I stuck out my chin and said, "Does it matter?"

"Maybe. If that's the reason we're dancing."

"You think I'd do that?" I brought my hurt wrist up to my chest, didn't pretend it was anything less than an accusation. "Fuck you to get out of Exile?"

"I might, if I were you," Tank said, and the words felt careful, measured. "It wouldn't make any sense. It's not as different Out There as you seem to think. But," he continued, despite my open scoffing, "if I were you ... if I thought it was the only way to get what I wanted. What I *thought* I wanted."

"The same way you'd kill Mother? If you were me?"

Tank nodded evenly, but his eyes weren't blank anymore. He knew I was going to spring something on him, and I grinned, grimly pleased that he was steeling himself against it. Against me. I worked up all the venom I could muster.

"But you aren't me," I said. "You're Tank Benavides, and before that you were Noé Benavides, and fuck knows who you were before that, 'cause unlike *me,* you got to start all over again. At age eighteen, after juvie, after foster care, after you killed *your* mom."

"What? How do ... What?"

His mouth worked for a few seconds, but he couldn't seem to breathe. He stopped to collect himself, and I was so vindictively proud I started to cry.

Tank's eyes were glossy, too, when he finally said, "You been talking to Puppy?"

"I am not fucking him!" Like saying it could prevent it.

Tank glanced at the ceiling, gave it a this-takes-the-urinal-cake smile. He sniffed. "Well, I guess he ain't got anything you want, yet."

"That's not why I'm here! Maybe at first, but not now. That's not why I'm with you!"

"'Course not." He looked at my wrist, not my face. "Now you're just trapped. Like the rest of us."

He stalked out of the room and down the basement stairs. A door slammed, and it sounded so final, I remembered my dream of Forrest, screaming his name through a locked door. Then I slammed my wrist into the counter to stop thinking at all.

Chapter Nineteen

I FELT MY WAY in the dark, fingers tracing dirt walls as I crept down, down the trench. I was making my way toward Father. What was left of him. My chest ached from sobbing.

Forrest caught up with me. I hadn't even known he was following. He tried to wrestle me from the trench, but his bullet-pocked hands couldn't grip. I whirled and punched. He smacked me, but it wasn't the knock on the chin that subdued me. His eyes looked wrong in his patchwork face: blue, not green.

Pounding. I thought it was my heart, or his, but the pounding came from the wrong direction. Something bit the inside of my elbow.

"Oww, fuck!" I said, and then I was awake.

On the kitchen floor, back to the cabinets, head slammed into a drawer pull. Paolo was straddling my legs, one hand still on my shoulder, the other on the inside of my arm. He'd pinched the ever-loving shit out of me.

"Oh, fuck no." I closed my eyes again. "Was I ...?"

Stomping up from the basement, Sweeney hollered, "Fuck yeah, you were sleepwalking again, you freak. Lemme guess which *S* you're missing." I opened my eyes as he swung into the kitchen. He scowled at me, then Paolo. "Dude," he said, slapping Paolo's head. "Get off her."

Paolo rolled off, trying to keep his weight off his bad foot. He pushed his shoulder against the oven and levered his way up.

Sweeney, fists at his sides, leaned over me. "You ever hear of locking your goddamn door? What the hell were you doing, anyway? Crawling 'round the floor, trying to tear up the lino ..."

Paolo braced himself against the counter and offered me a hand. I rolled the other way and scrambled up, avoiding their eyes.

"You okay?" Paolo said, breath ragged.

"Are you kidding me? No!" I pushed past them to escape the kitchen.

Sweeney dodged out of my path like I might spew pea soup. "Bad enough we gotta deal with those punks outside and your psycho mom, now we gotta worry about you attacking us in your sleep? Tank may've been willing to put up with your shit, but I ain't. You don't settle down, I'll fucking lock you in your room, you fucking wackadoo!"

"Sweeney!" Paolo tried following me. "Don't listen to him, Heidi."

"I'm not!"

I stumbled halfway up the stairs. Now that I was awake, my gross motor skills were perversely reluctant to cooperate. My deductive reasoning must've been on a ten-second delay, too, because it took that long for me to register the shrillness in Sweeney's voice. He was scared. Not because of me and my zombie antics, but because Tank hadn't come to the rescue. Sweeney went down to the basement to get him, but Tank had refused to come up ...

"Heidi," Paolo pleaded. "Wait."

"Leave me alone!" I yelled.

I went back to bed and cried. And I hated myself for crying, so I cried some more.

Paolo talked to me through the door. Each time he knocked, I threw something at it. Luckily, he gave up before I ran out of ammo. Later, I heard him rustling around in the study, and I wanted to tell him to keep his paws off my stuff. But more than that, I never wanted to speak to anyone again.

I lay there until I thought my bladder might explode, then I grudgingly used the toilet. Paolo took that as a signal, I suppose, because after laborious shuffling and a distant but acrimonious exchange with Sweeney, he hustled back upstairs and knocked on the door.

"What?" I said, slumped on the bed.

"I brought you a snack. Honey and apples."

"Leave it."

"No. I want to see you." Long pause. "C'mon, Heidi. We gotta talk. Sweeney's already taken one of Tank's shifts, and—"

"Why? What's wrong with Tank?" I said, moving to the door.

"He's in the panic room. I didn't know there was a fucking panic room. Haven't we been panicked for a while now? Anyway, he won't come out."

I glanced at the clock, didn't understand if it meant morning or night. Tried to remember what had happened after my fight with Tank: I'd slammed my wrist; I'd collapsed on the kitchen floor, sobbing; I'd stopped crying long enough to swallow the pills Paolo had given me. Ibuprofen, he'd said, but clearly not. I couldn't even be mad. I'd've slept forever if I could.

"What time is it?" I said, forehead to the door. "How long was I out?"

"You slept all day, most of the night. You probably needed it. And now you need to eat, so open up."

My hand was already on the doorknob, so why not? I peeked out at the apples—quartered, mottled red, drizzled with honey—and asked him, "Do you want to fuck me?"

Paolo coughed, tried to make it laughter. He cleared his throat, and I glanced at his Adam's apple, the spider webs laced over it, before lifting my gaze. He watched me like Tank had, waiting for me to spring something on him. It didn't make me proud this time.

Finally, Paolo tilted his head, tried a smile. "Is that a question or an offer?"

I rolled my eyes, reached for an apple. "Is it like Sweeney said? Are you only nice to me because you want to dance?"

He relaxed minutely and shook his head. "I'm nice to you because I'm a nice guy. And I like you ... And if you *did* offer, I wouldn't say no ... But you're with Tank. So it's kind of a non-issue. Right?"

I bit the apple wedge, listened to Paolo's short, careful sentences, and I wasn't sure—whether he was nice, whether he liked me, whether I was with Tank anymore, anything. My stomach cramped.

"Right?" Paolo prompted.

"How long's Tank been down there?" I asked.

≈

THE HOUSE ECHOED WITHOUT Tank, maybe like a hotel in the off-season. However he'd imagined the house fell short, while he'd moved within it, it had worked. Without Tank bracing its walls, filling its halls, it lacked—loud as a dropped coin never splashing in a well.

Near the end of my afternoon shift, the off-duty thugs climbed onto my parents' roof. That left five guys guarding the fence, but that was still too many, with Tank out and Puppy hurt. Sweeney had phoned Rain. Pops' crew still had half Tank's crew pinned. What's more, they'd jumped Moss and beaten 'em to a pulp and torched Jackson's house. Nobody was coming to our rescue.

I watched as Chazz's crew scuttled around on my parents' roof. *Parent's* now, to be more accurate. I'd missed Father's burn while I was doped and dreaming. Part of me was glad. Part of me didn't believe it, not until I saw the thugs up there, grimy from the ashes coating the shingles. They'd dropped their musical assault from ear-splitting to chest-beating, presumably so they could hear each other as they installed some bizarre home improvements. Sweeney clumped into the kitchen from the garage. I didn't want him near me, but I'd catch hell if I didn't mention the thugs' latest shenanigans. I called him over.

He stood beside the couch, chugging a bottle of water. He had a smear of dirt on his bearded jaw. "Metal brackets," he finally said. "What do you think?"

"I think brackets support shit, and those are some serious brackets."

Sweeney cursed under his breath, more creatively than with real anger or surprise. I chanced a closer look. The smear on his jaw was a bruise from Tank's punch the other night.

Perhaps drawn by our voices, Paolo limped down the stairs. "What's going on?"

Once we'd filled him in, he asked, "Shouldn't we get Tank?"

"Be my guest." Sweeney propped a boot on the footlocker and hunched over, forearm across his knee. "I've talked myself hoarse through the door down there, but I'm sure he'll come running out when you pretty please." He paused, didn't look at me when he added, "Maybe Heidi, though."

Before Paolo could hop on that bandwagon, I said, "He's got monitors down there. He knows what's going on. If he hasn't come out, he doesn't want to."

Sweeney pursed his lips in grudging agreement and scrubbed his head. He looked like a sad monkey. He mumbled about cleaning up and spur-jangled off.

Paolo flopped on the couch with me. "You should at least *try* talking to Tank. We can't afford to be divided now."

I smirked. "Status quo, baby."

I patted his knee—a silent "your turn"—and stood to leave. In one fluid movement he grabbed my waistband and pulled me into his lap.

"Doesn't have to be this way," he said, lips brushing my shoulder. "If you asked me to do something—anything—I'd bust my ass to do it. If you ask Tank to come up, how could he say no?"

I blinked at him, breath caught in my throat. Why did he and Sweeney think I had so much control over Tank? This whole femme fatale, power-through-sex thing? It worked so well, Tank had locked himself in the dungeon.

I reached back to pull Paolo's hand from my pants. He resisted, then saw it hurt my injured wrist. He let go of my waistband but curled his other hand over my knee, keeping me close.

"Have you met Tank?" I said.

"I've met you. And I've seen the way he looks at you. You could persuade him."

"*You're* his friend. Hell, you're the only one he didn't thrash the other night when I ran outside. Why don't you talk to him?"

"I would. But you're the one he had the fight with, you're the one sent him underground."

I squirmed at the phrase, imagined spiders and worms crawling all over Tank.

Paolo must've mistaken my squick for ambivalence. "Heidi, look, I'm confused, too. Any other time, I might not complain. I mean, I could never get this close if he were here. But we need all of us working on a way out, right? Whatever happens after that ..."

He rubbed his thumb along the inside of my knee. I squirmed again, this time equal parts squick and arousal. What was he implying? And why was it making me wet?

I pushed his hand off my knee. "I'll talk to him when I feel like talking to him," I said, jumping off his lap.

"Don't be stubborn, Heidi."

"Don't push me, Paolo."

I ducked into the kitchen, forcing him to choose between watching the feeds and harassing me. He let me go, but I hurried down the hall in case he changed his mind. The basement door stopped me. I really wanted to go down and talk to Tank. My heart threatened to burst through my chest if I refused. But I didn't want to run to Tank like a scared kid, and who knew what lures and innuendo I might spew in desperation? To hear Sweeney tell it, half the time I didn't even know I was working sex.

Instead, I forced myself to go out back. I sat in the nest of golden rectangles Tank had built, and I thought, *Fix me faster. Please.*

NIGHTS LATER, I GLASS-EYED the main feed, wringing my sore wrist to stay awake. We'd had to reorganize shifts, but I still got enough time to sleep. Problem was, I was afraid I'd sleepwalk. I didn't want to lock the door—what if Tank came up and couldn't get in?—so I tied one leg to the bed using a necktie. About as comfortable as you'd think.

Worse, the bed smelled like Tank. It made me so lonely and horny, I thought I'd never sleep again. Occasionally, I got up to work on my thesis, but then I'd remember Tank's face when he'd said my photos were only parts. Plenty of time to dissect that look now: revulsion, dismay, fear even. I assembled full-body portraits of Rob Lowe, Channing Tatum, Félix Rendón, but they seemed *less* real then, their bodies strangely blank, smooth, untested. Nothing like the men around me.

Tank's abandoned cell phone buzzed on the footlocker. Whoever was on watch was supposed to field those calls, but there hadn't been any in days. The phone claimed we were "Out of Service Area" more often than not. The fence or the feds fucking up our reception.

I snatched the phone and checked caller ID: Cantu. Finally!

"Hello?" I said, expecting Carlos, an update.

"Heidi! Oyes, chica, I got those UV tats I was telling you about."

I rubbed my eyes, felt whiplashed. "Romero?"

"Who else? You still at Tank's? I'mma come over and show you."

I bolted to my feet. "What? No! You can't! Chazz—"

"Chazz?" Romero snorted. "Fuck that overgrown gorilla. Can't keep me away from you."

"Romero, no!" I banged my shin on the footlocker, fought back a curse. "Have you been drinking? Where's Carlos?"

"Pues, working. Como siempre, mija." He spoke slowly, as if *I* were the drunk. "Algo de agua ... somewhere in the Outer."

"Again? And Sammy?"

"He's here. Dormido."

"You can't leave Sammy alone."

That, thankfully, seemed to sink in. "Then you come see me, baby. You come over."

I tugged at my earrings. If he didn't remember what was going on, he'd been partaking of more than his crew's Mexican moonshine. "I can't, Romy."

"Why not?"

I squeezed my eyes shut, took a deep breath. "You're messed up, Romy. Drink a detox and go to bed."

"Heidi ..." He said it with the Spanish intonation, soft and lazy as after sex. "You're so good. Always looking out for us. I mean, you can't cook, everything you make tastes like fideo ..."

"That's what Carlos taught me," I said, then shook my head. Might as well argue with Sammy.

He talked over me anyway. "... but I'll cook if you come back. Miss you so much, baby, all of us."

"Please, Romy." I stared at the tele—not that I could've said what I saw, all my attention willing him to shut up. "Please. Go to bed."

"Pero, te necesitamos, niña—"

"No, you don't."

"—Carlos the most. You know what you do to him—"

"Romy, shut up."

"Sabes que te ama."

Sweet Sue. He'd held it in for how many years, but he couldn't keep it to himself one more night?

"Stop it," I said. "You're always talking. You talk too much. I don't want to hear it. Drink your detox and go to bed."

"But it's not the same ..."

"No whining! And lie on your stomach. Don't you dare pull a Charlie Sheen on me."

"What? Wait!"

Hearing him so lost and confused, I softened a little. "I'll see your tats later, Romero. Okay? Now get some sleep."

"Wait, baby, wait—"

I hung up. And I turned off the ringer.

I SPENT THE REST of my shift blanked out, barely aware of the thugs' movements on the telewall. They could've strung up Red Sonja, and I might not have noticed.

I didn't need Romero drunk-dialing me with true confessions—I knew the boys cared for me; they didn't *need* me, not like Romy said—but having Carlos's feelings spelled out, obvious, unavoidable ... This thing I'd buried deep down in my stomach, in my lungs, in my stupid heart, all the way down into my bloodstream, where I didn't have to name it or face it—Romy, simply and brutally as ever, had dragged it to the surface.

I'd known the Cantus almost all my life. The last five years I'd spent most of my waking hours with them. And yet I'd never moved in with them, despite Sammy's begging and Carlos's unspoken agreement. I knew if I left Exile, Carlos would be devastated. That was why, after failing that last test, I'd broken up with them. I didn't trust myself. What if I asked Carlos, my buddy, the city liaison, to help me escape Exile? Whether he could or not, he'd try. And that wasn't fair; I couldn't do that to him.

And yet, I'd never stay in Exile, not willingly.

So I loved Carlos. I just didn't love him *enough*.

I caught motion out of the corner of my eye: Paolo shuffling into the bathroom. I sat straighter, smoothed out my expression in case the guilt corroding my insides showed on the outside.

Paolo emerged fifteen minutes later, freshly showered but bitching about the water pressure. I turned, neck creaking, eyes burning, and gave him a once-over. Habit.

A white T-shirt hung over his shoulder. I ignored his abs, tried to ignore the way his pelvic bones beckoned from his low-slung jeans. The line of ginger curls that started under his navel was impossible to ignore, though easy enough to roll my eyes at. But maybe because I was tired, seeing his good foot sticking out from his soft, ragged jeans—the rippling veins blue as denim—*that* triggered a pulse in my crotch. I scowled.

Paolo stopped in his tracks. "What? You should be thrilled to see me. I'm here to relieve you."

"I'll bet," I said, still scowling.

He grinned and walked over to the couch. "Come on, baby."

He took my hand and yanked me to my feet. Head reeling, I stumbled into him. My cheek pressed his still-warm, still-damp chest. I squeezed my eyes shut, clamped back the sudden urge to vomit.

"Whoa." He teetered, caught his balance, held us up. Hands cupping my elbows, he said, "You okay? Hey, look at me. Show me those Bambi eyes."

I fought to focus, to glare against the unwelcomed intimacy as he palmed my temples. I wished I wasn't propped up by his warm torso, that I couldn't smell his sweet, sandy scent under the skim of soap.

"When's the last time you ate?" he said.

I remembered Romy's crack about my cooking. My eyes watered. "Bite me."

Hands returning to my arms, Paolo lowered me to the couch. "You wait here." He tossed his shirt in my lap and hustled toward the kitchen. I threw his shirt on the floor and pawed water drops from my cheek.

He brought back a glass of orange juice fizzing from a detox tab, and a jar of peanut butter. I split-second considered—last time I'd taken medicine from him, he'd roofied me—but I drank the juice, half hoping I'd spew it back up all over him. The peanut butter was harder to get down, but he threatened to spoon-feed me.

"So," he said. "You're not eating. Are you sleeping?"

You try sleeping with one leg strapped to the bed, I thought. "Buzz off," was all I said.

He sat facing me, one hand on the back of the couch, the other on my knee. With his good foot tucked under his knee, his leg pressed a hot line against my thigh. "You better start taking care of yourself."

I sneered. "You'd better watch the feeds."

"Nothing's happening out there."

"Nothing's happening here, either." I pulled my knee out from under his hand.

"I wouldn't be so sure." He bumped his forehead against my temple, whispered, "I could pull you right into my lap. You're in no condition to fight it. And I don't think you want to."

Thankfully, I was weak and queasy. It kept me from soaking my panties. "Try it and die."

"Try and stop me." He licked his lower lip and smiled when my gaze followed his tongue. Smug bastard knew he'd won because he looked at my spoon, and ordered, "Eat."

Sweeney staggered in from the den, his yawn cut short when he saw Paolo crowding me.

"Sweeney," I said, relieved.

Paolo jerked back like I was a hill of fire ants.

I breathed deep, marshaling my resources to stand. "I'll put this away," I said, capping the peanut butter.

Sweeney followed me into the kitchen. He gripped the cupboard door when I tried to close it. "Really, Heidi? Really?" His beard shortened his overlong face, softened it. His eyes remained hard, yellow stones.

Fighting for control of the cupboard door, I ended up slamming it. "No, Sweeney. Not really!"

"Then what the hell?! What if Tank came up and saw that?"

"Saw what?"

"Puppy all over you and you not doing anything to stop it."

"I don't know, Sweeney. Could we be any more fucked? On a scale of one to ten, with one being we're stranded in a toxic fucking town with no hope of ever escaping and ten being we're stranded in said town with my fucking mother trying to kill us and my father dead and Tank throwing a tantrum because Puppy got his cooties all over me and ... and ..."

I held off a sob and sagged against the counter, rubbed the stupid tears off my shame-hot cheeks. Sweeney said nothing. He said nothing for so long I finally looked up, almost laughed when I saw how high his eyebrows had gone. His mouth hung open, soft and vulnerable in the depths of his beard. I hitched for breath.

"Relax, Sweeney. I won't tell Tank you made me cry. I mean, if he ever comes out of his pity party."

Hesitant, Sweeney lifted one hand like he might touch my shoulder. I turned to toss my spoon into the sink.

"Sorry," he said.

"Yeah."

When I turned 'round, he said, "No, I mean it. Not just

'bout this. 'Bout all a it. Your dad, the things I said. I'm sorry."

My stomach clenched at the mention of Father. But Sweeney was trying to make up, and I was so, so tired of fighting. I rubbed my nose on my good wrist. "Let's not get all sentimental," I said, forcing a smile.

"No, 'course not. That's for when I'm drunk."

Thankfully, his grin was more convincing than mine. I felt my wickedness rekindling.

"Think we can make vodka out of the quinoa?" I asked.

Chapter Twenty

THE NEXT DAY, AT the ass-crack of dawn to be exact, I said, "Screw insomnia," and returned to my thesis. But after desk sex, sitting in the study was as bad as lying in bed, so I transferred my text to the reader. I was heading downstairs to work at the dining table when Paolo hollered "Ho, crap!" from the couch.

I hurried downstairs to check the tele. Sweeney had already gotten there and swiped the remote from Paolo. He moved the picture to the center of the tele, magnified it.

In the smutty morning light the roof of my parents' house appeared to have grown a carpet. I squinted, and the carpet resolved into a tangle of rubber hose. Three people (including Thing One, a hockey mask pushed up on his head) stepped over and around the coils.

"What is that? What's Chazz carrying? What are they doing?" Paolo said.

"Compressed air tank?" Sweeney backed up to get a better look.

"It's a blowback tank from an old boiler," I said.

Chazz and another guy lowered the tank to the roof. The brackets bolted to the roof kept the rusty cylinder from rolling off onto the yard like the telescope the Things had fought over so long ago.

"He's used it before," I added.

"For what?" Paolo said.

"Air cannon."

Someone out of sight behind the house handed up a crate to Theo. He passed it to Chazz's minion and reached down again, this time coming up with a long PVC barrel. As he swept it through the air, its black eye glared at the camera.

I backed up to stand beside Sweeney. "It shoots tennis balls faster than five hundred fifty miles an hour. It blasts plastic water bottles through cinderblock. You don't want to know what it can do with a frozen Coke can at one hundred twenty psi."

"Actually, I kinda do." Sweeney tilted his head to study the contraption.

"Let me rephrase that," I said, suppressing a smile. "You don't want to find out when it's pointed at us."

He *tsk*ed wistfully. "Aim any good?"

I shrugged. "Good enough when he's aiming at shit in the alley behind the house."

The minion looked to Thing One for orders—Theo giving orders, Sweet Jaden Smith!—and kicked hose aside to make space for the crate. Theo notched the PVC barrel into a slot in the crate and pivoted the barrel, aiming at different parts of Tank's house. He gestured, and the minion hauled the crate a few inches this way, a few that, forward and back, before Theo nodded. Then Chazz and the minion pulled hammers from their belt loops and knelt to nail down the turret.

Sweeney threw the remote at Paolo. "Stay here." Ignoring Paolo's yelp of dismay, Sweeney turned, grabbed my arm, pulled me along as he jogged into the kitchen. "Go get Tank?"

It was a plea, not an order, and that alone was as good as a billboard: *Now Entering Very Deep Shit*. I shivered. "I'll try."

I ran for the basement. Sweeney ran to the garage. Behind me, I heard hammering. Even halfway down the stairs, I thought I heard it, then I realized it was my pulse ramming my eardrums.

"Tank!" My feet hit the cold cement floor, and I ran to the panic room, slammed a palm against the metal door. "Tank, you gotta come out. They're prepping a fucking cannon. You hear me?"

My hand stung from slapping the door, but the metal didn't so much as quiver. I didn't hear anything on the other side.

"Tank? Are you awake? Listen to me. You see the vidfeeds? You see that monster on my parents' roof? That can punch a hole through a window, even one of your windows. It can probably blast through the garage door. And if they breach the garage ... Damn it, Tank!"

I pounded the door with my fist. Could he hear me? Could he still be sulking? Or did he not care what happened to us? Tucked in there, he was safe enough.

Upstairs, Paolo yelled, "They're done hammering."

"Fuck! Tank! Enough of this hissy fit! This is serious!"

Overhead, Sweeney slammed the door connecting kitchen and garage, stomped into the living room. "Here!" Steel slapped skin; metal parts clicked. Great. The guns had come out.

"Heidi?!" Sweeney yelled. "You coming?! Tank?!"

I turned and stared at the ceiling. I didn't know whether to keep begging or go get armed.

"Your mom's outside," Paolo yelled.

I whirled and pounded the door. "Tank, you asshole, please! I'm sorry I want to get out of here so bad, I'm sorry I used my orphan eyes on you, I'm sorry I want to fuck you sixteen ways from Sunday and twice that on Tuesdays, I'm sorry I know your secrets, I'm sorry I can't help but scheme and connive and plot even when it doesn't do me any good, even when it's you—" My vision started to darken. Scurrying black spots spread across my sight, and I had to force myself to breathe.

"Heidi?" Sweeney's voice cut through the dark. He didn't sound panicked. Just a bit revved. "Could use a little help up here. You gotta be a better shot than Puppy."

"Tank!" I turned and kicked the door with my heel. "I'm sorry! But you're a miserable mess, too, you jerk!" I ran for the stairs.

"They're aiming for the front door!" Paolo yelled, and I hadn't gotten halfway up before metal punched metal, followed by a squealing shudder.

I ducked and looked behind me. Still nothing from Tank.

I stumbled up the stairs, hollering, "What was that? What got hit?"

"The garage door," Sweeney yelled back, laughter hinted at the end. I might've laughed, too, giddy with relief at my brother's bad aim, but the Stingray was in peril. I spun into the kitchen, where Sweeney peeked into the garage, a sawed-off tucked to his shoulder.

"It's holding. For now," he said, slamming the door. "But there's a dent the size of Albuquerque in it."

"And you know Albuquerque from your ass?"

Sweeney grinned and whipped a pistol from the back of his jeans, tossed it to me. I clapped it between my hands, instinctive, and hissed at the jolt to my hurt wrist. A Ruger, said the stainless steel slide. An ugly, snubby, black resin-gripped thing I couldn't quite get my hand around. Well, if I couldn't hold it well enough for shooting, I could always brain someone with it; fucker weighed about two pounds.

I followed Sweeney into the living room, Ruger pointed at the ground. I remembered hanging off Romy while shadier elements of the Cantu crew talked guns, remembered enough to expose the full ten-round clip and snap it back in before glancing up. Theo took up the whole telewall. The rising sun turned his hockey mask Phantom of the Opera as he prepped the air cannon for a second shot.

Paolo, eyes bright and wide, shotgun dangling from his hand, said, "How fast can he reload that thing?"

"Not fast," I said, estimating. "Five minutes?"

"Pan out," Sweeney said. "I can't tell where he's aiming."

Paolo adjusted the picture, and Mother leapt into view. Dark in battle gear in front of the house, craning her neck to watch Theo. More steel-toned streaks gleamed in her hair than I remembered. Her arms pumped as she flung orders that, for once, no one acknowledged. Everyone's attention was riveted to Theo.

The buckled garage door seemed to have altered my brother's strategy. He aimed the cannon barrel at the front door again, but he seemed to be looking at the garage. Hard to tell at that distance. And with the hockey mask.

There was a rifle propped against the stairwell. Sweeney swapped it with his sawed-off. "Five minutes?" he said, heading for the stairs.

"About," I replied.

Paolo had trouble dragging his attention from the vidfeed. "Where are you going?"

"You expect me to stand here and wait for him to bust a hole in the garage?" Sweeney jogged up the stairs. "I'm gonna go take the shit out. Guard the entry points."

Paolo's attention swung to me. "Take him out?" As if he hadn't heard right.

"Wait," I yelled after Sweeney. "He's ten years old!"

"He'll stay down if he wants to see eleven," Sweeney yelled back.

I felt Paolo's stare on me. I fiddled with the Ruger's safety; it was too stiff to do it more than a couple of times, and once I'd finished, it was like I'd used up all my brain power. When I said nothing else, when I didn't run after Sweeney, Paolo called, "You sure that's a good idea? What if you hit the air tank?"

"Boom." Sweeney's voice came from the study, in the vicinity of the sniper slits.

I fidgeted between kitchen and living room. Guard the entry points. I should've been standing in the doorway to the garage, but I felt tethered to the tele. I needed to see

Theo. Anyway, I didn't trust Paolo to guard the front door. I'd never seen him fight.

I smeared sweat from my forehead onto my shoulder, shook my right arm loose—damn heavy gun—before flexing, ready again. Paolo said something, but I ignored him. On the tele Theo reached back and down. From a ladder behind the house, a thug handed him fresh ammo: a steel canister slightly larger than a Coke can bulging with what I guessed was frozen water. Canister in his gloved hands, Theo came around the front of the cannon. He slid the can into the PVC pipe.

My stomach double-knotted itself. I shook my arms loose again. No sexy warmth unraveled my thighs now; I was tense all over. If Sweeney did take a shot, I might startle and blow a hole in the wall. I moved my finger from the trigger.

My brother scurried back behind the turret. He hunkered down and braced himself against the crate. He looked very small—like the ten-year-old he was. And this wasn't like what had happened with Thea. Sweeney had a rifle ... this would be deliberate ...

"No, wait," I said, a squeak not even Paolo heard. "We can't."

The shot glanced off the blowback tank. I jumped, teeth rattling. Chazz dropped belly-down on the roof. His minion ducked and whirled. Theo fell backward, started to slide down the slope of the roof.

"Oh, crap!" I raised my hand to my mouth. The scent of gun oil teased my palate.

Theo kicked a hole in the crate turret. His snagged boot kept him from surfing off the roof, and I nearly gagged with relief. Upstairs, Sweeney cursed.

While everyone else caught their breath, Theo wrestled himself into a sitting position. He reached and—"Stupid, stupid boy," I hissed. "Stay down!"—he twisted the tank's spigot.

Before Sweeney got off another shot, the cannon exploded. Plastic shards arrowed everywhere. Theo screamed, an arm flung up too late. I cringed, almost covered my eyes, but the Ruger bumped my cheek. PVC chips embedded my brother's mask, glinting like Thea's baby teeth. The minion screamed and started ... dancing, I thought. He hopped on one leg and slapped at his other thigh, as if he were on fire instead of stabbed with plastic. Idiotic, inevitable, he stumbled over the rubber hose and sailed off the roof. The thugs on the lawn scattered, shouting. The minion didn't get up.

Chazz had nearly rolled off the roof before grabbing a metal bracket. He sprawled, cheek plastered to the shingles, chest heaving, plastic poking from his leather jacket. Theo, still screaming, writhed on his back, boot hooked in the turret. I shivered, as if *my* bunching muscles could push the plastic shrapnel out of *his* skin.

A few thugs fled into the street. Grateful for the distraction, I tracked the movement to its source, felt a little less grateful.

Hands gripping her hair, head bowed, Mother groaned. Low at first, and I could only tell because of the way her shoulders shook. Fury spread through her body until she quaked. Then she lifted her head, opened her mouth, and I heard her *baying.* She hardly sounded human. The full-throated horror went on and on.

Scrambling movement on the roof commanded my attention again. Chazz had gotten to his feet. With one hand on the crate and the other on Theo's belt, he tried to free my brother without letting him slide off to crack his head open in the backyard.

Finally, Mother ran out of breath. She whirled around and shoved a straggling thug back toward the electrified fence, back on duty.

I sagged in relief. Then somebody fired—Sweeney, must've been—and the bullet zipped close enough to

Mother that she dodged behind a barricade. Before I could scream, two thugs guarding the fence shot back. Paolo and I flinched; but within seconds, Keith screamed, and the barrage stuttered to a stop.

My fingertips ached. I was clutching the Ruger tight enough to embraille the stippled grip on my palm. I gulped and knocked the back of my head against the door frame, trying to kickstart my brain. Man, Carlos was going to be pissed about the shooting.

Sweeney stumbled downstairs. He stopped on the landing, met my eyes. Wary. Bracing himself. "You see that?"

So he *had* taken the shot at Mother.

I nodded, numb but for a useless tingling in my fingertips, the ache in my wrist.

"We gonna have a problem?" he asked, face tight.

I shook my head, skin sweaty but cold. He relaxed and strode into the living room.

I glanced at Paolo. He looked at me—in my direction, at least. His blue eyes were glazed over like a train wreck survivor's. We stood there panting, the three of us, and said nothing. Not relieved. More stunned. By the explosion, yeah, and the fuckery of the guns, but more by the sudden absence of threat.

Beyond that stunning absence, I felt my toes dangling over an even deeper abyss.

Tank hadn't come out to save us.

≈

TWITCHING WITH ADRENALINE, SWEENEY and I left Paolo to watch the feeds while we reinforced the dented garage door. First, we wheeled the three motorcycles out the back and parked them under the deck.

As we returned to the garage, Sweeney stopped short, and said, "Wait a minute. Stop the fucking presses! Heidi's left the building."

I'd half turned at his faux-awed tone. Now I made a frog face and jabbed at his ribs. Hands greasy with motor oil, he grabbed my fist and pretended he'd topple me backward.

"Seriously," he said, releasing me smudged. "You never leave the house. Hardly ever left your parents', either. Hard to believe you want to get Out There so bad."

"I might go out more if I didn't have to worry about being mowed down in the street," I said, returning to the garage. "Or if the feds weren't eyeballing us all the time with their panopticons."

"Their pan what?"

"The watchtowers."

"I don't buy it. You ain't scared."

He gestured at Tank's six-foot-tall steel tool chest. I nodded, and we started rolling it from its pride of place against the back wall.

"You're tough as any mutant here," he continued, as we pulled the chest outside. "Tougher than some."

I blinked, disconcerted by the compliment. We had to finesse the chest over a gap in the concrete, and after that, Sweeney motioned for a break. I asked him, "Don't you want to leave Exile?"

"You assuming I can?" He appeared to be squinting at me. Then I realized he was smiling, the tweak of his mouth obscured by his deepening beard.

"Aww, baby, you're dumber than dirt," I said, absurdly proud when I got him to laugh. "No, this is purely hypothetical."

"Oh, *hypothetically*." He finished chuckling. "Well, my folks never beat me too bad when I was a kid. Doesn't seem asking too much that I stick around, look after them when they're old, you know? Then there's Serena. She's smart, pretty, lets me in her bed regular. At least—" he cupped his crotch, adjusted himself as I sighed in exasperation "—she does when I'm not stuck here. And thanks to Tank, I got work when I want it. Got a bike for fighting when I don't.

I've got my health more or less, except for these spots on my X-rays that ain't done nothing in years. Scintillating conversation with you." He shot me a wink. "Way I figure, lots of folks don't have half as much—even Out There."

"But some folks have more." I thought of med school, cineplexes, art museums, bookstores, coffee shops, bookstores *with* coffee shops. I thought of mountains and canyons and volcanos and skyscrapers and the ocean ... "Don't you want more?"

He shrugged. "I ain't greedy."

Amazingly, it didn't sound accusatory.

I started pulling my end of the chest again, and he followed my lead. "You trying to convince me to stay?" I asked.

"Don't think I got to. You been spinning in circles, tighter and tighter, for years now. Since you were seventeen, I bet. Here's good," he said, stopping, setting the brake. "You'd be gone by now if you could, right?"

I nodded, gaze skirting his as we returned to the garage to deal with the Stingray.

"The people on the other side of the trench?" he said. "They're as messed up as we are. Don't you watch the news?"

"Of course, I do," I said. "But a lot of that's theater. The media make it look worse than it is for ratings."

"You sure about that?"

We put the 'Ray in neutral, tucked our shoulders under her roof, and coaxed her front fender up against the wall. Meanwhile, I thought about Tank's old scars. I thought about Tank and Paolo tossed around like three-card monte in foster care. Maybe Sweeney was right. But then I thought about Theo's thumbless paws, Thea's jagged baby teeth, the Cantus' cousin ET with her open, anencephalic skull. I thought about Sammy, taller than his brothers but brain like a seven-year-old's. I thought about how Mother changed after the Spill and how Father did, too, but slower, and how Forrest turned himself off ... I forgot to say anything.

"Get the kill switch?" Sweeney said.

I did and then the only light came from the open back door.

Sweeney jammed the garage door by wedging a long pipe between the rollers and the tracks. If the thugs tried to lever the door up, it wouldn't budge. We retrieved the tool chest and rolled it flush against the dented door. In addition to the Albuquerque-sized dent, a scattering of hobnail bumps pitted the door, but it held. No holes.

I brought Sweeney a ladder, then spotted him as he looped titanium rope through the garage door tracks. He was odiferous, but so was I from the fight-or-flight sweat.

"You think Tank'll mind a little redecorating?" he said.

"He didn't mind an air assault."

I wondered what Tank was doing down there. Unable to work, lift weights, or run, probably stuck on a cot, head next to a composting toilet ... It sounded like juvie all over again. And he was punishing himself that way to get away from me.

"You think he'll ever come out?" I said.

"'Course, he just needs time. How he is."

"But how do we even know he's down there? You sure there's not a trapdoor or a secret passage he used to escape?"

Sweeney paused, biceps flexed. He shot me a radioactive glance.

"Okay," I said, arms crossing. "But what if he's hurt?"

"Don't be stupid." Sweeney shook his head, went back to cinching the rope. "Ain't room down there to slip and fall, let alone get up the momentum to brain yourself."

"No, I mean ..." Suddenly, I felt Forrest breathing down my neck. I realized I was hugging myself. "What if he *hurt* himself?"

Sweeney slowed, gave the knot a last tug before hopping off the ladder. Quickly, as if to paper over the silence, he said, "Tank? Please. When he gets pissed, he goes off by himself for a while. But we're stuck in his house, so where's he got to go?"

"Doesn't he fight when he's mad?" I watched Sweeney heft the ladder to the other side of the tool cabinet and climb up again. "Isn't that what the street wars are for?"

"Naw. That's more like a timed, pressure-release thing. He goes into the street wars cold ... calculating."

The word rattled around my head for a minute, circling like a ball bearing going down, down, down a funnel until it plopped. "Was Tank calculating when he killed William? Did he do it on purpose?"

"No, Heidi. I'm sure it was pure *chance* your brother's neck got in the way of Tank's *axe*."

I felt like shaking him from the ladder. "You know what I mean."

He smiled, because yeah, he did; he was messing with me. "Tank might keep a mental list of folks who don't deserve their organs," he said, returning to his task. "Keeps it simple on the street, y'understand. But he didn't *plot* to kill William."

"Serena thought he killed William for me," I said archly. "Where'd she get that idea?"

"Probably one of those stalker romances she watches on the chick flick channel."

"I always knew she had terrible taste."

He started to nod, then caught on. "Hey!" He made to kick me, but I knocked his boot aside easy. "*Any*way," he intoned. "Good luck or bad luck, that's all it was. Luck."

"If you say so." I believed him, though. By some creative logic that'd never hold up in court, I figured, if Tank hadn't set out to kill William, then it was less likely he'd killed his mom. I wanted to believe that more than anything.

"He was glad when you tracked him down, though," Sweeney added. "He's got a soft spot for ya. Why, I'll never understand."

"Moxie," I reminded him.

"Moxie," he repeated, jumping down. He busied himself with closing up the ladder. "So if he ever comes back up, if we ever get out of here, maybe you won't badger him about Out There? I mean, I don't know what happened to him, why he'd want to stay here, but I'm sure he's got his reasons."

I nodded, quirked my cheeks. "Be nice if he told us some."

"Shit, don't I know it," he said, avoiding my eyes.

≈

INSIDE, I GRABBED A soda. I'd've preferred water, but we were running low on the boiled stuff.

"Any news?" Sweeney hollered.

"They hauled away that one dude's body," Paolo said.

I followed Sweeney into the living room, stiffened when I saw Paolo standing at the table, holding my thesis.

Paolo looked up at me. "Who's Hemsworth, and why'd you write five pages about his widow's peak?"

"No word from Carlos?" I said, plucking the reader from his hand.

"Nope."

"Not even to yell at us?" I said.

"Finally!" Sweeney said, standing next to me. "An upside to no phone service."

I bent one leg behind me and kicked his rear. "Maybe he doesn't have anything to say," I retorted over Sweeney's half-hearted curse.

"After all that shooting?" Paolo said. "The feds must be chewing him out. Only a matter of time 'fore he passes it on."

I shook my head. "The feds don't care. What's it matter if they're going to wipe us off the face of the earth? And soon."

Paolo scoffed at what he thought was the usual Exile paranoia. But Sweeney, eyebrow raised, asked, "You serious?"

"It's the only thing that makes sense." I chugged the last of my soda. "Remember last time we started shooting? Two months ago, they would've torn Carlos a new one for that. Instead, they let it slide. Meanwhile, the borders keep getting tighter and tighter. The day I met Tank I was walking down Gatling Drive, and the alarms went off for nothing. At Mute's, Cam'n'Zak said they couldn't get within three feet of Gatling Drive without setting off the alarms. And Pops' boys said my father didn't even get that close before the Gatlings got him."

With Sweeney's eyes riveted to me, I spewed every detail Tank and I had been hiding from him and Paolo. As I explained, Paolo tuned in, began to grok how serious I was. Sweeney's posture stiffened while mine wilted.

"They're trying to get us to riot," I finished, weary yet strangely certain. "Then they'll fire up the Gatling guns and send in stormtroopers. Kill as many of us as they can, jail the rest, commit 'em, I don't know. We're an embarrassment, not to mention a money suck."

"When'd you figure all this out?" Sweeney said.

"I don't know." I wondered if he was mad. I would've been if I'd thought he'd been holding out on me. "Tank and I figured some things, me and Carlos put together other stuff. And I've had plenty of time to think, you know? Things make sense now ..." Now that Tank wasn't around to torque my sex drive into overdrive. Now that I wasn't wasting ninety-eight percent of my brain power trying to weasel out of Exile.

Sweeney must've figured I was beating myself up enough because he settled for fist-bumping my shoulder. "Go get some rest, girl. You look like hell."

"Still better than you," I muttered, automatic.

Upstairs, I lay down but couldn't rest. I was too sugar rushed from soda, too amped from the gunplay and the feds' machinations. And too scared. Theo could've been killed. Sweeney had shot at Mother. If Tank wasn't going to help us break siege, I had to think of something. No reason for anyone else to die. No reason for Sweeney and Paolo to starve in here because of me, because of my dead brother's dumb crew.

Maybe I could surrender. Go out and tell Chazz I'd be his medic so long as he kept Mother away from me. Of course, he'd want access to more than my medical skills. He'd probably expect the whole crew to get an all-access pass to my ass. Didn't matter. While I distracted Chazz's crew, hashing out deets for an arrangement that'd never happen, Sweeney and Paolo could scale the back wall and make a run for it. Well, Sweeney could. Paolo would rip open his stitches again, possibly break a leg trying to get over the wall with his bad foot. Sweeney would have to help him—if I could convince Sweeney to leave Tank behind.

The idea of ditching Tank opened up a black pit in my gut. But I guessed that was how he wanted it.

And me? Maybe I could hold Chazz and company off until ... what? Sweeney came back to help? But if Tank was done with me, wasn't his whole crew? The Cantus then. I could drag out the negotiations with Chazz. The longer my surrender took, the more likely they'd be to hear about it, come and get me. But what if Chazz's crew was still toting their guns, still itching to see insides? I might be igniting a whole new feud. And sweet Sue, when would the Cantu boys stop suffering for my mistakes?

All right, who knew if Sweeney'd go for this plot, anyway? First things first. Stop stinking up Tank's bed and go take a shower. I shuffled to the bathroom, peeling off clothes. But when I turned the knob, the pipes shuddered. A blast of rusty water shot from the showerhead, then dribbled to a dirty stop.

Damn it.

≈

258

HEAD SINKING TO THE back of the couch, Paolo groaned. "Please tell me you're shitting me."

"Didn't know you were into that sort of thing." I noticed I'd mis-buttoned the fresh shirt I'd yanked on to come downstairs, and turned away to fix it.

Paolo said, "How can you even ...?" and from the strain in his voice, I knew he was craning to look at me where I stood, near the kitchen. "What are we going to drink, how will we shower—"

"What do you care?" Sweeney said. He was in the kitchen, stirring a pot of quinoa to see if all the mango juice concentrate had been absorbed. "With your busted foot, you sit around in the A/C all day."

"But you don't," Paolo retorted. "You're out in the sun all day or greasing up in the garage. And I don't even want to think about flushing."

"'Stead of bitching, why don't you come up with a plan?" Sweeney hollered.

I finished fussing with my shirt and turned to see Paolo limping to the table. Hopefully, that meant less yelling. After my panicked plotting upstairs, my blood pressure was high enough.

"What if we cut the power to the panic room?" he said. "Then Tank would have to come out, right?"

"You seen any wires to that room?" Sweeney stepped toward the dish cupboard, but I waved him back to the stove, got out the bowls myself. "For that matter," he continued, "have you seen any circuit breakers? 'Cause I've only seen one for the garage."

"Okay, well," Paolo said to me, "what if Carlos cut the power to the house. He can do that, right?"

"Well, yeah," I said slowly.

"Man, think!" Sweeney said, slamming his spoon on the counter. "This is Tank we're talking about. He's probably got a generator in the panic room."

"You're assuming we can reach Carlos," I said, handing

Sweeney a bowl. "It's been days since we've gotten a call in or out. Even if he did cut the power, how long before the thugs realize our security's down and attack?"

"There's still more of them than us," Sweeney reminded him.

"Well, what about Rain and the others?" Paolo said.

"What about them? We supposed to use mindpowers to communicate with them?"

"Sweeney," I said. Warning and plea.

"Don't mom voice me," he said. "Screw it, I ain't even hungry anymore."

After he'd slammed out the back door, I dished out the quinoa, handed a bowl to Paolo.

"I'd better get back to the feeds," he said, hobbling toward the living room.

I started to sit at the table, but Paolo said, "Hey, come keep me company. Or are you pissed at me, too?"

I could've been. That whole force-feeding me thing the other day? But then I'd been upset about Romy's phone call, cranky, and exhausted. Maybe I'd misread things.

"No, not mad," I said slowly. In my hurry to get downstairs and report the water situation, I hadn't bothered with a bra. Now I was very aware of the button-down shirt brushing my nipples, the cool air sneaking up the leg holes of my boxers.

Paolo tilted his head to look at me. Stingy lips slightly parted, eyebrows raised quizzically. "Then is it because I'm watching *Little Orphan Annie* in Spanish?"

I laughed a little, shaking my head. It didn't matter what I was or wasn't wearing—I wasn't going to *do* anything—so I joined him. As we chewed in silence, I checked the feeds alongside the dubbed cartoon. Two thugs were playing a painful version of flashlight tag.

After a few minutes, Paolo set his bowl in his lap. "You know, that rule about not jumping the back wall, that's Tank's rule, not ours."

I threw him some serious side-eye. "He's your *chief.*"

"Yeah, but if you and me even *try* to jump the back fence? I bet that'd get Tank out quick, me running off with his girl."

I cocked an eyebrow at him. "I wouldn't count on it. Not if it's Tank you're really after."

He chuckled low enough to make me shiver. "Sweetheart," he said, squeezing my thigh, "I'd love to run away with you. But what I'm after is a prison break. If there's anything we can do to get Tank out here strategizing with us, shouldn't we do it?"

I thought about it. And I thought about the healed scars on Paolo's fingers, how much friction they could create. In a weak-willed compromise, I jogged my leg, and said, "I've had enough death-defying adventures for today, thanks."

"Maybe tomorrow?"

I didn't think Tank would care if I turned myself over to Chazz, much less jumped the wall with Paolo. But the convo was making me nervous, so anything to shut him up. "Maybe," I grunted.

"Fair enough." Paolo's focus shifted to the screen. His hand did not shift from my leg.

We lapsed into silence.

What lying in bed could not achieve, the sweetened grain heavy in my belly did. Eventually, eyelids drooping, I leaned forward to set my bowl on the footlocker. And pressed my breast to Paolo's knuckles. He gave an appreciative murmur. I sat back and smacked his chest. It'd been an accident, but no use denying the sneaky warmth spreading from my cunt. He chuckled again, his hand on my thigh, stoking the heat. I thought about telling him to move his hand. But it felt good to be touched, and I was warm and full; and he smelled like sweet sand I wanted to roll in.

"I know I'm comfy," Paolo teased. "But you should sleep with me, not on me."

I blinked, lifted my head from his shoulder. *Danger, Will Robinson!* I hadn't meant to doze off.

"I can sleep near anywhere," I said, scooting to the other end of the couch. "When I was little, I slept in closets, cupboards, the dryer. Even under the house."

He started to smile, but paused, confused. "You're kidding, right?" When I shook my head, he said, "Why?"

"William was a biter." Why I was telling Paolo, I don't know. Maybe just 'cause I was so strung out. "He liked to sneak into my room and chomp on me."

"No shit?"

Paolo sounded disgusted, but that didn't make sense. This couldn't be the weirdest thing he'd ever heard, not the way he grew up? And when had I closed my eyes again? Yawning, I sat up to show him the Morse code of old stitches on the inside of my calf.

"Used to drive Father crazy. He never knew where he'd find me passed out. First thought was always 'She's dead!' Wishful thinking, I guess."

Paolo leaned over and touched my leg, squeezed it to see the scars better. "Crazy."

"Not the craziest. Not by far." My eyes were crossing, I was so tired. I wasn't getting back upstairs tonight, but maybe I could get to my side of the couch. "Can I have my leg back?"

"Wouldn't you rather wrap it around me?" he said.

"Right." And I meant it sarcastic, but then the rest spilled out. "Maybe once you've broken me out of Exile."

"So it's a deal?" He kissed my calf.

My heart did something, skipped a beat or doubled up. Whatever it was, I needed more space. "Shut up," I said, and put my head on the arm of the couch, so our faces weren't so close.

"Come on, Heidi. You lure Tank back upstairs, we break out, and if he doesn't take you away from all this, I will. Deal?"

Did he mean it? Or was he too stupid to know not to joke? Or had I fallen asleep again?

"How?" I said, searching his eyes for the catch, some sign I was dreaming.

"We'll worry about that after we get out of here."

He ran his hand higher up my leg, and I shivered. I'd been right about the friction of those scarred fingers.

"Heidi, Tank ditched you. And he'll do it again. You know he's got a life Out There. Once we've broken out, he's going right back to it."

My chest ached like he'd poked his fingers in my heart. "You don't know that."

"I do. I know where he comes from. He can't stay in one place, he can't trust people, and it's not your fault, but after this fight? He won't help you, Heidi."

I closed my eyes to avoid the intensity of Paolo's gaze. But then I was alone in the dark with his stroking hands, his throaty words.

"You need him, and where is he?" he said. "You need something right now, don't you?"

My head wobbled—a nod if I'd admit it. I shivered again, famine between my legs, a black hole in my heart. I wanted. So much, so badly, more than I could ever say. More than his body or mine. More than my parents' house, this smoke-cloaked radius, this town with its three shrinking borders, this slow-motion death spiral. More than I could imagine—I just wanted ... more. I wished he'd crawl on top of me, hold me down, fuck me into the couch springs before the need swept me insane.

"Your skin, you're on fire," Paolo said, kneading my thigh. "And where's Tank?"

The cliché afforded me a streak of lucidity. I cleared my throat, opened my eyes. "Chazz could set fire to the house, and you wouldn't notice."

I meant to glance at the tele to make my point, but I couldn't pull my gaze from Paolo. Far as I got was the spiderweb over his carotid, his heartbeat throbbing there.

"Would *you* notice?" he said.

Only if the fire brought Tank back to me, I realized. My body was a traitor. But *only* my body. I tried to pull away. Paolo's grip tightened enough to hurt, and he raised one eyebrow: *You really want to test me?*

I didn't. Because that would mean admitting the conversation was worth fighting over. All I wanted was to fall sleep and pretend the whole thing had never happened. I forced myself limp, and his hand relaxed, slid down my leg, wrapped snug around my ankle. Better. My blood stopped pulsing in my clit, some of the screaming need abated. I could live with the rest; I'd been doing it all my life.

I huffed and flopped onto my side. "I need to sleep. You need to watch the feeds. Try not to get us killed, dumbass."

Chapter Twenty-One

Sweet William, two years old, grinning at me like a cannibal clown.

That's what I saw every time I closed my eyes, every night after he bit me. I'd sleepwalk to new hiding places, and I'd sleep better ... for a while. Once I woke up in the truck bed as Father was driving to the junkyard. When I knocked on the rear window, he nearly ran off the road. But the absolute worst, last straw was when I burrowed in under the back porch.

That morning, early spring, I woke with dirt musty-soft beneath my cheek. Eyes still closed, I smiled into the cool dark, pleased as Goldilocks to have finally found the right bed. Safe from William and out of Father's way. Free to sleep until refreshed, free to wake up on my own.

Then something tickled my foot.

William! I thought. *William's gonna eat my toes!*

I bolted up, slammed my head on the underside of the house. White fireflies swam around my face.

I fell back, flailed, tried to backstroke away. But the tickle advanced up my leg, multiplied, covered *both* legs. I screamed, feeling jointed ... *things* ... scurry up beneath my pajama pants. I couldn't roll over, not in that tight space, so I kept scrabbling backwards. I slammed my head against foundation posts, water pipes, cobwebbed planks. I couldn't see behind me, but I couldn't stop, and I couldn't shimmy my way out. Was I going in circles? Where was the porch?

My hands squished in something. I slapped at my pants, tried to scrape the slime off my hands, the tickling whatever-they-weres from my legs. Under my grody fingers, I felt distinct crunches. That's when I completely lost my shit.

"Whoa, whoa, Heidi! Hush!"

The words cut through the black static and brought me back. I shivered in my parents' backyard, the crew-cut grass needling my back. My pajamas were ripped open and studded with smashed spiders. Father crouched over me, his chest bare. He was using his T-shirt to scrape jointed legs and worm pulp off me. My head throbbed like a soccer ball.

"Daddy?"

I reached for him, cringing, ready for him to recoil, slap my hands away with his ruined shirt. Because that's what he did. But instead, instead of his grunt of disgust—"Ugh! No! Damn it, Heidi, you'll be the death of me!"—firm hands clutched my shoulders, shook me.

"Heidi, wake up!"

I blinked, still shivering, but I wasn't on the ground, naked. I was on a couch, my sweaty shirt pasted to me. And it wasn't Father—no, of course not—kneeling between my legs, holding me up. Father was dead. But Father's face wouldn't get out of my head.

"Shhh," whispered the blur above me. "A bad dream, that's all. Don't wake the others."

Carlos? I shivered as my eyes slid shut. Then "the others" were Romero and Sammy asleep in their room.

I felt a kiss on my damp forehead. I tilted my face up: *More?* The kisses tickled down the bridge of my nose, brushed one cheekbone, then the other, nudged open my mouth, licked heat inside.

"You okay?" he asked against my lips.

"Cold," I stuttered.

"I'll warm you up, but you gotta calm down."

I sagged a little, relaxing. "But," I said, because something was still ... off.

"No 'but.'" He pressed his thumb to the dip in my lower lip, eased me back. "Be good for me. Lie down. That's it." He shifted, rubbed warm circles on my chest with one hand, stroked up and down my thigh with the other.

"But ... wrong," I whined, drifting. "Something ..."

"No, I got you. Everything's good." He shushed me again. "I'll make you feel good."

Spanish, I thought. Carlos would be speaking Spanish.

And then I slept again.

I CREPT DOWN THE basement stairs, which I knew was wrong because our house didn't have a basement, but I had to get away from William. He was in my room, in my bed, his hand under the sheets, stroking my leg, preparing to strike, so I rolled out of bed and tiptoed through the moonlit room, blue as a bay I'd never seen. William moled under the sheets, looking for me, a piece to bite, so he didn't see me in the hall, didn't hear my feet on the stairs to the basement we didn't have.

I crept through the dark, one hand frail in front of me, but I knew my way, so I wasn't scared until a light flashed. Something huge blocked me at the foot of the stairs. I blinked, blinded, hand going up to shield my eyes.

"Please," I said. "Let me through."

I tried to inch around the shadow, stubbed my toes on rock. The shadow rumbled, and I remembered Father, how he yelled at me for sleeping under the house, so I tried to explain. "But William's in my bed, and when he doesn't find me, he's going to scream for Mother."

I looked behind me, and it was too late. Mother was coming. She was the blanket of tarantulas that would hold me tight while William crept closer and closer, she would soak up the blood he spilled. I opened my mouth to scream, turned to run ...

Tasted blood.

My head ached. My face. My mouth.

Wait a minute, I thought. *This is familiar.*

I gingerly touched my cheek, swallowed blood. I stood at the foot of the basement stairs, one hand out to keep my balance.

I looked up. "Sleepwalking?" I asked, mush-mouthed.

Tank nodded, a dark cloud in the fluorescent brightness.

"And you slapped me again?"

"Yeah."

I wobbled my jaw, tongued the cut inside my cheek. "And what? You figured you might as well get in a good one?"

He shrugged. At his side he shook his left fist open. "Most of us got it coming, anyway."

I guessed I was lucky it'd been a slap, not a punch. I nodded and swallowed more blood. Still dazed, like a neuron-fried lab rat. "Was I screaming? Is that why you came out?"

An expression passed over his face faster than I could decode it. "Go back to bed, Heidi."

He turned away, and my heart seized up.

"Come with me," I said.

He stalked toward the open panic room. "Go upstairs. To the bedroom," he said, verbal underscore. "And lock the door behind you."

"But how will you get in?"

He paused, head cocked like he couldn't believe what I'd said. "I ain't gonna."

"Tank, wait!"

He entered the panic room, and I swear I tasted my heart. I stumbled forward, synapses smoking as I beat my brain for the words to make him stay.

"Noé!"

He turned around, murder in his eyes. "Don't. Don't you dare!"

"Why the hell not?" He was looking at me. Relief loosened my tongue, let the crazy come spilling out. "Thanks to Sweeney, you know every punk I've ever fucked. You killed my brother, you know my bra size, and I can't even call you by your given name?"

"Fine. What?" Like each syllable cost him a pound of flesh.

I wavered. Had I hurt him that much?

"I just ..." I took a deep breath. "Sweeney was wrong. If you wanted to leave, if you asked me to go with you, I'd have told you about my three *S*s. Maybe you could've helped me, vouched for me, smuggled me out of here, I don't know, but I never would've pushed it. I thought about it, yeah, of course, but I couldn't bring it up. I couldn't do it."

"Yeah? And why not? 'Cause you cared so much?"

I care now! I wanted to scream. But he wouldn't believe that. He was too mad.

"I ... no. I got distracted. Because I don't plan well—can't you tell?—and because I'm a coward. Because ..." My voice faltered, my throat giving me one last chance to shut up. "Because," I insisted. "The last person I even *thought* of asking killed himself."

Tank frowned, not quite meeting my eyes. "Forrest Vai?"

I nodded. Wished the name back from Tank's lips. Wished it was still my private pain.

"You don't think he ..." He trailed off like fingers skipping over a bruise. "... because you *thought* about asking him."

"No? Well shit, Tank, thanks for clearing that up. Now I can stop dreaming about him. I can stop sleepwalking and trying to save him, stop cutting him down and digging him up and stitching him back together—"

Tank recoiled, a tension more than a movement, and I slapped my hands over my mouth. *Creeping Cary Grant, get ahold of yourself, Heidi.* I took a minute to breathe. When I almost trusted myself, I uncovered my mouth.

"Tank, you don't know. I came so close to asking him. But it's like he already knew. And instead, he told me he had something important to do when he went back and not to feel bad."

Tank shook his head. "You can't blame yourself. People do what they do."

"People do what they do?" I almost laughed. Or cried. "Where did you study philosophy? University of Popeye?"

He shook his head but stepped closer, gaze cutting. "Didn't your friend's death teach you anything?"

Hearing Forrest called my "friend" threw me. Everyone else called what me and Forrest did "dancing" or "fucking." Like you couldn't fuck a friend.

"Um?" I said, trying to focus.

"The fact that Forrest made it out, like you want to, but he killed himself, anyway? What does that tell you?"

"That ... the psych assessment is bullshit?"

A ghost of a smile curled under his scruffy cheeks. I breathed a little easier. He didn't smell bad for how long he'd been down here: sleep and a faint musk under the residue of antibacterial wipes.

"What I meant," he said, "is that it's not that different Out There."

"How can you say that?" My shriek echoed off the concrete walls. "I would love to live where I can cross the street without getting knifed or shot or bludgeoned or run over. I'd love to see a real movie in a real movie theater with real butter-flavored popcorn. I want to go to med school, I want to walk into a bookstore—better yet, a library!—and smell the books. I want to see your buildings, Tank, and skyscrapers, the fucking beach—"

"And yet you think," Tank said, stepping closer, "in that same Out There fantasy world, I killed my mom? When you were nosing around my past and talking to Puppy behind my back, didn't that world sound strangely familiar? You think the bastards Out There have to pass your 4-S test?"

I remembered Tank's circle scars, remembered Sweeney insisting the same thing: it's not that different. My blood felt hot, poisoned in my veins. But if I wasn't fighting to get out of Exile, why was I fighting at all?

Before futility clogged my throat, I said, "We weren't talking behind your back. Paolo, he just slipped, all right? And I only went nosing into your past because you scared me. You started talking worse than an Exile, all that 'let's kill your mom' and 'it was the best thing I ever did'—"

Tank's eyes widened. "I didn't say that!"

"—and then I found out Noé Benavides didn't exist before age eighteen—"

"I didn't kill my mother! I hardly even saw her after I turned seven."

"Well, why not?"

"Because CPS took me away from her!"

"Finally, we're getting somewhere!" I said, arms wide. "Now why?"

Tank yanked off his T-shirt, pointed at the scars on his side. "Her fucking boyfriend."

I didn't speak. Couldn't. My heart felt heavy as cinderblock.

"Fucker didn't even smoke cigars," Tank said, teeth gritted. "Only bought 'em 'cause they made bigger burns."

"And your mother didn't stop him?" I thought vaguely of Father.

"She didn't know. At least, that's what she told Child Services." He twisted his shirt in his hands. The muscles in his arms and chest rippled, as if he were still trying to escape the burning. "Same as when they asked about the neighbor kids using me for shoplifting, sending me out on drug runs."

"How old were you?" It didn't matter, but I wanted to keep him talking.

"I don't remember. Five? Little enough nobody thought to look under my hoodie. They'd ruffle my curls, chuck me under the chin. 'Cheer up, kid, nothing can be that bad.'"

Shit, I'd have shaved my head, too. "But someone figured it out?"

He nodded. "Neighbors finally got busted. I was there, made a run for it. A cop grabbed me, sank his fingers into a fresh burn ..." He shuddered, pulled his shirt back on. "I passed out."

"And they took you away, you never saw your mother again?"

"Couple times. Wish I hadn't." He crossed his arms. "She disappeared when I was ten. It was easier that way, for both of us."

I nodded, processing.

"Anything else you want to know?" he said, grudging but resigned. "Any other wounds you want to fuck?"

I deliberated, wondering whether to push my luck, and then, before I was quite done, I asked, "Who's Jenna?"

He paled under his beard. But tough guy, he kept his eyes locked on mine. "How do you know—"

"You talk in your sleep."

His eyes widened again; his cheeks went slack.

"Not a lot," I said, seeing how upset he was. "We can start a sleep disorder group like AA. Now, tell me, who's Jenna?"

He shook his head. "Hang around long enough," he said, eyebrows sinking to a defensive ridge, "you'll probably find out."

"Really." I tongued the cut in my mouth, not subtle.

He rolled his eyes. Under other circumstances, it would've been funny to see him reduced to such an adolescent expression. "She fostered me when I was fourteen, okay? She was twenty-one, hardly an adult herself. I was her 'favorite.'" The way he said it, I heard the ironic quotes. "I'd never been anyone's favorite before. It was nice ... at first."

"And then?" I prodded.

"And then it wasn't! And when I asked the social worker to move me, Jenna was furious. I'd been in so much trouble by then, and I was big, near six feet already. People looked at me and saw the scars, these hands like shovels, shoulders like a linebacker ..."

I remembered his reaction to my thesis pictures. The parts, not wholes. My stomach tried to curl in on itself.

"It was her word against mine ... not hard to see why I ended up in juvie." He made a noise like laughter, eyes shining with something else. "You know she came to visit me? The only visitor I ever had, and I refused to see her."

He scrubbed his hand over his head, surveying the corners of the room, the ceiling. I waited, stomach still twisting itself in exotic knots.

"Then, when I was in college," he said, "she tracked me down, said she was sorry. I was struggling. Being on my own, finally ... it wasn't what I'd dreamed of, not by a fucking long shot. I was confused, a hot mess."

I squeaked in disbelief. Tank, a hot mess?

He misunderstood, held up his hands. "I know, I let her get to me, and I shouldn't have. I figured that out right quick, but it was too late. So I moved. And she found me again. And again. I thought Exile might be the only place short of hell she wouldn't follow me."

"Oh." So that explained why he hadn't finished the office pavilion Out There. Jenna, his crazy ex-foster mom stalker.

"Ohh," I said again, because it also explained why he'd moved around so much during college. But the way he talked in his sleep? The way he'd said her name and cuddled me? That wasn't the way you talked to your mom.

"Ohhh ..." I said, finally beginning to understand. Her *favorite*.

"You stuck?" Tank raised an eyebrow. "You need a technical tap?"

"You still want to slap me?" I said absently, still processing.

"Kinda."

I thought about how I'd wanted to wipe Forrest's name from Tank's lips. I steeled myself from the shoulders down, raised my head, tried to keep my jaw loose.

He rubbed his eyes, a slight retreat. "'Course," he grumbled, "I feel like hitting a whole lotta people right about now."

"How about some rough sex instead?" I asked.

He looked at me, his ghost of a smile returning. "You got some nerve, girl."

"Thought you liked that." I toyed with my shirt collar, hoping to bring his smile all the way back. "Not even a *little* tempting?"

"You're always tempting. But then, I always want to jump off bridges, too."

That stung. A lot more than the cut in my mouth.

Maybe he regretted it. He reached for my shoulder, pulled me closer. "Faulty wiring aside, there ain't time. I got a plan, and we got to move."

≈

"HEY NOW, LOOK ALIVE," I said, striding into the living room. "Tank's coming up."

Paolo bolted over the side of the couch to stand in front of me. "Sweeney was right! You *do* have superporn powers."

I flinched, taken aback by his sprightliness. "It's 'porny superpowers.' And they have nothing to do with it. Tank was coming up, anyway."

Paolo's grin didn't falter as he gestured to his cheekbone. "What happened here?"

I mirrored him, felt my face. My cheek was bruised, probably looked worse than it felt. "Oh, I was sleepwalking again. Speaking of which, you're a lousy lookout."

"I thought you were awake!"

He looked guiltier than I'd intended, but before I could ask why, I heard Tank's voice in the kitchen. It wiped my mind clean. A minute later, Tank came out holding an open can of peaches, and he so filled the room, I wondered how we'd endured the emptiness.

"Listen up," Tank said. "We're gonna make a break for it. I ordered supplies, but—"

"How?" Sweeney said. He'd followed Tank in from the kitchen, must've been tooling around the garage. "We haven't been able to get a signal for days."

"This was last week," Tank said, pausing to sip from the can. "Even then, I had to set up an autodialer and run it night and day."

"You can do that?" Paolo said.

Tank nodded. "Learned in a group home."

Sweeney arched an eyebrow. "You were in a home?"

"Actually, not a home," Tank amended. "More an illegal call center that paid in shitty room and board—if you met your quota."

Sweeney's eyebrow went higher. That was a lot of sharing for Tank.

"Once I got UTL on the line," Tank continued, "they said the feds wouldn't approve any drop-offs because it's too dangerous. Feds claim they can't make contact with the liaisons, but Carlos tells me that's bullshit."

"You talked to Carlos?" I said, astounded. "You use autodial for that, too?"

"No, landline. Old timey phones?" Tank looked at me same as when he'd made that Skinny Puppy joke back at Mute's. "I tapped into the old phone lines when I built the panic room. Everybody uses cells and voiceover these days, so the feds don't monitor that dinosaur of a system. It's not even blocked."

"I didn't know the Cantus had a landline," I said.

"Maybe they don't, but Mute does," Tank said. "I called

him, and he told Carlos to scrounge up a handset and plug in."

I'd wondered what Tank was doing down there this whole time. Apparently, the answer was thinking, planning, working. I felt a charge of sweet satisfaction. That was the Tank I knew.

"So these supplies ..." Sweeney prompted.

"UTL's champin' at the bit. They strongly 'suggested'—" Tank made air quotes around his can of peaches "—if they heard directly from a liaison, that might satisfy their safety requirements."

"Because they get paid for every drop-off," I said, remembering the courier's gripe. "The company wants every last penny before the feds wipe us out."

Tank nodded. "Carlos said he'd green light a delivery to the roof this afternoon."

"Whoa, wait a minute!" Paolo said. "This afternoon? What's the rush?"

"You have prior commitments?" Tank paused to sip again. He'd probably been subsisting on protein bars in the basement. "I ordered food, water, first aid, all basics. No need to raise any flags. But more important, that big yellow chopper's gonna be a big yellow distraction to Chazz's crew. And they're less likely to shoot in front of UTL."

"What about Pops' crew?" Sweeney said, starting to sound revved. "Did you talk to Rain? Are they going to be here?"

"I asked Carlos to contact Rain, tell her the plan."

Tank paused, perhaps expecting Sweeney to object. Sweeney glanced at me, mouth pursed, as if holding back a gripe, but he nodded for Tank to go on.

"As for Pops' crew, I don't know. But between our crew and the liaisons and UTL running interference though they don't know it, I think we got a chance. I want to be on the roof thirty minutes before delivery.

"Sweeney, you're my backup. I want you," Tank said, looking at me, "and Puppy in the panic room, watching the feeds, talking in our ears."

Sweeney and I nodded, too stunned by Tank's sudden appearance to object. Paolo, on the other hand ...

"Are you sure? I mean, you said yourself we can wait them out, they're bound to get bored—"

Tank shook his head. "It's too late. We're running out of food, water. Long since ran out of patience."

"But why *now?*" Paolo insisted.

Tank's attention lasered onto him. I took a sliding step away from Paolo. If I got between those two, I'd've been zapped bad as from the fence outside.

"What do you mean, 'why'?" Tank said.

"Oh, I don't know." Paolo bristled with sarcasm. "Because you've been down there for days, weeks even? And now suddenly you're back, and we're about to go off half-cocked?"

"I needed *time.*" Tank's voice boomed. "To cool off, to arrange the pieces, set this plan in motion. You got a problem with that, there's the door."

Sweeney let out a low whistle. I knocked him in the ribs.

"It's not a problem," Paolo stuttered. "It just seems sudden."

Tank scoffed, dropped his glare from Paolo like releasing a bug. "Well, things aren't always what they seem, are they?"

Chapter Twenty-Two

I FIDGETED OUTSIDE TANK'S bathroom door. After the fuss with Paolo, he'd called a timeout, said he had to wash up before he crawled out of his skin. News of the water outage didn't faze him. If we had any of the boiled stuff left, he'd said, he was damn well gonna use it. He hadn't invited me in. He'd half closed the door, but he kept talking to me over his splashing.

"Moss is in pretty bad shape. Bad enough Carlos heard about it. Gave as good as they got, but they won't be riding any time soon. Belen moved in to Moss's place after they burned her trailer down—"

"I thought it was Jackson's house that got burned down."

"Belen's, too. Neither Pops nor Chazz is taking credit for it, which I don't see why not. It's no worse than anything else they've done, but she has an asshole ex, so maybe he did it. Anyway, she and Moss are working something out."

When he paused, I edged away to study my bruise in the closet mirror. It didn't look bad, yet. Kind of like a streak of cheap blush. I stank, though, like I'd gotten sweaty in my sleep. A flicker of a snippet of memory zipped through my head—*Daddy?*—but disappeared too quickly to make sense. I went to the bedside table where Tank had left his snack and gulped down a peach slice like an oyster.

Tank toed the bathroom door open wider. Towel knotted around his waist, he poured the last of the water into the stoppered sink, then leaned over to shave his scalp. Evidently, his kit had been there all along, hidden out of reach.

"Meanwhile, Pops' crew has formed a vigilante border patrol," he said, chin to his chest. "Ever since Gatling Drive, Pops insists the feds're getting ready to launch an assault. So odds are we won't have to deal with Pops during delivery."

The oblique reference to my dad's death should've shut me down. Instead, I let it sink under my heart for later. "You could've told us that downstairs," I said, coming closer. "Might've calmed Paolo down."

He swished his razor in the dingy water. "Yeah, but there's no telling what Pops'll do one minute to the next. Didn't want to give y'all false hope. 'Sides, ain't my job to calm Paolo's delicate nerves."

I made a noise in my throat, trying to agree but not quite clearheaded. I studied Tank's body, visually traced the water drops bisecting his lats. He was so close, so nearly naked. He tilted to look at me, masseter muscle flexing, then went back to shaving.

"Think you were right to be suspicious of those recall warrants. Even Carlos can't get a line on the feds anymore. Cell phones silent, water mains erupting ... something's going down."

He kept talking, and I stood there nodding in all the right places, taking inventory (ripples, ridges, scars), making sure the Tank in front of me was the Tank I remembered, that he hadn't morphed somehow while out of sight. Knowing what I was doing didn't make it any easier to stop. He was out of whack, too. All that talking, like he could make up for days in an hour.

Between sentences, he shaved off his beard. When he strode into the bedroom, heading for the closet and his body armor, I willed his towel to fall.

He half turned, ducked his head to catch my eye. "Hey." He pointed to his face. "Up here."

Sheepish, I looked up. He'd been explaining something. Hell if I knew what.

He checked the alarm clock by the bed, and said, "Shit. I've never jumped off a bridge, so why can't I stop jumping your skinny bones?"

"The landing's better?"

He actually laughed. For once I felt proud of blurting out the first thing to come to mind.

"Ten minutes," he said.

"Twelve," I countered. Instinct.

"Ten," he said, walking to the foot of the bed.

I met him there and yanked that damn towel off. He leaned down to kiss me, and I held his jaw, clamped him close, remembered the planes of his face. He pulled down my boxers. I locked my legs and shimmied so they slithered past my knees. I stepped free, hands still locked on his face. He tugged at the bottom of my shirt, fingers tickling at my waist, but I didn't want foreplay. I bullied him to the edge of the bed, pushed him down so I could straddle him. I licked my hand. He leaned back on his elbows and watched me jack him off. When I sank down on him, dry but frantic, he hissed.

"Shit, Heidi, we're not in *that* much of hurry."

"Sorry."

But I kept grinding until we were slick and tuned, and he didn't complain again. He sat up, coiled his arms under mine, grabbed my shoulders. He pulled me down, pushed himself deeper. I wrapped my arms around his neck, even though it slowed us down, because—goddammit—I needed to feel every inch of his skin branding mine.

Seven minutes.

Afterwards, we lay facing one another, our breath cooling circles in the sweat on our chests.

"You closed your eyes," I said.

"Huh?"

"Just something I noticed."

"You notice everything." Tank butted his head against mine. "Missed you, Heidi Heidi Ho."

"Oh? Were you gone?" I grinned to crack my face.

He spanked me, started to get up.

"Tank?" I knew it wouldn't make him laugh, but I couldn't keep it twisted inside anymore. "Why didn't you help us? When Theo used the air cannon?"

His head drooped. He didn't turn to look at me. I figured I'd blown it. He was gonna call off everything. Kick me to the curb, book it while my fellow Exiles tore me to smithereens, sonic boom through the checkpoint.

"Wanted to see what you'd do." His voice was so craggy, it took me a few seconds to translate. "I'd've come up if you were in real danger. I would've. But I wanted to see if it'd be any different, if you'd change your mind about your mom when you were scared. If it wasn't me doing the shooting."

"That's a creepy experiment. But one well-suited to Exile, I suppose." I sat up beside him. "You saw I caved. Why didn't you come up?"

"Wasn't done watching. And there was work to do." He retrieved his towel and offered it to me. From the rigid line of his mouth, I knew he wouldn't entertain more questions. Okay, then.

We cleaned up and put on fresh clothes. Before we headed downstairs, his warm hand engulfed my shoulder.

"Hold up," he said. "You still got that key I gave you?"

"Yeah." I nodded at the closet.

"Get it. If this stunt goes south—"

"Tank, we're on Antarctica."

"I mean it." He pushed me toward the closet. Once I'd grabbed the key and stuffed it in my pocket, he pulled me so we stood toe to toe. "If this goes wrong," he said quietly, "get to Mute's, show him the key. He'll let you in—only you—and you can stay there until the smoke clears."

He cut off my questions with one of his own. "You remember what happened when you were sleepwalking?"

I tilted my head like Red Sonja. "Yeah. I walked into the basement, and you slapped me."

"Before that."

I blinked at him, rewinding my memory. "I was dreaming about William. We were little kids, and he was after me again, crawling into my bed. And before that ... something about my dad?"

"That's it?"

"It was a nightmare, it didn't make sense. Why, what do you expect me to remember?" The chill spreading through my bones abruptly stilled when Tank took my hand, gave me his clean straight razor.

"Never mind. Keep this on you. No need to flaunt it."

"What's it for?"

He avoided my gaze, focused on the razor. "Anyone stupid enough to mess with you."

I thought about how he'd hidden all the sharps. "You sure you trust me with it?"

He sighed, folded my hand closed over the shiny steel. "I must be crazier than you," he said. "Because, yeah. I do."

I kissed him like my feet were on fire.

≈

Paolo squirmed beside me on the couch, antsy as Romero always was before that first hit. Sweeney leaned against the telewall, sometimes blocking our view of Cricket with his hip, Raven with his shoulder. Tank stood between them and laid out more of the plan.

"Carlos asked for a forklift," he told Sweeney. "I told him Rain'd give him one."

"What for?"

"Didn't ask." Tank studied the feeds—or pretended to. "All I care is he'll create another distraction while we're supposedly taking delivery."

Sweeney nodded, pushed off the wall, walked over to the couch. "So long as he don't turn the 'lift on us." And he kicked Paolo to make him stop twitching.

"What was that for?" Paolo snapped.

I patted his thigh, felt his quads jump, and realized I wasn't helping. I sat on my hands, and asked Tank, "What about Romero? The Cantu crew. They getting involved?"

"Don't know. Don't like to micromanage." But Tank raised an eyebrow at Sweeney, who stepped away from Paolo. "Besides, we'll be busy enough with our own agenda. If I get a shot at Chazz or Keith, or even," he said, looking down at me, "a shot at your mom, I'm taking it."

I swallowed. Sweeney didn't crow but pumped his fist in a silent "yes!"

"But ..." Paolo's gaze squirmed from me to Tank and back. No point appealing to Sweeney. "What about what Heidi said? How if you kill her mom, you might never get out of town?"

Tank shrugged. "We'll deal with it."

Paolo blinked. "We'll deal with it? What about the feds? Heidi says they're itching for a reason to attack." He turned to me, the whites of his eyes showing. "You're going to let him do this?"

I almost laughed. "*Let* him?"

Paolo reached for my wrist, faltered when his fingers touched my hip; I was still sitting on my hands. "Don't you want out?" he asked. Low, urgent.

Sweeney snickered behind him. Low, humorless. "Careful, Puppy."

Paolo's gaze cut away, fixed on the tele in frustration. I studied his profile, the pinch of his forehead, his nearly invisible lips. He had a secret. Not about me, I realized. Something more; I didn't know what.

But the razor sat in my pocket, warm steel certainty.

≈

TANK CARRIED AN EXTRA chair to the panic room, where he gave me and Paolo a crash course in the surveillance system. There wasn't audio, but he hooked us up with a set of walkabouts so we could speak with him and Sweeney when they went on the roof, even if we had to leave the panic room. Then Tank loomed over us like the Bad Cop in a police procedural, hands gripping the backs of our chairs while he explained which monitors corresponded to what cameras. He stressed the cameras overlooking Raven and Cricket, but I eyeballed the embossed labels on my left, opposite Paolo.

Tank really did have cameras inside the house. One in every hallway, one at each entrance, others in the den, kitchen, garage. This Jenna person was starting to scare me. But most unsettling was the camera evidently concealed in the telewall. Tank must've seen Paolo groping me on the couch and me letting him. I stifled a groan.

Over my shoulder Tank said, "Heidi. Focus."

I conjured a sick smirk. "Yes, sir." But my brain ran a mini-montage of every time Paolo had stroked, squeezed, or manhandled me. Of course, Tank couldn't know how often the attention had or hadn't slicked my skivvies. Come to think of it, I'd resisted often enough that Paolo's overtures might've looked unwanted, especially without audio. If it pissed Tank off, he could have intervened, but he hadn't.

Or had he? When I'd sleepwalked into the basement, he'd met me at the foot of the stairs. I wasn't screaming or banging on his door. He could've let me stumble around until I woke up or one of the guys retrieved me. I snuck a glance at Tank, now explaining how Theo's cannon had affected one of the cameras.

"Question?" he asked, not without menace.

"It'll wait," I said.

After the rundown we joined Sweeney in the living room for weapon assignment.

"No way," I said when he handed me the Ruger. "Not that clunker again."

"The kickback on the sawed-off will knock you on your ass," he said, pushing the handgun at me.

"I can't get my hand around the grip."

"So use both hands. You're not coming outside until the coast is clear, and if you're shooting in the house, you don't want to stop to reload a shotgun."

I pushed the Ruger away. "Fuck it, I'll go without."

"Don't be stupid," Sweeney said, cheeks blotching under his beard. "If anybody gets in, you need to drop them fast."

I looked at Tank for backup, but he was crinkle-eyed with amusement. "You two went and got cute on me," he said, rifle over his shoulder.

"Cute as the clap," Paolo muttered, hand out to Sweeney. "Give me the Ruger and the sawed-off. She won't have to shoot anything."

Sweeney checked with Tank. Tank nodded, his hesitation so split-second brief, only I noticed. I wondered what it meant.

Then there was nothing to do but report to our stations. At the door to the basement, Tank pulled me close, kissed the top of my head hard enough my knees bent.

"Gah, you're giving me sugar shock," Sweeney said, walking ahead.

No more subtle, Paolo tugged my elbow.

Tank offered me a press-lipped smile before striding after Sweeney. I swallowed hard—I just got him back and I was letting him go?—then started down the basement stairs. Paolo hurried after me.

"I can't believe you're letting Tank do this," he hissed. "This is insane!"

"Getting us out of here is insane?" I moved faster, trying to escape the convo. "I thought that's what you wanted."

"I do! But there's gotta be a better way." He grabbed my elbow, hooked me around to face him. "Not this blaze of stupidity, half our crew benched, and Pops joining Chazz! And what about the feds?"

"The feds are like the weather. And Tank's not taking a shot at Mother unless he has to." I imagined Tank on the roof, waiting to hear my voice in his ear. Every second I argued with Paolo was a second I lost with Tank. "It's not an unreasonable risk," I said over the *tick-click* of wasted time.

"Not unreasonable?" Paolo's fingers tightened on my arm. "It's the epitome of unreasonable! The feds get involved, and Tank might never leave town again. And you're okay with that? You're gonna let him abandon his life, his career, everything he has Out There?"

"Tank can design buildings here," I said, calm as I could with the *tick-click*ing in my head. "He doesn't have to be Out There to make buildings for them."

"Yes, he does! This isn't like your movie stuff, Heidi. He has people Out There who want him back. Clients. Partners." He leaned closer, and I practically smelled the panic rolling off him. "People willing to sink a lot of money into tracking him down. He can't keep running away."

"He's not running away from anyone!" I said, but stopped at a different kind of *click*—a things-falling-into-place click. I dropped my gaze so my horror wouldn't ticker-tape across my eyeballs. "He doesn't want to be found, Paolo. He doesn't want to go back."

"Not now, but what about later? This is ..." I sensed him looking over my head, searching for the word that might penetrate. "Irrevocable."

"He has his reasons. You'd know that if you were half the friend you pretended to be."

I yanked away and ran down the rest of the stairs. I didn't reach the panic room before Paolo grabbed me. His foot was definitely better. I should've checked it, after all. Who knew how long he'd been scamming us? He whirled me around and slammed me into the wall of lockers. Bracketed my head with hand and shotgun, breath heating my face.

"Okay, fine," he said. "Say he doesn't want to leave, ever. But what about me? I'm stuck in here with you guys.

Nobody's going to care whether it was Tank who pulled the trigger—"

"Nothing's happened yet!"

"—or me or you. I'll get stuck in the crossfire. Brick-shittin' feds on one side, Ragey Exiles on the other. What if I can't leave, either?"

Pinned by his glinting eyes and his knees in my thighs, the locker vents etching lines in my back, I might've felt trapped, too. But the straight razor sat in my pocket, warm and cunning.

"You said you'd stay," I whispered.

"What?" He shook his head, disbelieving—like I'd cut him already.

"You once said, if you were Tank, you'd stay with me."

"But ..." He backed off to get a better look at me. "What I meant ..."

I tilted my head. He seemed to think better of explaining exactly what he'd meant.

"Heidi, Tank has stuff to go back to. And I don't have a reason to stay."

"Stay for Tank," I said softly. "Stay for me."

"What?"

He lowered the sawed-off. Now we weren't touching at any point, but I still felt his dread, saw the sweat under his wide blue eyes.

"Remember, Paolo? You told me you'd bust your ass to do anything I wanted. Well, I want you to stay."

Eyes fixed on me, he shook his head. "Don't you try and pull that. *You* don't want to stay. You're just thinking with your pussy. So long as Tank's plugging your holes, you think you can put up with life in Exile. But I don't have a fuckbuddy. I don't have that kind of consolation, or delusion, or whatever. I'm stuck here because you two can't keep your fucking hands off each other."

I leaned forward. "Where do you *want* me to put my hands?"

His pulse throbbed under his spiderwebs. I'd reversed whatever spell he had on me. I could escape if I wanted. Instead, I waited. He clenched his jaw, eyes icing over.

"Cocktease. You won't. Not with Tank here. You think I'm gonna stick around so I can smell him on you all the time? Get over yourself."

I smiled as I swiveled into the panic room, the razor nearly singing in my pocket. "Then you'd better hope to naugahyde Tank doesn't get a shot at Mother. But if he does, you'd better hope he makes the shot. And every shot after that. Because if you want to leave town, you want us to win, fast."

Chapter Twenty-Three

SOON AS I OPENED the com channel, Tank snapped through the static, "What the fuck, Heidi? What's going on down there?"

"Paolo had to take a dump," I said.

Paolo smacked my shoulder hard enough Sweeney and Tank heard it. Sweeney snickered; Tank grumbled.

"You're the one full of shit," Paolo said, sitting in the chair next to me.

"Aw'right, cut it out," Tank said. "We're on the roof. Tell me what's out there before I stick my head up and get shot."

Paolo peered at the canted view from the camera facing Raven. "There's some kind of commotion on the east side."

The music-as-a-weapon stopped. I would've wept with joy, but most of the thugs assigned to the west barricade hurried to see what the fuss was about, and I had to follow them from one camera angle to another.

"Carlos drove up in one of the black Suburbans," I said, studying the same monitor as Paolo. Even with the grainy, black-and-white feed—from the camera slammed by Theo's air cannon—I recognized the front grill of the vehicle, one of three big-ass trucks on permanent loan from the feds. "He's getting out," I said, glad the camera zoom still worked.

Damn, but Carlos looked fine. Light glimmered pewter-oily on his armor. The feds had provided the suit—standard-issue metro police gear for cities Out There—when Carlos signed on as liaison. Romero had once teased that Carlos looked like Iron Man until we all got to work and punked that suit up proper. Carlos wore an earpiece but not his helmet yet, so I could admire the curve of his cheekbone, the wide expanse of his forehead notched at the temple by his shiny scar.

Paolo frowned at me, raised his hands "WTF?" before speaking to Tank and Sweeney. "Carlos is wearing armor, and so's the guy who was riding shotgun." He zoomed out in time to see sunlight flash off moving black steel. "I think Carlos has a couple more guys in the back. Maybe they're going to unload the forklift from a trailer?"

Tank grunted, waited for us to continue.

"Okay, Carlos is leaning over one of those trashed cars blocking Raven," Paolo said. "He's talking to one of their brass. Keith, I think."

"Would have to be," I said. "Chazz wouldn't talk to Carlos. So we got Carlos and Manny in charge, and behind them," I said, counting off on my fingers, "Jimmy J, Jimmy B, and Roach to drive the 'lift, I bet."

"Shit, Heidi." Sweeney sounded smiley. "For once I'm glad you know every guy in town."

"I live to make you happy, Sweeney. West end of Raven is almost completely unprotected."

"It's getting tense over here, east end," Paolo said. "Carlos is pointing at ... the generator? Hard to tell at this angle."

We waited, tense ourselves, for further movement.

"Wow, okay," Paolo said. "I've got visual on the forklift. At least, I think it's the 'lift. It's been substantially ... modified."

"Meaning?" Tank said.

I checked Paolo's monitor. "They replaced the forks with bayonets," I said. Tank and Sweeney would know what I meant, a cross between battering rams and spears added to a four-wheel vehicle. "And yeah, that's Roach. I bet they're gonna move the cars so they can reclaim the city's stolen property. Carlos has retrieved stuff before."

"Wait." Paolo held a hand in front of my mouth, cocked his head, listening. I resisted the urge to bite off his fingers. "Is that the chopper?"

Tank came on. "Naw, it's bikes. Should be coming up Raven from the west, Cricket from the south."

They motored into view. "Seven bikes approaching the Raven roadblock," I reported. "Looks like Romero and BlackJack teamed up with your crew. I see Rain, Cam'n'Zak..." I shook my head at their identical matte black bikes. "I can't believe those two aren't Exiles. Maybe Zeke? And that's Max in the back. Head of the Cantu crew." Watching the dragon green Honda bringing up the rear, I wondered who was taking care of Sammy.

"Coming from the west," Paolo said, leaning over to look at my monitors, "there's ... seven more bikes? Hard to tell, they're clumped together."

"Warriors from Mute's crew," I said. "Guess Rain called in some favors? That's Vanessa and her cousins, Rodney and Rascal, riding with Jackson, Dahlia, Kier, maybe Belen?"

Paolo turned back to his monitors. "Carlos is backing up, still talking to Keith. Well, shouting."

"Going up top now," Tank said.

"Be careful." Then—because how stupid did that sound?—I added, "Sweeney, if anything happens to him, I'm going to dissect your face."

"How's that for motivation?" Sweeney said, but I could tell he was smiling again. Street warrior through and through.

Glass buckled. Metal screamed. I whipped around to check out the east feeds. Roach had rammed the forklift's bayonets through some car windows; the noise shrieked through Tank and Sweeney's walkabouts loud and clear.

Beside me, Paolo winced, switched his bud to the other ear. "Look out, guys. Here come the guns."

Keith pointed and ducked. With that busted camera I couldn't see the thugs firing on his command, but I heard the crackle like a string of supersized Black Cats.

Carlos and Manny dodged behind the open doors of the Suburban. The forklift pulled back, no hurry, the ruined Pinto dangling in front of it and shielding Roach. The two Jimmys returned fire. The front doors of the Suburban slammed shut, and Carlos gunned the engine.

The left fender cleared the gap left by the Pinto, but its right fender crashed into a two-tone station wagon. The wagon whipped around, ass-end dragging along the side of the Suburban with a squeal. The truck veered right, over the sidewalk, and smashed into my parents' house.

"Holy Volvo," Sweeney laughed. So he and Tank were on the roof, could see everything.

"Bikes are moving," Tank said.

Sure enough, Rain's de facto crew swarmed on Cricket, readying to jump the roadblock. I checked the other feed and saw Jackson and company swarming, too. I hoped they had a signal, or they'd crack like billiard balls.

Romero glanced up at our roof. Sweeney asked Tank, "They waiting on us?"

Above, Tank must've given a silent answer. Max Cantu's dragon green bike cranked and zoomed. Paolo's attention whipped to my screens. I checked his. The Suburban's front doors were open. My stomach clenched. I couldn't see Carlos.

"Zoom out," I said, grabbing Paolo's collar.

"That's as far as it goes!" he said, pulling away.

The Jimmys jumped out the back of the Suburban, took a few shots—*Crack! Crack!*—and scuttled toward the generator, out of sight.

"Tank, we can't see crap," I said.

Not quite true. Chazz charged into view, helmet in hand, yelling over his shoulder. My gut twisted again. Chazz hated the Cantus as much as he hated me. If he'd gotten that far, where was Carlos? Bleeding out somewhere, suffering for my mistakes again?

Bikes bounce-snapped over the roadblock and into the street. Chazz took two steps more and then dropped, bullets torquing him down and around, smack into the ground.

"Shit," Paolo said.

"Don't worry. He's not dead, yet," I said, though a girl could hope. "Kevlar."

"Give me a minute," Tank said.

The back of Chazz's head exploded in a black blast. I jumped.

"Sweet!" Sweeney said. And Tank told me, "You're welcome."

Paolo glanced over his shoulder at the grin growing on my face. "You're all crazy," he said. Like it was finally dawning on him.

A warrior ran and crouched over Chazz's body. She craned to look at the roof. "Get down," I told Tank. "They see you."

"We've lost visual on the bikes." Paolo frowned at my screens. "They're in front of the house, too close to the palisades. Where's the fucking chopper?"

"Probably delayed while they surveil the 'activity,'" I said.

"What if they're not coming? What if the feds overruled Carlos?"

"Don't doubt Carlos." I stood, patted the walkabout clipped to my waistband. "Going upstairs," I told Tank.

"Be safe," he said.

In the study I balanced on the office chair to peer out a sniper slit. Paolo peered out the one beside me. Our allies zoomed up and down the street, flirting with the chain link fence. Every few feet, Max threw a Chinese star, testing for dead spots. With sparks flaring in his wake, he looked like a Mexican Zeus. Most of Chazz's crew—Keith's now, I guessed—had tossed aside their shotguns, probably uncomfortable with the ancient things, if they even worked. Now the thugs swung crowbars and baseball bats at the bikers. Keith and another thug wrestled the Jimmys for control of the generator. Meanwhile, the Suburban deflected stray projectiles like a glossy tank. Nobody bothered with it; the ignition key was Carlos's thumbprint. Carlos and Manny should've been easy to spot with their Iron Man outfits, but I caught no glimpse.

Between the scream of bikes and intermittent gun blasts, the crunch of metal and my heartbeat thudding in my ears, I didn't hear it at first, didn't understand what Tank meant when he said, "Here we go."

"Finally," Paolo said.

A shadow darkened the mayhem. Objects fluttered, as if the shadow had mass. Then a bright yellow blur buzzed my peripheral vision. *Finally* was right.

The chain link fence rippled and chimed, its serpentine movement drawing my attention to the generator. The Jimmys had overpowered Keith and the other thug, ground their faces into the street. Straddling the handcuffed thugs, the Jimmys looped plastic nooses around their necks, zipped the nooses to the cuffs behind their backs.

I checked my parents' house. Through the flying debris I saw a short person in a hockey mask—presumably Theo—climbing onto the roof. His black battle gear glinted with silver commas.

"Thing One's on my parents'—"

Sweeney cut me off. "Got it."

"You'd better," I said.

In the street BlackJack spun out. He ditched his bike, tore off his helmet, and surged back into the fray, where he promptly started whaling on that William wannabe kid.

I covered my mouthpiece. "You see Carlos?" I asked Paolo.

He glowered at me, covered his mouthpiece, too. "I can't keep track of all your fuckbuddies."

Dipshit. I peered down, watched two warriors tackle BlackJack from behind. All three collapsed in a kicking, punching heap. The first one to jump back up wore black leather bristling with fishhooks. Her dark, scraggly hair was shot through with silver. I thought of tarantulas, the light glinting off their hairy legs, and shivered.

"What now?" Paolo said.

"It's my mother."

"How can you tell?"

The woman yanked a T-shaped weapon from her belt. Shaken once, it telescoped to a full-length fiberglass spike maul. She jabbed the blunt end into BlackJack's ribs. A blast of air sent her curtain of hair flying. She turned to glare at the chopper, but for a second, I imagined she glared at me. I almost fell off my chair.

"You see!" I told Paolo.

"Yeah, yeah. I'm more worried about your brother."

Behind a new air cannon, Manny wrestled Theo. Theo shouldn't have been able to hold off Manny, who outweighed him by a hundred pounds, but those silver commas on Theo's suit were fishhooks like on Mother's battle gear. Every time Manny got a grip on him, Theo wrenched away and Manny bellowed, shaking his hands.

The barrel of the air cannon stared off to my left. But the kick on it, that would pull the blast up and over to the right. To the roof.

"Heidi?" Tank yelled. "Get away from the windows!"

"No, you get down," I said. "Theo's aiming at you!"

Theo threw Manny off again, and Manny stumbled back, pinwheeling. Theo dropped down and grappled with the blowback tank. Maybe the knob was stuck. He slapped the side of the tank. A thick white mist curled from the new PVC barrel, caught and frayed in the chopper's wake.

Sweeney shouted. "... courier ..." was all I caught over the chopper's roar.

Paolo wrapped an arm around my waist and hauled me off the office chair. I flailed, tipping us back. Paolo cracked his head on the edge of the desk. His curse turned to a groan when he landed on his back, the Ruger tucked into his waistband. The sawed-off landed a few feet away.

"Sweeney." I gripped my mic like that would do anything. "Stop my brother. Now!"

Sweeney replied but got drowned out again.

I rolled and crawled back toward the office chair. Paolo caught my ankle and dragged me across the floor. I kicked. He caught my arms and jerked them behind me.

"Goddamnit, Heidi! We need to get out of here. If you get hurt, Tank'll kill me!"

Collateral damage, I thought. Face smearing against the floorboards, I fought. Paolo straddled my legs. His hand slipped on my arm—he'd touched his head, gotten bloody—but he held me down.

Something slammed the roof. The house shook, windows rattling. Paolo fell on top of me. My earbud went dead.

I squirmed, craning to look out the sniper slit. I saw the courier, a spider tangled in her own web. I saw a growing shadow, a yellow wall ... I heard, outside, a rushing suck of wind like the breath I couldn't catch. Metal moaned, the sound drawn out so long, it melted into white noise. Then ...

... silence. Nothing from my earbud. Nothing from Paolo on top of me. Nothing, I thought, from my suddenly still heart.

And then the earth buckled.

Chapter Twenty-Four

I HELD THE MIC to my mouth, and screamed, "Tank?"

I couldn't even hear myself. The rotor blades of the fallen chopper thwacked the earth, shaking the whole house. A shadow darkened the study each time one hit the street. My posters fluttered around us, new ones dislodged with each jackhammer thud.

"Tank?" I screamed again.

Paolo rolled off, reached under me, waved the walkabout in my face.

"Gary Fucking Cooper." I grabbed it from him and rolled over, plugged my earbud back into the transmitter, knocked the box against my palm like a pack of cigarettes until the fucker started transmitting again.

"Tank?" I stared through a haze of drywall dust, wishing I could see through the ceiling, grateful I couldn't because that meant the roof was intact.

I heard static, then a tiny, tinny reply like an ant from beyond the grave. "Heidi?"

"Tank," I sighed. "Are you—"

"I'm okay." Mumbling to or from Sweeney. "We're okay."

"Where are you?" Paolo asked, getting to his knees.

Tank was breathing hard. "Near the west roadblock. We'll come up to the front door. Stay put, it might take us a minute." Pause for panting. "Sweeney's leg."

And I knew which one, the one he always messed up. "We'll get ready to patch him up," I said, rising.

Paolo covered his mic. "The hell we will! We gotta get to the chopper. There's the pilot, the courier—"

"Fuck them!" I said. "Let 'em fend for themselves."

He yanked his headset off, threw it at the wall. It nicked Steve McQueen, and I almost didn't care. "Heidi, they're here because of us!"

I pushed past him into the hall. Tank asked, "What's Puppy saying?" He didn't wait for an answer. "Don't come out here, Heidi. It's bad. Worse."

A screech from the earbud froze me mid-stride. "Was that Sweeney?" I asked, blood icy-hot in my veins.

"Yeah." Tank panted a second before adding, "Be ready."

"Heidi!" Paolo tugged at my elbow. He'd retrieved the sawed-off, had it pointed vaguely in my direction. I chose not to interpret that. "Wait a minute!"

I charged down the hall, saw a spray of black and bright triangles on the floor. Shattered glass, I realized, and leaped in time to avoid running across shards from the picture window. Something—one of the chopper's landing skids?—had punctured the steel siding and the tar-glopped window. The same thing had stabbed a new horizon across the wall. I squinted against the sunlit dust rolling in and raced on down the stairs. Puppy followed me to the kitchen, still bitching about the downed chopper.

"Enough about the tragic Outsiders!" I said, grabbing the first aid kit. "They're UTL, it's their goddamn job. They screwed up—"

"It's not their job to get shot down and slaughtered by you mutants!"

I spun around, not quite believing the last words from his lips. He stood in the kitchen entry, chest heaving, spit in his goatee, ocean eyes threatening to drown his face. He pointed the gun more definitively. At my chest. My fingers tingled.

"We're going!" he said.

"We're not!"

We stared across the kitchen at each other. I wondered if he could see my pulse pounding in my throat, the way I could see his.

"Carlos!" he finally shouted. Like, *Bingo!* "He's a city liaison, right? You think he's going to stand there and watch those maniacs ransack the chopper, maybe tear two Outsiders limb from limb? You want to find Carlos? That's where he'll be!"

He must've seen the answer on my face—I didn't give a damn about the Outsiders, and I didn't grok why Paolo did either, but Carlos ... Paolo lowered the gun and turned, certain I would follow.

"Heidi," Tank warned.

"I'm just gonna take a look," I said, heart feeling too hot for my chest. The kit banged against my thigh as I ran for the door. "I'll meet you back here at the house, Tank."

I ignored his roar of frustration. Wasn't the first time I'd heard it.

I hoped it wouldn't be the last.

≈

PAOLO YANKED OPEN THE front door, and everything came blasting in like a technicolor inferno. Billows of heat slammed my chest, followed by an almighty stench that nearly knocked me over. I ducked, gagging on fumes. Flaming diesel, charred cellulose, blistered paint, burnt rubber—Carcinogen City. Sweat sprung from my upper lip, prickled between my shoulder blades.

"Heidi?" Tank said. "You okay?"

I strangled off a retch, choked out, "I'm fine. Heading out, mic off." I turned off the transmitter before he could object, though I left the receiver on. I wanted to know what was happening to him but not vice versa.

Paolo coughed and hawked up more than spit. Eyes watering, he caught his breath, and hollered, "Move it!"

He charged out the door. I stumbled two feet after him, then staggered to a stop.

The chopper had ripped down the palisades in front of Tank's house. The splintered timber littered the street like giant Tinker Toys. I could see clear across Raven now, where—crumpled on its side—the helicopter blazed in the middle of a lot two doors down from my parents', its darkened belly pointing at Tank's house. The chopper's top rotor blades had sawn through the neighbors' faux brick-sided house. One blade had snapped off and disappeared: the world's deadliest lawn dart. The other had pierced the house's foundation, pinning the chopper in place like a burning butterfly.

I blinked through the roiling smoke, stunned by this new view, and stepped onto the gravel lawn—right onto a chunk of cracked safety glass. Shit, I was still barefoot. Not that wearing fuck-me pumps, the only shoes I still owned, would've been any better. I limped forward, hoping the glass would fall out as we ran.

Paolo helped me hike over split wood and concrete rubble. Underneath, the chain link fence smoldered, flattened. Bikes and thugs raced over sections of fence without bursting into flame, so I walked over it, too. I held my breath the first few steps, but I did it. I knew if I were lost in that chaos, Carlos would walk over live wires for me.

Out of the corner of my eye, I saw a warrior drag someone toward a concrete barrier, presumably out of harm's way. In my ear I heard Tank grunting with the effort of hauling Sweeney, and Sweeney cursing in a cracked voice. Hearing Sweeney so close to sobbing set my teeth on edge; I hated caring. Now and then, a scream or a motorcycle roar blasted through both my earbud and the air around me. My neck creaked with the effort of not whipping around to search for Tank.

People—I don't know whose crew—saw our first aid kit and tried to flag us down, but Paolo waved the sawed-off at them and dragged me to the chopper so fast I couldn't be waylaid by sympathy if I'd had any. A fresh flood of bikes zipped into the disaster zone. They looped around us easily, and the kids scavenging for parts and people in the streets scuttled out of our way, hardly looking. Red Sonja ran dazzled in yipping circles. Raven trembled under my feet, as if giants roamed a second out of sight.

Standing on the helicopter's fuselage, Manny gripped a bright yellow fire extinguisher in bloody hands. A steady stream of white glop pounded the flames into submission. Paolo climbed up beside him, then reached back to tug me up. When Manny saw me, he twitched, boots sliding a little in the foam. I frowned, puzzled. But then again, he'd been wrestling my brother on a roof minutes before. Could be he'd had his fill of Palermos.

From atop the helicopter, I spied frenzied action in the house: my neighbors yanking belongings from the new fault line in their rooster-themed kitchen. Then Paolo jerked my arm, pointed down at the cracked window of the helicopter's pilot side.

The pilot was unconscious. Hunched within, Carlos sawed at his seatbelt with a switchblade. Standing there, we blocked the sunlight, and Carlos looked up. His eyes fixed on me, and I felt born again. I would've kissed a Bible had there been one within five miles.

"Heidi!" he yelled. "What the hell are you doing here?"

"C'mon." Paolo jumped off and ran around to the front of the cabin. I followed, slipping on extinguisher foam, stumbling over crushed cardboard boxes stamped *UTL*.

Paolo stomped the glass shards ringing the windshield, and I yelled to Carlos, "Spiderman here wanted to rescue somebody."

"Well, Spiderman can help me get this bastard out," Carlos said. "But you go back inside. You can't treat this guy out here."

"Yeah," Manny added. "You're better off at Tank's."

"Who asked you?" I said. Then Paolo shoved the sawed-off at me, and I watched him squeeze into the glop-sprayed cockpit.

Dark patches stickied the pilot's chin, his stupidly yellow shirt. "Is he spitting blood?" I said.

"Yeah." Carlos grunted, shifting to make room for Paolo. "But he bit off a chunk of his tongue, so maybe that's all it is."

"That's all?" Paolo said, eyes bugging. "Fuck, never mind. What about the courier?"

Cramped inside the tilted cockpit, Carlos tried to shake his head. The seatbelt finally split, and he grabbed the pilot. "Dead." His vague shoulder jerk indicated the open cargo door behind him. "Strangled on her line first, if she was lucky. If she wasn't ..."

"You sure?" Paolo said.

"No, I never seen a dead body before, pendejo," Carlos snapped. "Shit, you don't pick 'em for their brains, do you, Heidi?"

"You'd know, baby."

I backed up to let them wrangle the pilot out through the windshield. Once they were through, I peeked into the back of the helicopter. A first aid kit was strapped overhead on one wall. It was twice as big as the one I had. I ditched the gun and went for it. I didn't think about the courier until I tripped over half of her.

I grabbed a hanging nylon strap to catch myself. I knew better than to look down, so I focused on the jumble of packages strewn through the cargo hold. Blood coated my feet like slippers. I shivered, swallowing hard against my gorge, and tried to get my feet on either side of the courier's squishy torso. I needed a good footing to unstrap the chopper kit without letting go of ours.

In the street, Carlos hollered, "Hurry up, Heidi! I ain't leaving you."

I emerged from the foam-frosted windshield with both kits. Manny had disappeared. I spotted Carlos's helmet on the lawn, and I squatted, juggling kits to grab it—it seemed more important than the sawed-off; it could double as a weapon. But then Jimmy B ran up to Carlos and Paolo, his freckles standing out like dried blood spatter on his sweaty brown face.

"Carlos! Romero's down!"

"What?" Carlos nearly dropped his end of the pilot.

"He got hit in the head," Jimmy shouted, pointing, but badly.

"Here." Carlos shoved the pilot at Jimmy. "Take him to Tank's. Heidi!"

He didn't have to bark at me, I was right behind him, my bare feet slipping in grue and diesel. Paolo called after me, and I heard Tank, too, bewildered in my ear, demanding to know where I was, what I was doing, who and why and ad infinitum furioso. But it was Jimmy's words that hammered through my panic.

"Make it fast," he yelled. "Can't keep the feds out much longer."

≈

WE FOUND ROMERO SPRAWLED between a concrete barrier and a trashed car, part of the west end roadblock ripped open by the warriors. One of his boots was missing. No helmet. Where was his fucking helmet?

Carlos fell on his knees beside Romero, grabbed the front of Romero's leather jacket. "Oh, hell no. Romy, come on!"

Dropping everything, I knelt beside Carlos. "Move!" I pushed him out of the way, closer to Romero's legs, so I could do a quick visual.

Crescent scab scraped off his face along with most of that cheek. He'd hit the street hard, no chance to block his fall. Someone must've turned him over. Leather motorcycle jacket raked. One wrist snapped—*his drawing hand*, I thought, like tattooing meant fuck-all at that moment.

I pulled back to see the bigger picture: the bloody bull's-eye darkening the asphalt around Romero's head. It felt like the farther I panned out, the more there was to see, an evil circle spreading all the way to the horizon. No way all that blood came from his scraped face.

Chest aching, I leaned over and pulled up his eyelids: pupils blown, unresponsive. Shit. I bent to listen at his mouth, to feel the thin skin over his carotid. Instead, I felt blood. *Fuck*. I slipped my fingers up and back to probe his skull. My fingertips sank into wet meat, brushed broken bone, hit an unyielding plane of metal, then slippery softness.

I remembered the Cantus' cousin ET. I remembered her open skull. I remembered that she died.

"What? What's wrong?" Carlos said.

I shook my head hard enough to blur my vision. I fumbled for Romero's carotid again. *Pulse*, I demanded. *Pulse Pulse Pulse* Please.

A warrior screamed, and Carlos pitched over Romero's legs. His forehead smacked the concrete barrier, and he slid down, dragging a bloody line. An arm wrapped around my neck, and I gasped, wrenched to my feet.

"You let your brother die in the street," Mother snarled in my ear, "but you're out here tending to the Cantu boys?"

I gasped. I cast about for landmarks, triangulated, tried to figure out how far we were from the house, how far I had to push Mother until she fried in her skin.

"I didn't *let* William die, you stupid mutant."

"You were supposed to look out for your little brother," she said, shaking me.

My headset went flying. William's fist, still dangling around Mother's neck, knuckled my spine. I tried to jerk away, but the fishhooks in Mother's sleeve sank into my neck. I cried out and flailed, hand smacking her spike maul.

I grabbed for it, but the shaft slipped in my fist, slick with Romy's blood.

"Get off me, crazy bitch."

Carlos groaned, tried to lift his head.

"You were the medic," she insisted. "You were his big sister, you were supposed to be his protector. But you were too busy looking out for yourself, you whoring cunt—"

"No!" I slammed my elbow into her gut almost by accident. The hooks at my throat tore free, gave me half an inch of stinging relief. Before she headlocked me again, I wedged my hand between her arm and my neck. "*You* were supposed to look out for William. And me, and the twins, and instead, you served us to the street on a fucking platter—"

I stopped, distracted by movement. Carlos had hauled himself to hands and knees, but now he faltered. He couldn't leave Romero. He blinked up at us, struggling to focus.

"Let her go," he panted at Mother.

My eyes burned. I squirmed around to face Mother. One of my earrings caught on a hook, but I yanked free. I ignored the blood slithering down my neck; it was better than looking at Carlos all wrecked.

"We took you to the clinic for every appointment," Mother snarled in my face. "Every vaccine known to man. We sent you to Miss DeeDee, we paid for your lessons, all so you could be a medic. And you didn't do shit for us. I should've pimped you out."

"You did! You made me William's slave! The minute you brought him home, he took over!"

I kneed her in the crotch, trying to get more space between us. Mother lurched, losing her hold on my neck. This time I got a better grip on the spike maul and fought her for it. I didn't even have to get a good swing with its hammered steel head. Just use it to push her far enough from the house ...

Carlos shouted my name. Still kneeling beside Romy,

he'd pulled a gun from the holster in his Iron Man suit. "Get down!"

"The hell I will," I said. "Get Romy—"

Mother regained her balance. She snagged my collar, yanked me so William's rotting fist butted my nose. "Don't you dare put this on William," she said. "You're the traitor."

I grabbed William's stinking fist. I snapped the leather strap around her neck and raised the fist high overhead. Mother reached up, tried to block, missed. I slammed the last chunk of William into the street.

"No!" she screamed.

"*You* killed William."

Her grip on the spike maul withered, and I managed to wrestle it from her, wacked it broadside against her chest. She swiveled around, away from the house. I started counting steps.

"*You* made him fight," I said. "You drove me out, you drove Father insane, you practically set fire to Thea yourself—"

She grabbed her weapon again, tried to rip it out of my hands. "No, they're all dead because of you!"

I wobbled on my feet, hairs tingling up my arms.

All dead? I must've said it out loud because Mother said, "Yes, all of them! William, Thea, Theo, your own father ... All of them dead—murdered!—because you cared more about fucking that mad dog foreigner—"

"Don't listen to her," Carlos yelled.

"But, when did Thea ..." My vision darkened, and I blinked fast, struggling to push past the blur. "No, not Theo. I saw him, he was on the roof, he was—"

"He fell off the roof," Mother snarled. "The chopper fell, and so did he. I found him crushed under that damn blowback tank. You know what that was like? To see my baby, my last ..."

Her grip on the spike maul faltered once more. That split

second of weakness, more than anything else, convinced me it was true.

My family. All dead. Because of me.

Mother sobbed once, cleared her throat for more fury. "Don't act so shocked, Heidi. What did you expect when you sicced your liaison scumbags on us? You *wanted* us dead, you ungrateful, unfeeling—"

I shrank behind my mental safety glass. I lost all sound like someone had turned on my dampeners. I kept my grip on the maul—but only by backbrain instinct. No wonder Manny had twitched when he saw me. I was walking death. Father had known: *There's going to be trouble*, he'd said. *Always is with girls like you.* How many times had I wanted William and Thea and Theo to go away, disappear, be gone? Never have *been*. All so I could be free. And now they *were* gone, but I was still stuck here ... with Mother. Or the monster that replaced her. Alone with Mother. Forever.

Something bounced off my shoulder. I slow-motion twisted 'round, spotted a small chunk of concrete quivering to rest on the street. As if squeezing through that crack in my shield, sound snuck back in by decibels: first, Carlos shrieking my name, then him begging Romy to hold on, then it all roared back, a periphonic blast that nearly knocked me off my feet.

"Everybody knows you're a fucking robot, Heidi," Mother sneered, and I wished I'd go deaf again. "No feelings, no loyalty, no honor or love. Just a black hole cunt, fill her up and watch her go."

"Shut up!"

"You broke your father's heart. He was so ashamed—"

I yanked the spike maul from her, went to slap her mouth. I missed, snagged my fingers on fishhooks. She retreated, and I followed, fingertips caught. Frizzed strands of her hair rose, writhing.

"I told him there was no point begging you to come home. What for? You suck the life out of everything. You kill everything you touch." She smacked my hand away, and my blood drizzled her face. "You were always jealous of William. You had him killed because I loved him best."

"I didn't!"

"Oh yes, William's dead because of you. And your father, you drove him to the towers—"

"No!"

"—like you did that pussy Forrest Vai—"

"Don't!" I clenched the spike maul so tight my shoulders shook. The filthy fiberglass stung my torn fingers. "Don't you say his name! Don't you even think it. I will fucking *kill* you."

"Oh, I'll say it." She grinned bloody, her hair a black halo. "Forrest ... Fucking ... Vai. That pussy couldn't hack it in Exile *or* Out There. And once he'd tasted your slutty rot, he *ran* to the wire. He couldn't get dead fast enough. And soon those Cantus, your precious perverts, we'll spray their brains all over the pavement."

Romy had traced a finger over my heart, drawn an invisible tattoo. *No one here gets out alive.*

"Even that retard's brains, whatever ground chuck he's got—

"No," I whined. "You can't. Sammy never hurt you. He never hurt anyone!"

"—and then? Then we'll take care of Tank—"

"No!"

Crunch!

Mother's nasal bone splintered under the maul's steel head. For a second I didn't realize I'd swung.

"Not Tank," I said, and swung again. Her maxilla buckled. "Never Tank." Her face caved in. "You will never touch him. I'll erase you before you can touch him. I'll destroy every trace of this motherfucking family. We shouldn't have lived, we shouldn't have survived. I'll bury you, I'll bury all of you, and you'll rot in the ground, no pyres for you you'll be eaten by worms and carried away by spiders and I'll crush the spiders under my boots and grind every speck of you back into this forsaken shithole of hell and it'll all bleed together your blood and my blood and the blood in the streets and it will cover everything and be black as this thing in my eyes and in my heart and my head and my lungs and my hair oh my hair—"

"Heidi!"

I blinked. The world was black-on-black. I hung over Mother's body, feet not touching the ground, dangling by my hair. Tank's hand clutched my hair, my collar, my hair caught in my collar—

"Heidi!"

He shook me, and I blinked again. Black-on-less-black. My arms hurt.

Tank lowered me, held me even after my feet found the trembling street. My eyelids fluttered, and he squeezed my arm. He peered into my eyes. A wisp of blackness receded, slunk away to hide under the porch again.

"You okay?" he said, voice deeper than the blackness.

I blinked a few more times. Black-on-static. Nodded. Started shaking.

He eased the maul out of my grip, threw it across the street, moved his hand from my collar, my hair, to my shoulder. "You sure? Romero needs you. Sweeney needs you." He tilted my chin, looked deep again. "C'mon," he finally said. "Feds are gunning for the Inner Radius. Gotta get inside."

"Mother—"

"She's dead."

"But she said—"

"Forget her! You hear me?"

I nodded, still shuddering, not quite understanding. Tank turned and helped Carlos lift Romero. Then he and Carlos looked at me. Gray-and-grayer.

Tank jerked his head at the house. "Go!"

I ran before the dark could swallow me up again.

≈

TANK AND CARLOS HAULED Romero into the house, laid him on the table. Someone else moaned. My head swiveled, and I spotted Sweeney's boots poking out from between the couch and footlocker. He was safe there, out of traffic.

Motion fishhooked the corner of my eye. Paolo leaned out of the bathroom with a dripping towel. He bent over the still-unconscious pilot who sprawled half in, half out of the bathroom. Paolo barked at me, but then looked over my shoulder at the table, at Romy. He gritted his teeth and settled for mopping the pilot's blood-smeared face.

Tank brushed past me into the kitchen, and his energy caught me, swung me around. Cam'n'Zak leaned over the sink to spit blood in unison. It was very red, the only color that registered. Then Tank spoke to them, and they turned, sliding apart, ready to obey.

"Heidi," Carlos said. Begging, hoarse. "What do we do? Tell me what to do."

I turned to his voice. Tried to blink away the black spots that crawled in front of my eyes.

"I need more light," I said.

Carlos screamed for light, a lamp, anything. Tank yelled something else. Cam'n'Zak bolted past me through the room and up the stairs.

I approached the table and leaned over Romero. "We gotta roll him onto his side," I said, squinting past dots. "I need to see the back of his head."

Carlos and I pushed and pulled. Romero's left side was stiff, his arm and leg hyperextended, so we had to roll him to the right. Somebody pushed gauze at me, shoved my hands out of the way. I looked up, and Tank shoved a squeeze bottle of saline at me, too, then helped Carlos wrestle Romero into position. Cam thundered back downstairs with a blanket. He and Tank wedged the blanket under Romero, balancing him on his side. Isaac thundered over with the lamp from Tank's drafting table, switched on its cold glare.

Gauze over my fingers, I brushed back Romero's thick black hair and searched for the edges of his wound. Everything was red or black or red-black, even the crinkled edge of embedded metal. "It's not enough," I said. "I need more light."

Tank hollered over my head. The gauze had soaked hot and black. I flicked it off and got handed a fresh batch. I wrapped it around four fingers like a mitt, then drenched Romero's hair with saline. Bloody runoff splattered the floor.

The telewall blasted pure white light. But the light cast strange shadows that melded with the darkness dotting my vision. "It's not enough," I said, blinking impatiently. "One of you, get a pulse tag on him."

"I'll do it. Where the fuckity fuck are the little motherfuckers?"

I glanced up: Isaac rifling through the first aid kit. I felt a flicker of gratitude, went back to flushing Romy's wound. Amidst all that black hair, the crest of twisted metal gleamed. I squirted it with more saline; the bloody antiseptic swelled up and out in a tide. I saw skull. Blood slowly seeped back, hiding broken bone. Another squirt of saline and I saw a tattered white frill: dura mater, the membrane that should've shrink-wrapped Romero's brain. Blood trickled back into the crater but not as much and much slower this time.

Jaw aching, I squirted the crater clear again. Saw the cheesy whiteness like grout in the cracks. Prayed Carlos didn't see it, though his head was pressed against mine, though the blood was sluggish, no longer pumping, no longer hiding anything.

Cloth ripped. Cam's arm bumped mine as he pressed not-quite white rags to Romero's head, framing the wound. On the other side of the table, Isaac flung the biosensor aside. "Shit! Goddamn thing is busted! Can't get a fucking pulse, BP, anything." He dug around in the kits for another tag.

"Don't bother." I set aside the saline, my hands shaking. "It's not busted."

"Well, shit. What do we do now? Defib? Reboot?"

I sensed Isaac looking at me. I shook my head.

"How long was he down?" Tank said.

Carlos sobbed, a stab to my stomach.

"Too long," I said.

I cupped Romero's head. I wanted to lean down and kiss his wound, wet my lips with his blood, nuzzle his cracked skull. I wanted to feel the last heat roll off his soul. I could hold it—like I'd held ET, like I held Romy during sex.

Rage flared in my chest. *Goddamnit, Mother.* If she hadn't found us, if she hadn't stopped me ...

But I'd sworn she wouldn't touch my boys, and she wouldn't. Not in this moment, not even in my memory. So I blinked past the black fractals obscuring my vision. I swallowed down the tightness in my throat. And I whispered, "Sweet Sue." Because Romero never would again.

I lumped the rags in a dirty pillow. "Help me," I said, and we rolled Romero gently onto his back. Outside, metal chimed as people ran over the chain link fence. Roach's forklift beeped, reversing. A distant PA squawked unintelligible warnings. Inside the house—utter silence.

I couldn't look at Romy's scraped face, his closed eyes so still. I looked at his hands, his broken wrist that didn't matter. Inflamed swoops and flourishes decorated his skin, disappearing up his leather sleeves.

"Those the UV tattoos he was talking about?" I said.

Carlos nodded, sobbed again, fell across his brother.

"Heidi." Tank touched my elbow. "I'm sorry ... but, Sweeney?"

"Yeah." I uncoiled the gauze from my hand, dropped it in a heap beside Romero. I touched Carlos's back, thought a kiss at him.

Then I turned to Sweeney. He wouldn't wait too long like Romy had. So long as I was still breathing, none of my crew would.

≈

"WHAT THE FUCK!"

I stared down at Sweeney's leg, at the sleek steel cylinder impaling his thigh. Couch cushions propped his leg and kept his thigh from dragging down the length of the rod run through him.

I whirled on Tank. He took a step back.

"When we fell off the roof," he began.

"Get the footlocker out of the way, get the couch back, bring me towels," I said. "Get the fucking lamp over here. I can't see better than a mole. Get me saline and a knife. Why the hell didn't anyone pull this thing out of him?"

"Afraid he would bleed out," Tank said, kicking the locker aside.

"Well, no shit, but it's not like Medevac is gonna come to the rescue! Damn thing's got to come out eventually. What is it, a curtain rod?" I fell to my knees and shuffled to Sweeney's side. "Did you give him anything for the pain?"

"I ran out to get you." Tank kicked the couch over and back.

"For fuck's sake, get his head up and get some pills in him."

"Heidi?" Sweeney moaned.

"Yeah, gonna take care of you. Give me a minute."

I studied the steel piercing his thigh. Maybe it was from the helicopter. Didn't matter. I squinted past black blobs, the imaginary ones in my eyes and the real ones on his pant leg. Cam dragged the lamp over, and the steel rod gleamed like Excalibur.

"You okay?" Sweeney said.

I looked up. Tank knelt behind him, propping his head while Isaac shook pills into Tank's palm. Sweeney's gaze was blurry, kept slipping off me, but his forehead was rippled, his slanty eyebrows droopier than ever, his mouth a downturned pucker buried in his beard. He looked worried. About me, Walking Death.

"Well ..." I tried to laugh. "I don't have a cool pipe sticking out of me, but yeah, I'm okay." I ran my hand through my hair. My fingers caught in blood-clotted knots, and the knots yanked at my ripped ear. Fresh blood trickled down my neck. *Great*. "Suds and gloves," I told Isaac.

"You did good, girl." Sweeney paused to take the pills Tank pressed to his lips. "You're a good girl."

What that meant coming from Sweeney, I had no idea. He was probably delirious. "You won't think so in a few minutes," I said. "That pipe's gotta come out, and we don't have any way to shorten it."

Isaac handed me Betadine, and I doused my hands and wrists. My ripped fingertips stung like hell. "I'm going to cut the jeans," I told Isaac. "Give me your belt for a tourniquet. Is there a local in the chopper's kit?"

He gave me the surgical gloves, turned the first aid kit to read vials. "Fuck yeah. 'Bout time something went right 'round here." He passed the kit to Cam, suddenly beside him again. Isaac unbuckled his belt.

"After we stick him, we'll roll him," I told Isaac. "The short end of the rod's underneath, so you'll have to pull it out the front."

"Yeah, right," Cam said, kneeling across from me. "And then he'll titty fuck the Virgin. Zak's squeamish."

"I don't care who does it or who he fucks once it's over. Just do it!"

I finished fanning my hands, pulled on the surgical

gloves. Cam handed me scissors, and I started sawing at Sweeney's pant leg. As I ripped the last bit of denim away, I glanced at Tank. He had one arm clamped around his middle, as if cradling cracked ribs. But more worrisome, he was biting the insides of his lips, a nervous tic I'd never seen from him before.

"Sweeney needs a bit," I said to distract him. "Somebody's belt or jacket."

Isaac gave Cam his belt for the tourniquet, then shrugged out of his leather jacket, and passed it to Tank for the bit.

"What is this, strip poker?" Sweeney mumbled.

"Can we get the light closer?" I said. "Before I fall under the porch?"

"What?" Tank said.

"Zak, get over here and hold Sweeney's legs. Close your eyes if you have to but don't fuck it up."

When Cam pulled the rod out, Sweeney screamed through his leather bit. Then he fainted. Then he pissed himself. Luckily, gravity took care of that while Cam and I stanched the blood flow. I irrigated the wound, poked around a bit to account for major blood vessels and such. That was harder than it sounds, given the black blossoms that squirmed across my vision, the smoke and dust seething through the gouged wall above us. I figured it was best not to stitch up the holes on either side of his thigh, in case I needed to purge an infection later. Still, it felt wrong to leave him open like that, so we packed the wound with scar jumpstart and plastered on antimicrobial patches.

"Get more blankets," I said, falling back on my heels. "Wrap him up, keep a pulse tag on him, watch his temp."

"You going somewhere?" Tank shifted Sweeney's sweaty head to the floor.

I took a deep breath, closed my eyes, wished the blackness away. Pointless, given my track record with wishes.

"The pilot," Paolo said behind me.

"The pilot," I sighed.

Cam helped me to my feet, which I couldn't feel, and wrapped my hands around the chopper's first aid kit, ransacked as it was.

"Come on." Paolo edged between me and Cam, took my arm. "I got him into the spare bedroom. He's starting to wake up."

Tank said, "Heidi?"

I turned. "Yeah?"

He stood there, holding his ribs in silence. I realized it hadn't been a question, not really. It was permission. To not go, to curl up in a corner instead, hide somewhere and grieve. And it was an offer. He'd cover me, even guard me, if need be. I almost accepted, though I couldn't admit the weakness, even to myself.

"I should wrap Tank's ribs," I said, leaning in his direction.

But Paolo dug his fingers into my arm. "First, the pilot. Then we'll take care of Tank."

His echo of Mother's threat sent a dark lightning bolt up my spine, dimming my vision again. *You will never touch him*, I thought. *Not you or Mother or anyone. I will take care of Tank.* Same way Tank had rescued me from my family, I'd rescue him. I was the only one who could—I was the only one with an inkling of what had really brought Puppy to Exile. The only one who'd keep Tank's foster monster a secret.

"Of course," I said, yanking my arm from Paolo's grasp. "First, the pilot." Despite the fury clouding my vision, I tried to smile at Tank. "I'll get your ribs later. You'll be all right," I said. "I promise."

Chapter Twenty-Five

"LIGHT," I SAID, FOLLOWING Paolo into the spare bedroom. My veins felt stripped. My filthy feet stuck to the floor, making every step an effort. The pilot moaned, eyes closed.

"The light's already on." Paolo lingered by the switch, uncertain.

"Then I need more," I snapped. "You get a tag on him?"

"Yeah, I'll be back," he said, swinging out of the room.

The pilot lay on the floor, a towel folded under his head, another one beside him arrayed with paper towels, a bowl, saline, gauze, scissors, needle, and thread. Fucking Paolo. Always so sure he could make me do exactly what he wanted. But why did he want me to do this particular thing so fucking bad?

I knelt beside the moaning man. His eyes rolled behind his lids, but he didn't wake. He was small, about 5'7", and neat as a clown accountant, bright yellow pants still crisp-creased despite the blood. I squinted at his tag. Decent vitals, despite the presumed concussion that had knocked him out. Talk about a lucky SOB.

I sighed and sat back on my haunches. Paolo jogged in with the drafting lamp.

"We need pillows to prop him up," I said. "Or he'll choke on his own blood. Any sign of the tip of his tongue?"

"No." Paolo plugged in the lamp.

The sticky soles of my feet gave a soft velcro rip as they peeled from my pants. I threw a leg over the pilot's chest. "Maybe he swallowed it."

Paolo froze, lip curled. "You think?"

"No. Forget it." I pinched a square of gauze and reached into the man's mouth, moved his maimed tongue from side to side. His neck stiffened in a slow-mo flinch, and I jammed my other hand into his mouth to keep him from biting me. "I probably couldn't stitch it back on, anyway. Best I can do is dope him and close him."

Which is what I did. I'd never even pierced a tongue— more Romero's domain than mine—let alone stitched one, and my vision was clouding again. But I made it up as I went along, and not giving a shit actually improved my confidence. Whether it improved the guy's prognosis ...

Paolo knelt behind the pilot's head, holding it tight, fingertips locked on the guy's jaw. "So," he said, voice thick, tired. "Did we win?"

We? I resisted the urge to stab my needle into one of Paolo's impossibly blue eyes. I held my breath as I curved thin steel into thick meat. When I pulled the thread taut, I breathed out, and said, "My whole family is dead. And Chazz. Maybe Keith. So yeah ... I guess we won."

"Your whole family? How?"

"No thanks to you." I kept my gaze focused on my bloody task. "Don't worry, your conscience is clean."

"What about the feud?"

My arms ached, my shoulders ached, my back ached. From beating my mother to death or from the effort of *not* beating Paolo to death? I took a deep breath, concentrated on my shaking hands, the needle threatening to spear soft palate.

"Who's left to care?" I said. "Keith? His crew? By the time they get organized, the feds will've cracked down."

"What do you mean, 'cracked down'?"

"Can't you feel the streets shaking? Can't you hear the PAs? The feds'll breach the Inner Radius any minute if they haven't already." I shifted closer to the pilot, my knees bumping the couch cushions that propped his head. I felt

Tank's key in one of my pant pockets, his razor in the other. I blessed that warm solid line, too clean for Mother.

"But they're here to restore order, right?"

"Right," I drawled. "And when they're done, we'll be orderly as a graveyard."

He sniffed, a weary attempt at scorn. "If the feds wanted you dead, they'd have razed Exile a long time ago."

I squinted at him past the black spots. He didn't look as certain as he probably wanted. "Maybe," I conceded, starting a new stitch. "But the feds do a lot of shit that doesn't make sense. You think we know half of what's really going on? For that matter, you think they're going to take the time to sort Outsiders from Exiles?"

He smirked. "They will when I'm toting this guy to safety."

Damn it all to hell, motherfucker had me repairing the pilot so he could use him as a bargaining chip.

"I'll kill him," I blurted out. "Then what'll you do? How you going to get the feds' attention without a hostage?"

"I don't think so," Paolo said, cocking his chin at my hands. I was surprised—more like pissed—to look down and find my hands had gone still again, training turned to instinct. So much for being Walking Death.

"You're almost done," he said. "And you're being so careful even after that stupid threat. Why you think that is?"

"Shut up, Puppy."

"Oh, so *now* I'm Puppy." His mouth opened for a silent laugh. "You got a hero complex? You trying to make up for the patient you couldn't save?"

Rage throbbed behind my eyes, burned my vision black as motor oil. How dare he speak of Romy. "What do you care?" I said, jaw tight as a vise. "So long as I fix your bargaining chip, right?"

He held my gaze, calculating. Apparently, I was a simple equation, or he was getting lazy. He looked at the unconscious pilot. "You're right. I don't give a shit about your complexes. Just finish him up so I can get the hell out of here."

"What about Tank?" I said, struggling to keep my voice steady.

"Far as I'm concerned, you freaks are welcome to each other."

I blinked my eyes clear, then continued stitching, the muscle in my thigh dry humping the sleek metal in my pocket. "And those people Out There? The ones who want Tank back. They're going to forget him?"

He snorted. "Gonna have to. You think the feds'll let more Outsiders into Exile?"

I wasn't sure there'd *be* an Exile come morning. But punching through gristle, I said, "Maybe it doesn't matter what the feds do. Rules and visas might stop architects, but desperate people don't think like that. And Hell hath no fury, right?"

I glanced up to see him regarding me with a raised eyebrow.

"Tell me. What is it, Heidi? Is it the muscles, or the Neanderthal brow, the steely silence? 'Cause I really don't get it. What about Tank brings all you psycho chicks running?"

My stitching hand trembled with frustration. Was that as close as he'd get to admitting it, that he'd been sent by Jenna? I switched hands and shook out the tremors, tried to shake off the urge to clock him.

"Puppy, you lowdown, duplicitous sack of shit," I said. "Is that any way to talk about a client?"

He held my gaze, giving me freezer burn even through the black squiggles. I couldn't believe I'd ever compared his baby blues to the ocean. I dropped my gaze, switched hands again, pretended to concentrate on the pilot.

"I'd bet Tank would love to know about the psycho chick paying you to flush him out," I said.

"And I'd bet he'd love to know about the deal you and I had."

My hand stopped; my eyes darted up. "We never *had* a deal, Puppy. Just a lot of what-ifs and flimsy promises."

"Heidi, you backstabbing, conniving whore," he said, and I was so glad I'd ditched the sawed-off outside. "If that's your story, then you'd better keep your mouth shut about mine."

Nostrils flaring, I considered. Tank wouldn't stop to hash out me and Paolo's "he-said/she-said" crap. He'd hightail it out of Exile like his ass was on fire, feds be damned.

"Fine," I snapped. "But what if—" I couldn't say her name; it blocked all the other words for a moment like a rock in my throat. "What if she sends someone else?"

"Not my problem, sweetheart." Mockery twisted Paolo's stingy lips, and I wondered how long he'd had to practice the guileless smile and puppy eyes that took me in. Fool me once ...

"Fair enough."

I finished the stitch and tied off the last knot. Then I snipped the thread and wrapped the leftover around the needle, pinned it through the nearby towel. Standing, feet bracketing the pilot's ribs, I said, "We need this guy back down and on his side for at least five minutes before you run off with him, got it? You grab his shoulders and hold him up. I'll move the cushions out from under him."

Puppy rose on his knees. While he hefted the pilot, I stuck my hand in my pocket. The blackness in my eyes jumped to the periphery of my vision, giving me a pinhole of clarity.

"Wait, I forgot something." I brought the razor out. "Hold him still?"

"What?" Puppy frowned, neck tendons splayed with effort.

I flipped open the razor, leaned in business-like, and raked it across Puppy's throat. Squinting against arterial spray, I jabbed the blade into a spider web. Puppy dropped the pilot. I dragged the razor halfway across his neck again before he grabbed my wrist.

I planted my free hand on the wall and fought to keep the gurgling, grappling puppy off the pilot. I'd just fixed the guy, after all. Teeth gritted, I rocked hard and shoved Puppy off my blade. He smacked the wall, slid to the floor. His legs scissored, that useless impulse to run I'd seen over and over again in the streets. I panted over the pilot—dirtied again, poor fuck—and watched blood pump over Puppy's T-shirt, his jeans. The pillows, the floor. It was a lot of blood—and dark.

When the puddle stopped growing, I followed the trail upriver, past the spider web massacre. I studied the lines of Puppy's pretty face, trying to find the hiding places for all his lies. But my pinhole of clarity was shrinking, the blackness encroaching, combining with all that blood. And Puppy had been so pretty, hidden so many lies.

It would be easier if I had a grid, I thought. *Like on my thesis pictures.*

I lifted the razor, and I made one.

I ENTERED THE LIVING room, eyes finally clear. The room was so bright I wondered where the angels were. But the light didn't hurt my eyes. It didn't warm me, either. I kept shivering.

"Hey." I tried to find a person to focus on in the crowded room. Cam and Zak, Vanessa and Rascal, Jimmy B and two other guys, they all turned to me, but their eyes were so round it was disconcerting. "Hey, is Manny around?" I said. "Or Tank? Where's Tank? We need to get the pilot somewhere safe for the feds."

Zak's gaze skipped over me—up and down, left and right—before zeroing in on my right hand. "Son of a bitch," he said. "Is there anything left of the motherfucker?"

"What?"

I glanced at myself, the spot that seemed to rivet him. The razor, dripping with every shiver. Red Sonja darted out from between their legs to lap at the puddle.

"Oh. The pilot's fine," I said. "I mean, as fine as he can be after falling out of the sky. But I had to put Puppy down."

"No shit." Zak nodded slowly. The others in the room mumbled nothing I could make out.

Cam came forward, eyes locked on mine. "Tank's helping Carlos get his bro home. Had to haul ass 'cause the goddamn feds are pushing through what's left of the roadblocks."

Now that he mentioned it, the metal-dragging, glass-cracking ruckus outside *was* too loud to be Roach's work.

"Manny's out trying to corral warriors," Zak offered, nudging Sonja away from her sauce. "Organize a defense a some kind."

Huh. That sounded pointless. Maybe as pointless as trying to save the pilot. I headed for the stairs with the first aid kit.

"Fine. Deal with the pilot, would ya? Ditch him somewhere the feds'll see his clown suit."

"Hey, Heidi?" Zak said. "We heard something about your little brother ...?"

I froze on the first stair. All the mumbling in the room stopped.

"I don't want to hear it," I said.

Cam tried, "But they said Mann—"

"I don't want to hear it. You understand me? Not now, not ever."

"Okay, then," Cam'n'Zak said in unison.

In the upstairs bathroom I shed my bloody clothes. Dropped the razor and key in the sink. Stopped my teeth chattering long enough to swallow a bunch of pills from the kit. Calculated, then gulped a few more. Then I turned the shower on full blast and waited. The showerhead coughed for almost a minute before I remembered: no water.

I sat in the tub, anyway—as good a place as any to wait for the pills to kick in—and stared at the tiles. They formed a neat, taunting grid. Much neater than anything I'd managed downstairs. And for all that, I still hadn't found a golden rectangle, the Fibonacci sequence, any magic ratio or secret formula for Puppy's pretty multiplicity. I'd lived in my parents' house too long, let my brain get mangled by haphazard additions and convoluted booby-traps. I hugged my knees and rocked. I wished I could drift away while sitting tight.

A thump on the door startled me. I'd lost track of time. Before the echo dissipated, before my fog cleared, Tank barged in. His voice thundered in the small space. "You wanna tell me what the hell happened down there?"

No, I thought. I tucked my forehead to my knees.

He jerked the shower door open. "Did Puppy hurt you?"

"No," I mumbled, not looking up.

"Look at me, Heidi. Did he try something again?"

I felt a flicker of annoyance—what was he talking about?—but not enough to ripple my pharmaceutical chill. "He didn't do anything to me," I said, loud enough to compensate for the muffling.

"Then why'd you turn his face into a fucking jigsaw puzzle? I gave you the razor to protect yourself, not so you could play Jack the fucking Ripper."

"I took care of him for you."

"For me?" The shower door rattled. "What do you mean?"

I turned my face, uncurled enough to see the torn knees of his jeans. "He wasn't your friend." The words sucked and resisted like cold motor oil. "He was a merc. He was supposed to find you and make you go back."

"Back where?"

"Out There. To Jenna."

A crash in the street sent shivers through the walls. I peeked up. Tank was staring at me. One hand still gripped the shower door, the other his ribs. I felt guilty. I should've wrapped them by now. He shouldn't have had to haul me off my mother, or carry Romy, or—

"Puppy tell you that?" he said, voice craggy.

I closed my eyes, leaned back, imagined water slicking down my hair. "Almost."

"*Almost?* What does that mean? You knifed him and cut his face to the bone for 'almost?'"

"Tank ..." *Noé*, I thought. My forehead sank, unbidden, to my knees again. Despite being cold, I felt seconds from melting down the drain.

"Tell me *exactly* what he said!"

"What does it matter?" I said, voice liquefying. "The feds are here. They're on our street. We're never getting out. Not out of this house or the Inner Radius or Exile. We're all dead."

Tank squatted by the tub and growled, "Not yet we're not, but Puppy sure is."

Outside, a bullhorn blurbed orders. Why was Tank still here? Why were we still fighting? What were we fighting for?

"Leave me alone," I said. "I'm tired."

"You think I'm not? Damnit, Heidi, did you take something?" He shook my shoulder, cursed louder when my head lolled. "What did you take? Talk to me!"

"Stop slapping me," I think I said. Tried, anyway. "You're always slapping me."

"Don't you dare leave me," he said.

I would've felt bad for breaking my promise, but I was already gone.

Chapter Twenty-Six

I TWITCHED AWAKE.

I looked around. In Tank's bed. Alone. The sheets kicked and rumpled, bloody in places.

I shifted. Something on my wrist snagged on the sheet. I brought my wrist up nearly to my nose, blinked at the biosensor tag registering my vitals. The numbers didn't make sense. But apparently I was alive.

I noticed my sleeve. I was wearing pajamas. Flannel pajamas with stupid pink flowers on them. *Fuck me.*

I flattened my palms to the bed and pushed up. My blurry vision went blurrier, and I sank into the pillow, whimpering. My back hurt like I'd been flogged with a fire hose. I panted, listening to the roar of my heartbeat. Eventually, I registered the rumble of heavy trucks outside, the occasional zip of a bike followed by a patter of small arms fire.

I was alive, and Exile was still fighting.

I heard voices downstairs. I eased myself into a sitting position. Then I took a break before I slid my legs over the side of the bed and inched up, braced against the nightstand. Took another break. Then I traced the peninsula of the bed, though it took longer than walking a straight line, so I could anchor myself. Bed to nightstand; nightstand to wall; more wall; finally, door. Forehead sweaty against the jamb, I listened but couldn't hear enough. I turned the knob, opened the door a crack, then slid to the floor, exhausted.

"Just as well." Sweeney's voice, slightly slurred. I wondered if he was drunk, then remembered the house rules, figured he was hopped-up on painkillers. "This way Heidi won't miss it."

"She's in no state to attend a burn," Tank rumbled. "Let alone Romero's."

My stomach hitched. Romy. I'd been so worried about Carlos, so afraid Chazz had gotten to him, I hadn't even wondered where Romy was. Not until it was too late. My eyes burned, and I looked up, willing myself not to cry.

"She'll wake up, she'll be fine," Sweeney said.

"I know she'll wake up ... I don't know that she'll be fine."

"What you worried about, man? You worried she's crazy?"

"That's what you've been telling me all this time, isn't it?" Tank said. It was like he'd grabbed my guts in his fist. "The sleepwalking and the sleepin' around and the Frankenstein pictures?"

Sweeney scoffed—it seemed to take a lot out of him— then said, "Man, if she's crazy? She's crazy in the best possible way. She's willing to put up with your shit, right? And you're not the easiest dude to get along with, all stoic and sober and shit."

Maybe he *was* drunk. And on drugs.

"Yeah? So why do you stick around?" Tank sounded tired but amused.

"You're like power steering. Keep me from spinning out. Now Heidi didn't do nothing that didn't need doing—"

"You saw Puppy's face," Tank said. And suddenly I did, too: the red line of symmetry slicing through his philtrum, his stingy lips, the ginger goatee; the cross-hatching that went haywire through his punctured eyeballs. I yanked off my biosensor tag, didn't want to know how my heart was racing.

"Artistic flair," Sweeney said with an unspoken *Meh.*

"More like a meltdown."

"If that was a meltdown, it's the neatest one I ever saw. I mean, I didn't actually see it, and I guess it was really pretty messy ... but what I'm saying, man—"

"Yeah, what are you saying, Sweeney? You even remember?"

"I mean," he said, drunkenly indignant, "it was the most *controlled* meltdown this town has ever seen."

"Nothing controlled about what she did to her mother."

I almost remembered that, too. Remembered the spike maul in my hands, remembered hanging in mid-air, Tank holding me by the scruff of the neck. Remembered looking down, then ... darkness ... like a vat of black spiders.

"What she *did*," Sweeney said, "was what *you'd* been rarin' to do for weeks. Old bitch had it coming. Carlos told you the sick shit she was saying to Heidi. Anyway, that girl pulled it together, marched in here and out-Florence Nightingaled before she put Puppy down. You going to begrudge her some personal time with the body?"

"She pulls a pole out of your leg, and now you're best friends."

"Damn straight!" Sweeney laughed wheezily, then panted, "I know I gave you shit about her, man. But I was wrong."

"No, you were right. About her lying, using me to get out of here."

"She *thought* about it, she didn't *do* it."

"Because you busted her!"

"I don't think so, Tank. I talked to her while you were locked up, and ... if she was gonna use you, you really think she'd wank around so long, not doing a damn thing about it?"

Tank said nothing. I hoped it was 'cause doubt was creeping in, not 'cause he'd shut down à la Forrest.

"Give her a break, man. Try and imagine what it was like in that house. With those people. 'Course she's gonna have

328

crossed wires. But what you worried about?" Sweeney's tone changed to teasing. "She ain't ever gonna take a knife to *you*. Not the way she looks at that monkeybutt face of yours."

Tank muttered, and Sweeney yelped. After that it was mostly static and Sweeney bitching about fifty-seven channels and nothing on.

I tried crawling back to bed, but my arms and back hurt so much I gave up. I forced myself to my feet: wall wall wall, nightstand again. Then to bed and a deep sleep, but no peace.

≈

LATER THAT NIGHT, TANK checked on me. I pretended to be asleep while he pressed a fresh tag to my wrist. I didn't care if he knew I was faking. I wasn't ready to talk. The next morning, playing possum was harder. He made a racket. Once he was gone, I peeked. His computer monitor stared at me from the wall. A hub, remote control, and a bunch of flash drives sprawled on the nightstand next to a bag of saltines.

Thoughtful bastard.

I groped for a couple of drives. The labels read "Classics" and "Slashers" in tiny handwriting I didn't recognize. As I pondered, a door slammed. A minute later, the side gate cranked open, and the Ninja growled to life. Tank leaving the house; the war must go on.

Not needing as many breaks this time, I got up and shuffled to the bathroom. It stank of bleach, but there was no bucket for flushing the toilet. Feeling slow and stupid, I looked around, saw a sticky note on the mirror: WATER USE IT BEFORE WE LOSE IT. That blocky print, I recognized.

Too tired to soap, I slumped in the shower and relied on scalding blasts to power wash myself. Then I propped myself in front of the steamed mirror and examined my ear. Somebody—Tank probably—had mended it. Messy, but that was my own fault; I'd ignored the wound too long. I was lucky he hadn't had to cut off much before stitching. A bottle of Tank-approved pills waited on the counter beside electrolyte ade. I gulped a double dose.

Hair still wet, I pulled on a non-flannel, non-flowered shirt of Tank's. Changing the sheets was a workout I didn't have energy for, so I settled for stripping the bed and tossing a fresh blanket on the mattress. Then I snuggled under and slept. Dreamless.

≈

BEEP-BEEP-BEEP.

I woke to the sound of a reversing vehicle, the clank and thud of broken road scraped by metal. I wondered if it was Tank's forklift or the maggot feds, clean up or tear down. I wondered if Tank was home or fighting, safe or hurt.

Alive or dead.

Shivering, I shoved the Classics flash drive into the hub and queued the first film that came to mind.

Later, the Ninja roared down Raven, swerved around the corner and into the backyard. When the back door slammed, Sweeney exclaimed, and Tank rumbled in answer. Then Tank's heavy step thudded on each stair, nearly in synch with my pounding heart. I didn't roll over. I squeezed the blanket in my fists and watched George and Mary throw rocks, make wishes.

Tank opened the door. I felt him standing there, waiting. I smelled him, too: dirty denim and gasoline, smoke and sweat. Blood. Onscreen, George bragged about all the things he was going to build. Things he never did.

Tank closed the door, leaned against it. "I hate that movie."

"Me, too." I fought not to curl into a tighter ball.

"Then why you watching it?" He walked around the foot of the bed. Stared at the shifting pixels as he sat near my feet. "For Jimmy Stewart?"

I might've smiled if I hadn't been so fucking scared. "No."

He waited a few minutes until George offered to lasso the moon. "Then?"

I lowered the volume. Couldn't think up a lie and figured it was too late to start airbrushing now. "Forrest used to watch this movie."

Tank tensed on the end of the bed, but I soldiered on.

"He watched it over and over again. Like he was looking for an answer. Right up until the day he died. Until he killed himself."

Tank looked at me. It wasn't as bad as that time we fought in the kitchen or even our first date, but I had no idea what he was thinking. Did he blame me for Forrest's death? He hadn't before, but that was Before: before he caught me beating my mother to death in the street, before I killed and mutilated Puppy.

"That," he finally grumbled, "is the worst movie recommendation I've ever heard."

He reached over slow enough I could get away if I wanted to and pulled the remote from my hand. "Ain't no answers here, Heidi Heidi Ho. That's why they show it at Christmas time, when everybody's all eggnogged up."

Surprised to hear my pet name, I let him stop the movie. He erased it from the drive before scrolling through the other titles.

"Where'd you get the movies?" I said to stave off the silence.

"Serena."

"She was here?" How long had I been out?

"Naw, stopped by her place when I went out for supplies."

"And pajamas?" I said.

"Her idea."

I watched him sitting with tensely perfect posture, and I realized his ribs were wrapped. Hadn't stopped him from fighting, though. The light from the screen limned his dirty features, deepened the wrinkles that bracketed his mouth. He was chewing the insides of his lips again.

"Noé?"

He flinched, zipped through a scad of titles too fast to read. My throat tried to close up. Before it could, I asked, "What's your favorite movie?"

His scrolling slowed to a sensible speed. He frowned as if thinking, then said, "I like that one where the guy gets the girl at the end."

I felt a smile that didn't quite reach my face. "I think I know that one. And the girl doesn't stab the guy or cut his face into a checkerboard, right?"

"Yeah," he said, almost a sigh. "That's my favorite part."

"I like the sex scenes."

"Yeah, they're pretty hot." He stopped. "Here, we can handle this."

I waited for the opening credits, then said, "Godzilla?"

"*Godzilla versus Megalon.*" As if, lying right beside him, I hadn't read the words.

He cranked the volume so we could hear the bad dubbing over the street noise. The fighting didn't stop after dusk anymore. I didn't think we had time for this, fiddling while Exile burned. But I pushed that thought away and concentrated on Seatopia's plot for revenge.

When the walkabout clipped to Tank's belt buzzed, we both twitched. Tank muttered, "Damnit, Sweeney," and stood, turning it off.

"He your escape goat?" I said, half hiding in my pillow. "Your excuse to leave the room if I'm freaking you out?"

"No," Tank said, but he sounded caught out. He cupped the back of his neck, bit the insides of his lips again. "Heidi ..." he started.

"Yeah?" My throat strangled the word into two syllables.

"You remember what happened to Romero?"

"I remember." I swallowed hard. "I remember 'most everything."

"Carlos is waiting on you. He can't wait long—we pushed the feds out of the neighborhood." Tank swiveled, as if to see the battle through the wall. "But we only managed that 'cause of the chopper crash, 'cause people Out There are finally paying attention. Feds can't bring out the big guns, yet. But Carlos, he doesn't ... He doesn't want to do Romero's burn without you." He paused, as if wondering whether to say the next part. "Honestly? I don't know if he can. He's pretty messed up."

My chest tightened. "When did you talk to him? Is Sammy—"

"I can call him for you. Carlos, I mean. Let him know you're awake, that we'll be there?"

I began to nod, stopped. "*We'll* be there? You're going, too?"

He turned to me, eyebrows high. "After what they did for us? Of course. We're practically crew now."

"Oh." That was all he'd meant. Warrior honor.

He must've seen my disappointment. I was too tired to fake anything.

Palms up, he said, "I'm going, Heidi. Okay? I'm going with *you*. I'm going *for* you. Not just the crews, all right?"

I pushed myself to sit up. Though woozy, I nodded. Completely this time, despite my surprise.

"And when it's over," he said, voice rising, "when you know they're going to be okay—Carlos and Sammy—I want you to come home. Here. To me. You get that?" He dropped his hands, lowered his voice again. "But that's up to you."

I didn't understand the invite. He was obviously nervous around me. Had Sweeney guilted him into it? I went with what seemed a safer topic. "So you're staying in Exile?"

"Are you?" he said.

Like I had a choice. I wasn't fit to take the 4-S test. I'd beaten my mother to death in the street. Even if the feds never found out, I'd know. But from the line of Tank's jaw, I sensed he wasn't joking. It took me a little longer to realize, from the softness in his eyes, the patience in his stance, he was trying to say, "I'll stay, if you will."

"Okay," I said.

He didn't comment on my slant response. Instead, he strode to the door. "Fine. I'mma go down to the panic room to call Carlos."

"Come back?" I said. "When you're done?"

He faltered. I guess I was giving him the velvet painting orphan eyes. I couldn't help it. I didn't care.

"Or," he said, returning to the bed, "you could come, too. Sweeney misses you."

"Yeah?" I tried to smile.

"Yeah," he said. Like, *duh*. "Besides, you're the medic. Maybe you can give him something to knock him out. Dude's mouthy when he's bored."

My smile firmed up. Tank extended his hand, offering help, and—for once, no argument—I took it.

"Fact," he said, as I scooted out of bed, "lotta folks need a medic right about now. I doubt the clinic's open for business this month. You?"

I staggered, head-rushed and bemused. "Me, what? That a question or a request?"

He half-huffed, an effort to laugh. "A request, I guess. You up to patching people up? Once Romy's taken care of."

Taking care of Romy ... I fought off an image of the burn-to-come, and said, "I never wanted to be a medic."

Tank squeezed my hand. "I never wanted to be a warrior."

"But you're more than a warrior. You're a builder, too."

"And you're more than a medic."

"Yeah." I scoffed, eyes stinging. "There's my porny superpowers, right?"

"Heidi," he said, voice craggier than usual. "There's more to us than most people see. Nobody's ever looked at me half so deep as you, not without running away. Guess that's why I keep jumping off your bridges."

I legit teared up. Leave it to Tank to turn a cut-down into a compliment.

"I ain't saying it right," he continued, misunderstanding my tears. "But trust me, you're more."

And that's what I'd always been fighting for. For *more*. I'd thought I wanted to be Out There, living a normal life among normal people, but I didn't know what normal was—if it even existed—and I'd been killing myself pretending I did. What I really wanted was to see the world without watchtowers glaring back at me, without fences slicing the horizon, without an analytic grid between me and everyone I touched. I wanted the *possibility* of more. I wanted to want without setting off alarms or getting body slammed or having to fight off my brother.

Tank had taken care of that last one. Now I wanted him to live without looking over *his* shoulder. I wanted Sweeney to get his cigarettes and sex with Serena and the chance to bust up his other leg while Tank egged him on. For that matter, when Sweeney did bust his leg, I wanted him to have a doctor no matter what fucking day of the month it was. I wanted real food, coffee, chemistry sets ... so many things. Not just for me or Tank or our crew, but Mute's, too, and BlackJack's, and hell, every motherfucker in Exile, no matter how messed up they were. Because, mutants or not, we deserved it. We all deserved more.

I straightened, gripped Tank's hand tighter. "You trust me with sharp things again?"

He blanched. I couldn't help it, I grinned. In a manner less than reassuring. Probably less than sane. But I did take pity on him, didn't make him answer the question.

"Not like I got anything better to do."

Tank had cleared away the broken glass on the stairs and punched the starburst siding back, opening the view. He tried to hurry me past the window, but I resisted.

"No, I want to see the damage," I said, craning to peek around him. That, and my body needed a break. Walking down the hall felt like a workout.

Hearing my voice, Sweeney called, "Heidi Palermo? Come on down! You're the next contestant on *Sweeney Needs a Beer.*"

"More like *Sweeney Needs an Ass-Whuppin',*" Tank yelled back.

"More like *What Kind of Asshole Threatens a Crippled Man Who Just Needs a Goddamn Beer*?" Sweeney retorted, wheezing near the end.

Tank cocked his head, listening to make sure Sweeney was all right, then asked me, "You sure about this? It's pretty bad out there."

"So long as Exile's still there," I said, chin out, "I want to see it."

Tank studied me, as if taking my temperature by sight, but he was fast. Then pursing his lips in that facial shrug, he stepped out of the way.

The afternoon puffed its hot, carcinogenic breath over my face. I gritted my teeth, refusing to recoil. Below, Raven Street had been pounded into cube steak. The traffic barricades veered this way and that like scattered dominoes. Crushed cars junked up the lawns of bullet-pocked houses. Warriors on roofs catapulted chunks of asphalt and launched scrap metal arrows. Other warriors careened down Cricket. Some were on motorcycles, some were on foot—some were on fire—but all of them were bleeding. I watched a pair of women zigzag across the street, barely keeping each other upright. A herd of black-eyed kids erupted from behind cracked barricades and made a beeline for the women, darting over blast craters and bike carcasses.

"Shit," I muttered. "You didn't tell me the kids were fighting, too." I'd always considered my siblings to be freaks among freaks for joining the fray so young.

"Wait. Watch," Tank said, and I was surprised to hear approval in his voice.

The kids dragged the warriors back to their concrete shelter. They ripped open the women's perforated battle gear to strip them of it and take it back to their own crew, I thought. But they only yanked the women's gear open enough to get at the damage. I braced myself, expecting the feral pack to exploit their wounds, kill them the rest of the way. Instead, they pressed rags to bleeding limbs, hauled the warriors onto folded tarps.

"What are they doing?" I asked, watching four kids lift each tarp. "Where are they taking them?"

"Probably to an overburdened medic not half so good as you. Or as dangerous."

No time to elbow him in the side, which I shouldn't have been doing, anyway, considering his cracked ribs. "They'll never get away with it," I said. "There's too many of them, and they're out in the open. Easiest kill shots ever."

"Think again."

I zeroed in on the nearest rooftop warriors. None of them bothered to aim at the struggling kids. In fact, the warriors barely spared a glance to the streets below, once the epicenter of Exile's violence. They'd turned to a new threat.

Exile was still fighting, but instead of the suicidal spiral I'd grown up watching, the people were pushing back. The ring of tire fires between Inner and Outer Radius had been extinguished. A lumbering caravan of gray Humvees slogged through hastily dug trenches and over slag heaps, intent on piercing our neighborhood—now the strangely peaceful eye of the storm. But warriors with newly liberated semiautomatics stalked the feds from behind overturned cars and dilapidated houses. Exploiting the smoky confusion of IEDs, they ambushed isolated assault vehicles and battered their way inside.

I pulled my gaze from the scene long enough to frown at Tank. "Whose crew is down there?"

"All a them."

I thought I'd misunderstood his gravelly voice, but his smile suggested I'd heard right, and he was enjoying my confusion.

"Say what?"

"All of them. All the crews are fighting. Against the feds."

My mouth dropped open. Sweeney had been right. He'd said if the feds invaded, Exiles wouldn't keep beating each other, they'd turn on the Guard. But uniting against a greater threat? That was ... logical. That was ... impossible.

Ignoring Tank's chuckle, I said, "No way everybody's mended fences. No way Exile's a united front."

"Didn't say *that*," he conceded. "Everybody ain't working *together*. Not even close. But most've agreed not to skullfuck each other until the feds're out."

From our lofty lookout I couldn't distinguish Inner from Outer Radius anymore. There was just ... Exile. True, our noose had been cinched tighter than ever, but Tank was right. Most of my fellow Exiles were playing it cool. I resisted the urge to rub my eyes in disbelief. I might rub them all the way out.

"That's one reason I asked you to set up shop. It's a rattletrap alliance," Tank said. "If you medics can keep up with casualties, get folks back onto the streets, the truce is more likely to hold."

"What are you staring at?" Sweeney hollered. "Are there naked guys outside?"

"Are you volunteering?" I called back absently.

"Will it get me a beer?"

Tank shook his head, gestured down the stairs. "I'mma

go deal with him before he pulls something. Like my last nerve."

"Wait." I snagged his grease-stiff sleeve. I'd spotted shapes hovering beyond the watchtowers. "What are ...?" I pointed.

Tank glanced over his shoulder, and the smug look on his face ... I didn't know whether to pinch him or blow him.

"TV choppers," he said. "I told you, folks are paying attention. That's as close as the feds will let 'em get, but they're probably filming an eyeful, anyway. That's why the feds ain't nuked us, yet. Don't want the massacre on the five o'clock news."

"So we might be able to get a message out," I said, half to myself.

Romy's burn was going to be smaller than he deserved. There wasn't so much a *front* line as *one* line of resistance. Exile couldn't spare many mourners. But maybe we could prevent the feds from crashing the funeral. Communicate with the TV crews, explain our rituals, generate some sympathy ...

Tank knocked my hand before it reached my torn-up ear, before I realized I'd been reaching for earrings that weren't there anymore. "What are you thinking?" he said.

I shook my head, not ready to talk about the logistics of Romy's burn, yet. Too real. "I've seen enough for now," I said.

"Those big eyes had their fill?" Tank raised an eyebrow. "That's a first."

"Well, brace yourself. If that business down there's anything to go by, we got many more in store."

As I limped down the stairs, Sweeney belted out his own version of "Roadhouse Blues." He replaced almost every word with "BEER!"

"We need more dope," Tank muttered.

I laughed. It hurt like hell—I must've pulled all six hundred and fifty named muscles in my body and most of the unnamed ones, too. Tank waited beside me as I clutched the railing, trying to catch my breath.

"You up to this?" he said.

"This, what?" I wheezed, thinking, *Join the revolution or be your medic or ...?*

"Going down the stairs."

I laughed again. "Fuck, if I stopped doing stuff 'cause it hurt ..."

"But if it hurts too much," he said. "You sure?"

I shook my head. "I'm sure. Are you?"

He shrugged. "It's all downhill from here."

With that craggy deadpan, I couldn't tell if he meant the stairs or our situation, good or bad. But his hand hovered near the small of my back, so I took the first step.

If we were going down? Least we were going down together.

About the Author

A queer Tejana raised on the Texas-Mexico border, Lisa M. Bradley now lives in Iowa with her spouse and their teenager. Her speculative fiction and poetry explore boundaries and liminal spaces: real, imagined, and metaphorical. Her first collection is The Haunted Girl. Her work also appears in numerous anthologies, including *Sunvault: Stories of Solarpunk and Eco-Speculation*, *The Moment of Change: An Anthology of Feminist Speculative Poetry*, and the forthcoming *Rosalind's Siblings*. Online, you can read her work in *Uncanny, Strange Horizons, Fireside Magazine*, and soon *Beneath Ceaseless Skies*. In articles and conference presentations, she honors the often-overlooked speculative elements in work by Latina poets such as Gabriela Mistral, Sara Estela Ramirez, and Alfonsina Storni. Follow her on Twitter (@cafenowhere) or visit her website: www.lisambradley.com.

Acknowledgments

I thank my publisher, Bill Campbell of Rosarium, for taking a chance on a book that others said was too dark, too violent, too sexy, or too difficult to market.

I thank Joseph C. Hager for his invaluable DataFace website, www.face-and-emotion.com (currently between web hosts), which gave me the technical terms for Heidi's cataloguing of faces; I may have made mistakes—I certainly took liberties—but DataFace was an amazing resource.

Thanks to the Dragons of the Corn (the best SFF critique group in southeast Iowa!), especially Deborah Coates, Catherine Krahe, Sarah Prineas, and Dorothy Winsor; to my writing buddies Jennifer Crow, Olivia Fowler, Francesca Forrest, Gwynne Garfinkle, and Virginia Mohlere; to Erin Cashier for savvy guidance; to Julia Rios and Sabrina Vourvoulias for their shining examples and kind words; and to all my friends at the pub for, well, everything!

Special thanks to my found family: Courtenay Pogue and Erica Seemann, who have always supported my work but, more important, have nourished my soul over years of loyal friendship. And I can always count on Rose Lemberg, Bogi Takács, and Mati for tea and sympathy, professional advice, and joyful family feasts.

Thanks to my therapist, who helped me change my life.

Finally, big thanks and bear hugs to all my family. I'm glad not to have lost any of you in the street wars. JJ, you are truly mi media naranja. Ash, thank you for blessing my life.